COME BACK TO ME

By

Jenna Avery

2025 Author's Note

Revising this book and redoing the cover in 2025 was quite the choice. When I was deep in the trenches in 2021, I started hating this book. It was my second fiction book ever, so I was still figuring out my writing process. Unfortunately, I prioritized the goal of publishing instead of making sure everything looked good. It was riddled with more typos than I was comfortable with, so in 2025, I said "fuck it" and here we are.

Adeline's story is rough. I didn't want this story to turn into trauma porn, but even doing a re-read, I icked myself out and I wrote the damn thing. So make sure you tread carefully, okay?

Also, the first edition had the letters between Adeline and Kennedi at the beginning, but they've been moved to the end. You can go find those before you start—they don't contain spoilers—but I didn't want to possibly turn off a potential reader with them at the beginning. You can find them here.

Thank you for being a part of my journey as an author and giving Adeline's story a chance.

Trigger Warnings

This book is dedicated to my fellow humans—your inner fire exists.
Just light the fucking match.

It is gone, it is lost, never to return.

For childhood and time are the things we cannot repossess.

Give me your love, your heart, your most profound regrets.

Living inside you is where I belong.

CONTENTS

THE PARTY

Addie's eighteenth birthday party was nothing short of extravagant. Addie's father always went all out, but he'd really outdone himself this time. Crystals and glitter sparkled in the curated lighting. Toward the stage, an ethereal live "mermaid" smiled demurely at guests while pretending to sunbathe on a fake rock.

Guests filled the ballroom, yet Addie had never felt so alone. Upstairs was an unfinished letter that she was eager to send. It felt like a part of herself was absent without Kennedi. Though there were dozens of teenagers here, they belonged to her father's business associates. She didn't even know their names.

She sat on a chair in the corner, sipping a spiked orange juice. The soft fabric clinging to her body was a sheer, shimmering pink dress. The neckline plunged to an inappropriate depth, emphasizing her breasts. It was a custom design from some fancy designer and a bit too provocative for her liking.

It was her father's choice, like everything nowadays. Before her eighteenth birthday four months ago, he'd allowed her free rein with everything. Whatever she asked for was here. No hesitation. Now, he picked out what she wore, where she went, and even who she spoke to.

The beautifully dressed wives in the room chatted in small clusters—all perfectly decorated and coveted for their looks. How glamorous their lives must be, she thought. She'd spent her whole life watching the wives of rich men titter and gossip in corners, stealing glances with their secret lovers while the men crowded in clumps around the center of the room, trading business tips and discussing sports. Some of them, familiar and not-so-familiar, eyed her in between sips of beer.

She knew she looked good—the boys at school had always hounded her, begging for dates. Her dad had never allowed her to accept their requests, telling her to save herself for someone truly special. Now that she was eighteen, the plan was to move out and start a life without his watchful eyes.

The idea of living out on her own was thrilling. She was strongly considering joining Kennedi in that tiny town. The big city never called to her, but helping at a bookstore? That sounded glorious.

Ice slid across her lips. She looked down and saw that her drink was empty. Sighing, she stood and started toward the drink station. Her journey was interrupted by a wall of black stepping in front of her.

Gasping, she looked up into the deep pits of nothingness that were Alexander's eyes. Alexander was her father's terrifying right-hand man. Built like a bull, he filled her vision, black tux cut to his frame making him appear far more cultured than he was.

"Uh, hi," she squeaked, offering a friendly smile. His face remained emotionless, as usual.

"Your father wants to see you in his study." He had a thick accent, though she'd never known from where. His skin was milky white, which clashed with his obsidian hair and eyes. He looked like a demon corpse that lifted weights. A lot of them. Tonight, he wore an all-black suit. He could have been Lucifer himself, for all she knew.

"But the party isn't even done," she said, pouting. In truth, though, she didn't care about the party; it wasn't really for her, anyway. But Addie was tired of being bossed around, especially by Alexander.

"Do you want me to tell your father you disobeyed?" Alexander sounded hopeful.

She shifted, uncomfortable with his predatory grin, and the way his eyes trailed along the top of her dress.

Stepping back, she said, "Okay, I'll go."

Alexander turned, and Addie followed him up the curved, black marble stairs. She avoided looking at the painted portraits on the walls, each depicting every male relative in the Oremen lineage. Their eyes watched her as Alexander led the way. He glanced back every few seconds, smirking. More than once, his eyes lingered on her breasts, a fact she would inform her father about. This sudden creepiness was inappropriate.

They stopped in front of her dad's study, the deep brown wood door rising twelve feet. Alexander brought up a massive fist and knocked with surprising reverence.

"Bring her in," her father barked. The brusque tone made Addie flinch. Alexander swung it open. He leaned in and smelled her as she passed. The door closed with an ominous click.

Firelight lit the room, dancing across his features. Despite his gently coiffed salt-and-pepper hair swept back, reminding her of old '50s Hollywood actors, he resembled a devil prepared to make a deal.. Lucas Oremen, known as a ruthless businessman, lounged on a massive leather chair beside the fireplace. The tuxedo encasing his muscular form was custom made, the material shiny and shimmering in the firelight.

When she was younger, her imagination convinced her it was leather from human skin, ripped from his adversaries. His reputation lent believability to her imaginings. At school, her classmates whispered words like *mobster* and *criminal*, but to her, he had always been sweet and doting. Knowing he was only soft with Addie made her feel protected and special.

"Come closer, pet." He motioned with a meaty hand. Noticing her nervous smile, he offered a dazzling grin in return—one usually reserved for successfully closing a deal. It flip-flopped her stomach.

She crossed the room, anxiety sparking. The new term of endearment was troublesome; he'd always called her "princess" or "darling." She paused a few feet from him, the warmth of the fire licking her bare arms. His fingers thrummed the armrests as he inspected her. She made her hands into fists, resisting the urge to pick at her thumb. His eyes flicked to her hands and then back to her face.

"How was the party?"

A smile came easily as she said, "It was a beautiful party, Daddy."

His blank expression was disconcerting. Instead of responding, he stood and strode over to her with an unfamiliar urgency. She faltered, taking a step back. He narrowed his eyes. Mixed with his normal scent of pine was an acrid layer of bourbon.

"Are you nervous?" He cupped her face, his thick thumb running along the underside of her jaw.

"No, of course not, Daddy." With one of her nails she picked at a crystal sewn into the dress.

He gently turned her face, inspecting her features as he would a horse. She wriggled her head, freeing herself from his proprietary hold. A shadow skated across his expression. She looked away, inhaling quietly, hoping to stave off the budding nausea.

"Look at me." His tone was scathing, as if he were chastising an employee.

Uneasy tingles crept up her spine. The crystal on her dress fell off, and her fingers immediately felt for a new one. She continued to stare at his shoes. This time when he grabbed her face, pain flared.

"Daddy, that hurts." She jerked her head, but he held on tight. What was happening? He snapped her head up and squeezed her cheeks. She hissed in pain. He squeezed so hard she had no choice but to pop open her jaw.

"Look at me," he repeated, the tone more demanding. Her eyes locked onto his. He gave a slow, feral smile and let go. She rubbed her cheek, moving her jaw around. Tears burned, and her heart thumped with fear. He circled her. She tracked him with her eyes. Something was different—his observations stripped away all of her dignity. What was he doing? It was difficult to keep up with this alternate version of him.

"You're a woman now, and absolutely beautiful," he crooned, stroking a knuckle down her arm.

"Th-th-thank you, Daddy." Her thoughts raced, trying to figure out what was happening. This wasn't her dad; he had never treated her like this. Like she wasn't even his daughter. Like she was a piece of meat.

His face split in a sinister smile. A rolling ball of terror slammed against her sense of self-preservation. Trembling, she played with another crystal. He reached into a pocket and pulled out a pocketknife. The dark metal glinted with deadly promise. She stiffened.

"Do you know what that means?"

She shook her head, eyes locked on the weapon. Her knees knocked together, and a bead of sweat slid down her spine. A log cracked and groaned under the heat. He dragged knuckles down her arm and swept them along her collarbone. The tiny hairs on the back of her neck prickled. He slowly turned the knife around in his palm. With his thumb, he pressed down on a button, and the steel blade popped out with a click.

She watched with horror as he dragged the wickedly sharp blade against the pad of his thumb, a thin line of blood appearing. Her heart stalled as he smeared the blood against her bottom lip. Instinctually, one of her hands flew up to wipe it away, but he slapped it down.

"My blood is yours. Don't fear it."

The blood smelled like dirty pennies, coagulating and mixing with her lip gloss. With legs like jelly, she stood there as he grabbed the back of her head roughly and slammed his lips onto hers. She fought against his hold, screaming against his lips, but the more she fought him, the harder he maintained his grip.

It felt like years had passed before he released her with a loud smack, his thick tongue licking his lips.

"Like cherries," he murmured.

She cried out and stumbled back. Surely, this was a dream. A really terrible dream. She took a step back. His grin widened as she raised her hands defensively.

"Daddy, I don't think—"

"Turn around." His voice was oily and demanding. Air froze in her lungs, and stars played at the edges of her vision. The implications of what was about to happen were painfully clear. He would use that knife tonight—she knew it in her bones as surely as she knew the sun would rise tomorrow. How she behaved would dictate exactly how it was used.

Turning, she squeezed her eyes shut. A wisp of air kissed her bare shoulders, and she cried out at the sensation of sharp metal biting into her spine. The tip of the knife skimmed her flesh and drew more blood. She could feel its warmth dampening the fabric.

There was a ripping sound, and the top of her dress slumped down around her. She gasped, gripping it to her chest. Bile bubbled in her throat as his lips brushed against the curve of her neck and trailed down her shoulder. With a squeak, she tried to step forward, but his hands clamped onto her biceps, keeping her in place.

"Daddy, w-what are you doing?" Terror clawed into her chest. He didn't answer, his lips busy with the soft parts of her back. Nausea thickened like quicksand in her belly.

"Daddy, please—"

The knife flicked up; the edge sliding under her chin. She froze.

"I've spent these past few years giving you everything you could want. It's time you helped your family. Now, turn and face me."

Her legs obeyed, robotically pivoting around the point of the knife. The hunger in his eyes made her whimper; this was the gaze of a starving wolf eyeing its fresh kill. His teeth bared in a mocking smile, a string of saliva stretching from his lip to his teeth. A mighty maw. Her insides shriveled up. She wanted to hide from his predatory gaze. A lamb desperate to bolt.

This wasn't her dad. This wasn't the man who had raised her. Her brain ached as it realigned realities. Her body dislodged itself from her soul as he yanked the dress down past her hips. Her hands cupped her breasts, trying to hide them, but he forced her arms down to her sides.

"You will not hide from me. I'm your father. It's my right to claim you. The kings called it *primae noctis*. Am I not your king?"

When she didn't answer, her tongue thick with fear, he slapped her. Stars exploded in her vision; the sound of it rang in her ears. Devastation incinerated eighteen years of respect and love.

Reality rearranged itself as he screamed, "*Fucking answer me*: Am I your king?!"

This couldn't possibly be real. Her dad would *never* do this to her. A sob ripped from her lungs. This was a stranger. Hot tears rolled down her throbbing cheek.

"Yes."

"*Say it.*"

"You're my king."

That feral smile widened. "Good. Now bend over my throne." He motioned toward the leather chair. She walked over stiffly, trying to turn her brain off. *This isn't real. This isn't real. This isn't real.*

But it was very real. As he clawed at her hips and scraped down her back, she tried to think of her mama. Of the days when they ate ice cream together and giggled conspiratorially. She missed her so much. When the memories didn't work, she practiced saying the alphabet backward. The complexity kept her mind busy.

When he was done with his self-perceived rights as king, he called for Alexander. The door swung open immediately; he'd been waiting outside the whole time. He gazed at Adeline on the ground, where she lay as still as a corpse. His colorless eyes were dark pools of lust. She tried to sit up. Put up a fight, maybe. But everything hurt too much and there was no way for her to escape.

As her father dressed and poured himself another bourbon, Alexander began to teach her how to please men. The education lasted late into the night. When they were done, he forced Adeline to gather the pieces of her dress and walk to her bedroom completely naked. The maids kept their eyes averted from her bruised body as she brushed past them. Adeline didn't even feel their gaze. They could stare all they wanted—it didn't belong to her anymore.

CHAPTER ONE

Four Years Later

By now, there wasn't a book on Adeline's shelves left unread. Some of them were her favorite escapes, their pages creased and worn. They helped keep the threatening madness of isolation at bay. Her favorite stuffed bear, Jack, joined her for lonely dinners. He was the perfect dinner guest — entertaining her quiet, desperate conversations; never judging her for talking to the air. No, those soft brown eyes gazed at her with unconditional love, a needed distraction from the unrelenting eyes screwed into the corners of her room.

After spending the last four years eking out a semblance of existence, Adeline remained grateful for his civilized company.

At times, Adeline knew she was losing her mind. What person wouldn't, when all life has given her for these last 1,524 days is loneliness and pain? It delivered exceptionally well on the latter.

It was a pitiful existence for a twenty-two-year-old, and not by choice. Deadbolts on her door sealed off the world; the two keys in existence belonged to her father and an assigned maid. A small, square portal cut into the oak door delivered meals and toiletries through the door.

It'd been years since she'd prostrated herself at the door, begging the disembodied hands for a scrap of conversation. They could have recited a book on plumbing, and she wouldn't have cared. But the staff's fear of Lucas overrode their humanity, for she was a plaything — not a person. Kept in solitary confinement until he summoned her.

For that's what it was: a pretty prison. The periwinkle walls and midnight blue molding complemented the lush virgin-white carpet. It sank between her toes during the short journey between the bedroom to the bathroom.

The once a week, she changed the navy blue silk sheets that adorned the king-sized four-poster bed, the replacements shoved through the door. White and light blue damask curtains covered the large windows, permitting a view of the grounds from three stories above. The tasteful, twirling metal bars attached to the windowsill didn't block the proud spray of the garden's fountain. Some days, she'd watch it for hours.

Every day was the same until it wasn't. When it was time to leave her room and interact with the men, she would receive a beautiful outfit through the door with written instructions on how to prepare.

This morning, a fresh note shattered the five-day solitary confinement, the sound of the slot opening waking her up. A surge of adrenaline snapped Adeline upright, causing a cold sweat to break out across her skin. As much as she craved human interaction, the outfit delivered promised the unenjoyable kind. Adeline reached for Jack, who'd tumbled to the floor. Placing him carefully by her favorite pillow, she padded over to the silvery chiffon pile.

As she lifted the dress, matching silver shoes slid through the slot. Underneath lay a piece of white paper sitting on top, neatly folded. A farce of civility.

"Thank you," she whispered, knowing no one would answer her back.

Walking back to the bed, she laid the note by Jack and unfolded the dress, letting the soft material flutter to the ground. It was a stunning piece that would hug her curves and accent her dark brown hair, making her gray eyes pop. Lucas loved her in silver for that very reason. It was impossible to deny that he had good taste.

She placed it on the silk sheets carefully and picked up the note.

Chignon, silver locket, dark red lipstick, neutral-colored eyeshadow. Jasmine. Be ready by one.

Simple enough. She glanced at the clock, dismayed to see it was around 11 AM. She had slept for over ten hours. It happened more often than not, her brain desperate to escape from the monotony and the terror. Depression was a bitch.

Straightening, Adeline rushed to the bathroom and started the shower. Lucas expected absolute perfection, not a hair out of place. Time would slip by too quickly if she didn't hurry.

The two hours vanished in a blink, with five minutes to spare. Waiting for the door to unlock, she gave her reflection one last inspection. Just as she thought; the dress hugged her supple curves, the loose scoop neck gracefully hanging below her cleavage.

If one were to attach a price tag to her beauty, she'd be worth millions. many;, she knew exactly how many: bidding began at two. Whoever scored her for the day had a slightly lower bank account.

Right at 1 PM, the lock clicked. Adeline stood patiently as the door swung open, revealing Alexander. The disgusting beast in all of its glory. Head almost brushing the top of the doorframe, he stepped into the room. His sallow skin pulled taut against his severe cheekbones and square jawline. The dark holes one could call his eyes grazed across her skin with ruthless appraisal. Always eager to find a mistake—he loved punishing mistakes. Fortunately, she was flawless.

"Let's go. I don't have all day." A flicker of disappointment pinched his mouth.

Hands clasped in front, Adeline looked to the ground as she glided past. She held her breath; the less she inhaled his scent— cigarettes and a pungent soul—the better. He leaned forward. She refused to flinch as his nose grazed the sweep of her elegant neck.

"Ah, jasmine. I like it when you wear the jasmine."

Her stomach rolled as she dug her perfectly manicured nails into her palms. The years of abuse had beaten the fight out of her. On the inside, though, the raging inferno never ebbed. One day, he'd get what was coming to him. The thought kept her alive in the darkest times.

On autopilot, Adeline headed down the dark hallway to Lucas's office. She paused at the closed door, the sound of conversation on the other side piquing her fear. Alexander brushed up beside her, cupping her backside as he reached for the handle. He dug his fingers into her ass cheek; practice kept her face devoid of expression.

"Be a good girl, and it might go by quickly."

Doubtful, but she knew better than to say so. The beautiful iron handle snicked, pausing the voices. Alexander stepped aside, and as Adeline walked in, she took a quick inventory of the scene.

Lucas's office was as familiar as the palm of her hand, having spent an uncountable amount of hours being used on the different pieces of furniture: the piano, the overstuffed brown leather couch, the multiple supple leather chairs positioned around the roaring fireplace—all of them held a piece of her shattered soul. She couldn't stand looking at the beautiful Turkish rug anymore. If her bedroom was a prison, Lucas's study was her personal hellhole.

At the farthest end of the room was an absolutely beautiful window, spanning fifteen feet in either direction. overlooking the manicured gardens. In front of the window sat an oversized antique desk made of black walnut. The home of Lucas' machinations and multi-million dollar schemes, throwing Adeline's name into contracts as a deal sweetener.

Lucas sat on his imposing black leather chair. Its back swept upwards like a shell, cupping Lucas inside—a cocooned throne. Even in the dim light, his rich, dark hair glowed. Seated, he appeared more physically imposing than he was.

As he rose, his head barely reached the top of his throne of dead flesh. Short and stocky, he was the embodiment of short-dick syndrome. Custom tailored suit. Perfectly trimmed beard And, of course, perfectly coiffed hair. It swept back like a '20s gangster with too much gel.

Next to Lucas stood Henry Summerton, his hair the color of spun gold and bright, too-large veneers. A gray Armani suit clung to his thick muscles. A foot taller than Lucas, Henry was imposing as he leered at Adeline, a smirk tugging at his softly curved lips. To anyone else, he was a devastatingly handsome bachelor who owned a football team and entertained a hefty addiction to fast cars. Adeline knew better—he was a man who enjoyed watching women fucking inanimate objects, and causing pain that would shatter most minds.

Despite her meticulous training, Adeline blanched. Knees wobbling, she stood by the door as Alexander made his way to Lucas's side. As he passed, he gave her a menacing look, silently demanding she behave. She bit the inside of her cheek, stared at the beautiful rug, and started mentally reciting the ABCs backward.

"It's good to see you, Adeline," Henry purred, voice like smooth whiskey. Unable to disobey, Adeline's eyes flicked up to his.

"It's always a pleasure, Mr. Summerton."

Z. Y. X. W.

Henry chuckled. She chanced another look and saw him give Lucas an amused expression. "Did you train her to be a liar, Oremen?"

Lucas offered a genial smirk and clapped Henry on the shoulder. "There's a fine line between lies and manners, Henry. You of all people should know this. I heard you convinced that Patterson woman to marry you. Which side of the line will you land on after the wedding day?"

A low chuckle rumbled. "Touché." Henry slapped his hands together and stepped forward, cobalt blue eyes lighting up. She knew that look. It took everything inside her to not fling the door open and bolt down the hallway. A small act of rebellion could be the difference between staying sane and finally shattering completely while her body was violated for the umpteenth time.

Before she could do just that, Henry said, "What are my limits today?"

Lucas brought a small hand to his soft chin and rubbed it thoughtfully. "Well, the deal stipulated eight hours. However, because we're long-time friends, I'll give you twelve. Have her back by one."

"And if she turns into a pumpkin?" They laughed at Henry's joke.

V. U. T. S.

"Make sure to not return her rotten. You know the rules: nothing broken. No scars. And I swear to fuck, Summerton, if you make her piss blood again, I'm going to sue."

"You drive a hard bargain." Henry scowled but nodded. He looked to Alexander, who continued to watch Adeline like a hawk. "Load her up in my Benz; I'll be there in a minute."

Alexander gave a curt nod and stalked over to her. Heart raging against the bars of its prison, she dared a glance at Lucas. He didn't even regard her as she turned and followed her prison guard out of the room and downstairs to the driveway. She was nothing but an asset. Bred, groomed, and kept like a pretty object worth the exact amount it took to make rich men salivate. Her entire childhood had been a farce, teaching her to wholly rely on him. Everyone around her had been so envious, and Adeline had the naïve audacity to be smug about it. She'd been unforgivably foolish. Thinking about it filled her with shame, so it was easier to not think at all.

The soft material of her dress grew damp with perspiration. She resisted the urge to wipe her palms—the moisture would be immediately obvious. Buzzing filled her ears, muffling the sound of her heels on the black marble floors. A famous designer decorated the mansion with masculine textures and styles: dark wood, black walls, and matching furniture.

The only hint of brightness came from the gigantic portraits that hung from the inky ocean blue walls, each lit with an accent light. The eyes of old men followed her down the spiral staircase. Had they done this to their children, as well?

R. Q. P. O.

The foyer was cold in every sense of the word. The sharp teeth of winter still bit, seeping through the walls and lingering in the dark energy of the mansion. Nobody came into their house with good intentions.

Alexander opened the large iron front door, bowing theatrically. "I do hope you have a wonderful time, princess. Make sure to think of me when he's riding that tight little body of yours."

N. M. L.K.

"So, I should think of stabbing you, too?" The rebellious words were ash on her tongue, immediately burned up in regret. They stared at each other, frozen in the foyer. The brilliant sunlight outside barely cracked the darkness. Alexander's eyes gleamed with malice.

"If you want. Won't matter much to me. I might not own you, but I'm allowed to borrow you any time I want. Keep that in mind on the way back home, princess."

She shivered, fear creeping down her spine like icicles. *You stupid fool.* Normally, she could come home from a date and go to bed after a scalding shower. Her hot-tempered mouth just ensured that wouldn't happen. It would've been wiser to try and run. At least it wouldn't be seen as a personal affront.

Alexander swept a hand out toward the pebbled driveway. She had no choice but to obey, tensing as she passed him. As expected, he slammed one of his hands into the back of her neck, squeezed it like a vise. Yanked her close—his onion breath made her eyes water.

"I can't wait to show you how to stab someone." He shoved her away, and she almost fell over, heels wobbling under the shift in weight. She steeled herself upright and looked forward, slicing the inside of her cheek with her molars and refusing to cry.

Henry's red BMW sat front and center, freshly waxed and gleaming in the sun. It was a beautiful car, and she knew from experience how supple the tan seats were. Alexander made her open the passenger door. Once inside, she stared at him through the window, watching as he continued to wait by the door. She took a deep breath, willing dread away. Even after four years of this, it never got easier. She wasn't sure it would be a good thing if it did.

The mansion's front door boomed. She jerked her head up, sucking her lower lip into her mouth to hide the way it trembled as Henry walked around the hood of his car. Whistling, he opened the door and slid into the driver's seat like a snake. Flashed her a grin.

"Good to see you again, baby. We're going to have so much fun. I plan on making my bonus hours count."

Time slowed as she held his gaze. Up close, she could see hairs coming out of his nostrils. Not so perfectly wrapped after all. He tapped a finger to his cheek. She obediently leaned over and kissed the spot.

The words felt thick like tar on her tongue as she said, "I've been so excited. I've missed you."

He raised an eyebrow as the engine roared to life. "I'm going to make you choke on those lies, baby."

CHAPTER TWO

The cigar smoke was suffocating. It felt like burning cotton balls on her eyes as Lucas Oremen blew another puff into her face. Her throat itched, but she swallowed the urge to cough—it would only make him laugh. And it certainly wouldn't stop him from what was about to happen. She'd failed him last night, and there was hell to pay.

They stood in the middle of his dark leather-and-wood office. He stalked around her statue-still body. She lifted her chin higher, eyes glued on a hideous painting on the opposing wall. Anything more than that simple show of defiance would result in swift punishment.

He stood a few inches shorter than her, stocky with a rounded gut. His salt-and-pepper hair—more salt than pepper—resembled a helmet underneath generous layers of gel. She'd inherited his sharp jaw, but thankfully, that was where their similarities ended. Her mom had gifted her with lush auburn hair, a plump lower lip, and long limbs. She wore a stretchy dress the color of summer clouds, and her breasts strained against the scooped neckline. Just the way he liked. And he was undoubtedly enjoying the view at this moment.

He blew another puff in her face. "Summerton told me you defied him last night."

Her knees trembled. Henry Summerton was a sick fuck who enjoyed a flair of sadism. If it meant she avoided another belt around her neck, she'd gladly defy him again. Eventually, if allowed, Henry would kill her—he'd implied as much every time she saw him—and she wanted to delay this fate as long as possible.

"He wanted—"

Quick as a snake, Lucas struck her violently with a meaty hand. The taste of blood signaled a split lip, but she didn't dare to check. His thick silver rings cut into her soft cheek. She was so numb at this point, she barely felt it. Her father seethed. "Do you think I care what he fucking wanted, pet?"

"I imagine you'd care if I were dead," she spat, still looking above his head. She'd pay for it, but every day, she crept closer toward tempting him to kill her. It would be a relief to die.

He gave a dark chuckle. "This is true. It would cost millions if you weren't usable." He stopped circling her and stalked to his golden liquor cart. It held an extensive collection of alcohol, the most expensive the planet offered. He poured another brandy, muttering to himself.

Her feet ached in the impossibly high heels, but showing discomfort was the equivalent to a crime and this interaction was only just beginning. He took a sip of his drink and looked at her again. He smirked when he noticed her watching.

Nausea was like a fist clenched deep in her gut. He slunk closer, graceful as a cat. Despite his blocky stature, years of being a boxer had honed his body into a work of art. He motioned to his favorite burgundy leather chair—a command she knew well. Air froze in her lungs, but her feet moved forward automatically.

There was a knock at the door. Lucas looked at it with irritation. "*What.*"

Alexander opened the door. Adeline's body involuntarily shuddered. "Sir, there is something that you need to take a look at."

Lucas sighed. "Can't it wait? Pet needs some corrections."

Alexander looked genuinely regretful at the interruption. He knew what "corrections" meant. "Yes, sir. I'm positive you'll want to address this immediately."

Lucas sighed. "Take her back to her bedroom. I'll meet you downstairs."

Alexander opened the door wider, giving Adeline a stony look. When she didn't move immediately, her father marched up and pushed her forward roughly.

"Don't make things worse for yourself, pet. Be a good girl and go to your bedroom. I'll come back in an hour," he promised. Alexander leered as she brushed past him. He leaned in and took a deep whiff of her perfume—vanilla, with a touch of lavender. Another one of her father's choices.

He closed the door behind them and then strode ahead of her down the hallway. The walls were bone white, lit with warm-colored sconces that flickered like candles. Her bedroom was only four doors down. Alexander opened the door and forced her to walk past him again. He grabbed her ass as she stepped inside.

"I'll make sure to ask him if I can 'correct' you next," he purred. The door clicked behind her.

But it didn't lock.

Adeline held her breath, waiting to hear the deadbolt snap into place. To her shock, it didn't. She slipped out of her heels, continuing to listen: the sharp sound of expensive shoes rushing past her door, down the nearby set of stairs; the front door closing loudly. Her father and Alexander were leaving. Without locking her inside. *Holy shit.* This was the moment she'd been waiting for.

She fumbled for the zipper on her dress, almost ripping it apart. There was no way of telling how long they'd be gone—every second counted. The dress fell into a heap, and she rushed toward the dresser. Yanking open a drawer, she seized random pieces of clothing. Blood roared in her ears, the anxiety making it hard to think.

Without contemplating what she was grabbing, Adeline pulled her overnight bag off the table by her bedroom door and stuffed it with whatever she could. She snatched a frame containing the only photo of her mother and a couple pieces of jewelry worth pawning. Hurtling toward the bed, she dropped to her knees and shot an arm under the bed frame, frantically pawing for the shoebox of cash she had hidden—a meager year's worth of savings. Tips shoved into her palm when her father's "friends" were done with her. Hopefully, it would be enough. Finally, she grabbed the coveted letters from her childhood best friend, the ones she'd never been allowed to respond to. She'd read them so many times, she'd memorized every word.

Panting, she quickly took stock of what she'd grabbed. The small bag, barely full, would have to be enough. Slipping on a pair of flats, Adeline hurried to the bedroom door. Her fingers hesitated as they curled around the doorknob. What if it was a trick? It wouldn't be the first time they'd let her believe escape was possible. She blew out a breath when it turned smoothly and the door swung open.

Adeline poked her head out—the hallway was empty.

Her shoes squeaked loudly on the marble flooring as she swept down the ancient spiral staircase, the wood banister polished to a mirror-like shine. The suitcase smacked against the railing; the sound reverberated through the house. She tripped on the carpet that lined the stairs and barely caught herself, but not before the suitcase flew out of her hand and crashed the rest of the way down. Each bang matched the slamming beats of her heart. When it finally settled at the bottom, a corner of the black plastic had cracked.

She held her breath. The mansion remained silent as a tomb, but that didn't mean it was empty. Apathetic eyes were everywhere. Her silent jailers, dressed as servants, couldn't stop her, but they certainly would report her behavior—soon.

Next to the dark wooden doors hung a set of car keys. She snatched them, their edges digging into her palm. From down the hall, the *snick* of a door closing. She startled, risked a glance. A flash of white around a corner told her someone lurked nearby. It didn't matter. She would be gone by the time whoever it was returned. She pitied the servant required to report her escape.

The heavy doors opened with a groan, revealing the dark gray pebbled driveway. It was a beautiful day, the sounds of nearby songbirds a jarring soundtrack to her moment of defiance. The sun reflected off the deep koi pond nestled in the center of the massive driveway. Beads of sweat prickled her brow, a drop sliding down her temple.

Not bothering to close the door behind her, Adeline hurried over to a black coup and threw her suitcase into the backseat. She got in the driver's seat and stabbed the keys into the ignition, the pressure in her chest releasing slightly as the engine turned over. Shifting into drive, she peeled away, pebbles rattling against the fender and scratching the expensive paint.

She tapped the steering wheel impatiently as the iron gate ahead slowly opened. Every second was a wasted resource. The world didn't hold enough time for her escape. The only way she was even able to attempt to leave—again—was because she had already been planning another escape attempt. She was lucky enough to have recently swiped the key to the drawer that held her phone and wallet. It was strange that she was left alone in her unlocked bedroom, but Adeline wasn't going to look a gift horse in the mouth. She had no idea where Lucas had gone, but he'd be back soon.

"Come *on*," she cried out, urging the groaning iron gate to move faster.

Finally, the gate gaped open, and she put the pedal to the metal. She was leaving behind everything she'd ever known, but it didn't matter. At least he wouldn't be able to rape her tonight.

✳✳✳

Exhaustion crept into her bones the farther she drove. No one followed her—she obsessively checked the rearview mirror and took only left turns for the first hour. After a couple hundred miles, her eyes grew heavy. She gnawed on the inside of her cheek, tasting the tang of blood. Stopping now would be a mistake. *He'll find you anyway.*

That sinister voice, her only friend for the last few years, curled around her anxiety with thick tendrils.

She pushed and pushed, but after almost falling asleep three times, she gave in and pulled into a worn-down motel. One night of rest couldn't hurt. She'd continue running tomorrow. Who the hell knew where, but anywhere Lucas wasn't would be good enough.

The motel was the last place he would look, a complete shithole fit for "the lessers," as he called them. It felt like a familiar roadside stay, in the way that she had seen its twin in movies. Horror movies, more specifically. She shuddered and pushed the thought away. She'd never liked horror movies.

The motel was certainly less than impressive. A one-floor building with six rooms and an office attached. Its walls were painted a faded yellow, and the ancient doors were the color of puke. Every window showed thick layers of dirt. A lone beat-up truck parked horizontally in front of the dimly lit office. The flickering of a TV offered the only light inside. She parked next to the truck, and stepped out, glancing around warily. The air was thick and humid, springtime creeping in too soon. All around the motel were cornfields, the full moon drawing its light over the landscape. The miles of road in each direction were empty.

A bell above the office door jangled as she stepped into the chilly space. The foyer was spartan, featuring a worn brown couch with cushions that dipped into themselves.

It reeked of stale coffee and cigarettes. A wiry man, thin as a toothpick, looked up from his phone, eyeing Adeline's split lip and bruised cheek. His skin was sallow, untouched by sunlight. Partially balding with a paunch, he wasn't much to look at. His gaze burned into her flesh, those shit-brown eyes assessing. The nametag said Hubert. Hubert arched one of his brown bushy eyebrows at the tightening of her fist. Sighing, he put his phone down and turned to his dilapidated computer.

"How many nights?"

Staying in one spot for too long was risky. She reached for the small amount of cash she'd grabbed from the box and slapped a fifty-dollar bill onto the counter. His eyes flickered with surprise.

"It's only twenty a night."

"The extras are for your discretion."

The clerk paused, weighing his options. Finally, Hubert nodded and grabbed the money, shoving it into his pocket.

"Room six." He scraped a rusty key across the old wood counter. She snatched it, muttering her thanks. Adeline stepped back out into the night and took a deep breath. One of many steps left.

She grabbed the almost-broken suitcase from the passenger seat and patted her back pocket, ensuring the cash was still there. The door to room six creaked open, flecks of rust floating from the hinges. The lone deadbolt wouldn't hold against any force, but it was better than nothing.

She grimaced at the room. Scuff marks littered the dirty walls. She crinkled her nose at the smell of cigarettes infused in the cheap paint. The AC clearly wasn't working; the air was stuffy and thick in her lungs. The queen-sized bed squeaked as she tossed the suitcase on top of the faded brown comforter.

It was a far cry from the five-star hotels her father required. A motel like this would have enraged him. In other words, this place was perfect. He'd have no reason to look for her here, not his *princess*. His moneymaker.

Adeline unzipped the suitcase and fished out the small pile of toiletries she'd packed. Cringing at the stickiness of the flat carpet, she entered the bathroom. It was all white tile, although labeling the grout as white was too generous. The entire room needed a real scrubbing. Two relatively clean white towels hung from a rusted towel rack. The spigot sputtered with hot, clean water—a small blessing.

Steam curled around the room, fogging the mirror. She stripped, trying to avoid her reflection, but failed. Her ribs strained against a thin layer of flesh, and her hipbones jutted past her flat stomach. She desperately needed a few good meals. Food had become a weapon of control; she'd lost the war.

She stepped into the shower and sighed as hot water cascaded down her curved backside. She knew it would never be hot enough to clean her tainted body.

The water mixed with tears as something inside her heart split. The walls echoed with a keening noise that she realized was pouring from her mouth. Her knees buckled, and she collapsed into the tub, bringing her knees into her chest. Drowning in this tub would be a small mercy. That last breath would be the sweetest. At this point, there wasn't much in the world keeping her going.

When the water ran cold, goosebumps prickling her skin, she turned off the tap and wrapped a towel around her frail torso. Shivering against the chill, Adeline walked back into the room and reached for a pair of pajamas.

As she pulled up the soft pair of blue pants, the sound of a car pulling up to the motel made her heart putter to a stop. Her fingers froze, ears perked for any sign of danger. There was the sound of murmuring voices, a small chuckle, and the ringing of the office bell. She slipped an eye around the curtain and saw an unfamiliar car in the parking lot. It was a nondescript compact car. Certainly, nothing her father would ever be caught dead in. She was still safe—for now.

Pulling back the threadbare comforter, she inspected the sheets, hoping there were no six-legged visitors. They seemed clean enough, so she wrapped herself into the fabric like a cocoon. Flashes of memories clouded her brain, making it hard to relax. Unwelcome hands on her flesh, digging into tender spots. Not an inch of her body had belonged to her these past four years.

Trying to lasso her thoughts, Adeline closed her eyes and sucked air into her lungs. In for one, two, three, four. Out for four, three, two, one. She'd seen it in a movie once and practiced every day.

Her thoughts slowed from a gallop to a trot, and eventually to a meander. Outside, a cricket chirred. Adeline focused on the comforting sound, visualizing the cricket absorbing the white light of the moon and releasing it back into the world as a melody.

Adeline smiled and nestled deeper into the bed. Tomorrow, everything would get figured out. She'd get in the car and continue driving until she found a place that felt safe. Maybe she could even try calling—

BAM!

The door splintered, exploding inward. Adeline screamed and clutched at her stomach as a sizeable chunk of wood flew into her hip. Alexander, dressed in black combat gear, pulled back his thick boot.

His beady eyes narrowed as she tried to scramble out of bed. His large canines gleamed as his mouth peeled apart in a smile, a dark chuckle making the hairs on her arms stand up. She didn't care if he heard her hysterical sobs, watching her frantically kicking free of the comforter.

She had to escape—*now.*

As Alexander stepped through the destroyed door frame, she eyed the small window inside the bathroom. If she could just make it in time and prop something against the door, then maybe, just maybe…

Her hands slammed onto the disgusting carpet as she kicked free from the fabric, but in the end, she was too slow. It took three strides for Alexander to close the distance between them. He yanked her upwards by her hair. The separation of her scalp and skull was pure fire. Adeline dug her nails frantically into his wrists. He tossed her onto the mattress like a bag of trash. She lunged for the bathroom again, and this time he wrapped his thick sausage fingers around her throat. Clawing at them only made him squeeze tighter. A dark chuckle rumbled.

"He's *very* angry," Alexander purred. Lifted her up until her toes skimmed the floor. He scoured her with his eyes, from her mouth to between her thighs. A tear escaped down her cheek. It'd been foolish to think escape was possible.

He licked it off slowly with an insidious hum. Her mouth snapped open and closed like a suffocating fish, but he didn't relent.

"He says I can have you after, if I want."

Desperation spun like a tornado—she lashed out with her nails again, raked his ominous eyes, even as the world around her tunneled. He snarled and threw her back with such force, her brain rattled as it hit the wall. Something cracked. For a moment, the world went black. She sucked in slivers of air as she tried to orient herself. Stars danced in her vision. Maybe this was the moment. Maybe it would all finally end.

Then he walked in.

Her father's squat but powerful frame loomed in the shadows, lit by the headlights of the non-descript car. Where Alexander was the appetizer, her father would be the main course.

Adeline crawled on her hands and knees, unable to get away. She screamed as loud as she could, but it only came out as croaks. Her father's cold dark eyes crinkled with amusement as he glanced around the room. Alexander stood up straighter and took a small step back in deference.

"A bit below our price range, isn't it?" Lucas clucked his tongue in disappointment. He made a show of sniffing the air, and a feline smile curled along his thick jowls—the smell of her fear was an aphrodisiac. Tears streamed down her face, spittle flying through the air. His mouth quirked as he stepped closer. She eyed the gun at Alexander's waist. He noticed and placed a massive hand on it.

"Adeline, Adeline, Adeline." Her father never said her name. This was going to be *really* fucking bad. The last time she had tried to escape, he'd found her and ensured that every inch of her body hurt for days. She raised herself up on her knees, squared her shoulders. All she had left was her dignity.

He took a deep breath, as if he had all the time in the world. Eyes full of death quickly turned feral. Terror thickened like a pool of tar in her gut.

"My sweet pet, did you think you could escape? I *let* you escape. I never tire of this game you insist on playing. You're such a naughty little creature."

He took another step forward, close enough now for her nose to brush against his pants. Her neck ached when she craned up to look at him. The air crackled with his rage, his eyes narrowing into deadly slits, focused entirely on her stomach.

"It's time, my sweet pet, that you learn exactly what it means to be my property."

At the word property, she felt rage boiling from deep within. Years of festering, oozing, pure fury ready for a target.

"I *hate* you," she snarled.

He laughed. "I don't care. Hold her up."

The order froze the fire in her veins. She screamed again, hoisted up by the hand gripping the back of her neck. She kicked out at him, missing by an inch as he stepped backward. He laughed again, the sound dark and cold with hate. He cracked his knuckles and closed the space between them again.

His stench was oily and sharp, like burning gasoline. It made her gag, too many memories of that scent filling her nose late at night. He bared his teeth like a grinning hyena. She went to slap him, but he caught her hand at the wrist and squeezed. Adeline shrieked in agony as something crunched inside. She tried to yank it back, but he held fast. Leaning forward, he raked his nose against her throat, breathing in her terror. She tried to bite him, but missed. He snickered.

"I think our time together is at an end. I'm tired of your fight," he said, pulling brass knuckles from a pocket and sliding them onto his fingers. "You're getting a bit too old, anyway. So, consider this your last lesson in life: You never held a chance. All those times you escaped were at my leisure. I had hoped you would learn your lesson, but apparently not. It was nice working with you, pet."

He reeled back. The air exploded out of her lungs as the brass knuckles made contact. He was known for his uppercut. Adeline's insides turned into jelly. Wetness trickled down her thighs, her bladder unable to contain itself. She lashed out again with her bare foot, this time connecting with his groin. He grunted and stumbled backward, bellowing with rage. For a moment, she thought she had hit her mark, but he pressed a hand against the inside of his thigh, deadly promise flashing in those dark orbs of death.

"It was going to be quick, but you've changed my mind."

The last thing she saw were those brass knuckles hurtling toward her face. Then the world went black.

CHAPTER THREE

The smell of rotting food jolted Adeline awake. She tried to open her eyes, but only one would obey. She looked around—she was surrounded by moldy waste and utterly unspeakable things. The pain kicked in then. There wasn't a single atom of her body that wasn't screaming. She opened her mouth for more air and choked on the putrid smell of rot. *Where the fuck was she?* If this was hell, she hoped to die all over again, slipping into nothingness this time.

Adeline pressed her hands against the ground, and it gave way. Not ground—trash. Reality hit, another punch in the face: She was in a *dumpster.* Putting more weight on her palms, she hissed at her swollen wrist. *Great.* She gritted her teeth and pushed past the pain to sit up. It was a mistake. She cried out as her internal organs felt like they were reassembling themselves, pushing against each other in unfamiliar ways. This was worse than he'd ever done. She wondered if he even knew she was still alive.

To her relief, the lid to the dumpster was only a couple of feet above. All she had to do was reach up and push the heavy plastic lid high enough to shove herself over the edge.

No biggie.

She took it slow, taking time to sob in between wishing he had just killed her. In the last four years, she had contemplated slitting her own wrists more than once but never seemed to make it happen. She just wasn't brave enough. Adeline was a coward, and she knew it.

By the time she was high enough to lift the lid and peer outside, sweat soaked her entire body. It made her hands slippery. The sun was peeking over the horizon, hot pinks and orange clouds sweeping across the sky. She took a moment to appreciate its beauty.

Then her arm muscles cramped. *Hard.* She cried out and lost her grasp on the edge of the dumpster. The hand holding the lid slipped. She snatched both back before they were crushed. Back to square one.

By the time the morning sunshine was high and bright enough that it invaded every shadow, she had finally flung herself over the edge of the dumpster. Her body slammed onto the concrete below. Flipping onto her back, she sucked in gulps of oxygen, stealing a moment to rest. A rib twinged against her lungs. She brought up the hand that was in better shape and gingerly touched her face. It was surprisingly not as bad as it could've been—a swollen eye but that was about it. All of her father's rage seemed to have been focused on the rest of her body. Sighing, she looked around. The yellow walls of the motel were behind her. He hadn't even attempted to hide her.

It took what felt like an eternity to stand. One ankle felt more weak than usual, but mostly, she could walk if she shuffled like a zombie. Rounding the corner of the motel, she saw the splintered door to her room, its interior dark. Aside from Hubert's truck, the parking lot was empty—her father was gone, along with the car she had taken. Narrowing her good eye, she shuffled as fast as she could to the motel office door.

Wincing, her crooked fingers protesting, she opened the door and stumbled inside. Hubert dozed in his chair, legs up against the top of the desk.

"Hurbert." His name was barely a croak, and still he startled, almost falling out of his chair. His eyes bugged.

"Wha-what happened?"

Adeline turned to a mirror hanging by the door and took in her reflection. Her whole body was smattered with blotches of green and blue. One eye was swollen shut, and multiple splits cut into her lips. Her clothes were soaked with god knows what. She smelled like absolute shit.

"Uh, are you, uh—" Hubert stuttered, at a loss for words.

She bit back a sob. Staying at the motel again would be a mistake, in case Lucas thought better about leaving evidence behind.

"Oh, you know, I'm great. Can I use your phone?"

His caterpillar eyebrows shot up. "Are you going to call the cops? Because I have nothing to do with this."

"Hubert," she said impatiently, knees straining with pain. She leaned against the wall. "I don't care about whatever you've got going on here. I need to call someone before my father comes back."

Defying all odds, Hubert's eyes widened further. "Your *father* did that?"

"Yes. Now, can I please use your phone? Maybe have a change of clothes? I'll leave money, I promise."

After a moment's hesitation, he bolted for the desk and snatched the phone out from behind it. He tossed it over to her. She sucked in a sharp breath as she caught it with her good hand.

"I didn't know, okay? You gotta believe me."

She ignored him as she dialed the only number she knew by heart, thumbing through those letters from Kennedi every night. It was a shot in the dark. The number might not even work now after four years.

"Hello?"

Kennedi's beautiful voice threatened to crush her under layers of grief. That one word was the first light she'd experienced after years of darkness. Adeline bit the inside of her cheek hard enough to break skin. She barely felt its ember of pain in the cacophony of agony coating her body.

Flashes of memory filled her mind: red curls. Soft, freckled skin. A laugh made of bubbled joy. A sense of mischief that kept people guessing. Everything good in this world.

"Hey, it's Adeline." The silence stretched for so long, Adeline double-checked to make sure the call hadn't dropped. "Hello?"

"Addie?" Kennedi breathed with shock. "What's going on? Are you okay?"

A sob escaped Adeline's lips. She choked on it before saying, "No. I need help."

"Okay. I'm still in that small town we moved to ages ago. Menforth. Can you make it here?" No hesitation.

Adeline almost collapsed in gratitude. "Yes, but I could be followed. I don't know if I'm safe."

"I don't care. Is this your number?"

Adeline looked at Hubert, who heard the question and nodded. "Yes, this is my number for now."

He watched a drop of blood slide from her elbow to the nasty carpet but said nothing.

"Okay, I'm going to text you an address. I'll have a friend meet you—Mags. We will get you somewhere safe, okay?"

"Thank you."

She hung up and looked at Hubert's pale face. He fiddled with a pen as she said, "Thank you. Can I get some clothes? Please? I might not have a lot of time left."

He hustled out of the room, past a door. She heard a curse, the sound of something falling, and a drawer slamming. There was a glass of water on the desk. Adeline pitched forward, reaching for it. She guzzled it greedily, relishing the cool liquid down her throat, ignoring the coppery taste of blood. Hubert reappeared and froze in place, his eyes on the smear of blood at the lip of his glass. Ignoring the look, she reached for the clothes in his hands.

"I'm going to take a quick shower in the room. I'll leave money on the end table and try to clean up what I can."

"Don't worry about it," he assured her. "Won't be my first time."

She didn't want to know. With a grateful dip of her chin, she hobbled to the door. She paused, turned to look at him once more. "Is there a bus station nearby?"

He reached under the desk, jingled a pair of keys. "Take my truck. I've been looking to get a new one. I'll report it stolen in two days, so get rid of it. Just take care of yourself. Hide."

She gave a grim smile. "Thanks, Hu, for everything. I really appreciate it." The office door closed behind her. Leaning heavily against the nearby wall, she stumbled into her hotel room, past the splintered door, and aimed straight for the bathroom. After a quick shower, hissing as the water burned her wounds, she dried off and dressed quickly. The ticking of an invisible clock thrummed in her blood. Time was running out, and she needed to disappear.

Slipping into the clean clothes, Adeline pulled out cash from her bag and left it on the end table as promised. She avoided looking at the destroyed room or the stains on the floor, and willed her feet toward the truck.

The worn, soft leather seats gently hugged her as she slid inside. She put the key in the ignition and turned it. The truck's engine purred to life. She pulled out the cellphone Hubert had given her and put in the address from Kennedi's text. Menforth. Wherever the hell that was.

CHAPTER FOUR

Stomach growling, Adeline stopped for a few minutes at a truck stop. It was way past lunch, and she hadn't eaten since breakfast the day before. She bought an energy drink, chips, a first aid kit, and some pain meds.

On second thought, she grabbed some heavily tinted sunglasses. To her amazement, few truckers gave her appearance a second glance. After chugging the energy drink, she inspected her wounds in the bathroom.

Deep, swollen bruises marred her ribs and stomach. There was a familiar, sharp pain every time she inhaled—a bruised or broken rib, no doubt. With the energy drink buzzing through her veins, she went to work cleaning the scrapes and cuts.

Hissing through clenched teeth, Adeline cleaned the cut above her swollen eye. It was deep red, and nothing could hide it. Sighing, she put a large patch over it. Sufficiently caffeinated and cleaned, she piled back into the truck and continued the long drive while holding ice to her face.

By the time Adeline reached Menforth three hours later, her adrenaline was swiftly fading. It was late afternoon, bright sunshine lighting up the thick maple forest—the primary industry there was maple syrup. *Menforth: Home Sweet Home.* The jolly wooden welcome sign showed a pile of pancakes drizzled with syrup. Her stomach grumbled at the sight of food.

She texted Kennedi: **Here. Where do I go?**

The response was quick: ***Look for a woman named Mags at the coffee shop. You'll know her when you see her. I'll see you in a couple of hours.***

The town of Menforth was quaint. Colorful shops lined the streets, with tiny tables dotting the sidewalks. There were a fair amount of people going about their day. Adeline pulled into a parking spot and shoved her back into the seat with a huff. She slowly stepped out of the truck, trying not to hold her aching ribs as she moved. A few curious bystanders stared, eyes flicking to her obvious bandages.

Adeline attempted a friendly smile, but people averted their eyes. Her knees and ankle barked with protest as she hobbled over to a coffee shop, painted light purple with yellow shutters. The surrounding shops were all different colors, creating a vibrant backdrop to the already sunny day. If she hadn't felt like death, it would have been charming.

Opening the door, she jumped at the small bell announcing her presence. As her eyes adjusted to the light, Adeline spotted a collection of cozy couches and small tables. Soft muzak played over a speaker. A young woman with a dark complexion looked at her curiously from behind the counter. In fact, all of the patrons had stopped mid-conversation to stare.

Their attention stripped her bare, and the urge to bolt was overwhelming. Lucas almost never let her out in public—this was the largest crowd she'd seen in years. *No one is going to hurt you at a coffee shop.*

Stretching an awkward smile across her teeth, Adeline made her way up to the counter.

The barista gave her a warm greeting. "Welcome to Gerald's Place. You new in town?"

It wouldn't be wise to give too much information—there were eyes and ears everywhere. "Yep. Maybe passing through. Maybe staying for a spell."

"What happened to your face?"

The blunt question caught her off guard. Adeline pretended to study the baked goods, laser-focused on their labels. "Uh, fell off a bike. Can I have a cinnamon cake?"

The woman didn't move. She was still examining Adeline; she clearly didn't believe the bike excuse. "Looks like quite the nasty fall. Are you staying with anyone here?"

Adeline glanced around, noticing everyone waiting for her answer. "Uh, yeah. Kennedi Murphy invited me to stay with her friend, Mags?"

"Oh, Kennedi!" The barista's eyes lit up. "She's amazing. Well, let's start off with a coffee, huh? My name is Jean, by the way."

She noticed how Jean didn't say the same about Mags. "Adeline. Can I have a latte with cinnamon?" Used to the standoffish customer service from high-end establishments, Adeline was wary as she pulled out cash from her back pocket. She handed over some dollar bills but Jean waved them away.

"On the house. I sense you need one of my famous lattes, and newcomers always get a free sample." Jean winked and turned her focus to the coffee-making gadgets lining the counter. In record time, Jean had a steaming cup in front of her with a star stenciled into the froth. "Sugar and cream are to the right. Try it first, though. I'll bring your cake over."

"Thank you." Adeline grabbed the hot mug gingerly and took it to an empty table by one of the large windows. It gave her the perfect vantage point from which to take in the town center.

True to her word, Jean made an incredible latte. Adeline savored it, letting the soft touches of sugar and milk slide down her throat, warming up her ice-cold insides. It'd been years since she'd been allowed to drink one.

Jean looked at her eagerly from across the room. Adeline inclined her head in approval, and Jean beamed and then turned around and started restocking the pastry display.

Outside the window, Adeline watched the passersby in the town square. Spring still teased the senses, but it was warm enough to wear shorts. The sidewalks were clean, and the storefronts shined, all occupied by average-looking people.

Adeline was accustomed to seeing primped and Botoxed rich people. Here, there wasn't a briefcase in sight. A little girl with hair the color of molten gold visibly strained at her mother's arm in an attempt to drag her somewhere. Adeline watched as the mother sighed and gave in, following her daughter to the ice cream shop.

Adeline looked away as Jean slid the cake in front of her. Thankful, she dug a fork into the sugary bread and had a bite. She had to hold back a moan at the exploding sweetness. Desserts have been a rarity these last few years. She savored each bite while continuing to stare out the window.

At the center of the town square was an old courthouse. It was typical brown brick but with large pillars at the front and small gargoyles perched atop the roof. On the steps of the courthouse sat an older woman with frazzled gray hair, red-rimmed glasses that hung on for dear life at the end of her nose, and a large sandwich in her hands.

Despite the warmer weather, the woman wore a pair of old jeans and a red flannel shirt. She popped the last bite into her mouth and her bright eyes scanned the sidewalks.

The woman startled and then glanced down, reading something on her cellphone. Too late Adeline realized she was staring. The woman jerked her head up and made eye contact with Adeline as she slowly chewed and swallowed her last bite. Adeline looked down at her almost-empty mug, hoping the woman hadn't seen her gawking.

Her heart skipped when she saw the woman strutting up to the coffee shop, staring intensely. A car almost hit her, the driver yelling something, but the woman just flipped him the bird and continued on.

The bell rang as the door burst inward. Conversation paused again, but this time, everyone was a little more tense.

"Hey, Mags, how ya doin'?" Jean called to the woman.

"Black coffee, Jeany," Mags commanded in a voice like rough sandpaper. She turned to look at Adeline with eyes the color of summer skies, taking stock of the injuries.

Without a word, she plopped down at the table, splaying her legs and propping her arm on the back of the chair. Her graying hair was wild, tight ringlets exploding from her head. Up close, Adeline could see deep laugh lines carved beneath her eyes and around her thin mouth. She wore no makeup, and her nails were chewed down to small stumps with dirt caked underneath. Something about this woman was both terrifying and inviting.

"Um, hi?" Adeline squeaked. The urge to bolt resurfaced. Jean came up and placed a mug in front of Mags, who muttered her thanks. She took a sip of the coffee, wincing at the heat.

"She always makes this shit too hot." The faint smell of manure wafted over.

"You're Mags?" Adeline struggled to find something else to say.

"Yep. Kennedi sent me but didn't tell me much. Where are you from?"

Adeline's good eye darted around the room. No one seemed to look their way, but she suspected all ears were tuned to them. She cleared her throat.

"Here and there," she said, trying to sound confident. "Are you able to help me?"

"Yep. Are you okay with cats?"

"I don't know. I've never seen one before."

"I forgive you, and we'll fix that immediately. Are you being followed?" Mags' fingers thrummed the table, the pace sharing her impatience.

Adeline wasn't sure how much to share, especially in a public place. She lowered her voice as she said, "Maybe. Is that a problem?"

Growing up in a world where niceties and manners were paramount, this woman's personality was jarring. A touch refreshing, as well.

"No problem at all. As they say, Danger is my middle name. Come on, then." Mags stood, her chair scraping back loudly.

"I thought I would wait until—"

"Wait until what? Kennedi told me to keep an eye out for you. Come on, stop dawdling."

"Can you just give me a second? I've had to do some adjusting, and frankly, I'm tired as hell." Adeline said, overcome with frustration. It was all too much, going from being locked up in a life full of terror, to almost being killed, to now having a deranged old woman drag her somewhere.

Mags sat back down and leaned forward on her elbows. On her forearm was a small tattoo of a gray cat. Her eyes were the color of blue icebergs but turned the color of stormy waters when observing Adeline's injuries. Leaning to one side, she looked out the window and across the street, where the beat-up truck waited.

"This town is the size of a backyard. Everyone knows everyone. And everyone helps everyone. Kennedi called me and told me someone she knows needs help. Looks to me like you aren't tied to one place right now. Why don'tcha come stay with me for a few days? I have a guest room, too many cats, and a dazzling personality that is sure to keep you entertained." The darkness disappeared from her eyes, and a small smile tugged at her wrinkled mouth.

"Why?"

"Why, what?" Mags said impatiently, taking a deep drink from her coffee.

"Why help a stranger?" Kindness always came with strings attached. That's the way society works.

Mags tilted her head with curiosity. "You look like someone took their anger out on you. You're on the lam, and I know what that's like.

It's been quiet too long, and I need a little adventure in my life. My cats can be quite dull—don't tell them I said that—and my garden monotonous. Now, let's go. I don't like how much the townies stare." At those words, the other patrons snapped back to their conversations. Mags rolled her eyes and slapped a dollar on the table.

A burning sense of apprehension almost stopped her from following the woman. What if she was escaping right into another shitty situation? The deep, unending ache of exhaustion and terror just simply said, *what else could she do to you that hasn't already been done?* Instinct told her that Mags—and Kennedi—were to be trusted.

What was left to lose?

Standing, she walked out of the shop without a second glance. Gathering Hubert's keys and phone, Adeline followed.

A nearby green truck roared to life, and Mags hollered something out the window. It sounded an awful lot like, "Get your ass in gear."

Adeline climbed into the cab of her own truck, grimacing as she buckled up.

"What the fuck am I doing?" she muttered. Mags peeled out of the parking lot, gaining multiple irritated looks. Adeline had a feeling as she started the engine that this was only the beginning of the old woman's "dazzling personality."

***

Mags' house was an old Victorian-style home, painted different pinks and purples. It was hideous and charming all at once. In the front yard was an enormous garden lined with a rainbow-colored wooden fence.

Mags hopped out of her truck and stood on the sidewalk, weathered hands on her round hips. Parking behind Mags' truck, Adeline turned off the engine and climbed out, overnight bag in hand. She closed her eyes and took a deep breath, sucking in the smell of fresh-cut grass and wet earth. Rounding the front of the truck, she kept her eyes on the sidewalk. Her ankle buckled—she barely caught herself on the hood. Mags jolted forward but saw the look in Adeline's eye. Adeline didn't ask for help. She saw a flicker of respect in Mags' sharp eyes.

"So, what happened to you?"

Did no one in this town mind their own business? "Fell into a fist repeatedly."

"Been there. Who? Father? Brother? Pastor?"

Adeline paused, alarmed. "A pastor? Really?"

"Yes." Her tone was unapologetic. "You'd be surprised what men would do." She looked Adeline up and down. "Or maybe not. So, what happened?"

"Father. I think he thinks I'm dead, but I don't know."

Mags grabbed the bag from her hands. "Me and my cats are looking forward to hearing about it. Let's go."

Mags pirouetted and walked down the sidewalk past the flourishing garden with a nod to herself. She left the magenta-colored front door open for Adeline, letting her take her time through the garden.

With trepidation, Adeline stepped inside the foyer. She took in the quirky and vibrant decor—it looked like a rainbow had exploded inside the house. Colorful frames with different pieces of artwork were hung haphazardly on floral-wallpapered walls.

A set of stairs led to the second floor, two cats sitting at the top. Adeline gasped as something brushed up against her calf. A small calico looked at her, squinting in the bright light. Adeline's hand hesitated above the cat's arched back.

"That's Aslin," Mags announced. "Don't be afraid—she isn't the type to bite."

"They're softer than I thought." Aslin purred as Adeline's nails sifted through the silky fur. Mags watched the interaction silently, clenching her jaw.

"What's wrong?"

Mags pursed her lips. "How the hell have you never experienced the glory of cats?" She whirled around then and continued through the house.

The living room was to Adeline's left, filled to the brim with different colored pillows, a yellow couch, and at least a dozen quilts thrown all over the space. Three more cats curled up on different soft surfaces, staring at her silently.

"Stop dawdling and close the front door." Mags appeared on her right, inside what would typically be the dining room. Instead, the floor held canvases in various states of creation. Tarps were laid out on the floor. Splashes, splatters, and methodical shapes coated the canvases and the walls. It was beautiful chaos. Adeline closed the front door behind her, ensuring Aslin was still inside.

It was then that Adeline noticed the house smelled of nutmeg and coffee.

Mags looked down at Aslin. "Don't mind her. She's a house cat. I found her in the garden as a kitten, soaking wet. She refuses to go outside now. Now that one—" she pointed up the stairs to a fat orange tabby, whose green eyes flicked to Mags with haughty indifference. "That's Todd. He's an asshole. Do *not* let him outside. He won't come back, and he needs medication every day. Follow me."

Mags walked through the art room—the only way to explain the artful insanity—and led Adeline to a massive kitchen. Unlike the rest of the house, this room was peace incarnate. No solid colors, only muted tones complementing white walls and tile. Adeline gasped in surprise. Mags gave her a knowing look.

"All chaos needs balance. This is mine. Are you hungry?"

As if on cue, Adeline's stomach growled loudly. She offered a sheepish look. Mags chuckled. "Sit tight. A lasagna is callin' your name."

Adeline sat at the gray wooden kitchen table. She noted the deep scratches on its surface. Running a finger through one of the tinier grooves, the sides felt smooth from wear.

There was clearly a history worn into this piece of furniture. She'd never been around something that was intended to last through generations. Her father demanded only brand-new things, minus his Civil War-era desk.

Mags pulled out different containers from the pale green fridge. Adeline watched her spoon something red and orange onto a plate before throwing it into the microwave.

"Do you live here all alone?"

Mags hummed thoughtfully. "Yep. Me, the cats, and the occasional lover to keep things spicy."

The microwave beeped. Mags retrieved the plate and placed it in front of Adeline. "It's a three-day-old lasagna. Hope you're okay with that. It's still good. Want a beer?"

Adeline nodded and dug into the dish. It was delicious. She'd never had a home cooked meal infused with care and love. Food cooked by expensive chefs wasn't the same with artistic plating and a too-strong focus on foods most people couldn't pronounce. Bottle caps snapped off and clattered to the ground. Mags sat down across from her and slid a brown bottle her way.

She raised her bottle to Adeline. "Cheers."

Adeline did the same and took a swig. It tasted unlike anything she'd ever had. Extremely hoppy with a nutty aftertaste. "This is amazing."

Mags smiled. "Thanks. So, what's your story?"

It had been an incredibly long day. Underneath the bruises, Adeline's heart ached. A hot bath and a warm bed sounded like heaven.

Mags' face softened as Adeline struggled to find the right answer. She dragged her eyes from Adeline's face and continued down her body. The T-shirt was two sizes too big, swallowing her narrow body, and her arms were bare. Around her wrists she noticed old bruises from restraints. Fresh ones bloomed elsewhere.

It was difficult for Adeline to not tuck herself into a ball. She wanted to hide the wounds. Tears burned as she looked down into her lap.

"I don't know if I'm ready to say. It isn't safe. Are you sure you want me—"

"You're safe here."

Adeline jerked her head up. Mags was like unbending, hot steel, but her expression softened. "If anyone tries to come in this house, I will not only sick my cats on them, they will also be greeted by my twelve-gauge. Do you need any medical attention? It looks like you're relatively patched up, but I have some skills."

Adeline shifted in her seat, wincing at the twinging in her ribs. "No. I cleaned everything, and I don't think there's much to be done about my rib."

Mags nodded thoughtfully. "I'll make sure to get you some pain meds. Bring that swelling down in your face. But don't hesitate to ask. I know a guy that can zip right over and patch you up."

"Thank you." The offer of kindness, though simple, made Adeline burst into tears. She expected Mags to do something comforting, like try to hug her, but instead the woman sat in her chair, watching with sympathy.

Mags somehow knew Adeline didn't need—or want—hugs. Not yet. The thought made her cry even harder. She just needed someone *there*. In four years, no one had been there for her.

When the tears had dried, Adeline chugged the rest of her now-warm beer. Mags gave a small smile and did the same.

Mags stood. "Well, let's show you to your room."

Adeline nodded, relieved that the inquisition had been averted. She followed Mags upstairs to a small bedroom. It was simple, with light blue floral wallpaper and a queen-size bed in the center.

All normal furniture was present: a dresser, a desk, and a chair. Nothing fancy. The room was the size of her old walk-in closet, which strangely enough lent it a cozy feeling. Turning the light on, Mags strode over to the bed and pulled back the comforter. She glanced around the room and shrugged.

"It's nothing much."

"It's perfect," Adeline breathed.

"Great. Do you need anything else from the truck?"

Adeline looked down at her feet, her cheeks warming. "I don't have anything else."

Mags stared at her long enough to make Adeline shift uncomfortably. Her ankle was throbbing, but she refused to show it. A clock ticked somewhere. A cat mewled. Finally, Adeline gave an exasperated sigh.

"Are you going to stare at me all night?"

A muscle twitched in Mags' jaw. She went past her, into the hallway. "I have some clothes packed up, from back when I was a lot less round in the middle. I'll get them for you."

Adeline gaped at the receding back of the woman, easily the most fascinating person she'd ever met. Mags reappeared moments later with a heap of clothes in her hands and a fresh towel.

Adeline reached for the pile. "Thank you. Really, I appreciate it. I need some rest now, though."

Without waiting for a response, Adeline hobbled to the bathroom. She closed the door behind her, catching Mags' gaze honed in on Adeline's ankle. There was a conversation brewing. Adeline just needed sleep first.

Reaching for Hubert's cellphone, she texted Kennedi: **With Mags. I'm exhausted. I need to sleep. Can I see you tomorrow?**

The response was instant. **You sure? I just wrapped up some emergency work and was going to head over.**

Yeah. I'm no good right now.

Three dots appeared, then, **Alright. Text me immediately if you need anything.**

Throwing the phone down on the nightstand, Adeline grabbed some clothes and a towel. After a quick shower, Adeline pulled on some of the clothes Mags had offered. They were a bit too big, but they were clean. The sun was still high in the sky when she crawled into bed. As soon as her head hit the pillow, she was asleep.

CHAPTER FIVE

It was past two in the morning, and Adeline shivered in a corner, waiting for the verdict.

Her father had Alexander rip all of her clothes, minus the expensive lingerie the maids delivered the day before. Afterwards, she was left standing in the middle of the room, covering her stomach with her arms, waiting for him to say something. Her father and Alexander left seconds later, commanding her to go stand in the corner and wait. It had been over an hour since.

She leaned against the freezing stone wall, attempting to blend into the shadows of the dark study. Maybe they would finally swallow her whole and drag her to hell. It couldn't be any worse than this place. Being Satan's mistress would be a relief when compared to being Lucas Oremen's whore.

The massive fireplace glowed, its heat filling the room, touching everything but her skin. She ground her teeth together as she shifted in place, taking one side of her body off the ice-cold stones and giving her other side a turn. Her shivers turned into full-blown shakes.

She jumped as the doorknob turned. To her dismay, all four of her father's closest business partners filed in after him, their gazes surveying the room until finally they found her. She shrunk back, silently begging God, the gods, Satan, Zeus—anyone—to come save her. Adeline choked on a sob as Alexander closed the door behind him before taking his place beside her father. The business partners stood silently, hands clasped in front, eyes locked on her body.

The man standing directly next to her father was Sean McBride. McBride was deeply invested in oil and backdoor weapons dealings. He had strawberry blond hair, tousled in a boyish way. His brown eyes were soulless and hungry as a demon's. The last time she'd been in the same room as him, she could barely chew for a week afterward.

Down the line, next to Sean, was Henry Summerton. Hair the color of spun gold and bright, too-large veneers. He had a fetish for women fucking the stick shifts in his expensive cars.

Next to him was Carl Lambert. He was almost as tall as Alexander, covered in tattoos, and with rings on each finger. He packed a mean right hook. Her neck still twinged from that night.

Finally, next to Alexander stood the reason they were all there: Hunter Bastern. He was gorgeous enough to be a supermodel, with perfectly arranged hair the color of milk chocolate. She'd heard he dabbled in modeling when he was younger, but now he focused on horse racing and cryptocurrency. A scratch slashed across his cheek; the blood dried into small rivulets—pieces of him were still underneath Adeline's nails.

Her father stepped forward, and her body tensed. She no longer trembled because of the cold. He crooked a finger and motioned for her to come closer. Her knees wobbled as she stood, a hand moving to her rib, where Hunter had landed a solid punch after she scratched him. Hunter smirked, victory electrifying his turquoise eyes. She stood in front of the six men, the roaring heat of the fire at her back. Their faces glowed menacingly, and she struggled to keep her eyes open. She had enough nightmares already.

"Do you know why you're here, pet?" her father crooned. She looked down, chewing the inside of her cheek. "Look at me," he barked, causing her to jump. Carl snickered and cracked his knuckles. She cringed but somehow found the strength to drag her eyes up to meet her father's gaze. Shorter than the other men, she had to look down at him, but his fury and might still towered over her.

"Yes, sir."

"Why?" he said impatiently. "Can you explain to the group what you did to Mr. Bastern?"

"Hunter—"

Her father cut in, "He's Mr. Bastern to you."

"Yes, sir. Mr. Bastern took me on a date—" She swallowed hard, trying not to heave. There was nothing romantic about their relationship, but her father

insisted on calling her experiences "dates." She continued. "He took me on a date and wanted me to do something I couldn't do."

Her father raised an eyebrow. "I broke and trained you myself, pet. What on earth could there be that you cannot do?"

This is where the other men all smirked. Even Alexander's eyes flared with anticipation. Panic bubbled, surging through her like a tornado. She should've just agreed when Hunter demanded she fuck all of them at once.

Whenever she refused to do something, the punishment was always whatever that thing was but somehow, always, made worse. Reality coming at her like a train wreck made her want to die. If she could move an inch, she'd throw herself into the fire and be done with it.

"Well?" her father barked. Everything inside her turned off. Her soul curled up into its secret corner, closing its eyes, hiding until later. Hopefully. She fully expected it to never return one day. To just leave, disappear, die—whatever it was that ruined souls went through. Maybe she'd be lucky, and she'd black out again.

"Mr. Bastern wanted me to have sex with Mr. McBride and Mr. Lambert at the same time as him." She looked at each man as she named them, keeping her face as neutral as possible.

Hunter narrowed his eyes and touched the cut on his cheek. She looked away.

Lucas sighed and checked his watch. "I don't understand what the fucking problem is, Adeline. Tell me why you cannot accomplish this task."

She was absolutely in deep shit if he used her name. "Because they wanted to see if they could all insert themselves . . . into me . . . at the same time."

Lucas's eyes raised in surprise. He tapped the deep cleft of his chin. Turning to his colleagues, he cocked his head. "Inventive. Have we done this before?"

Sean shook his head fervently. "No, and honestly, I've always wanted to. I love the way they look so stretched out when I watch porn."

Carl nodded, licked his lips. "I want to really take this baby for a ride. See what she can really do."

Lucas looked at Hunter expectantly. He crossed his arms. "Where did this idea come from?"

For a second, Adeline thought maybe they had stepped over a line. Lucas appeared reluctant; maybe it was too far, even for him. She'd been forced to take two men at once, but three? That was too many. She'd be injured beyond belief, and her father valued his belongings.

Hunter's mouth curled into a cruel smile. He glared at Adeline as he spoke. "Because I want to make her cry. She never cries. I want to use her tears to wet my dick. I want her so ruined, she cries when she hears even the hint of my name. And now that she scratched me, I want permission to fuck her skull in."

Adeline's eyes burned. She bit her cheek deeper, drawing blood.

Lucas chuckled. "I understand that desire, Hunter. But Orwell Nielson wanted her this weekend for a couple of days. He paid extra for the 'sleep over.'" He air-quoted the word, because they knew she wouldn't be sleeping.

Hunter sneered. "I'll pay triple whatever he's paying, and tell him I'll pay his fee, too."

Lucas froze. A night with her—a beautiful, compliant, and skilled gift— was worth an amount that in any other consensual circumstance, would make her proud. Triple that? Plus, not losing a dime from having to delay a different customer? Lucas couldn't refuse. He had no reason to. It's not like he would pay the true price.

"Done." Lucas stuck his hand out and shook each man's hand firmly. He turned to Adeline then, gave her the kind of smile a fox makes when he catches the hare: pure predatory satisfaction. "Now, my darling, you know there is a price to pay for your disobedience."

"What, fucking three men at once until I beg for death isn't a steep-enough price?"

The room fell silent. Even the fire seemed to quiet under her words. All Adeline could hear was the blood rushing to her ears, pounding behind her eyes. Fear was a living thing, snaking through her veins, squeezing her nerves.

Lucas tilted his head, face emotionless as he assessed her. This level of rebellion hadn't appeared in well over a year. For many, many good reasons. Lucas glanced at his friends, and then nodded to Alexander. To her horror, all five of them began to undress. She gaped with terror as Lucas loosened his tie.

With poise, he said, "I'm curious: If three at once seems like a lot, how does six sound?"

While they began their ministrations, she sank into the dark depths of hell to visit her soul.

It appeared in front of her, a glowing being permanently aged at fifteen. She wore a simple T-shirt and shorts, with a scrunchie in her hair. Pure and optimistic. It was her, frozen in time, back when she still had any semblance of innocence.

Adeline sat down beside her soul and grabbed one of its tiny unblemished hands. She couldn't actually feel any texture, but the uncanny sense of familiarity let her soul at least feel semi-real. Her younger self squeezed her hand tightly.

"It's bad today, huh?"

Adeline stared blankly ahead. "Yeah."

A tear trickled down her soul's golden cheek. "I'm not sure how much longer I can go on. It's getting harder and harder to stay."

"Please, don't leave me here all alone," Adeline whispered. So they waited there, clinging to each other, desperate to stay together.

***

Adeline bolted upright, squealing at the pain that flared in her ribs. Her heart pounded; it was a struggle to catch her breath. Sweat soaked the sheets and her pillow. One of her worst living nightmares haunted her dreams regularly. Even now, the ghosts of that memory clutched and ripped at her body. She shivered, rubbing her arms.

It's okay. It's over. It's not real. They aren't here.

One day, that dream would never appear again. Something to look forward to, even if it meant she was dead.

The room was pitch black; not even pale moonlight streamed through the windows. The house was disturbingly quiet. Even the most nocturnal cats were asleep.

It was an oddly comforting feeling, as if she were the only living being in the world. Adeline took a deep breath and slowly exhaled as she looked at the digital alarm clock on the nightstand—it was almost dawn. She had slept for over fifteen hours.

Her bladder pressed painfully against her pelvis. Gingerly scooting out of bed, Adeline limped to the bedroom door. She was shocked to find the sweet calico curled up outside her door. The cat blinked blearily and yawned.

"Well, hello little one," Adeline whispered.

Aslin stood and stretched, then promptly strutted into the bedroom as if she'd been patiently waiting for hours. By the time Adeline returned from the bathroom, the cat had snuggled under the comforter. Loud purrs filled the room as Adeline tucked the blanket around herself and the cat. She fell asleep against Aslin's soft fur, feeling safe for the first time in a very long time.

***

Hours later—maybe even a day—Adeline woke again. Pale sunlight streamed through the thin white curtains.

She groaned. Her whole body was stiff, and it felt as if she could barely move. She tensed and relaxed the muscles in her legs. Gritted her teeth as she rolled her shoulders, stifling a cry at the way her muscles screamed.

Getting up to pee again would be challenging. Aslin mewled at the bedroom door. It took longer than she'd like to admit, but she finally got out of bed and shuffled to the bedroom door, releasing the cat. In the hall, next to the doorway, were a tray of muffins, some fruit, a glass of water, and some butter. The kindness almost caused her to break down.

After seeing to her needs, she bent down and picked up the tray. It took several long, excruciating seconds to do so. She brought it over to the dresser, where she chugged the water and stuffed half a muffin into her mouth. Then she crawled back into bed, yanked the blanket over her head, and fell back asleep. This time, there were no dreams.

CHAPTER SIX

Adeline's mind stumbled as she woke up. She blinked, trying to figure out what had woken her. Downstairs, a pot smashed against the stove.

She winced and turned over on her side. More sleep sounded amazing, but the quilt was suddenly too rough on her skin. Her stomach grumbled; she'd picked clean the tray of food that had been left for her. Time to journey downstairs.

Adeline pushed herself up and scooted to the edge of the mattress to look out the window next to the bed. Through the glass, she could see large oak trees stretching for the windows.

The sky was a dark gray, the morning light too soft to break through. The clock showed it was almost 7 AM. Somewhere, a single bird chirped. Adeline sniffed the air and smelled coffee. She attempted to stretch, but a rib pinched painfully and she gave up.

Groaning, Adeline stood and shuffled to the door like an old woman. Her ankle was more stable, so there was that. In fact, she was overall less sore than before. How long had she slept? At least it was easier to pull on clothes this time, the soft smell of detergent easing some of the tension.

The door creaked as she opened it. On the other side sat Aslin, staring up with bulbous yellow eyes. She mewed, and Adeline smiled.

"Hello again, sweet girl." She bent down and scratched behind the cat's silky ears. Aslin leaned into the touch, her purrs like a rusty engine.

Straightening, Adeline gently sidled along the banister, descending carefully one step at a time, following the humming coming from the kitchen. Aslin chittered as she popped down the stairs past Adeline, pausing at the bottom as if to offer her an escort. Adeline smiled, charmed by the tiny feline. It felt nice to have a friend.

Aslin guided her into the kitchen and promptly sat next to an empty red bowl, glancing down at it and looking back at Adeline.

"She's a filthy liar. They've all eaten." Mags held up a coffee pot. "Want some?"

Adeline nodded eagerly and sat down at the table.

"How long was I asleep?"

Mags glanced at her as she pulled two mugs from a cabinet and placed them on the pale granite counter.

"Over thirty-six hours."

Kennedi. Adeline's stomach dropped; her friend "Oh my god, does Kennedi know? She was going to come over, but I fell asleep."

"I let her know and told her to give you some time. We've been texting. She said if you woke up today you could come visit her at the bookstore."

Adeline shook her head in disbelief. Thirty-six hours was an insane amount of time to sleep. Her stomach growled loudly as if to make a point. As Mags poured the coffee, Adeline took a better look around the kitchen. The space was all soft light bouncing off white surfaces. Adeline could see outside the huge bay windows. She sucked in a breath—the backyard was stunning. It was at least half an acre, speckled with tiny groves of what looked like orange and lemon trees. Closer to the backdoor were rows of garden boxes exploding with various types of greenery. Right outside the door was a large patio with quaint patio furniture. From the awning hung three bird feeders, where birds currently feasted. Mags followed her gaze and smiled as she positioned a mug in front of Adeline. A pitcher of milk and a bowl of sugar cubes sat in front of the mug.

"That's my pride and joy out there."

"It's beautiful." She gave Mags a grateful smile as the surly woman filled her mug. Adeline took two sugar cubes but ignored the milk.

Mags snorted. "It's a lot of work, is what it is. You can help me with it later."

"Later?"

Mags sat down in the chair next to her and started pouring generous amounts of sugar and cream into her own mug. "Yes, later. You're welcome to stay as long as you'd like, but you are going to earn your keep. Savvy?"

The image of digging her fingers into soft earth was an oddly pleasant vision. "Savvy." Adeline took a sip of coffee and sighed. It was easy to ignore the way Mags observed her. Unspoken questions hung in the air, and Adeline refused to offer a single answer. The pain could wait a little longer. Today, she needed to focus on finding Kennedi and getting rid of Hubert's shit. She played with the deep groove in the table.

Mags broke the silence first. "So, what are you going to do today?"

Adeline shrugged. "Hopefully go find Kennedi. The phone I have is dead, and I don't have a charger. Plus, it's not mine."

Mags looked down at her mug, fiddling with the handle. Her red-rimmed glasses slowly slid down her narrow nose. "Do you need money?"

"I have some I can use."

Mags looked up and nodded slowly. "Okay, but you let me know if you need anything, okay? Do you want me to walk with you to the bookstore?"

A part of Adeline wanted to beg the woman to be the buffer in her reunion with Kennedi. Adeline bit her lip and looked out the bay window again. Was she ready for this? It would be impossible to express the depth of her regrets and the horrors she'd endured the last four years. Would Kennedi turn away in disgust? Would she scream and accuse Adeline of being an asshole? The imaginings pushed against her seething, ever-present fear. But if she was going to somehow push forward, she needed to deal with it—all of it.

"I think I'll be okay. Can you give me directions to the store?"

"Sure, but before you go, I need to show you something." Mags stood, beckoning Adeline to follow. She led her down the hallway and turned left into the art room.

They stepped into the chaos, the plastic tarps rustling loudly under their feet. Adeline didn't know why the tarps were even there when splashes, splotches, and spills of paint covered the walls and even the ceiling.

Mags walked over to a large dark wood easel situated in the center of the room. In front of it was an adjustable swivel chair. On the easel sat a rectangular blank canvas. Next to the easel was a raised table with fresh brushes, bottles of paint, and one of those flat, weird circular things Adeline had seen Bob Ross hold. Was it called a platelet? Pronation? *A palette!* She reached for it, slipping a finger through the hole. Mags stopped next to the chair and turned to face Adeline.

"You might not want to tell me what happened yet, but that doesn't mean you don't need to get it out. Ain't no better therapy than some paint ruining a perfectly good canvas."

Adeline gaped, eyes flicking between the canvas and the ridiculously presumptuous woman standing in front of her.

"I don't need to—"

"Yes, you do." Mags crossed her wiry arms, her red-rimmed glasses slipping down her nose again. She was a couple of inches shorter than Adeline but seemed to tower above her all the same. "You don't want to talk to anyone, fine. But whatever the hell happened to you—" Adeline opened her mouth to protest again, but

Mags held up a hand. "Whatever the hell happened to you needs to get out or you'll turn as dark as whoever did that to you."

The idea of turning into her father made Adeline gulp loudly. Maybe this psychotic old woman had a point. "Fine. But I need to go find Kennedi first."

Mags waved her words away. "You don't have to start right this minute. Go find the girl. Do whatever. But I expect a new painting in the next two days."

Who the hell was this woman to make these kinds of demands? Adeline nodded, hoping it would appease Mags enough to leave her alone. Satisfied, Mags stomped back into the kitchen, muttering about her stack of never-ending dishes to clean.

Adeline stayed in the art room, staring at the blank canvas. It wasn't a large one, maybe a couple of feet tall. She suspected it was chosen to be less intimidating. Having never painted before, she didn't even know where to begin. That was a Future Adeline issue, she decided.

Walking out of the room, she trudged upstairs to grab Hubert's phone and car keys. That's when it hit her: Hubert had probably reported the truck stolen. She sighed and headed back downstairs.

"Mags?"

"What?"

Adeline walked into the kitchen to see Mags elbow-deep in a sink full of suds. "Hey, where can I get rid of a truck?"

Mags' eyes narrowed, her mouth pinching. "Get rid of a *truck*?"

Adeline bit the inside of her cheek. "Yeah, uh, it isn't exactly mine . . ."

"Who in the hell is it?" Mags yanked her hands out of the water and began wiping off the bubbles, eyes sharp as knives.

Adeline shifted uncomfortably, picking at a scab on her arm. "Um, some guy named Hubert."

"What in the world . . ." Mags huffed and tossed the hand towel onto the counter before stomping past Adeline. She stopped at the front door and peered out the window to where the old, rusted jalopy waited. She whirled around, eyes wide with shock.

"Girl, what the absolute hell have you gotten yourself into? You show up basically unannounced, beaten to hell, and in a *stolen truck*?" She crossed her arms, looking ready to charge—like an enraged bull. Adeline squared off in the kitchen, their stares clashing. Adeline gave in first. Pressing a hand to her belly, she shook her head.

"I can't, okay? Not yet. I'm not ready. Can you please just help me?"

Mags' mouth twisted in a grimace when she noticed Adeline's defensive movement. Her shoulders dropped and she shifted.

"I know a guy. It'll be gone by the end of the day." Mags waved her away as she headed into the living room and went over to the phone there—a landline. "Go buy a phone. See the girl. Get out of your head, ya hear? I'll take care of that hunk of junk out front."

Adeline's eyes burned. She gave a slow nod and ducked her head. "Thank you."

Mags offered an understanding nod. "I'd say don't mention it, but I wasn't kidding about requiring the story."

CHAPTER SEVEN

It was easy enough to buy a phone at the local drugstore. It was a three-minute walk down the street, Mags' safe haven still visible. Slipping Hubert's phone out of her pocket, crushed it to a pulp under her heel and tossed in the trash.

She turned on her new phone and texted Kennedi's number, hoping she wasn't too busy.

Hey, it's Adeline. New number. Can you hang out?

The response was immediate: ***At the bookstore. It's a few stores from the coffee shop.***

Glancing at the magenta Victorian house, Adeline hesitated. The coffee shop was just around the corner, but she had to go out of sight of safety. Taking a deep breath, she steeled her nerves. Each step away from the house was a step forward into something new. Something better. Lucas couldn't take this from her, too.

Heading to the town square, Adeline fidgeted in her too-big shirt, pulling at a loose thread. Her anxiety was a living thing, jellied and restless in her belly.

The sun was warm on her skin as she played through every scenario in her head: She might walk in only for Kennedi to verbally tear her apart. Maybe she just pitied Adeline and told her to come to Menforth but didn't really want to see her.

Before she knew it, Adeline stood in front of the door to the quaint bookstore, a large pane of glass reflecting her hesitation. Her auburn hair crowned her head in a messy bun, untouched by a brush for days. Her body was gaunt, her arms like malnourished limbs. The clothes Mags had let her borrow hung loosely. In other words, she looked like shit. *Trauma chic.* She sighed, anxiety pinging around her stomach like tennis balls, and pushed open the door.

The smell of books was both jarring and delicious. It was a cozy space, with books piled high along full shelves. There were so many towers tucked in corners and along the aisles. At the center of the store was a small reading space containing two deep purple couches and a tattered black leather chair. A brown wooden coffee table sat between them.

"Kennedi?" she called out.

"Be there in a sec!" The voice hit her full force, and her whole body tensed. *Get your shit together.* She ground her teeth into her cheek, using the pain to focus. The was the sound of something heavy falling, followed by *"Shit!"*

Around one of the long aisles popped a mass of curly red hair, followed by a short and curvy woman strutting down the aisle in a pair of worn overalls with a short white crop top underneath. In her arms was a pile of books.

It was as if the sky had opened up and struck Adeline with lightning. Kennedi was still the most beautiful woman—or person, really—she'd ever seen.

Time had melted the childhood chubby cheeks, highlighting high cheekbones. Time hadn't added height though; Kennedi barely reached the fourth shelf of the bookcase next to her. Adeline could only gawk with awe, reveling in her dreams coming to life.

Kennedi drew closer, her expression inscrutable as she took in Adeline's appearance. Kennedi dropped the pile of books onto one of the purple couches before moving quickly to Adeline with outstretched arms. Adeline stiffened at the unexpected touch but relaxed at the familiar smell of her friend—strawberries and warm bread. Old, familiar electricity zapped when they touched, lighting up the space between and around them. *Home.*

Adeline broke in half, chunks of splintered grief lodging against her skin. Kennedi was *real*, in the flesh, and she was *touching* her. It was the kindest physical touch Adeline had experienced in four years.

At that thought, she lost it. Her knees buckled and Kennedi fell with her, never letting go, even as they collapsed into a heap. Adeline's rib twinged, but she didn't care. Kennedi hugged her fiercely, an anchor keeping Adeline in place as she transformed into a bawling disaster.

Of all the scenarios she had visualized, being embraced by Kennedi as she dissolved into a snotty mess hadn't been on her radar. The longer she breathed in Kennedi's heady essence, a deep yearning appeared, as if her body strained to meld with the one person for whom they had always ached—like two souls finally colliding. Kennedi's hands swept slowly along her back, and the gentleness made her cry harder. She spent years ignoring the gnawing desperation of being touch-starved.

All there was in the world was Kennedi.

The bookstore darkened, and still, Kennedi held her. Adeline quieted, her tears spent for the moment. When it was clear she was calm, Kennedi shifted back onto her haunches with a wince. Adeline couldn't take her eyes off the red lion's mane. She was desperate to spend hours gazing into Kennedi's moss-green eyes.

Kennedi stumbled as she stood back up. She held a hand out to Adeline, helping her to her feet. Kennedi brushed the dirt off her overalls and gave a grim smile. Adeline could only take in shaky breaths.

"So . . . do you want to tell me what happened?" Kennedi's eyes flicked to the bruises.

Adeline grimaced. The swelling wasn't as bad now, thanks to ice and sleep, and the bandage was long gone, but her father's beating would still show for at least another week or two. Adeline looked away, shame burning her cheeks. Kennedi stepped forward and gently touched her elbow.

"You don't have to talk about it if you don't want to."

Adeline's head pounded at the thought of sharing, but the experience begged it. She nodded. "A little bit. Are you busy? Do you have time?"

Kennedi pointedly looked around the empty store. "I'll go make some tea. Take a seat on the couch and I'll be back in a jiffy."

Adeline walked over to one of the purple couches and sat. She shifted a few times before finding a position that didn't make her ribs upset. Finally, she settled with one leg tucked under her body, the other dangling over the side. Pulling one of the books from the discarded pile, she flipped through the chapters, the words a blur as her mind raced.

If he found out she was still alive, he'd come for her. Every moment was on borrowed time. Lucas was always a step ahead of her, and for all she knew, this was another one of his tricks. He could be waiting on Mags' porch when she returned. Alexander would kill Mags without a second thought.

Her hands trembled at the thought. She put the book down.

"We have to let it steep for five minutes."

Kennedi's voice was like an assault—Adeline gasped in terror, hands flying up defensively. Kennedi froze at the end of the aisle, alarmed. In her hands were two clay mugs, steam snaking from them.

Adeline lowered her hands. "Sorry. Instinct."

Kennedi swallowed hard. She gently placed a mug on the coffee table then moved the pile of books and sat down next to Adeline. They sat in silence for a few moments, neither able to figure out what to say.

"I—"

"You—"

They stopped, and for the first time in a long time, Adeline smiled. The muscles in her face ached, unused and forgotten. Kennedi motioned with encouragement. "You first."

Adeline looked down at her tea and grimaced. "I don't even know where to begin. I don't want to scare you or put you in danger."

"What kind of danger? Does it have to do with why you look beat to hell?"

Adeline bit her lip. "Like, the kind that involves my father being a psychopath hell-bent on torturing me until I come home?" She choked on the words. Paused, closing her eyes. *It's okay to share.* Besides, Kennedi deserved to truly know what could be coming. "I . . . I think he assumes I'm dead—he's the one that beat me to hell—but I can't be sure. If he finds out I survived, he'll come for me. Guaranteed."

Her eyes shimmered with tears. She looked down, picking at a thumbnail, her heart racing. Rejection was simply something she couldn't handle at the moment. A part of her was immediately disappointed when Kennedi didn't object to the concerns. She looked up to see Kennedi watching her contemplatively. Then, Kennedi gave a firm nod.

"I'll help you however I can. Say whatever you want or need, I can take it."

Now comes one of the hardest parts of the conversation. "I'm sorry I never responded to your letters. I wasn't allowed to write back." She thought of the letters tucked into her suitcase. Her most prized possessions. "My father just let me read them as a form of punishment until they stopped coming. He knew it broke my heart. He took great joy in watching me…" She swallowed hard. "In watching me cry."

Kennedi's hands stilled, the mug halfway to her mouth. She slowly lowered it and said, carefully, "The letters helped him do that? I never meant for them to hurt you."

A sinking feeling dug itself into Adeline's gut. "It isn't your fault. If anything, his plan backfired—they let me know you still cared. That maybe you felt the same way, and that maybe one day, I'd be able to see you again."

Kennedi's eyes watered. "I never expected to see you again, but I hoped every day. I stopped sending letters because I wasn't sure they helped, but I never stopped hoping we'd come together again."

"Mmm." Adeline sipped her tea. The heat bit, but she enjoyed the burn. "You remember how my dad started acting weird after you left?"

Kennedi nodded sympathetically. "He was a creepy fuck. He gave you whatever you wanted, but I hated how he would watch us."

Adeline huffed a small laugh. "Yeah, well, he had plans. He turned me into what he called his 'deal sweetener.'"

Kennedi's brows pinched. "What does that mean?"

"He would give me to his business partners as a token of gratitude for a well-made deal."

Kennedi's face turned to stone, her brilliant green eyes like shards of sea glass. "Are you for fucking real?"

Adeline nodded. It was strange how much weight seemed to fly off her back, by just saying those words. The silence abuse required was always a heavy burden. Unfortunately, Kennedi looked as if she had taken on the weight instead.

She brought a hand to her mouth, eyes squeezing shut. Kennedi ducked her head and breathed. Her eyes were rimmed with red. "I'm sorry I stopped writing, Addie," she croaked.

She leaned over and put a tentative hand on Adeline's leg. The nickname was a warm balm on Adeline's shredded heart. She brought her hand down on Kennedi's and gave it a gentle squeeze. They sat like that for a minute or two, a mournful gaze between them.

Finally, Kennedi sat up and reached for her tea again. Clearing her throat, she asked, "Was this your first escape?"

Adeline's spine drooped with resignation. "No. It was my sixth. Before I understood his influence; *truly* understood." She gave Kennedi a stern look. "And before you ask, yes, I tried to tell people the first year. He told people I was unhinged, on meds, prone to hysterics. Everyone believed him, because who would think philanthropist Lucas Oremen would do such a thing? When I didn't stop trying to escape, he would lock me in my room for weeks at a time. I was only let out for what he called, 'dates.'" The word was pungent on her tongue.

Kennedi's eyes narrowed. "Dates?"

Adeline shifted, aiming to relieve a sore spot in her back, and took a sip of tea. "Yes. If the men bid enough during their business dealings, Lucas would throw me into the deal. I guess the idea of defiling one of Lucas's belongings, after getting screwed in their deal, made it all worth it."

One hand to her heart, Kennedi looked ready to shatter. "I feel awful, Addie, about not continuing to write. I just didn't think you cared. And instead, you were living in the most fucked-up situation." Her voice caught and she grabbed her tea, busying her hands. She blew on the steaming liquid before admitting, "I'm not sure how you're still sane."

Adeline wiped her runny nose with a napkin. "I don't either. I just couldn't find it in myself to give up. I thought of you a lot, but it really just felt better to fight than to give up. I think he wanted me to give up, even though he loved when I fought back,"

"I . . . I . . ." Kennedi bit her trembling lower lip. "Is there anything I can do? I know Mags is a hard pill to swallow, but I still live with my dad and we only have two bedrooms. I figured an actual bedroom, and not a couch, would be better. But if she gets to be too much, I'll sleep on the couch and give you my room."

Adeline finished her tea and set the cup on the coffee table. "No, it's alright. Thank you for the offer. I'm just grateful to be away from him." *Even if it's temporary.* Eager to change the subject, she asked, "What have you been up to all these years?"

Kennedi shifted in her seat. She bit her lip and paused, clearly uncomfortable with the shift in topic. "Not much. We moved here. My dad bought this store. I got a degree in business, but I can't figure out what to do with it. Maybe get an MBA, but I can't afford that right now. Instead, I'm *still* trying to convince my dad to let me expand the shop. I'd like to really make this bookstore into something. Add a café, like I've always wanted. Book readings would be cool, too. But the man is more stubborn than a mule."

Adeline looked around the space. There was definitely space available for a café, as long as some of those book towers tumbled onto a shelf elsewhere. In her letters, Kennedi had been so excited about the store. And she's gotten a degree! Adeline missed so many things. The sense of loss was enormous and almost impossible to process. Kennedi had never stopped thinking about her. Someone remembered she existed, all this time.

Exhaustion layered too thickly on her mind to entertain the grief—those tears would have to wait.

Kennedi sipped her tea. "That's mostly it. Not really exciting." She looked around the store. "Actually, I need to get back to inventory—these damn books don't shelf themselves—but I can walk you back to Mags's place?" Right on cue, Adeline's stomach growled. Kennedi grinned. "Or maybe you can get something to eat?"

Adeline patted her stomach with a small smile. "I haven't eaten a lot lately."

Standing, Kennedi held out a hand, helping Adeline stand. "I don't want to overwhelm you. I won't lie: I have no real way to understand what you've been through. So if I bumble around, just know I never mean to offend you. But I'm here for you, okay?"

Adeline's throat tightened. "Thank you. I'm just happy you aren't running into the streets, screaming to everyone what a broken freak I am."

Kennedi's face dropped. "I would never. Ever. *Ever.* Do that. You aren't a freak, Addie." Kennedi stepped closer, using a finger to tip Adeline's chin up. "Look at me. You aren't a freak, okay? You aren't broken. I may not know a lot about the world, but I do know none of that shit was your fault. And if I have to spend the rest of our time together convincing you of that, I will happily do so."

Adeline wiped away a tear. "If it all becomes too much—"

"I'll tell you," Kennedi said firmly, dropping her hand. "In the meantime, tell me what you need, whenever you need it. My whole life is this bookstore. I'm here everyday but Sunday."

Adeline raised a brow. "What does your dad do? I thought he owned the place."

Kennedi laughed. "I made him stop coming. He's a dreamer, but not the best business owner. He drives me insane with the things he gets caught up on, like needing all of the books to be on shelves."

Adeline huffed out a chuckle. "What an odd thing to be obsessed about."

Kennedi winked. "I know, right? What a psycho, wanting an organized bookstore. Now he just stays at home, puttering in the shed, making things out of wood. Do you need me to walk you back to Mags's place?"

Adeline took a deep breath and shook her head. "No, I want to get something to eat. Is there a spot nearby?"

Kennedi glanced out the large window into the town square. "Yeah, but are you sure? Menforth is super safe, but your day—"

"I can't spend my freedom holed up, terrified." The words were far more confident than Adeline felt, but she didn't want to impose any further than she already had.

Kennedi gave a long look before saying, "The diner down the street makes amazing food. Tell Zelda I sent you, and to make you the Tallylicious Tater Special."

"The . . . what?"

Kennedi wiggled her eyebrows. "You heard me. Come back and thank me when you're done. If you hate it, drinks are on me tonight. If you love it, drinks are on me tonight."

***

Seeing Kennedi after all these years put an impressive pep in Adeline's step as she walked to the diner. She didn't know why she had even worried about how Kennedi would react.

When they were kids, Kennedi had been the easy-going one, always up for an adventure. Adeline had been the opposite, always cautious and afraid of making mistakes. It was something she had loved about Kennedi, how they balanced each other. And Kennedi always supported her, whether it had been helping her study for a test or when things got dark after Adeline's mom died.

She still wasn't sure it was fair to involve anyone, especially Kennedi, in this clusterfuck that had become her life, but she was too selfish to just walk away. If Lucas suddenly showed up, snatching her from this newfound freedom, she wanted to be able to say she hadn't squandered the chance to live.

As she passed the different shops, she vowed to herself to live as fully as possible going forward.

Adeline stepped lightly as she walked to the diner. A patron held the door for her, and she walked in, sucking in the smell of grease and fried foods. Her stomach roared with eagerness. When was the last time she was allowed greasy food? Unfamiliar faces turned to look at her, the conversation pausing.

Hopefully, this stopped happening the less she looked like a black-and-blue painting. The swelling in her face was mostly gone, but the black eye was still clear as day. Why hadn't she brought her sunglasses?

She halted, willing herself to not bolt. So many eyes. So many curious stares. She felt exposed, laid bare in front of these strangers. But she couldn't make a vow to be brave only two minutes before and then run in a moment of discomfort. Yet, she found her shoulders curling inward, wanting to shrink away from the attention.

"Guys! Stop staring! Eat your damn food!" A jolly-looking guy came out of the kitchen, his round face flushed from standing over a hot stove. He gave her a toothy grin and motioned to an empty booth. "Have a seat, honey. I'm Tally."

Saved by a stranger. She stepped back when he got too close; he noticed and paused. She smiled. "I'm Adeline."

Tally blinked when she put space between them, but then gave a toothy grin. "Nice to meet you, Adeline. Zelda will be with you in a sec."

He walked back into the kitchen, the silver door swinging behind him. The sounds of conversation returned, but noticeably quieter. She slid into a booth facing the front door. Everything inside was different shades of either brown or cream. A large counter stretched from one side of the diner to the other, with a dozen stools underneath the counter's lip. Under the windows were other brown booths with worn cream Formica.

A waitress bustled past with a tray full of plates layered with pancakes oozing syrup. Adeline caught a whiff of bacon, and her stomach grumbled. For the last four years, her diet had been strict. Bacon certainly never appeared on the trays of food—too fatty.

"What'll it be, honey?" A short and compact woman sidled up to the table, pen and pad in hand, *Zelda* scrawled onto a plastic name tag attached to her shirt. She had fluffy black hair with strands of gray, kind but tired eyes, and silver rings on every finger.

"I've been told to get the . . ." Adeline thought of the strange words. "The Toyalicious Toga?"

"Tallylicious Tater Special." Zelda smiled. "Want a chocolate shake to go with that?"

"Yes, please. What's in the special?"

Zelda wrote the order on her notepad and smirked. "Now, you wouldn't want me to ruin the surprise, would you?"

She walked away before Adeline could say anything else.

She sighed. The last hour was draining, to say the least. Even a hot meal in her belly wouldn't fix this never-ending exhaustion that had dogged her heels for years. Kennedi seemed to take the news in stride, but who knew how she really felt? It wouldn't be the first time someone pretended to care.

Adeline unwound her hair and redid the messy bun. She grimaced—a spot near her temple was still tender. She wished there was some magic balm to fix injuries immediately.

The silver door swung open a few moments later, and Zelda walked out, beaming and holding a tray of hot food.

"All right, one Tallylicious Tater Special."

Zelda placed the shake and culinary behemoth in front of her. Adeline gasped in shock. Between two buttery and crispy pieces of brioche bread was a thin beef burger crowned with a large, round hash brown as thick as her thumbnail.

On top of the hash brown were three thick slices of bacon, cheddar, and what looked like gruyere cheese, melted down below the beef. Right below that was a bed of onion rings—three round, golden pieces of heaven.

Hot damn. Kennedi was right. Adeline's mouth watered in anticipation.

"Thank you. It looks . . ."

"Life-changing. Or so they say. Enjoy." Zelda walked off, hips swaying.

Biting into the burger was easier said than done. The corners of Adeline's mouth cracked as she tried. The explosion of flavor, though, was perfection. The hidden ingredient, thickly slathered onto the bread, was a buffalo aioli. It was everything she didn't know she needed. Kennedi *definitely* earned a night of beers, on her.

When she was done, she left Zelda a hefty tip and gave her compliments to the chef. She walked out of the diner then and strutted back to the bookstore. Kennedi startled at the door swinging open. She saw the look on Adeline's face and smiled. "How was it?"

"Tonight at eight, you said?"

"That good?"

"Drinks on me."

Kennedi winked. "See you then."

Adeline hummed a happy tune the whole way home.

CHAPTER EIGHT

Adeline agonized over her limited clothing options. With a deep sigh, she settled on a black oversized T-shirt and a snug pair of jeans. Sneakers would have to do. She brushed and braided her hair and swiped mascara onto her eyelashes. Simple but not hideous.

With a final inspection, she brushed her fingers against the T-shirt, anxiously picking at a cat hair.

Mags looked up from the couch while knitting a green blob of yarn, three cats precariously perched in her lap. Aslin trotted over to Adeline and rubbed up against her jeans. Adeline crouched down to rub Aslin's ears.

Mags thoughtfully petted one of the cats, eyes skimming Adeline's outfit. "You look good. Not too flashy, not too underdressed. Good date attire."

Adeline stood. "I don't think it's one of those."

Mags hummed. "Sure. Do you want me to walk you to the bar? It's getting dark."

"I'm going to try, and go out by myself." Adeline picked at her thumb nervously.

Mags pursed her lips. "Well, just be home at a decent hour. Call me before you head home, so I know when to expect you. Keep your head on a swivel."

Adeline smiled and walked to the door, grabbing the house key Mags had made for her off the table by the door. "I won't be out late. By the way, what happened to the truck?"

Mags waved her question away. "Don't worry about that. All that matters is it's gone. Have fun."

Adeline closed the door behind her and shoved her hands into her pockets as she walked. Dusk settled on the horizon, the pinks and purples of the sky deepening. Adeline passed a thicket of trees, enjoying the vibrant green leaves—spring was no longer creeping in; it had arrived. A small bluebird chirped a song. Adeline smiled, halfway hoping it would fly down and perch on her shoulder. Like Snow White. Not that she was any sort of princess.

So far, her first full day in Menforth had been eventful. Now, headed to her first bar experience, genuine hope fluttered. Maybe she could make a home out of this small town. It was already clear why Kennedi had never left. Menforth just had that Disney charm.

Snap. The sound of a twig snapping inside the thicket caused her to jerk her head up. It came from somewhere deep in the trees. There was another flash of movement, another twig snapping. Adeline's breath caught, heart pounding against her ribs. She could hear her blood throbbing, making it hard to focus.

"Hello?" No one answered and nothing moved. She felt exposed on the sidewalk. Adeline willed her feet to move, hustling as fast as she dared without revealing her budding fear. *It's just a dog. Or another bluebird.* No matter how she tried to reason it, she struggled to believe it herself—birds don't break twigs.

She breathed a sigh of relief when she saw the lights of the bar twinkling in the distance. The sound of music drifted over, calming her nerves. It felt as if there were eyes following her down the sidewalk, but after years of constant observation, the paranoia was familiar to her.

The name "O'Malleys" was lit up in flashing green neon above the nondescript wooden door. A patron stumbled out, laughing with his friends. Adeline froze, nerves already beginning to fray. The sounds of raucous music and laughter twisted her stomach with anxiety. It was too busy for comfort. She whipped out her phone and texted Kennedi.

It's a bit loud and too much. Can we go somewhere else?

Adeline stepped aside as a group of men poured out of the bar, laughing uproariously. The sound prickled fear down her back. Her phone pinged.

How about the garden out back? I'll bring us drinks. A beer sound good?

Adeline sighed with relief, resting a hand over her heart, coaxing it to slow down. Looking around, she saw a small path on the side of the bar and bright lights leading the way.

Yeah, sounds good. I'll find a table.

Adeline tucked her phone away and followed the string lights to a dark garden lit by more string lights and a fire pit in the middle. Picnic tables, benches, and random lawn chairs littered the space, a few of them occupied—patrons bent toward each other, murmuring.

It was quiet enough to hear crickets chirring. Adeline's shoulders relaxed, and her heart eased. In the corner of the yard, against the fence, was an empty picnic table.

Adeline weaved through the random lawn ornaments, including an oversized gnome drinking a beer by the fire pit, and scooted into a seat at the table. Moments later, the back door swung open, loud music following Kennedi as she strode over to Adeline carrying a beer in each hand.

Kennedi flashed a playful grin. She wore a pair of tight-fitting overalls that hugged her curves, and a long-sleeved shirt. Her red curls were swept into a bouncy ponytail, her face devoid of makeup. Even in the dim light, she radiated sunshine.

Kennedi placed the beers on the table and tucked into it. "Sorry, I wasn't exactly thinking when I invited you to a bar. I'm sure you're not looking to be shoulder checked by some drunk dude." She slid one beer to Adeline. Adrenaline lit up her nerves, a voice in her head screaming, *you'll get in trouble.*

Adeline accepted the drink, examining the bottle before lifting it to her lips. Beer had been considered *uncouth* in her circle, so this was only her second one, ever. Fear and guilt flirted in her chest, and she almost flung it away, just in case someone was watching.

Her fingers clenched around the bottom. *No. It's okay. It's okay to enjoy this.*

So she did. The nutty flavor exploded on her tongue, fizzling down her throat. She definitely liked beer.

"It's all right. I should've thought of it, too. I'm just shocked to be out of the house, on my own, so it might be smart to take it slow for a bit. This is my first time at a bar, and it's a little much for me. "

Especially with all of the happy, drunk men. They were minding their business, but all men did … until they didn't.

Kennedi took a sip, watching Adeline the entire time. "I can't believe he kept you locked up this whole time. It's wild to think a parent could do that."

Adeline looked down at the grainy, worn wood. Someone guffawed, and she flinched. Her palms started to sweat. This might have been a bad idea. "Yeah. I had a really long adjustment period where I tried to escape. A lot. In the beginning, I tried to talk to Lucas, to try and appeal to his fatherly side. It didn't work, obviously."

Kennedi scooted closer to the fence and leaned back against it, one leg stretched out on the bench. "How did you escape this time?" She paused, then said, "You don't have to tell me anything you don't want to. I just spent years thinking you might be dead. Or hated me. I never imagined this and... I'm just having trouble processing what happened to my best friend." She frowned. "Annnnnd now I'm making it about myself. I'll shut up now."

"I know what you mean."

Gathering the energy to share, Adeline watched a group of people to their left: two men and three women, all laughing and toasting to something she couldn't hear.

So carefree. The kind of life she'd probably never have.

"It was pure luck," she said. She motioned to her bruised face and laughed bitterly. "You might say it wasn't a very successful one. I think he thinks I'm dead—I don't know why else he'd let me go. He and Alexander beat the shit out of me and threw me into a dumpster. Why would he do that if I were still alive?"

"A *dumpster?*"

Adeline flinched at the loudness of Kennedi's response. People looked at them with surprise. She lowered her voice. "Sorry. I just didn't expect that. A fucking dumpster? Jesus, Addie. I can't even imagine what you went through. You said you were a deal sweetener?"

The term echoed in Adeline's mind, crawling over her skin like an unwanted touch. "Yeah, but I've decided I don't want to talk about that right now." Her cheeks warmed with shame. "He used that term. I hate it."

Kennedi paused, looking around the garden. "Okay. So, is it appropriate and okay to ask if you discovered or experienced anything good in the last four years?"

Adeline took a long drink, contemplating. It wasn' ta straightforward answer. "I saw a sunrise in Budapest that made me cry. One guy brought me to London, and we had some of the best Peking duck of my life while there. The staff at the mansion weren't allowed to speak to me, but one of the chefs who'd known since I was a kid would sneak me French toast sometimes." And that was it. Everything else was tainted with fear and dread. A yawning ache stretched painfully against the constraints of her soul.

At that moment, a burly man in a green T-shirt walked up. The bar's logo was stitched above his heart. His face was ruddy but bright with friendliness, and he had blond hair so bright the dim lights reflected in the strands. Kennedi perked up and stood to hug him. He towered over her tiny body, enveloping her with meaty arms.

"Hey, Ned! How's it going?"

He grinned with crooked teeth. "Oh, you know, livin' the dream. Friday nights bring in all the townies, and some have forgott'n what it means to be in polite society." He looked to Adeline and raised a brow.

Kennedi took the hint and motioned to Adeline. "This is Addie. She's a friend, and she's staying with Mags right now."

Ned squinted. "Your face okay?"

Adeline's cheeks burned. She looked down. Did literally no one in this town know how to pretend everything was normal? "Yes. It's fine."

"Ned." Kennedi smacked his arm. "Don't be a rude asshole. Go get us two more beers as an apology."

Ned dipped his chin, properly chastised. "Sorry, Ken. Sorry, Miss Addie. Was just curious is all. I'll go get those beers, on the house."

Kennedi sat back down as he walked away. She shot daggers at his back before looking at Adeline. "Sorry, they're busybodies around here. Some are more blunt than others. Everyone has known everybody for years, if not their whole lives. Took me two years to fully ingratiate."

Adeline scanned the area, squinting into the shadows. It felt like eyes were everywhere. "I hate everything about it, but at least they ask. Most people don't. It's refreshing to have someone care, even if it's a bit rude."

Kennedi finished her beer, and Adeline did the same. They sat in silence for a moment, but it wasn't uncomfortable. They had never been uncomfortable together—it was one of the things Adeline had only truly appreciated after Kennedi left.

"Do you remember that time we decided to bake cookies, but put in salt instead of sugar? Then fed them to the entire staff and my mom?"

Kennedi laughed loudly. "Yes! Oh my god, everyone's face! Your mom was so shocked, she spit it out on the table. That butler almost choked. One of our finer moments, for sure."

Adeline chuckled. "My mom wasn't a happy camper, that's for sure. I was banned from the kitchen for a month. And that butler always glared at me after."

The moment grew somber again. Kennedi picked at a piece of wood sticking out from the table. "I miss your mom. She was a good person."

Adeline's throat tightened. She tried not to think about it too much. "She was. I miss her every day. Lucas didn't seem to miss her at all."

Her mom died right after graduation, a drunk driver careening through a red light; no prison sentence would ever compensate for what he stole from her. The funeral wasn't even an open casket. Everything good in her life died that night, except for Kennedi.

Kennedi, who spent every weekend night over at the mansion, comforting her when it turned dark in Adeline's mind.. Without that unwavering support, Adeline probably would have walked off a roof.

Eager to change the subject, Adeline asked, "Have you dated anyone?"

Adeline watched Ned walk up with two fresh beers. "Sorry again, Miss Adeline. Let me know if you want anything else."

"Mozzarella sticks?" Kennedi looked at Adeline for confirmation; Adeline nodded eagerly. She hadn't had fried anything in so long. Ned grinned and shoved a finger into the air.

"One order of mozzy sticks, comin' right up!"

As he walked away, Kennedi lifted her beer. "To fresh starts and fried foods."

Adeline clinked her bottle against Kennedi's. "I cannot tell you how freakin' excited I am to have them. It's been too damn long."

They both took a swig. Then Kennedi said, "Back to your question. I've dated a bit. Sometimes I gotta go to the next town over. It's not like Menforth is chock full of single people."

"No, I suppose not." Adeline smiled. She liked knowing Kennedi hadn't been entirely alone, but it hurt to know it could have been her. There had been moments during their time together, moments that turned in Adeline's head late at night, that had made her wonder.

Adeline's heart thumped hard. "Anyone super serious?"

Kennedi brushed back a rogue curl. Her eyes clung to Adeline's face. "Not really. One lasted almost a year, but she lived over an hour away. It became hard to make that trip regularly enough, and honestly, I didn't like her that much."

"Oh. Yeah, that sounds hard. Anyone right now?"

Though she'd escaped only days earlier, it was hard to not have hopes and dreams about the one person that had kept her going, whose letters had given her life during the darkest of times. That was so much to pin on one person, on stale memories, but survival didn't always make sense.

Kennedi took a drink. "Nah. I've been focused on work. And I started riding at a nearby stable. Keeps me busy and drama-free. Well, as long as I'm not doing the store's taxes, it's drama-free."

Adeline laughed. "I genuinely don't know what that's like, but I've read about it."

"So, tell me about what you've been able to read." Kennedi leaned forward, bracing her elbows against the table. Her tongue played with her lip ring, spinning it again and again. Adeline's eyes narrowed on the thin piece of metal.

Sighing, Adeline quirked her mouth. "So many. And movies. Kept me busy and distracted."

"Tell me all about it," Kennedi ordered, smiling. "I wanted to know everything."

And that's how they spent the rest of the evening, trading stories and hobbies. As the moon rose into the sky, Adeline felt like she could finally relax. Tomorrow, life and the truths she actively avoided would still be there. But in that moment, all that existed was Kennedi, beer, and fried foods. And that was enough.

CHAPTER NINE

After three weeks of freedom, Adeline was growing increasingly antsy. Everywhere she went, it felt like there were eyes nestled into every corner and shadow, following her every movement.

It drove her crazy; made her skin itch under the weight of anxiety. Even spending afternoons with Kennedi at the shop, helping her stock shelves and drink too much coffee, wasn't enough to stave off the feeling.

The not knowing of it all, if Lucas knew of her survival. kept her up at night, picking at her fingers. And if he showed up, how would she fight back? Fighting back never worked; it always hurt more later.

Death was more appealing than returning to servitude.

So, when Mags offered to teach her some hand-to-hand combat, Adeline eagerly agreed, ready to feel a sense of empowerment.

Which is how she found herself slammed on her ass, dazed, Mags' face peering down at her. They were in the backyard, the sun high overhead. The grass scratched Adeline's bare arms and legs, sweat clinging to her skin.

They'd been sparring for only ten minutes, following thirty minutes of cardio and bodyweight exercises. Mags' arms were wiry and built from whatever it was she did during her younger days. She shook out her hand, and Adeline saw the honed muscles flex.

Adeline's cheek stung.

"Girl, you need to duck," Mags chastised. Adeline groaned and sat up, holding a palm up to her face. Mags held out a hand, helping Adeline stand. "I'm pulling my punches, weakling."

The thought was boggling. "Where the hell did you learn to do this?"

Mags smirked and stepped back, putting a few feet between them. Put her arms back into position, ready for another round. Adeline bit back a groan. She was exhausted down to her bone marrow. Another match and she might pass out. The injuries on her body still bothered her, but at least she could breathe without pain now.

Mags shrugged. "I lived a different life a long time ago. Picked up a few tricks. Fought a few nasty men—worse than your father, I'll bet. Now, hands up."

"I can't keep going," Adeline complained, arms still dangling at her sides. "Can't I get a break? Please?"

"Don't be a ball sac." Mags took a threatening step forward, forcing Adeline to bring her weary arms back into position. "How about this: If I win, you have to tell me what you're running from. If you win, I'll make you a feast for dinner, and I'll rub your shoulders."

"That's not fair." Adeline gave a heavy sigh. "I'm clearly weak right now."

"Oh, well." Without warning, Mags leaped forward and slapped Adeline on the cheek. Adeline hissed and attempted to lunge, fist hurling toward Mags' eye. She cried out with pain as Mags deflected her punch and slapped the other side of her face.

"What the *fuck*," she yelled. "You're taking advantage of my situation! You know I'm not capable of fighting back properly yet."

"Sounds like a 'you' problem." Mags smirked again, looking quite pleased with herself. She wiped a wet gray curl from her forehead. "Now, let's go have some lemonade and you tell me a thing or two about why you need to learn how to deliver an uppercut."

Adeline trudged behind the short, surly crone, steaming with frustration. Living with Mags had proven to be a challenge. The old woman didn't ask anything of Adeline that she wasn't capable of, but most days, all Adeline wanted to do was curl up and sleep.

When she admitted as much, Mags had shaken her vehemently and said, "Absolutely not. A lazy body equals an overactive mind." If that insistence weren't enough, she also continued to ask Adeline what she was running from, wearing her down until, finally, lemonade felt like a solid trade.

The kitchen was cool, the blessed air conditioning drying the sweat against her skin. Mags walked to the fridge while Adeline sat at the table. Her thighs shook as she lowered herself into the chair. Walking tomorrow would be a bitch.

Even in that moment, life felt surreal. Three weeks before, someone would have punished Adeline for defending herself. Conversations with anyone but her father and his associates were impossible, not that they could be called conversations.

Now, as Mags placed two glasses on the table, Adeline realized what a gift it would be just to share her story. Sure, Kennedi had listened intently and held her if she needed to cry, but Mags would be a different sort of sounding board. Something told her Mags would offer solutions instead of just support.

Lowering herself into a chair, wincing at her own fatigue, Mags poured the lemonade. "So. Tell me one or two things. Or all of it. You can't and won't scare me. I spent years as a war photographer—there's not much that shocks me anymore."

Adeline reached for her glass. She took a deep gulp before speaking. "You know, the usual: Father takes daughter and makes her body a tool in closing business deals. Daughter stays locked up for four years, used by rich men with sick minds until she's able to escape to a small town and live with a crazy bitch who likes to slap people for funsies."

Deadpanned, Mags retorted, "Sounds like a fairy tale. And that crazy bitch sounds like the fairy fucking godmother."

Adeline rolled her eyes, wincing as she lifted the glass. The ache in her weary muscles slowly seeped in; by the end of the day, she'd be lucky to be able to lift a fork. "Yeah, yeah. I get it. You're not easily impressed. But it's true."

"I believe you." The sincerity in Mags' voice caused a lump to lodge in Adeline's throat. "How did you escape?"

Adeline filled her in on the past four years—an abbreviated version—and her escape. Retelling the story felt like slogging through mud, weighed down by the horrific, unforgettable truth. She wondered if the smell of that dumpster would ever fade in her memory. By the time she was done, she felt like a wet bag of cement covered in dog shit. The lemonade was gone; Mags seemed to have exhausted all of her questions. Almost.

"So, your father, a millionaire, used you in his business deals. And when you became too rebellious, he chose to try and kill you instead?"

"That about sums it up."

Mags tapped a nail against her empty glass. "Where's your mom?"

"Killed by a drunk driver at the end of my senior year."

Mags' face fell. "I'm very sorry to hear that. A child deserves to have a mother. A mother deserves her child."

"Did you ever have kids?"

Mags' jaw set. "No. It wasn't in the cards for me. I have someone in my life who I love very much, but I've never married. Sometimes men love to crush beautiful things, just to see if they can. I vowed at a young age to give no one the chance." She leaned over to pick up a cat. "My lover is exempt—and maybe six others in the world—men are awful and generally deserve crushing instead."

"Ooookay." Adeline sat back in her chair. "So, what I'm hearing is that you're one bad bitch who might be able to take on my psychotic father?"

Mags' blue eyes glittered. "If your father walks into this house, he's not walking out."

Adeline looked around. "Is there a security system?"

Mags refilled her glass, hand still steady. "In a way."

"In a way?"

"My, you're quite the parrot right now. The windows are wired with a hidden system. There are cameras at the front and back doors. I have a few weapons and some angry cats I can toss like grenades."

A laugh burst out of Adeline as she tried to imagine Mags hurling a cat at Alexander. "What kind of weapons?" Adeline reached for the bottle of whiskey on the table and took a swig.

Mags patted her hip, where her belt held a pocket knife. "This and that. Why? Do you want to learn how to use some of them?"

Adeline eyed the knife. "Yeah, I think I do. When I'm not so damn sore and exhausted." She stood, groaning. "I'm going to take a bath and then sleep for another week."

Mags grabbed the whiskey bottle and took a sip. "I have a surprise for you tomorrow. I'll show you after breakfast."

Adeline bit back another groan. "Is it more sparring? Because I seriously need a rest."

Mags raised an eyebrow. "You think bad guys wait for you to be feeling well?"

"Mags…"

The old woman chuckled, looking down as a fluffy white cat strutted into the kitchen. "Fine. No, it's nothing physical. Just mental."

Adeline narrowed her eyes. "I'm not in the mood for games."

Mags held up her hands. "I swear, you might actually like it. See you in the morning."

***

Every single little muscle in her body ached, but it was a good kind of ache. Adeline gently shuffled into a seated position, bracing against the mattress, hissing with every inch.

Looking out the window, she could see the sun already high in the sky. She threw on clothes and padded downstairs. Mags muttered and hummed to herself as she put away groceries. Adeline cleared her throat. Mags glanced over and closed the fridge door.

"Come 'ere." She flicked a finger, motioning for Adeline to follow. Curious, Adeline followed her to the art room. She gawked as Mags motioned to a box full of fresh brushes and paints. They were the same ones Mags showed off when Adeline first arrived. Adeline stopped at the door, unable to move forward.

Mags adjusted the stool in front of the easel.

"What's wrong?" She asked when Adeline didn't step forward. She looked down at the brushes and paint. "Do you need anything else?"

Adeline sucked in a deep breath, tears pricking her eyes. "It's just... so nice of you to do this." She chewed her lower lip. "What's the point of painting, though?"

Mags motioned to the cushioned seat in front of the easel. Adeline sat down on it, her knees almost brushing the virgin canvas. Her fingers skimmed the tips of the dry brushes, their silky strands tickling. Mags pointed to a wooden box of paints on the floor. She picked up a bottle of purple acrylic paint and handed it to Adeline. The bottle was smooth and cool in her palm.

Mags said, "It isn't safe to do talk therapy with a professional right now, so I thought maybe some art therapy could help. When I was healing, art was the one thing to keep me sane in this lonesome, too-big house. Maybe you can get some value from it, too."

"Thank you," Adeline said, staring at the bottle of paint while trying—and failing—to hold back tears. She looked up at Mags. "This is amazing, but how do I do it?"

"Just take a feeling or memory and paint it out." Mags leaned over and plucked out a paintbrush. She offered it to Adeline. As Adeline's fingers curled around the pale wooden handle, Mags lifted a fresh painter's palette. "Put paint on this to mix and use. Just do what feels right. It doesn't actually have to be a memory; it can be a feeling or a place. Or a person."

Adeline hesitated. Her eyes flicked to the box of paint, every color of the rainbow available. The choices were overwhelming. With a small shake of her head, she put the purple back and chose the deepest black. Mags' eyebrows shot up, as if surprised by the choice. She walked away, turning back around at the doorway.

"Holler if you need anything. I'll be in the garden, weeding."

"Thank you, again," Adeline whispered, hands already shaking with anxiety.

Mags dipped her chin in acknowledgment before leaving.

Adeline stared at the canvas and took a few deep breaths. It was time to take the emotions that had eaten her alive for over four years and drag them into the light.

Finally.

CHAPTER TEN

Then Adeline had only been "working" for Lucas for a year when she first escaped—or thought she had. Until that point, he'd been careful, ensuring there was an escort around the clock.

After only six months of servitude, Adeline stopped begging for him to see reason. The more she pleaded, the more painful the corrections. When she fought back or tried to run, Lucas beat her and starved for days at a time.

The burning rage inside her broiled, scalding her insides with nowhere else to go. It caused unexpected outbursts—the kinds of outbursts Lucas was determined to quell with copious amounts of corporal punishment.

In the beginning, he informed her that, in no uncertain terms, he was confident she could never escape. He laughed when she'd tried to bolt and put bars up on the windows when she tried to climb out. The first time she successfully reached the front door, he locked her in the bedroom without food for four days. The only relief provided was the water she had to slurp out of the faucet.

A part of her died during that time.

Any hope of success was never fully extinguished, though. She kept watching. Waiting. Observing. Lucky for her—in the most ironic sense—not a lot of men could afford her as a prize, so she was only used once or twice a quarter; however, her father still enjoyed parading her around town, making men salivate. Wolves will always crave the lamb; more so when it's hard to get.

When she was compliant, after a year of him doing what he called "breaking in," Lucas brought her out of the mansion to join him at a dinner with other businessmen. Alexander always hovered within ten feet, ready to spring into action if she so much as looked at a door.

The first dinner outside of the mansion was incredibly stressful. She was plucked and scrubbed to perfection. Lucas also forced her to sit down and memorize the names of the men attending, making sure she understood how paramount her performance would be. Failure would equal severe consequences.

After a year of his flavor of training, Adeline knew it would be pointless to disobey. So, she let the professionals groom her like a prized show bitch, practiced the flashcards until her brain ached, and tucked away her humanity into the darkest parts of herself.

The evening started easily enough. Primped to perfection, Alexander escorted her down to a limo, where Lucas waited. As Alexander slid in next to her, his frame almost crushing, Lucas admired the final product.

He wore a dark green suit, his hair perfectly styled. Those cold, dark eyes actually flickered with approval when he saw the satin emerald gown. It tucked into her curves, cleavage dipping an inch past inappropriate. Her hair cascaded in an old Hollywood style, and the bling around her neck was worth at least five middle-class salaries.

She loathed h0w much his approval caused pleasure to sluice through her, warming up her chilled insides. She was like a puppy begging for some form of praise. Praise meant he wouldn't hurt her—yet.

"Smile." The command was simple enough. She stretched her red-stained lips, showing off her pearly white teeth. He nodded with satisfaction.

"You look beautiful."

She gritted her teeth, trying not to cry. The words were a balm to her frayed nerves, and she wanted to scream because of it. She bit her cheek and said, "Thank you."

He turned his attention back to his phone, fingers a blur as he typed out emails. Alexander leaned in, his breath hot on the nape of her neck as he whispered, "You look good enough to fuck into a coma."

Silence. Any response other than a *yes please* would be met with retribution. The henchman's ego was fragile, a lesson she'd learned long ago. He gave a dark chuckle and leaned away from her.

Adeline turned her head to look outside the window, watching the world stream by like an untouchable dimension. A part of her ached for death: the concept of nothingness, the flame of her soul extinguished with a single breath of the universe's will… It sounded like absolute bliss. The men she was about to meet were motivated to purchase time with her. She'd be meeting her future rapists.

The idea was nauseating.

The limo crawled to a stop in front of a restaurant, a black awning reaching to the sidewalk. Adeline scanned the surroundings, taking stock of who and what was around. It was in the middle of the city; the block lit up with restaurant and store signs.

People pulsed around each other in crowds, absorbed in their own lives. None of them gave her a second glance as the door swung open and she stepped out of the limo. The fresh air was crisp in her lungs; the smell of fall deepened the ache inside her heart. It used to be her favorite season; now it meant nothing. Not much meant anything to her anymore. Except for those letters, tucked away safely in a drawer in her cage.

"Welcome, Miss Oremen." The valet greeted her with a beaming smile, not even bothering to hide his appreciation of her cleavage.

She looked down at him, at his pimpled cheeks and pale blond hair, and sneered, "Keep your eyes to yourself."

It felt good to take some of her anger out on someone deserving. The valet's cheeks bloomed with humiliation. He stepped aside as she walked the carpeted stairs that led into the restaurant. Turning, she searched the surroundings for someone, anyone, who could help. A policeman. Someone who looked trustworthy.

Maybe if she tried hard enough, she could convince a stranger of the danger she was in. But Lucas had bought everyone. Through him, she had learned at a young age that everyone had a price. *Everyone.* So, if she was going to try something, she needed to be damn fucking sure it would work.

Seeing nothing, she sighed and watched as Alexander unfolded from the limo. He perked a sharp eyebrow at her, silently taunting her to try something. With what she hoped was a perfectly bored expression, she pretended to examine her manicure.

Lucas stepped out next, straightening his suit jacket as he rose. His eyes passed over Adeline once more before he stalked up the carpet, giving the young valet a glare when he didn't bolt up to the door fast enough to open it for him. The valet's cheeks were beat red and words of apology came out in a fluster. Still pissed at his gawking, Adeline offered only a haughty glare as she passed.

With Alexander at her back, she followed Lucas past the hostess—who looked ready to object but thought better of it—and weaved through tables to a back room. Everyone in the restaurant watched them pass, the women sending Adeline envious glares. *If you only knew.*

Adeline would trade places with them in a heartbeat.

Sure, she looked glamorous and rich, but the cost was too high. When she was younger and more innocent than she deserved to be, Adeline would have stared the women down until they looked away. Now, Adeline was the first to look away.

Lucas led them into a room with a heavily tinted sliding door. The room was dim, lit by a handful of pin lights above a long table. At the table sat twelve businessmen, all talking animatedly, drinks in their hands. The moment Lucas stepped into the room, they fell into silence. Their eyes skipped to Adeline, crawled over her body while barely looking at her face, as if her body were a piece of art so beautiful, the rest of it wasn't worth examining. Everything they needed to know about her was held in that satin emerald dress.

She sat in the chair to the left of the empty chair at the head of the table. Alexander sat across from her, to Lucas's right. Half the men stared at her, while the other half watched Lucas with rapt focus.

A waiter swooped in from the shadows to take their drink orders. Adeline was about to order a martini when Lucas interrupted her: "She'll have vodka and water."

Adeline refrained from making a face. That sounded terrible. The waiter paused, waiting for her to refute the order. She looked down at her lap. Lucas ordered a brandy, and Alexander stuck with his glass of water.

The room stagnated in silence until the waiter returned. Lucas raised his drink into the air.

"To money and success."

The twelve men around the table murmured their agreement and sipped their respective drinks. Adeline took a small sip of her own, the vodka searing her tongue. She'd barely eaten since the day before, nerves seizing her stomach into submission. It scalded her belly, warming her up immediately. Her vision swam, forcing her to stare intently at the golden charger and plate in front of her.

"So," Lucas began, catching Adeline's attention. He looked each man in the eye before continuing. "We're here today because we all want to invest in the Alburton development. It's an investment like no other, and we stand to make millions. *Each.* As you're aware, I am heading up this project, but I would be delighted to add your company and personage to said investment. It will take five years to come to fruition, with an estimated one hundred and twenty percent return. The catch is: you must agree *tonight.*"

He sat back and sipped his drink. Adeline watched as the men murmured to one another, some even checking their phones. Finally, an overweight man with a bulbous nose looked up with concern.

"Oremen, the math doesn't add up. You're asking more than is appropriate. What's the catch?"

Adeline's stomach sank as Lucas smirked. Sliding his eyes to her, Lucas said, "I'm offering to sweeten the deal. One night with my pet, who will do anything you ask of it. In exchange, I'm asking for twenty percent more than normal investment. The returns speak for themselves, and I assure you, one night with her cunt will make up for any perceived losses."

Fourteen eyes fell upon her face, drilling into her humiliation. To him, she was a long-awaited investment, ripened for exploitation when the time was right. When her mother was out of the picture.

Adeline squirmed. All twelve strangers undressed her with their eyes. She had never felt more naked.

A rail-thin man with a receding hairline—Justin Loupren, CEO of an illustrious bank—spoke first. "Oremen, we aren't about to hand over an extra three million for some premium pussy. That's insane. The amount of whores I could get for that would fuck my dick off for years."

Adeline couldn't agree more. The trade didn't make sense in most instances, but definitely when millions of dollars were involved. Except Lucas put her through a stringent training regime, ensuring she would satisfy men.

The mogul, already tipsy, said, "I assure you, my pet is well trained. In fact, I invite you all to take a taste."

A taste. Adeline's blood turned icy. Did he mean right here, in the restaurant, where anyone could catch them? He was daring and unhinged enough.

"A taste?" A fat, sweaty man—Robert Prestlin, owner of a successful gas company—licked his chapped lips, eyes locked on Adeline's breasts.

Lucas signaled the silent waiter for another drink. While he waited, Lucas spread his hands on the table and looked Robert in the eye. He looked like a king commanding his court.

"Yes. A taste. I will let each of you stick your dick in her, right now, bent over this table. Three pumps. That's it. If you find yourself uninterested afterward, I'll consider a renegotiation, but with a significantly lower stake in profits."

Adeline's breath caught in her throat, threatening to choke her to death. The words were absolutely, entirely, and completely insane. Did he truly expect her to do this? In the last year, she'd been given to only ten men. None of them had actually taken her overnight, preferring to drill her right on top of her bed, rushed and business-like. Far more tolerable than a whole night. But now? Now he wanted her to let twelve men pump their cocks in her, just for a taste?

She couldn't possibly do it. There was no way. Not realizing she'd done it until it was too late, she shook her head in disbelief. Lucas gave her an ice-cold glare. Under his breath, so none of the men could hear, he said, "You will fucking do this, because if you don't, I'll find that red-headed bitch and make you trade places. Do you understand?"

Kennedi. The threat wasn't new, but it wasn't untrue either. He'd do it. Hell, he'd take Kennedi and force them to live together, side by side being raped. It was the most successful control device he'd found. Once he realized how desperately Adeline clung to those handwritten words, her rebellions were burned to ash.

She needed to escape. If she could just escape and warn Kennedi…

The air thinned in the room. The twelve men gossiped amongst themselves, surveying her with hungry eyes. An idea popped into her head. Looking at Alexander, she said, "I need to pee."

Alexander peered at her, cocking his head to the side like a dog trying to understand. "And that's my problem, why?"

Lucas's eyes flicked to her, then Alexander. Adeline hissed, "Because I highly doubt you want me pissing on these men's tiny pricks and ruining any damned motivation they might have."

Alexander's mouth twisted with disgust. He looked at Lucas, who gave a quick nod in approval. Alexander stood, and Adeline rose steadily to her feet. The burn of the vodka in her empty stomach provided focus. Terror gnawed at the edge of her consciousness. All she needed was some space to breathe. To think. To scheme.

The walk to the bathroom was slow, her heels catching on the hem of the long, sweeping satin. Alexander hounded her heels, baring his teeth at any man that stared at her.

The bathroom was multi-stalled, so Alexander was forced to stand outside the door. Positioning himself across the door, hands crossed in front of his groin, he hissed, "Don't try any funny business, bitch. You won't succeed." He leered down her neckline.

She bit back a scathing retort and entered the bathroom. As soon as she was inside, she leaned back against the door and closed her eyes. She started sucking in deep breaths, trying to wrangle her thoughts; they scattered like manic ants.

This was an entirely new low for Lucas. It felt impossible to bear. How could she possibly force herself to walk out that door and do what he asked? Was she really expected to literally lay down and take it? Quietly? With a smile? Maybe a well-placed moan or three?

She exhaled and pushed her shoulders back. It was a beautiful bathroom, with a black-and-white aesthetic. A round sitting couch sat in the middle, swathed in black velvet. To the right were three stalls, all empty. On the opposite wall were mirrors and black sinks. The far wall held a window. A *window*.

She shoved off the door, her heels clacking loudly as she walked to the window. It was about five square feet, with sheer black curtains hanging on either side. The window led to an alley, with a dumpster right underneath. She checked the door, considered locking it, but Alexander would most likely hear it if she did. She shoved the window upward. A soft breeze floated in, caressing her.

Sticking her head outside, she calculated the distance between the window and the dumpster. It was about five feet—short enough to not break her ankle. Alexander warned her to not do anything stupid, but it was easy to argue that walking out of the bathroom to please a room of twelve men was equally stupid. She spent every day swallowing her desperation—she wasn't about to waste any opportunity.

Adeline lifted her satin skirt and unbuckled a shoe. She dropped it to the ground and unbuckled the other, fingers moving with urgency. She hooked a finger through their straps and leaned over the edge of the windowsill, awkwardly lifting a leg to crawl over the edge.

"What are you doing?"

The voice startled Adeline and she nearly pitched forward face first. She straightened up so fast she knocked her head against the metal frame. With a seething hiss, she held a hand to the back of her skull and looked to the voice.

One of the waitresses, someone she didn't recognize, stood by the door, hands on her hips. She was tall and slim, wearing the requisite black pants and button-up shirt. Dark brown hair swept into a ponytail. Her nametag read "Holly."

Adeline attempted a placating smile. "Just needed some fresh air."

The woman narrowed her eyes, looking from the window to Adeline's face. "There is a front door, you know."

Adeline chuckled. "You're right. I just didn't want to be bothered by anyone. Thanks for stopping me from doing such a silly thing."

She made like she was heading to a stall, hoping the waitress would leave, but Holly stepped in front of her. She had a mole on her dusky cheek and dark eyes that quickly assessed Adeline. "That lunk outside waiting for you?"

Adeline hesitated, glancing at the door again. "Oh, yeah, he's just, um, super protective." She rolled her eyes, hoping her anxiety didn't layer her tone too much.

Holly's eyebrows furrowed. "Are you in trouble?"

And there it was—the moment she'd waited a whole year for. Adeline weighed the situation: Holly seemed nice enough, but was she trustworthy? If she was caught or if Holly turned her in, she'd be in for a world of hurt. But wasn't that already waiting for her? The pain and abuse would never stop; she had try and get away.

Adeline lowered her voice to a whisper, heart hammering. "*Yes.* Please, help me get out of here."

Holly's shoulders tensed, and she looked away. Finally, she said, "Alright. I can create a diversion. Go out the window and make a left. It'll take you away from the front door."

"Thank you." Adeline impulsively grabbed the woman's hand. "*Thank you.*"

Holly squeezed her hand and motioned to the window. "Go. Hurry."

Adeline didn't hesitate. She rushed over to the window and hiked her dress up. Swung a leg over and lowered herself onto the dumpster. The feel of cool plastic against her toes made her heart skip with excitement. She was doing it!

From above came the sound of the bathroom door opening and closing. Lowering herself a little more, she was finally able to stand on the dumpster. She hopped down, hissing at the sharp ache of gravity slamming into her ankles. Looking then to both ends of the alley—no one was around—she leaned down and strapped her heels back on before turning left and hurrying down the alley. Sweat pricked her armpits and forehead, the anxiety nearly unbearable.

Reaching the end of the alley, she looked both ways again. All clear. Across the street was a gas station. Outside, by the front door, was a pay phone. There was a solid chance it didn't even work. If so, she'd beg the clerk to call the cops. Surely, once she explained her situation, they—

"There you are," Alexander purred. He sidled up to her and put an arm around her waist. She'd hesitated for too long. She stepped forward, preferring to have a car hit her, but his grip tightened.

"Don't you dare." His hot breath in her ear. She turned away, sickened. He chuckled. "That waitress acted real funny-like when she left the bathroom, so something just told me to take a walk around the neighborhood. You think you would actually have gotten away?" He tsked. "After all this time, you're still so hopeful. It's cute. Now, come on. The gentlemen are getting restless."

Adeline watched the traffic speed by, tempted to fight him hard enough to make a scene. Maybe even make it to the front of a city bus going fast enough to at least disfigure her. But she grew up watching Lucas pay off powerful people—he'd have the situation in hand almost immediately, and for what? More desperation and humiliation? She already drank gallons of those feelings every day. Body sagging, Adeline hung her head and let Alexander steer her back toward the alley, where a brick propped open the backdoor.

He led her through the kitchen, ignoring the bewildered looks of prep cooks and chefs. She kept her gaze down, wishing the ground would open up and swallow her whole. The sounds around them changed, more muted and pleasant. In the corner of her eye, she saw Holly and looked up.

The waitress looked between her and Alexander, frowning. Adeline knew Holly might even call the cops, but it'd result in nothing happening. Lucas had the entire city tucked tightly in his pocket.

Too soon, they were back at the door to the private room. Alexander slid it open and subtly pushed her inside. Instead of heading to his seat, he positioned himself at the door.

Adeline stood in front of him, her feet cemented and weighed down under the gaze of so many eyes. All of them starved for her body. Lucas stood at the head of the table and held out a meaty hand.

"Come, pet."

Howling winds thrashed her insides, the world tunneling to a pinpoint. Her consciousness escaped her mortal body and rose above the scene. Adeline floated through the ceiling and into the warm embrace of sunshine. She'd have to go back to her body eventually, but not yet.

Not yet.

***

Now

Adeline sat with the memory of her first escape attempt. She poured her feelings of loss and betrayal onto the canvas, each paint stroke peeling away another carefully laid layer of protection.

She doused the canvas with black paint, letting gravity do the work. It slid down like thick, demonic tears. She closed her eyes and treaded into the vault where she hid the worst moments of her life. It was a voracious vortex, a dark abyss that yawned with endless hunger.

Closing her eyes, she reached into that darkness and brought her fingers to the canvas. She spun her hands in different directions, feeling the cold paint coat her fingertips. She opened her eyes and took in her creation.

It needed red.

Instead of pouring the paint into a bowl, she squirted it out onto her palm and then smeared her hands together. Opened them wide, fingers splayed—it looked like she had committed murder. She slapped them against the canvas and spun them, creating an ugly color that reminded her of a vile sickness.

She stopped and stared at the creation. It needed one more thing. She reached for a narrow paintbrush and squeezed out some bright gold paint. Dipping the very tip of it into the paint, she brought it to the canvas. The black and red swirled together like a whirlpool, and she placed the little bit of gold right at the center, where the swirling came to an end—a spinning tunnel leading to something unattainable.

By the time she was done, beads of sweat dampened her forehead and an unfamiliar sense of satisfaction budded inside her heart.

"What's the gold?"

Adeline turned and saw Mags leaning against the door frame. Her cheeks went red; she held back the urge to cover her obvious pain and shame. Instead, she took a deep breath and blew it out.

"What's left of my soul."

Mags hummed and crossed her arms. "At least there's something left. That means there's still hope."

"That's one way to look at it," Adeline muttered, putting the bottles of paint back into the box. Her fingers were caked with it, splatters drying on her clothes and face. She looked to Mags again, who wore an expression of determination.

"Girl, that's the *only* way to look at it. Otherwise, the world would turn us mad."

CHAPTER ELEVEN

Two hours later, Adeline found herself at the bookstore, smelling like soap with not a speck of paint in sight. Her brain was fried to a crisp, a headache throbbing at the base of her skull. All she wanted—needed—was Kennedi, and some drinks.

Kennedi looked up with surprise, then laughed as Adeline lifted a white paper bag filled with donuts. Kennedi's hands shot out, and she grabbed for the bag.

"Thought I would surprise you with some breakfast," Adeline said as she stuffed one hand inside and pulled out a Boston cream donut wrapped in a napkin, which she passed to Kennedi.

Kennedi bit into the warm donut and made a sound of appreciation. A dab of cream sat at the corner of her mouth. "Just the right amount of sugar and cream."

Adeline's eyes flashed with mischief. "That's what she said."

Kennedi furrowed her brow before barking out a laugh. "You're always so dirty and nasty."

"That's what—"

Kennedi held up a hand. "I know where this is going—you can go on for hours. Instead, why don't you come and sit for a spell?" She motioned to the couches.

Adeline glanced over at them, more mischievous thoughts causing her cheeks to blush. An old flutter stirred in Kennedi's chest. It was as if no time had passed between them.

Adeline tilted her head. "Actually, do you want to get a drink? I've had a rough morning and need to blow off some steam."

Kennedi blinked slowly. "It's noon."

Adeline shrugged and stuffed the last of her donut into her mouth. "Haven't you heard of brunch?" she said, her mouth full. She motioned to the donut chunk still in Kennedi's hand. "There's the requisite breakfast. Now let's go get some booze. I bet the bar is empty at this time of day. We can drink inside."

Kennedi looked around the empty store. "All right. I can take a long lunch."

After locking up, they linked arms and walked to Ned's bar. At the front door, Kennedi made a show of sweeping open the door. She offered a tiny, reverent bow. With a British accent, she said, "After you, m'lady."

Adeline lifted her chin, glaring at Kennedi with mock disapproval. "You didn't bow nearly deep enough."

Kennedi laid it on thick with her accent. "My deepest regrets, m'lady. But if you could kindly get the hell into the bar, I'd be oh so grateful."

Adeline chortled and walked inside. At that time of day, the bar only had a couple of day-drinkers. Kennedi walked around Adeline and headed for the long bar over to the left. Ned stared out into space as he absentmindedly twisted a beer mug around a towel. He was startled when Kennedi plopped down in front of him and slapped the bar top.

"Ned! We need a morning-appropriate drink."

Ned nodded, trying to catch Adeline's eye. "Nice to see you again, Miss Addie."

Adeline sat down next to Kennedi. "Nice to see you too, Ned." After a quick glance around, marking the exits, she took in the collection of spirits lining the glass shelves behind the bar.

"Wait, not me?" Kennedi pouted, crossing her arms petulantly.

Ned chuckled and spread his arms across the bar top. "Miss Murphy, you always bring extra spice. What'll it be?"

Adeline tapped a nail against the wood. "I want to get blitzed and feel fancy while doing it. Do you have any champagne?"

"Sure do." Ned ambled down the bar and reached under the counter. He pulled out a dusty green bottle and popped it open. "It's a bit old though, and not cold."

Adeline tapped her chin. "Do you have cold orange juice? We could do mimosas."

Ned gave a toothy grin, and he placed the bottle in front of them. "I like where your head is at, Miss Addie. I think I have some in the back. Lemme go check." He walked away.

Alone again, Kennedi raised an eyebrow and leaned against the bar top. "Soooo… What happened earlier? Why are we getting blitzed?"

Adeline cringed. "Mags had me do some art therapy and… I thought of a memory I needed to work through."

Kennedi shook her head. "Art therapy? Is that even a thing? What was the memory?" She held up a hand. "You don't have to share if you don't want to."

Adeline bobbed her head. "Just the first time I tried to escape. It was…" She trailed off, momentarily locked in the memory as if an out-of-body experience. "I thought I had escaped, and I hadn't. When I was caught, my father punished me in some of the worst ways possible." Her throat tightened, and she grabbed the bottle of warm champagne and started guzzling as much as the warm fizz allowed. It warmed her insides, causing the festering feelings to bubble away.

Kennedi tugged at a red curl, twisting it around a finger. "I'm sorry to hear that. I'm here to listen, no matter what." She grabbed the bottle and took a swig. "Do you think you've actually escaped this time?"

Adeline took a deep breath, ignoring the racing of her heart at the mere mention of Lucas possibly looking for her. "I think so. But what if he's just fucking with me? What if this is all part of an elaborate game?"

Ned reappeared carrying a chilled bottle of orange juice. Kennedi straightened up and clapped exuberantly, causing Adeline to smile. Ned puffed out his barrel chest. He swiped two wine glasses off a shelf and plopped them onto the counter.

"Sorry, ladies, but I don't have champagne flutes. This'll havta do."

Kennedi propped herself up on her elbows, watching as the liquid swirled in the glass. "No problemo, Neddy. The job gets done regardless."

Adeline moaned, the sweet tang of the orange juice exploding on her tongue.

Ned walked away again, said to holler when they wanted more. Once he was out of earshot, Kennedi inched closer to Adeline. Her breath was sticky and sweet. Adeline leaned in, wanting more.

"I say we take the afternoon and just catch up some more. What's brunch without some salacious stories?"

Adeline grinned. The idea of pretending the outside world wasn't still out there, lurking, sounded perfect. "Deal."

In less than an hour, they'd polished off three mimosas each. The more they drank, the louder they got. Kennedi regaled her with dating stories, each one worse than the previous.

"You're telling me that you dated this woman, Rebecca? Raquel? Rianne?"

Kennedi rolled her eyes. "Richard."

"Right, you dated a woman named *Richard*." Adeline made a face that clearly communicated her thoughts on the name. "And by date five, she was proposing marriage? And you said yes until you found her stealing shit out of your house. Which was only two months later."

Kennedi scoffed. "Well, when you put it that way… But I swear, it felt right at the time!"

"Where's the ring?" Adeline gave a pointed look at Kennedi's bare ring finger. Kennedi jerked her hand back defensively.

"I sold it, okay? She stole my entire closet! I needed to replace it!"

Adeline cackled, partially collapsing on the bar top and almost knocking over an empty champagne glass. She rushed to catch it before it fell.

"Whoops." Adeline grinned, eyes shining, her heart fluttering. A strand of Adeline's dark hair fell forward, and Kennedi leaned over and swept it back around the shell of Adeline's ear.

They both froze as their bodies made contact, and a zap of energy passed between them. Adeline's face went slack, eyes widening as she turned her head slowly into Kennedi's hand. Her warm breath rolled over Kennedi's forearm, goosebumps erupting along her limbs. Time stood still, suspended between them.

Adeline tried not to cringe as Kennedi's eyes moved over her body. She knew what Kennedi could see: Tiny scars covering different parts of her skin. A nick across her throat. One below her right eye. An almost invisible one on her left cheek. Kennedi sucked in a breath as she moved her hand along Adeline's jaw, slowly tracing its smooth edge. Her thumb glided over the faint cheek scar. Adeline closed her eyes and instinctively pressed her face into Kennedi's palm. Something deep clicked into place. It was the most immovable feeling in the world. Nothing could destroy it.

They pulled away from each other slowly. Adeline cleared her throat and motioned to the empty glasses.

"What on *earth* is in that cheap champagne?"

Kennedi chuckled. "I don't know. You want some more?"

***

By the time Adeline got home, she was wobbling on her feet. The champagne pumped through her veins; she felt like she was floating. Kennedi returned to the bookstore, albeit a little unsure how productive she'd be, and promised to call later. Adeline smiled to herself. She was on a high that had nothing to do with the alcohol.

Mags snuggled three cats on the couch in the living room, knitting something small and odd looking. Adeline closed the door and plonked down in the seat beside her, eyeing the cobalt blue mess of yarn.

"How was your afternoon?" Mags side-eyed her, a smile playing at the edges of her wrinkled mouth.

Adeline sighed loudly, patting her bloated belly. "Full of champagne. What on earth are you making?"

Mags snorted. "Mr. Binxs wanted a new sweater for the winter."

"Winter is months away," Adeline pointed out.

The clinking of knitting needles stopped. Mags pointed to an extremely fat white cat with blue eyes. "Tell *him* that."

Adeline looked at Mr. Binxs. With a very serious tone, she said, "Mr. Binxs, you are made of glorious fur. Why do you need a sweater?"

"Bitch," Mags said in a voice that sounded like she'd inhaled helium. "Don't question my needs."

Adeline burst out laughing. "That's his voice, huh?"

Mags nodded solemnly. "Yes. I've known him for years."

The shrill ring of Mags' cellphone interrupted whatever Adeline was about to say. Mags stared at the offending black object on the end table to her left.

She sighed impatiently and answered with a curt, "Whatever you're selling, shove it up your ass."

Silence.

"Who is this, and why are you wasting my time? I have a cat sweater to ruin." She put it on speaker.

Adeline's blood ran cold as a silky, menacing voice answered: "How far one falls from saving children caught in gunfire to making, what was it? Cat sweaters?"

Mags narrowed her eyes. "Who the fuck is this?"

Adeline was close to throwing up. Mags looked at her and tilted her head as if to ask, *is this who I think it is?* Adeline gave a jerky nod. A too-familiar chuckle rumbled. "Your file said you were smarter than that, Magda Deanlight, also known as Mags, affectionately called Thunder Cunt by ex-military comrades."

Mags' face turned a deep shade of red. Not of embarrassment but rage. Despite her reaction, Mags kept it cool. "Is this Dukas Boreman? I'd say it's a pleasure to meet you, but I'd hate to tarnish my cunty reputation. What the fuck do you want?"

"The name is Lucas Oremen, and I want what's mine," Lucas said icily. "Adeline has been with you for quite a few weeks now. Reports say she's settling into some form of life with you and that *whore* from her childhood. I knew she'd run to that red-headed slut. But I want her back."

Adeline balled her fists, nails digging into the flesh of her palms. He could say whatever he wanted about her, but speaking about Kennedi that way—it was too far. And how the absolute fuck did he find her?

Mags snorted. "Then come get her. Or are you too much of a little bitch to do so yourself, Mucus Goreman?"

"Don't test me, Magda," he hissed. "I'm no fool. I know you won't take my money. But I will tell you right now that if you don't convince Adeline she needs to return, hell will rain down on everyone she's befriended. I will burn down that entire town if it will teach her the right lesson."

Adeline jolted upright. He didn't make empty threats, but returning to Lucas would be a death sentence.

Mags' knuckles whitened. "Why did you even let her go? Why not come get her right now?"

He chuckled again. The sound made Adeline gag. "There's a certain pleasure in watching your pets enjoy themselves. You're their god, and you allow them to run around and revel in their false sense of freedom. Dogs will behave for treats. Even cats will be friendly for a good snack. See, Adeline is my prized pet. I spent years making sure she understood her place."

"You used her as a broodmare."

Lucas scoffed. "Actually, I ensured she never foaled, if you want to use such an odd metaphor. I gave her a life of luxury, and all I asked in return was for her to earn her keep."

"By fucking your friends."

"We all have our purpose in this world," he purred. "I gave her an amazing childhood, something most people don't get. Now she has to pay me back. I don't think I'm asking too much." He sighed loudly. "I bore of this conversation. Will you help me or not?"

Adeline eyed the stairs, feeling the temptation to bolt, to pack her things and try to disappear. Fear was already slithering down her spine, settling in her gut like wet cement.

Mags snapped viciously, "Thank you so much for calling, like a psychopath, but I'm not interested in helping you keep your daughter as a prostitute. Please kindly fuck off and enjoy your coffee."

Adeline watched with bulging eyes as Mags ended the call and tossed her phone across the room onto another seat. No one had ever dared to taunt the monster she called father. Mags glowered at the cat sweater, then looked to Adeline with eyes the color of stormy tropical waters.

"That motherfucker seriously needs to die."

Adeline burst into tears. "What am I going to do?" He was going to come and steal her. Drag her back to his home and bury her in that beautiful garden. She'd literally be pushing up daisies. Each passing second marched her closer to hysteria. She stood and paced the span of the room.

"He's going to hurt you, Mags. And Kennedi. Don't assume he makes empty threats, because he doesn't."

She halted and looked at Mags, who watched her with a thoughtful expression. Throwing her hands in the air, she cried, "Well! Aren't you going to say something? Toss me out on my ass? I would if I were you. I'd wish me luck and lock all the doors."

Mags stood and marched to Adeline, bracing her hands against Adeline's shoulders. "Girl, you're not going anywhere. He'll remove you over my cold dead body."

Adeline wrenched out of Mags's grasp. "Mags, *he'll make that happen*. Don't you get it? He owns cops and judges. He's richer than a god and has gotten away with more things than you can imagine. I can't do this."

Adeline began to pace again, ignoring Mags. "He's going to come. He'll bring me back. Maybe do worse. I need to leave, Mags. It isn't safe for anyone." Wiping away hot, angry tears, Adeline looked out the window. "He could even be watching right now."

Mags snapped her fingers a couple of times, catching Adeline's attention. "Hey. Stop. Take a breath."

Adeline started to hyperventilate, hands clutching her knees while she gulped deep breaths. "I'm trying. But he's coming, Mags. He's coming for you and Kennedi and me and—"

"*ADELINE.*" Mags barked her name like a command. Adeline straightened, swiping at snot.

"Mags, you really don't—"

Mags clapped loudly, surprising Adeline. "Addie, stop. Right now. Breathe. We will come up with a plan, alright?"

"What kind? There's nothing we can do. He's coming for me. *He's coming for me.*" Hysteria shredded her senses; air was impossible to inhale. "I can't go back. I'd rather kill myself, do you understand? *I'd rather be dead.*"

Mags sighed heavily. She'd stopped trying to slow Adeline's spiraling. Instead, she stood a few feet away with hands on her hips. "Don't you want to live, girl?"

Adeline gaped at Mags. "Excuse me. Do I want to *live*? Have you heard *nothing* about what he's done to me? If he takes me back, it'll be worse than death."

"So let's prepare for his arrival."

Adeline shook her head in bewilderment. "How? He has Alexander, and besides that, he used to be a boxer. I don't stand a chance."

"When you arrived at my doorstep, you didn't stand a chance," Mags corrects. "But we've been working every day on your fitness and self-defense. And we will continue to do so. I'll teach you how to use some weapons. We'll make sure you have someone with you as much as possible. I can't speak for Kennedi, but I for one can't wait to filet this fucker. I might be an old bitch, but I'm not afraid of him."

"You should be," Adeline argued. But Mags's words were seeping in. She *did* know more now. She was stronger and faster than ever. If anything, her developed skills could take them by surprise enough to escape or buy time.

Aside from that, she vowed to not continue being afraid. It gave Lucas too much power. And if there was one thing in this world she was done doing, it was giving him any more power. The tears dried up and Adeline took her first deep breath. She wasn't weak anymore— she had a real chance.

Mags grinned. "You're seeing reason, eh? Come on, let's go have a drink. Then plan the next few training sessions. Tell me about some of their go-to moves, and we can work on counteracting them. How does that sound?"

Adeline cracked a weak smile. "I'm still tipsy, but the day is young."

"Thatta girl.

CHAPTER TWELVE

A week later, Adeline stared at her latest piece of art. It was a far cry from her first piece—this one was all color, puffs of clouds caught in rainbows.

Her inspiration came from what she envisioned a perfect day might feel like. She took gold paint and swooped slivers of it along the edges of some of the colors. She hummed a nameless tune, lost in thought.

It had been almost two months since she'd arrived in Menforth, and the art therapy was doing its job; she was turning into a new person.

No, that wasn't quite right. She was turning into an *actual* person.

For the first time in years, she could go anywhere she wanted, eat whatever she wanted, and even choose what to wear. She learned she liked jazz music and loved pancakes. Using some of the cash she'd stolen from Lucas, Kennedi dragged her to the nearby city to go shopping. Adeline filled her closet with sundresses, jeans, and tank tops—clothes banned by Lucas. She bought her first pair of sneakers since she was a teenager and took up running in the mornings, followed by sets of push-ups and shadow boxing.

When Lucas did show up, she'd at least have a fighting chance. True to her promise, Mags ramped up their training, going over more Krav Maga-style fighting. Every day, she worked at learning more and refusing to let his looming shadow haunt the future.

She was going to live life fully until then. Even Kennedi joined them. After Adeline confessed all of the threats Lucas had made—she knew Kennedi needed to make the choice for herself—she was relieved to see the steely look in Kennedi's eyes when she declared she'd learn how to fight too.

Making the final touches to the painting, adding tiny speckles of yellow, she thought about how it might go down. Would he try to kidnap her? Trick her? Hurt someone? The best she could do was prepare herself as much as possible.

She sat back in satisfaction, admiring the finished piece.

"That's fantastic."

Adeline whipped around to see Mags leaning against the doorway, arms crossed and smiling with approval. She pushed off and walked over, critical eyes skimming the still-drying paint. "I like how you used a different technique here, between the colors, but it still somehow blends together. What does it mean?"

"Who I want to be," Adeline said simply.

Mags nodded and motioned to the wet canvas. "I hope to see you turn into whatever this is."

"Me too." Adeline raised her hands over her head and stretched. She glanced at her silver watch—a gift from Mags. It was scuffed to hell. When Adeline had asked what happened to it, Mags was cagey about the answer, saying something about the watch "seeing some shit."

"I need to head to work." Adeline yawned. "I stayed up too late reading. It's going to be a long night."

Mags followed her out of the room. The old woman had been more clingy than usual the last couple of weeks, but Adeline didn't mind the mother henning. It was nice to have someone care about her well-being.

"Do you want me to walk you to the bar?" Mags asked with a hint of anxiety. Adeline had been working at Ned's for about a week. He'd needed the help, and she needed to keep busy—it was a win-win.

Adeline shook her head as she grabbed her purse hanging on a hook by the door.

"No, I've got it. It's only a block away" She smiled. "I'll be back later, okay?"

Mags looked like she was about to argue but said nothing. She glanced down the hallway to the coat closet. "All right, but text me when you're about to leave, all right?"

Adeline opened the door and took a deep whiff of the summer night air. It was warm and smelled of fresh-cut grass. "I promise."

She closed the door behind her and headed down the sidewalk, completely missing the dark sedan parked down the street.

***

Adeline stepped into Ned's bar and took in the busy space. A Dolly Parton song played from the old jukebox. She smiled at Ned cleaning an empty glass with an old rag. She had never seen him anywhere except behind the bar. She suspected he had a pull-out cot under the kegs. He might even be a bar troll, just no one had figured it out.

"Hey, Miss Addie! Glad to see ya."

"Hey, Ned. Happy to be here."

She rounded the bar and placed her purse on a hidden empty shelf. Next, she grabbed a short black apron hanging on a hook and tied it around her waist. The bar was already half-full, and happy hour hadn't even started yet.

"Table seven needs refills." Ned walked up, bumping his hip to hers. She smiled.

"Got it."

Ned always played waiter during the day, relying on her to take over on weekend nights while he slung drinks to the larger crowds. She was more than happy to help out.

After a few hours, she took a quick break to scarf down some mozzarella sticks. Then, just as she was cleaning up, Ned ambled up to her with a grin.

"Mind doin' me a favor?"

She nodded. "Of course. What's up?"

Two large bottles of vodka appeared on the bar top. "Can you bring these to Zelda? She has a party this weekend and asked me to get her some bottles on the down-low."

Adeline smiled. The way everyone helped each other out in Menforth was really growing on her. "Sure. At the diner?"

"Actually, at her home. She might be working, but I highly doubt Rick would approve."

"Rick?"

"The chef-slash-owner."

Adeline recalled the guy who'd come to her defense the first time she was in the diner. He didn't come out of the kitchen too much, so she'd never had the chance to introduce herself.

"Sure. Want me to come back after?"

"Nah. You did great today."

Adeline's chest expanded with pride. Compliments were becoming a drug for her. Grabbing her purse and the bottles of vodka, she gave Ned one last grin before heading outside. She texted Mags to let her know what was going on, but didn't hear back immediately. It was only two blocks away—a quick walk. It'd be fine.

All around her, fireflies flirted with the night, their light blossoming every few seconds. An owl hooted somewhere in the trees. Adeline took a deep breath. She felt at peace.

Adeline turned a corner and started down a street lined with houses, each one unique. Nothing like the rows of identical homes found in modern suburbia, every house ordered to look the same by some over-lording homeowner's association. Overgrown bushes covered in soft-smelling flowers made her hum with happiness. Menforth wasn't so bad. It held a magnetic charm. Maybe she would—

BAM!

The world exploded into stars and darkness. A boulder the size of Rhode Island slammed into her back, emptying her lungs of air. Her body flew forward a few feet, the jugs of vodka flying even farther—they hit the ground and shattered. She caught herself right before she slammed into the cement, but her wrists buckled as her full weight hit. Shards of glass bit into her palms. She tried to scream.

A rough hand slapped over her mouth. A fist ground between her shoulder blades, pinning her to the ground.

A familiar voice hissed, breath like onions: "He's going to come soon, little mouse. He'll play his game, and when he's done, he'll eat you up."

Alexander. Memories assaulted her brain, his voice hot on her ear. Mags had drilled into her how to defend herself, but with his weight on her spine, she could barely think. She tried to scream again, but the meaty hand clamped down harder, pinching her nose at the same time. Her lungs burned, and every nerve ending was lit up in terror.

Think! Think! Think!

Adeline tried desperately to think of a way to defend herself, but the lack of oxygen created an all-consuming terror that made it impossible to assess the situation objectively.

Then her mind calmed. This is what Mags had been preparing her for. They hadn't covered this exact situation, but she wasn't helpless.

She wasn't powerless.

He was just a man, with the same soft spots as all the rest.

He spoke again, this time licking her ear. "Be a good pet and just come home. Otherwise, you'll regret it. You hear me, bitch? He'll carve up your new friends and feed you their tongues."

Opening her mouth wider, Adeline felt his meaty palm slide between her teeth. She bit down as hard as possible, tasting blood. He roared, yanking his hand back.

Adeline sucked in a breath. He reared up, and she used the shift of his weight to bring an elbow up in the air. *Crunch.* The satisfying feeling of his nose collapsing under the impact made her smile.

He roared and stood up. She flipped onto her back, baring her bloody mouth in a vicious grin. "You taste delicious."

His face twisted in fury when she threw his words back. Blood slipped through his fat fingers. "You stupid fucking bit—"

"Hey! What the fuck! Get the fuck away from her!" A male voice roars, boots pounding on the pavement. Alexander paused.

Glaring at her, he growled, "This isn't fucking over. I'll see you soon."

She heaved in a gasp of fresh air as Alexander fled. Her lungs sang with relief, expanding fully with each desperate gulp. Gasping, she tried to look around, searching for him, but her back spasmed in protest. The sound of boots grew louder until black leather soles appeared in her vision. A man crouched down, brushing hair away from her face.

"Are you okay?"

She sat up with a groan and spit out the blood coating her mouth. A pair of firm hands reached for her shoulders. A dark-haired man squatted in front of her, eyes wild with concern. Even in the dark, she could see his caramel-colored eyes in stark contrast against his tawny skin. He wore a burnt orange and blue plaid short-sleeved shirt and dark jeans. A soft scruff of beard darkened his chiseled jaw.

"Are you okay?" he repeated, fumbling with his pockets. "What's wrong with your mouth? Are you hurt?"

She shook her head. "Not my blood."

A part of her was disappointed—now she had to continue playing this fucked-up game. But the other part of her was thrilled that she not only fought back, but truly hurt Alexander. Finally.

"Here, take this. I'm calling the cops." He brought a cellphone to his ear, handing her a hanky from his pocket. She continued to suck in air, wiping away the blood on her lips. She held up her hands, inspecting the glass embedded in her palms. Wincing, she picked each piece out using just her nails.

"Hey, it's Ryker Avila. I'm on Maurant Street, by Zelda's house. I have a woman in front of me who was just attacked." A pause. "Yeah, I'll stay here."

He hung up and tucked the phone into his back pocket. Noticing what she was doing, he gently grabbed her hands to stop her. She resisted the urge to snatch them back, enjoying the rough warmth of his palms.

"An ambulance is on the way. Let them do that, okay?" His voice was deep, patient.

She nodded. He peered around, watching for anyone else. He focused on her again. "Can you tell me your name?"

Tone robotic, she said. "Addie Oremen."

He shifted, glass crunching under his boots. "Can you stand, Addie?"

"I think so."

He hesitated. "Can I help you up?" She nodded, biting back a cry of pain, her spine protesting with every inch of movement. Her thoughts clamored against each other, demanding attention, but she couldn't focus on a single one. Alexander was *here*. And she *fought back*. The dark-haired stranger—Ryker—wrapped a hand around her waist and lifted her as if she weighed nothing. He tucked her close, letting her lean against his torso. An ambulance wailed in the distance.

"Is he gone?" she whispered. She looked up then and saw Ryker glance around again.

"Seems like it. Did you know him?"

When she didn't answer, he repeated the question. She sighed, resisting the urge to ball her fists. His proximity made her nervous.

What if he's a part of it?

The sinister voice taunted from a dark corner of her mind. He could have been a plant, swooping in like a hero to lower her guard. And yet… She'd been around so many kinds of men. Something about him felt easy. Maybe even safe.

As the red and blue lights swept across the houses and lawns, she focused on the dancing fireflies in the pockets of darkness. Nearby, a dog howled at the abrasive noise. Curtains fluttered as people peered out from their homes. By morning, all of Menforth would know what had happened. There would undoubtedly be a mob carrying pitchforks parked in front of Mags' house, demanding she take her drama elsewhere.

The ambulance stopped in front of them, and two paramedics hopped out, rushing over to her. Ryker pressed her tighter against him.

"What happened?" One of the paramedics, short with sandy blond hair, inspected her outstretched hands. She flinched when he tentatively turned them from side to side, examining the damage. He looked up and offered a brief smile. "Looks like it's all superficial. You'll be good as new in a couple of days."

"Is the ambulance really necessary?" she asked. The paramedic turned away without answering.

Ryker's grip loosened. He said quietly, "Do you think you can stand on your own?"

She tested her legs, easing away when they proved strong enough for her to stand. He continued to stand beside her, anxiously looking between her and the paramedic, who was heading back.

A cop car rolled up behind the ambulance, and a man wearing a sheriff's uniform stepped out. Adeline watched him survey the scene as the paramedic took tweezers and plucked out the glass from her palms.

She bit the inside of her cheek, trying to focus on what pain she could control. The sheriff strode over, pulling out a pen and a notebook. His uniform was crisp; his brown hair shellacked with gallons of gel. He looked to be in his forties but was unexpectedly fit. Laugh lines were deeply embedded in his tanned face. Sharp eyes swept across the scene.

He offered a comforting smile. "Howdy. I'm Sheriff Bill Teerman. You can call me Bill." Flipped the notebook open, pen poised. "Mind tellin' me what happened?"

She told her story as the paramedic gingerly wrapped her hands. When she was done, she noticed Bill's brows stitching together.

He glanced at Ryker. "Avila, you live around here, right?"

Ryker shifted, shoving his hands into his pockets. "Just came down the mountain. I was headed to the bar. Heard her scream and ran over as fast as I could. Scared the guy off."

"What'd the man look like?" Bill looked between them again. Adeline looked away, which caught the sheriff's attention. "You know who he is?"

Silence. Then Ryker said, "He was huge. Over six feet and probably around two-fifty. Black shirt and pants. Dark hair. Surprisingly fast."

The paramedic walked away, murmuring something about keeping the wounds clean. Adeline wiggled her fingers, surprised at the lack of pain. Bill stepped closer. She looked up warily.

"Ms. Oremen, do you know who he was?"

She weighed her options. On one hand, telling the sheriff what has happened—or what would continue to happen—could be helpful. She doubted the sheriff could do anything to actually prevent something from happening. All it would do is brand her as a troublemaker. The last thing she needed was more eyes watching.

She cleared her throat. "No, I don't think so. I'm not sure what he wanted."

Sheriff Teerman sighed and gave a look that said he didn't believe her. Thankfully, he didn't press. He stepped back, looked over his shoulder. Motioned to a deputy standing nearby before turning back to them. "I'm going to have someone drive you home. Mags would have my head if I let you walk."

"You know I live with Mags?" she blurted.

He sighed again. "Yes. Everyone knows Mags. God help the ones who don't but someday will. Regardless, she told me you might have some trouble. I've been keeping an eye out."

So, he knew she was lying and still didn't press for answers. She tried to ignore the shame that slithered down her body. How much had Mags told him?

The sheriff looked at Ryker. "You good to go?"

Ryker grunted. "Yeah. You sure she's okay to go home?"

Bill gave a wry laugh. "You clearly land on the 'don't know Mags' side of the situation. I once saw her scream very particular words at a squirrel eating her garden—words I won't repeat. If she brings a fraction of that attitude to protecting Ms. Oremen, I have no doubt she'll be just fine."

Ryker's shoulders relaxed. He looked to Adeline. "Will you be okay?"

Adeline huffed out a weak laugh. "The sheriff is right; Mags would make anyone regret coming into the house."

Ryker assessed her a little longer before dipping his chin. "Is it cool if I check on you tomorrow?"

Sheriff Teermen turned to the waiting police cruiser. Adeline started after him. "Yeah, sure," she said over her shoulder. "Thank you for helping."

"No problem."

As the cruiser pulled away, Adeline in the backseat, she watched Ryker, whose eyes only left her face when the cruiser turned a corner.

CHAPTER THIRTEEN

As the squad car pulled up in front of the magenta house, Mags bounded out the front door faster than Adeline thought she could move. She stood on the sidewalk anxiously as the deputy opened the door for Adeline. Mags was on her in an instant. Adeline didn't have a moment to speak as Mags squeezed her tightly, refusing to let go.

"I'm so sorry. I'm so, so, *so* sorry, Adeline. I should've been there. Are you okay? Where are you hurt?" Mags pushed Adeline back, frantically scanning her for injuries. She paled at the bandaged hands.

"What happened?" she demanded. She turned to the deputy. "What happened to her? Doesn't she need to go to the doctor? And why the *hell* is she in the back of the cop car?"

"Mags, I—" Adeline tried to interrupt her, but Mags sent her a wilting look.

The deputy, to his credit, didn't crack under Mags' venomous tone. "I'm not a doctor, ma'am, but I doubt they would have sent her home if she was in grave danger. And with you as her guard dog, I'm sure she'll be fine."

Adeline thought for sure Mags would be insulted by the reference, but instead, Mags squared her shoulders and gave a firm nod. "Yes. She's safe here. Thank you for the escort."

And just like that, the deputy was dismissed. Mags began pulling Adeline toward the house, but Adeline dug in her heels. She gave the officer a tentative smile. "Thanks for the ride."

He tipped his head. Mags pulled Adeline forward. Every second out of the house was a second she was in danger. Mags didn't release her steel grip until they were safely back inside. She pointed to the couch. Adeline trudged over and collapsed onto it. It felt amazing to sit down in a safe space; anyone stupid enough to attack her here would be ravaged by an old woman's wrath. And possibly rabid feline demons.

"I'm going to make tea. Go sit down. Have some cats." Mags leaned down and grabbed two curious felines and deposited them into her lap.

As she marched out of the living room, the cats settled into Adeline's lap. Their purrs soothed her frazzled nerves. She stared out the big bay window, the void of night threatening to swallow her whole. Maybe someone was out there, staring back from the shadows. Obviously, *someone* had been. The thought made her shiver. Aslin slunk into the living room and jumped onto the couch, hissing the other cats away. Adeline smiled as Aslin made biscuits with her thighs.

"Hi," Adeline said softly, enjoying the unconditional love. Aslin's brown ears were silky soft as she shoved her furry head under one of Adeline's hands. Mags swept into the room, holding two steaming mugs of tea. She set them down on the coffee table and sat down on the other side of the couch.

"Here, drink up." Mags passed a mug to Adeline. Holding it carefully in her bandaged palms, Adeline inhaled the scent of jasmine. She took a small sip, barely feeling the tip of her tongue burn. Mags popped up suddenly and violently jerked the curtains shut. Then she resettled onto the couch, gaze drilling into Adeline.

Mags leaned forward. "So, what happened?"

Adeline sucked her tongue after scalding with another sip. She shrugged. "I was attacked. Luckily, some guy showed up and spooked Alexander."

"Some guy?" Mags echoed. "Who's Alexander again?"

Adeline swallowed. "My father's lackey. Or right-hand man. Or fixer. Depends on the needs of the day."

Mags scoffed. "A loyal dog, then."

Adeline blew on her tea before taking another sip. "That's certainly one way to put it."

Mags ran her fingers along the top of a cat's head, staring at a portrait on the wall. "So, what did you do?"

Aslin purred louder. Pride welled. "I broke his nose and took out a chunk of his hand."

Mags guffawed, scaring away the cats. "Are you for fucking real?"

Adeline held up two fingers. "Scout's honor."

Mags hooted, slapping her thigh. "Girl, you never cease to amaze me. How did it feel?"

"Like I kicked the bogeyman's ass."

Mags shook her head, looking at Adeline in wonder. "Oremen's a total pussy for sending some threatening hulk to attack a defenseless woman. Or someone he thought was defenseless."

Adeline barked out a laugh. No one had ever called Lucas Oremen a pussy. Give it to Mags for being the first. "Yeah, well, I don't know what to do now. Should I leave? I don't want to put any of you in danger."

A glint sparked in Mags' icy blue eyes. "No. Let's keep you here. Home turf and all. If we're lucky, Alexander will be walking across a crosswalk right when I suddenly go senile."

"He'd make quite the mess."

Mags scoffed. "That's all men do: make messes." Standing, Mags lifted Aslin and tossed her to the floor. "Come on, les' go. Time for a hot bath, some wine, and sleep."

Adeline placed her mostly-full tea cup on the coffee table and stood. "That sounds heavenly." She hesitated. "What happens if Alexander followed me here?"

Mags patted Adeline's arm, her hand rough and warm. "That's between me, him, and the gods. Now les' go."

***

When Adeline opened her eyes, her brain was blissfully blank for a few moments. Sun streamed through the white chiffon curtains, with a bluebird chirping outside. She smiled, luxuriating in the soft sheets. Then she moved. Every muscle in her body was as tight as a strung bow. A knot of anxiety made quick work of her false sense of safety. She was an idiot to let her guard down. A damn fucking idiot.

She pulled on a pair of loose shorts and a deep red tank top. Over the last few weeks, she had become more comfortable showing the tiny scars that speckled her body. Even the three cigarette burns on the soft skin of her thighs.

Throwing her hair up into a ponytail, she dared a glance into the mirror. She liked the way her body filled out with new curves. If her father had known how shapely she could be, he would've force-fed her.

Thinking about him roiled her insides. Even if he came for her, storming through the door like havoc incarnate, she didn't regret anything she'd done in the time since she'd taken her freedom.

Mags stood in front of the stove, wearing a bright green painter's shirt and khaki shorts. A large brown butterfly clip held back her silver-gray hair. In front of her was a pot of grits and a pan of eggs; she stirred both simultaneously. The smell made Adeline's mouth water.

A floorboard squeaked as she stepped into the kitchen. Mags glanced over her shoulder.

Below her eyes were dark purple crescents. Had she even slept? "Morning, sleepyhead. How'd you sleep?"

Adeline shrugged. "Fine. No nightmares, thankfully." She sat down at the kitchen table, wincing at the twinge of pain in her hips.

Mags slid a handmade mug in front of her, the steam from the fresh coffee dancing into the air.

"Breakfast will be done in a jiffy," Mags said cheerfully. Adeline looked down at her coffee, willing the warmth to reach her bones. No luck.

Mags hummed as she finished up the scrambled eggs. She placed a tower of them in front of Adeline, followed by a bowl of grits, a slab of butter still melting over it. "Eat up."

Adeline continued to stare at her coffee. "I don't feel like it."

Mags leaned against the table's edge, her mouth pursed. "And I hate wearing underwear, but I do it anyway. *Eat.*"

Adeline stabbed the eggs with her fork, making an exaggerated show of taking the first bite. Mags clicked her tongue. "Look at me like that all you want, but you need to eat. Your body needs to recover after that kind of adrenaline rush."

She huffed and collapsed into a chair next to Adeline, chattering about the weeds in the garden and the plumpness of her summer squash. Adeline managed to swallow a few bites. The grits were heavenly, as usual. She'd asked Mags what made them so creamy, and Mags had whipped out a container of goat cheese from the fridge. Adeline wouldn't eat them any other way ever again.

When her stomach was full to bursting, she pushed the plate away. Mags harrumphed in satisfaction and sipped her coffee.

"How do you feel?"

Adeline snorted. "Like shit."

"Have you talked to Kennedi?"

Adeline groaned. She wasn't used to having a phone or texting anyone. "Oh my gods, I totally forgot. She's probably worried sick. And I think my cell phone flew out of my back pocket last night."

Mags held it up. "A deputy dropped it off this morning."

Adeline picked up the plate, deposited it into the sink, and made her way to the front door, snatching the phone out of Mags's hand.

"Where are you going?" Mags demanded.

Adeline glared over her shoulder. "To the bookstore."

Mags bolted upright. "The hell you are. I'll drive you."

"I need to move, Mags. My muscles are stiff, and movement will help."

The old woman rushed down the hallway. Her cats scattered. "Fine. I need a walk, too."

Behind her, Mags opened the closet door and reached inside. Adeline turned to see Mags tucking something into her back pocket. "Okay, then let's go, ol' biddy. Hope you can keep up."

Adeline almost immediately regretted her words. Mags charged down the sidewalk, head swiveling side to side and occasionally over her shoulder. What did this woman think she could do against someone like Alexander? Lucas mentioned on the phone she was a war photographer, but what did that really mean?

Glancing at Mags, Adeline asked, "What did you do as a war photographer? Why did Lucas say those things about you?"

Mags's mouth tightened. "A lot of different things, sometimes not photography related at all. I wasn't known for my ability to stay objective."

"Is that how you learned how to fight?"

Mags narrowed her eyes. "Yes, and other things. I'm not big on talking about it. I spent years reclaiming my sanity." Adeline scoffed. Mags smirked. "You're right, but believe it or not, I used to be even crazier."

The thought was disturbing.

By the time they reached the worn, wooden door, Adeline had beads of sweat dripping down her neck. She leaned over, hands on her knees, trying to breathe.

"Jesus, Mags. Are you trying to kill me?"

Mags smirked. "Oh, did this lil ol' biddy walk faster than w'ittle ol' Addie could keep up?"

Adeline's eyes flashed with irritation. "Fine. Point taken. You're as strong as vintage whiskey."

Mags grunted in appreciation and looked side to side, examining the surrounding area. Nothing seemed out of place—no strange cars or enormously tall lackeys to be seen. Adeline could see the gears turning underneath the gray frizz. She straightened up and put her hands on her hips.

"Mags, you can't protect me twenty-four-seven, and I can't live my life in fear. You're the one who told me that."

Mags bared her teeth. "When you're done with Kennedi, you call me. Do you understand? *You call me.*"

Adeline stepped past her and opened the door. "Got it. Loud and clear."

Mags huffed loudly and stomped away, muttering something about getting an actual guard dog. Adeline smile.

Kennedi stood behind the counter dressed in overalls and a baby pink bandeau top. She bounded around the counter and flung herself around Adeline's shoulders, sobbing into Adeline's ear.

"I'm so glad you're okay."

She pushed Adeline away, zoning in on the bandaged hands. She reached for one and looked up at Adeline again with watery eyes. "Why didn't you call me? I was worried sick! Lucky for you, Mags texted me before I heard from someone else. All I wanted to do was come and find you, but she told me to wait."

Adeline looked down, shrinking under Kennedi's tone. "I'm sorry… I didn't think…"

"Hey. Wait." Kennedi brought a finger to Adeline's chin, tilting it up. "I'm not mad. I'm sorry if I sound that way. I've just been so worried. I know that Victorian monstrosity you and Mags call home is secured like a bunker, but still."

Adeline giggled. "It's a good house. Might need a new paint job."

"Don't tell her that. She'd paint it orange out of spite."

The thought of a baby poop-orange house sobered Adeline up. "You're right. I vow to never say that again." She looked at three large piles of books on the counter. An empty delivery box was on the floor. "What's going on?"

Kennedi smiled and walked over to the pile. She picked up one of the books. It had a dark blue cover with gold foil twisting in different shapes. "New book day! I was just about to put these away. Want to help? We can go get lunch after."

Adeline lifted a pile, wincing at the pain in her hands, but it felt good to be useful. "Where to, boss?"

Kennedi grabbed another pile and started down an aisle. "Follow me."

The back of the bookstore was darker, lending the space a cozy feel. It reminded Adeline of a library. It was even as silent as a library. For all she knew, a librarian skulked around the corner, waiting to shush them. Kennedi had no such concerns and pointed out some of her favorite sections.

"Over there are serial killer stories. My favorite is definitely Elizabeth Bathory. Did you know she would bathe in virgin blood? And that section is full of horror novels. Some of the best society has to offer."

Adeline felt queasy. "Your *favorite* serial killer?"

They stopped in front of the romance section. Kennedi motioned for Adeline to put her pile down next to hers. She grabbed a book off the shelf and examined the other authors' names. "Yeah, I like horror."

Adeline grimaced. "Not me. I've seen enough blood to last a lifetime."

Kennedi paused before returning the book to its spot. Her cheeks reddened. "I'm sorry. I wasn't thinking. Of course, you wouldn't want to read or watch anything like that." She scanned the shelves. Her eyes lit up, and she snatched a different book. "Ah-ha! You might like this one. It's about two people who love one another, but life circumstances keep them apart. It's a happily ever after, too."

The corner of Adeline's mouth twitched. "Sounds familiar."

Kennedi laughed loudly. "Yes, I suppose you're right. Although..." She paused, chewing on her lip ring. "I mean, we used to say we loved each other, but we were kids…"

Those three words had remained unspoken since Adeline's arrival in Menforth. It would have been weird after four years of no communication. But life was short—that's the biggest lesson Adeline had learned over the years. The night before had been a stark reminder. When Alexander's hand threatened to suffocate her, a part of her thought of Kennedi's devastation if she died. She would never leave Kennedi ever again, if she had any say.

Adeline stepped forward. The regret she felt stabbed at her, forcing her to finally admit the truth. She brought her hands up and cupped Kennedi's face.

"Kennedi, I love you. I've *never* stopped loving you. The thought of you out there, living a wonderful life, that's what kept me going. Even if we are just friends for the rest of our lives, I never want to leave you, ever again."

Kennedi's eyes shimmered. Her mouth hung open. Adeline's heart thundered; she could feel her pulse throbbing in her throat. If

Kennedi rejected her… But she didn't survive four years of horrific abuse to hesitate any longer. Her father was coming, and there was nothing they could do to avoid it. It was time to seize the moment.

Their faces were only inches apart. She inhaled Kennedi's unique scent of fresh bread, punctuated by the smell of old books. Adeline stroked her thumb over Kennedi's smooth cheek. Kennedi leaned into it.

"I don't want to be just friends," Kennedi whispered. Her hands came up and held Adeline's elbows. "I thought of you every day. It broke my fucking heart when you disappeared. I love you, Addie. And I will always love you."

Adeline's heart felt like it was about to explode. Her fingers began to shake. "Is this a dream?" She closed her eyes, afraid to pinch herself and find out. Kennedi's sweet breath rolled over her face. She opened her eyes and saw hunger glinting in Kennedi's eyes; saw her lick her lips. Kennedi brought her hands to Adeline's waist and squeezed the soft curves.

"If it is, then let's make it the best fucking dream we've ever had."

Their lips collided at such velocity that it stung. Neither cared. Kennedi's lips were pillow soft against Adeline's mouth, the metal lip ring creating an interesting texture.

She hadn't kissed anyone—willingly—in four years. Kissing slobbering men was entirely different from kissing a woman whom she worshiped. She groaned into Kennedi's mouth, her core a raging fire. She grazed one of Kennedi's breasts. Kennedi raised her chest. Without hesitation, Adeline cupped the ample flesh, her hips thrusting forward as Kennedi yanked her closer.

Letting go of Kennedi's face, Adeline reached for a shelf and forced Kennedi back against the bookcase. Books tumbled to the ground. Keeping one arm braced, Adeline's other hand wandered down to the exposed skin between the side of Kennedi's bandeau top and her overalls.

The flesh was silky smooth and hot under her touch. She shoved her hands down Kennedi's backside, above Kennedi's panties; cupped an ass cheek and squeezed, hard. Kennedi gasped and did the same, grinding her pelvis against Adeline's. More books fell.

Kennedi's hands became frantic, roving at a fevered pace as she reacquainted herself with Adeline's body. Adeline's hips furiously undulated into Kennedi's, desperate to be skin-to-skin.

"I need to fucking feel you," Adeline growled. She slid her hand down Kennedi's ass to make a point—this time, underneath her panties. Kennedi's body jolted, and she moaned loudly. She gave a vague shake of her head in weak protest.

"We're at the bookstore. We shouldn't do this here."

They both gasped for breath as Kennedi peppered kisses down Adeline's neck. Adeline removed her hand from inside Kennedi's overalls and brought it to the apex of Kennedi's thighs. Even through the denim, Adeline felt the intense heat of Kennedi's need. She slowly trailed a finger over the inseam. Kennedi's knees wobbled. Adeline raised an eyebrow, a deviant smile.

"Why not? It's lunchtime on a weekday. Who would even come in here?"

And then the universe laughed. They froze as the bell above the front door jangled. Adeline swore under her breath. What were the fucking odds?

"Hello?" called a rough, leathery voice.

Reality splashed like ice water. Kennedi's eyes bulged. She gave an apologetic look as she headed down the aisle, squaring her shoulders. Adeline was left standing there, arms at her sides, watching Kennedi walk away from her.

Adeline took her time walking to the front of the bookstore. A man the same age as Mags stood near the counter wearing a large, tan button down, khakis, and a faded baseball cap. He looked over his shoulder as Adeline passed the couches.

"Oh, hello there." His voice was gruff but warm.

Adeline smiled. She approached him and held out her hand. "Hello. I'm Addie."

He cradled her hand in both of his. His grin was wide, showing off perfect, pearly white teeth. The laugh lines were deep, and his eyes sparkled. "Bruce."

Adeline liked him instantly. She looked to Kennedi, whose expression was impossible to decipher. Bruce followed her gaze to Kennedi, then he looked to Adeline again, then back to Kennedi.

"Ah."

That's all he said: *Ah*. Kennedi's cheeks bloomed the color of ripe tomatoes. Adeline felt even worse. Adeline liked Bruce immediately, but she wished he had never shown up. There had been some real magic cooking and, without meaning to, he'd gone ahead and ruined it.

Bruce smiled again. "Well, I don't want to interrupt. I'm sorry you don't have that book. But if you get it, where Bigfoot is a zombie, please call. My nephew raved about it." He went to the front door and brought a hand up to his cap, tipping it at each of them. His eyes twinkled, and he flashed a boyish grin. "Have a good one, ladies."

He whistled as he walked outside. Adeline let out a breath. In just thirty seconds, he had filled the room with a warmth that left Adeline feeling a little bewildered. She gave Kennedi an incredulous look. "Well, Bruce is certainly something."

Kennedi cleared her throat. "He would have to be. He dated Mags."

Adeline stared, utterly gobsmacked. "He... *dated* Mags?"

Kennedi laughed and grabbed more of the books on the counter. "Yep. Turns out, there *is* someone out there for everyone."

CHAPTER FOURTEEN

The spell broke, and as much as she craved exploring Kennedi's body, the bookstore wasn't the best place for it—Bruce had made sure of that. After a quick kiss, Adeline promised Kennedi she'd call before she headed back home. The world was brighter than before, continuing more hope than it ever had. Life was suddenly worth living.

Mags' head jerked up, hand thrust between the couch cushions, when Adeline opened the front door. Her eyes turned to slits when she saw who it was.

"How did you get home?" she demanded, pulling her sun-spotted hand from between the cushions. Adeline grimaced; she forgot Mags had demanded to be her escort.

"I walked…." she said slowly, looking down the hallway to the kitchen. It was a foolish, utterly stupid mistake. She'd been so wrapped up, thinking about Kennedi's mouth against hers, she simply walked home in a loopy, grinning daze.

And Mags was rightfully pissed.

Maybe she could bolt fast enough to the shelf full of booze and toss some of it into Mags' mouth while she ranted. Some way to appease the furious old crone. Mags stood abruptly and stalked over to Adeline.

"Girl, I'm of the mind to give you a thrashing. Do you not even value your life? Here you are, hands scratched up, and it's like you don't even notice."

Adeline brought her hands up and stared at her loosely wrapped palms. "That's probably because this is very mild. Honestly, I'm not even sure why I still have these on. With my father, this could've been a normal Monday morning. I mean, he didn't make me crawl through glass, but trust me, a punch to the gut hurts more."

Mags gave a stern look. "I don't give a shit. Under my roof, you're going to listen to me."

"Mags, I don't think—"

Her cell phone rang in her back pocket. They both paused, exchanging a glance. Adeline reached for the phone—an unknown number. She turned it so Mags could see. Mags motioned for her to answer.

She brought it up to her ear. "Hello?" She tried to hide the shaking of her voice.

"Did I fuck you up last night?" Alexander groaned like he was possibly touching himself. "It felt nice to have you under me again, even if you broke my fucking nose. I'll make you pay for that later."

Adeline was instantly furious. "I'll do more than that next time, you sonofa—"

The line went dead. Adeline stared at the black screen, knuckles white as she gripped the phone. She exhaled a shaky breath. A mix of emotions twist up her insides. She broke his nose and wasn't completely helpless. But that groan… Nightmares would be a companion tonight.

Mags inched closer. "Who was it?"

"Alexander."

Mags' blanched. "That man needs to die. Maybe we should make that happen."

So matter of fact. Adeline hesitated. "Mags, we can't just kill them. They're huge and powerful. No offense, but you are the size of a large child. Alexander could crush your face with two fingers."

Mags gave a rueful laugh. "Child, you have no idea what I've done in this life and the men I've dealt with. Men like your father and that Alejandro guy—"

"Alexander."

Mags rolled her eyes. "That's what I said—Alfredo. Men like that are a dime a dozen. Powerful men and lackeys are a dime a dozen. But they all bleed."

Adeline opened her mouth to argue, but there was a knock at the door. They both jumped. Mags rushed to the hallway closet. Adeline gasped as the tiny old woman reappeared brandishing a massive shotgun. She propped the butt against her shoulder, the silver barrel pointed to the wooden floor.

"What the hell are you doing?" Adeline hissed. Mags gave a tiny motion with the gun.

"Open up."

"What if it's—"

Mags's glasses slipped down her narrow nose. "One could only be so lucky. Open. Up."

Adeline sucked in a breath and opened the door. To her shock, there stood the man from the night before. What was his name? Digging through the traumatic memory, she remembered: *Ryker.*

In daylight, she could make out more of his features. Inky black hair fell loose across his forehead, a curl swooping just above an eyebrow. He wore a faded blue T-shirt with a small hole at the bottom. His jeans were well-loved, hugging his massive thighs. His skin was a deep burnished gold, and his almond-shaped eyes sharpened at the sight of Mags' shotgun.

"Who are you?" Mags commanded.

Ryker rubbed the stubble on his jaw. "I should be asking you the same thing. I'm… the guy from last night. But you can call me Ryker. Do you maybe want to point that thing somewhere else?"

Mags' hard expression melted into a genial grin. She lowered the barrel. "Well, hello there, handsome. So, I have you to thank for saving Addie."

"Yes, ma'am." Ryker dipped his chin.

Mags huffed. She rested the shotgun against the wall. "Well, thank you. Come in, have a drink."

Adeline did a double take. Mags saying "thank you" was like a cat barking: absolutely weird. Adeline moved aside, offering a tentative smile. Even on the other side of the door, he was imposing. She saw old scars along his arms and wondered where they could have come from.

Ryker entered, stepping past Adeline. He started looking around, eyes widening at the sight of the painting room. Mags quickly closed the door.

"So… what's your story?" she asked. She tipped her red glasses forward and made a show of looking him up and down.

"Mags, leave him alone." Adeline waved Ryker toward the kitchen.

Mags stepped back, pouting. "Well, fine then. Go see who you came for. I'm just the old hag with cobwebs in her crotch."

He gave a throaty laugh as he walked into the kitchen. Adeline followed him, breathing in the scent of pine. He stood straight, taking up all the air in the room. He felt friendly, but there was an edge to him, too.

Ryker's head swiveled as he took in the gadgets and beautiful stainless steel features. The room was phenomenally different from any other space in the house.

Adeline stepped past him. "Pretty different from everything else, huh?"

He nodded. She motioned to the empty spot at the table. He sat down with predatory grace, stretching out his long legs as Mags swept into the room, hell bent on pretending the spotless counters needed a rubdown.

"Would you like anything?" Adeline offered.

"Coffee? Milk? Booze? Tea? All of it?" Mags chirped. Ryker turned to look at her, the corners of his eyes crinkling in amusement. Adeline hesitated before returning the smile. If he passed Mags' inspection, then Adeline knew she could lower her guard. Sitting across from him at the table, she picked at a groove in the wood.

Ryker glanced at her. "Coffee, please."

"Me too, please," Adeline said.

Mags scurried around the kitchen, snatching up a mug and whipping out the milk and sugar. She cleared her throat.

"So, Mr. Hero Boy," she said while pouring the coffee, "before you tell us about yourself, I'd like to ask you one question."

"Let'r rip." He grinned again. Adeline's neck heated. His eyes were like bronze dunes, edged with black lashes so thick it looked like he had on eyeliner.

"What's your deepest, darkest secret?" Mags placed the mug in front of him. It was white with the words "Too fucking tired for your shit" painted on the side.

Ryker took a sip, with a contemplative look on his face. "That's a bit deep for breakfast with a stranger."

Mags shrugged. "I've been on this Earth long enough to learn there are three different answers to this question."

"And they are?"

Mags offered an inscrutable look. He exhaled and put the mug down, then settled deeper into the chair. "If you insist. But you might want to kick me out after. And you can't call the cops."

Mags cackled. Adeline stared at him, wide-eyed. What game was Mags playing? The old woman's face lit up. "I promise to never tell a soul. Adeline won't either, right?"

Adeline gave a dumbfounded shake of her head. Ryker studied her face. "Well, I'm a lumberjack. Grew up in a family that harvests trees for a nearby paper-making company. Well, my dad does. My mom is a therapist. I enjoy cutting wood, so I'm usually down in the dirt with our employees." He paused, gauging their reaction. Mags' face shone with anticipation.

He continued. "Anyway, there was this quiet guy, Joe. Kept to himself, never caused a fuss. But when he got drunk on gin, he word-vomited. Admitted to an entire bar of how he beat his wife, Becca."

Mags' face turned downright sour. "What did you do to him?"

Ryker gripped his mug tightly. He gave a thin smile. "I'm a believer in karma. I sent him on an errand one day, and while he was gone, I poured some acetone on his ax, where the blade and wood are joined. When he came back, I sent him to chop some firewood to sell. He lifted the ax and went to swing. When he brought it down again, the blade slipped off the wood and landed on his foot. Sliced straight through. He lost three toes."

Only the sound of the clock ticking and a cat purring invaded the silence. Adeline held her breath, glancing at the mercurial old woman. Mags' mouth hung open, eyes wide. She stared at Ryker. He boldly held her gaze, face blank. Finally, Mags' mouth morphed into a wolfish grin. She slapped the table and roared with a deep belly laugh. Adeline startled at the sound, then clutched her chest as she sucked in a sharp breath. Exhaling, she let out a tremulous chuckle.

Mags laughed again. "Boy, that was a good one." She shook her head. "An ax to the foot. I might have to steal that one."

They both stared at Adeline, waiting for her response. She shrugged. "I've seen worse."

Ryker's eyebrows flew up. Mags gave an impressed nod. "So, you don't care?"

Adeline took a sip of her coffee, rolling the nutty flavor on her tongue. "Why would I? Sounds like the guy deserved it. Not enough men get what they deserve."

Ryker hesitated. Mags guffawed and pushed his shoulder. "Hear that, boy? In this house, we dole out just desserts to all men. Be forewarned!"

He offered only a flat look. "What other answers do you get for that question?"

Mags sat back, looking like the cat that got the mouse. "The first is liars claiming they don't have an answer. Never trust those. They've either never lived enough or are shysty. The second answer is usually something like, 'I don't want to share.' Because they're big babies afraid of authentic connection."

Ryker smirked. "And the third?"

Mags cackled. Adeline groaned. Mags reminded her of a crotchety witch, determined to not only raise hell but also rule it at the same time. Mags pointed at his chest. "The third is actually honest. I like honest people. You've passed the test."

He crossed his arms. Adeline spun her mug, needing something to do with her fingers. Bemused, Ryker threw an ankle onto his knee.

Mags' face brightened even more. "So, did they call him 'No-Toe Joe'?"

Silence, and then a raucous laugh burst from Adeline. Once she began laughing, she couldn't stop. Ryker and Mags joined in, the laughter so loud that Aslin bolted out of the room.

Surely, Adeline thought, there was something wrong with her, laughing at a man who lost three toes. She didn't care about what Ryker had done in the past. It sounded like it had been for the right reasons; not enough people received the retribution they deserved. Adeline looked down and smiled at Aslin. She patted her lap, and the cat leaped onto it, bumping her head into Adeline's palm.

Tears streaming down her face, Adeline felt so unexpectedly happy. She couldn't tell if the tears were good or bad—there hadn't been a moment in the last four years where she had laughed like this.

Once the thought took root in her brain, though, it swept in and scrapped out the happiness, replacing it with regret.

Her laughter turned into straight-up sobbing. Succumbing, Adeline cried for the time and life stolen by her father. She should've had years filled with moments like these. She was too broken; spoiled goods. No one wants such a dirty woman.

The thought choked her, and she made a keening sound.

Mags abruptly stopped laughing and whipped her head to Adeline. Ryker turned and faced her.

"What wrong?" he asked, voice hoarse. His concern just made it worse. A man hadn't cared about her in years. Once he knew anything about her, he'd leave in disgust. Adeline crossed her arms and dropped her head to the table, crying into the worn wood.

Between sobs, she heard Mags whisper to him, "She's had quite the time recently."

Adeline's face burned. Jerking her head up, she wailed, "Aren't you supposed to care that I'm *crying?*"

Mags scoffed. She took another sip of her coffee, then placed the mug on the table. "Girl, all that's happening right now is grief. It's going to keep coming, whether you want it to or not. I can't do anything about it. He can't do anything about it."

She pointed to Ryker, then Adeline. "*You* can't do anything about it. The best way to heal from grief is to march right through it with a machete. Clear a path. You can't get rid of it all, but you can learn to live with it. That's all we can ask of ourselves. If I comforted you every time you entered one of these cycles, how would you learn to move through them? You know I'm here, and I'm not going anywhere. But don't you ask me to hold your hand each time. Only you can heal yourself. I'm just here to help steer."

Adeline glared at Mags. For a split second, she hated the woman. *Hated her.* Then it disappeared, replaced with shame. Adeline wiped her cheeks dry and looked away. Mags was right, and they both knew it: only she could overcome her trauma. If she wanted softness, she'd have to go to Kennedi.

Mags gave a self-satisfied nod and turned her head to Ryker. Sizing him up, she said, "Do you think you can help us with the phone call Adeline just received?"

Ryker settled back and propped his knee onto his other leg. "I'm interested. Do share."

Adeline weighed her options. She wasn't prone to trusting strangers, but if Mags approved of him, that was a solid start. If he were somehow tied to Lucas, none of it would be new information. Taking a deep breath, she began the story of her fucked-up life.

Two hours later, Ryker was caught up on everything. Through it all, he'd stayed quiet and hadn't shown too much emotion. It was impossible to gauge his reaction.

At one point, Mags walked to the alcohol cabinet and grabbed a bottle of liquor the shade of Ryker's eyes. Not bothering with a glass, Mags took a deep swig, her throat bobbing.

She passed it to Ryker, who did the same, and then he passed it to Adeline. It scorched a runway for her words to more easily fill the silence. Once she started, she found it impossible to stop. People love to feel heard, and she was no exception.

It was a wonderful feeling.

Ryker sat back then. "So, your psychotic father kept you locked up, used you, and let you escape for a fun game? Am I understanding that right?"

Adeline sighed heavily and took another large gulp of the liquor. Her vision swam. "Yeah. Exactly. It's as fucked up as it sounds."

"We were talking about possibly killing him," Mags chirped, reaching for the bottle again. A cat jumped on the table, and Mags scratched its ear thoughtfully. "We could use a strong man to help us out."

"Mags!" Adeline blanched. "You can't just—"

"I'm listening."

Ryker's words froze her mid-admonishment. "Really?"

He shrugged and rubbed the back of his neck. "I mean, sure. Like, I said, I'm into karma. If it doesn't sound like a good plan, I'll be on my merry way and I won't tell anyone."

And just like that, an idea began to form in Adeline's head.

CHAPTER FIFTEEN

The smell of horseshit was an unexpectedly nostalgic perfume. Adeline took a big whiff of the fresh air as she crept along the dirt driveway. Gravel crunched under her tires and spat up into the air.

The afternoon was bright, the sky full of cotton candy clouds. Adeline had spent the morning painting before sliding on a pair of jeans and brand-new boots, and headed out to ride with Kennedi.

The smell yanked up a memory of her mom from the days when they rode together at a nearby barn. Before her mom died, Adeline had ridden in cross-country competitions. Sometimes, Kennedi had joined them. So, when Kennedi invited her to come ride, Adeline had to stop herself from squealing with elation.

A quick fifteen-minute drive in Mags's truck, Adeline's excitement mounted with each passing mile. She passed through the large iron gate and wiggled her hips impatiently. The winding driveway led to a thirty-acre ranch, shouldered by tall, lush oak trees that bowed toward the road.

Beyond the oaks, white wooden fences swept into the distance, the vibrant green grass speckled with grazing horses. She slung her arm out the window and felt the light breeze dance through her fingers. The scent of sweetgrass brought a smile to her face.

The long driveway ended in front of a barn, white with red trim. Horses popped their heads out of windows, and a ranch hand wheeled out a wheelbarrow full of dirty shavings.

Kennedi waved from crossties installed in the side of the barn, tacking up an almost-white palomino mare. Adeline turned off the engine.

"Glad you found it!" Kennedi turned back to the horse, cinching its girth to a pale brown western saddle. Next to the palomino was a blood bay chewing on a crosstie. Adeline laughed.

"Wasn't too hard. Hope I'm wearing the right stuff."

Kennedi inspected the jeans and boots with a nod of approval. It matched her own outfit, though she also wore half-chaps. Adeline rolled up the sleeves of her dark blue long-sleeve shirt, enjoying the feel of the sunshine on her still-pale skin. These last few weeks, she'd experienced more sunshine than she had in a long time, but she still remained closer to the color of the pale palomino.

Kennedi reached for a bridle and unhooked the halter. The mare politely opened her mouth. Kennedi patted the horse's neck. "This is Sandy. She'll be your ride. I'm over on Rebellion, although we call her Rebby, so as to not encourage more mare bullshit."

The blood bay shook her head impatiently. With a final look over the saddle, Kennedi handed Adeline the reins. "Do you remember how to ride?"

Adeline smiled uncertainly. "Like riding a bike, right?"

Kennedi chuckled and walked over to Rebby. She grabbed the nearby bridle. As Rebby avoided the bit, Kennedi said, "Sandy is a push-button, so you'll be fine." She glared at Rebby. "Unlike this bitch. Reb, quit being a twat and accept your fate."

While Kennedi and Rebby argued, Adeline walked Sandy over to a mounting block. It was all-too-familiar, swinging a leg over the pommel and settling into the soft leather. A memory brushed against her consciousness. The last time she'd ridden with her mom was only a couple of weeks before she died. They'd galloped in a field, laughing the whole time while their mounts raced like the wind. She hadn't thought of that moment in years. It was a welcome memory.

Sandy waited patiently while Adeline reacquainted herself with the equipment and tall view above the ground. Her body, now strong and filled out thanks to daily workouts, flexed as Sandy shifted. It had been too long since Adeline had felt the familiar sensation of invincibility horses provided.

Kennedi finally won the battle and mounted Rebby, fussing as the mare walked forward while Kennedi hoisted up over the pommel.

"Rebby!" She hissed at the horse but grinned. Kennedi caught Adeline's wary expression and chuckled. "I like them feisty. She isn't the right fit for the horse therapy program, obvs, but I love her anyway. I really want to buy her, actually. No one else here likes her."

Kennedi clucked the mare forward, waving Adeline to follow. "Let's go on an adventure, shall we?"

Adeline nudged a boot into Sandy's side, and the mare eased into a meandering trot, one ear flicking backward every few seconds. The rhythmic push and pull of the horse's movements relaxed Adeline immediately.

She followed Kennedi down a side path flanked by more white fencing. All around them, the landscape stretched into the horizon with random groups of trees breaking up the meadows. In an arena nearby, some students plopped on the backs of trotting horses, led by individual handlers.

"What are they doing?" Adeline watched as the handlers ran alongside the slow-trotting horses, offering encouraging words to the riders.

Kennedi glanced over her shoulder. "This place is an equine rescue and therapy spot. My friend Becca owns it. She goes to slaughterhouse auctions, bids on the ones she thinks will be a good fit, and brings them here. If the horse is a good bet, both the horse and the rider grow together."

Adeline understood the benefit of horses through trauma. Sandy's energy was a balm to Adeline's anxiety. She leaned down and scratched the horse's withers. "Do you come here often?"

Rebby jerked against the reins, trying to swipe a mouthful of tall grass. Kennedi kicked her forward, and Rebby pinned her ears, voicing her displeasure. "Yeah. Once a week, or at least I try to. It's a great break from the monotony of the bookstore." She pauses. "I love helping both people and horses overcome the hard parts of life."

Adeline frowned and urged Sandy to speed up so they could walk side by side. She turned to look at Kennedi. "I had no idea. How long have you been doing this?"

Kennedi held a firm grip on the reins as Rebby jerked her head down. "A few years. Almost right after we moved. There's isn't a ton to do around here, and I hoped being near horses would help me remember you."

Adeline bit the inside of her cheek. "You came here to remember me?"

Kennedi chuckled. "Well, not entirely. I love it here. It's rewarding to help people regain their confidence. I've seen all sorts of things. One woman wept on horseback while she cantered for the first time. Later, she said she was working through the memory of her husband beating her. She went off to buy that same horse and entered the show ring with it."

"Wow." Adeline was impressed. Not just at the ability of horses to heal but to know that maybe, just maybe, she could do the same. "Do you want to work here full time?"

Kennedi shook her head, holding the reins with one hand and resting her free hand on a thigh. "Nah. I like the bookstore. It's like the best of both worlds. A woman doesn't need much more than books and horses."

Adeline chuckled. "Truer words have never been spoken. Also carbs."

Kennedi motioned to her body. "It's quite clear I've enjoyed those, too."

Adeline laughed freely and leaned over close enough to pat Kennedi's thick thigh. Sandy shifted so she wouldn't fall. "Your muffins are my favorite."

Kennedi giggled. "You let me know the next time you want to sample my baked goods."

"All day," Adeline teased.

Kennedi led them down a small dirt incline into the woods, the path still wide enough for them to stay side by side. Kennedi tucked a loose curl behind an ear. "Can I tell you something?"

Adeline nodded. "Sure."

Kennedi looked into the distance, contemplating her words. "I feel like an asshole when I'm around you sometimes."

Adeline frowned. "How?"

Kennedi weaved through some trees. "Because my life has been pretty easy. My mom ran out on us, but I was too young to have it really affect me. My dad is pretty great, if not a little protective. I've been able to make a good life here, and I'd like to think I'm pretty happy-go-lucky. Maybe too much. Compared to what you've been through—" her voice hitched; she looked at Adeline with mournful eyes "—I feel like an asshole sometimes. Like I need to downplay the greatness of my life."

Adeline jerked her head. "Have I made you feel that way?" The idea that she'd somehow made Kennedi feel like she needed to shrink herself made Adeline sick to her stomach.

"No!" Kennedi shook her head vehemently. "Not at all. This is absolutely on me. I'm just afraid of hurting you. I just don't talk about myself much because I want to make sure you have the space you need."

"Please don't do that anymore," Adeline said quietly. "I can't stand the thought of you holding back for my own comfort. I don't even know if it would make me uncomfortable, so don't assume it would. I don't hate other people for having better lives than mine."

Kennedi gave her a curious look. "You aren't at least jealous?"

"I get envious," Adeline confessed. "But not jealous. Of course, I wish my life had been different, but not at the expense of others."

The conversation paused as they weaved in and out of the trees. The conversation troubled Adeline. She didn't want anyone treating or viewing her differently because of what she'd been through. She'd never be close to being normal otherwise.

They paused by a stream to let the horses have a drink. Kennedi reached into a leather satchel and pulled out a large chocolate chip cookie. She split it in half and handed Adeline a portion. Adeline bit into it and moaned.

"Damn, that's good."

Kennedi grinned, a drop of chocolate smeared on her lower lip. "Baked them myself. I'm a stress baker." She pulled out a canteen and offered it to Adeline. "Water?"

Adeline took it gratefully. The water was crisp on her tongue. It wasn't a cold glass of milk, but it'd do. "Wait, you're stressed?"

Kennedi threw her head back and laughed. Adeline loved how the sunlight curved along her cheekbones and lit up the splash of freckles across her nose. "I guess it's more of a hormonal thing. I start my period in a couple of days."

Adeline nodded, popping the last bit of cookie into her mouth. "I crave blueberry pie when I'm PMS-ing."

"Duly noted."

The horses began to graze. Kennedi urged Rebby forward through the stream. Sandy followed, pausing to paw at the water, splashing all of them.

"Pull her head up!" Kennedi urged, laughing. "She'll lay down if you don't."

Giggling, Adeline pulled the reins up, and Sandy stopped her splashing. "Yeah, no thanks. Although a swim wouldn't be too bad in this heat."

Kennedi lifted her shirt and wiped her brow. "No kidding. It's a bit too hot for my comfort."

They reached the other side of the stream, but Adeline pulled Sandy up short. "Then why don't we at least put our feet in?"

Kennedi paused, then gave a wide grin. "Doesn't sound half bad." She swung off Rebby and jabbed a finger at the mare. "Don't be a dick. Go eat some grass and chill."

Rebby bobbed her head, chewing on her bit. Adeline landed on the ground with a heavy thud. She groaned. "Oh my gods, everything hurts." Her thighs began to shake. Suddenly, the idea of getting back up onto the saddle sounded impossible.

Kennedi chuckled as she pulled off a shoe. Both Rebby and Sandy meandered to a nearby plot of grass. "Sounds like you need to come riding more often."

"That would be wonderful," Adeline said. They were both quickly barefoot and sitting by the stream, sliding their toes into the chilly water. Adeline jerked her feet back, hissing at the cold.

"Fresh mountain water too much for you?" Kennedi teased. She leaned forward, legs raised, and wrapped her arms around her knees.

Adeline stretched her legs out, letting her heels rest on the brown gravel while a trickle of water lapped at her toes. "I'm not gonna lie, being outside in fresh air with no one looming over my shoulder is almost too much for me."

Kennedi rested her chin on her knees, staring at the water. "I'm glad you're here then." She paused. "Are you still afraid?"

Adeline leaned back. "Absolutely. I try not to think about it. I figure either he'll capture me… Or he won't. I can only control how I react. I'm choosing to not let the terror affect how I live my life.

Hiding up in my bedroom would be an absolute waste of this opportunity."

Kennedi turned and looked at her, resting her cheek on her arms. In the sunlight, her hair was on fire. Adeline ached to kiss her. Impulsively, she did just that. She leaned over, cradled Kennedi's head in one hand, and brought their lips together gently. It was quick but tender.

Breaking apart, Kennedi bit her lip. "I was lonely before you showed up."

Adeline smiled softly. "Are you still?"

Kennedi's eyes danced. "Nope." She popped the last part of the word. "Believe it or not, I haven't always been this relaxed or happy. Life has been good, but it certainly hasn't been perfect. When I moved here with my dad, I fell into a deep depression. It wasn't what I thought it would be—I was crazy to think small-town living would be for me. And then your letters stopped, and I thought you were gone, too. It was hard to dig out of that."

Adeline's eyes burned. "How did you get out of it?"

Kennedi jerked her chin to the feasting horses. "I discovered this place. It gives me an escape, and helping with the kids sometimes helps stave off the empty feeling inside, of being purposeless. I work at the bookstore more than my dad and try to create monthly themes. I invite kids from school to come and get free books. But it's never been quite enough."

She smiled softly. "And then you reappeared. It's been amazing, being around you again. Like that piece of the puzzle I didn't realize was missing. Even if we stay just friends, I am so happy you're here."

Adeline's cheeks warmed. The admission, all of it, made her heart sing. Knowing how much Kennedi was part of the community was a revelation. "Do you like kids?"

Kennedi stretched her legs out, fully immersing her calves in the water. "Yeah. I also want some one day. You?"

Adeline's body tensed. "I don't know. I haven't been around any since we were kids."

Kennedi's happiness dimmed a little. "But do you want any?"

What a difficult question; one Adeline had never thought about or had to answer. Did she want to be a parent? Her mom had been too good for this world, always attentive and present. Her father, though…

Adeline blew out a heavy breath and whispered, "I don't know. I… I don't want to become him, you know? What if he wasn't always like that? What if he has a mental illness or something?"

Kennedi's head jerked up. "You could *never* become him. Lucas is fucking evil incarnate. Something like him is born, not made."

Adeline's thoughts were still plagued with doubt. She didn't respond. Instead, she stood and reached for her shoes. "Want to go canter?"

Kennedi stood, wiping her hands on her jeans. "Absolutely."

Adeline's thighs immediately barked with protest, but she somehow found herself back in the saddle. Turning the horses back down the path, Kennedi kicked Rebby into a canter, their earlier conversation shelved. Adeline let the rhythm of Sandy's strides loosen her hips and heart. Worries were for later. Life could be on pause for a moment.

Her demons could wait just a damn minute.

CHAPTER SIXTEEN

Two days later, Adeline sat in a rocking chair on the royal purple front porch, watching as Mags dug her wrinkled hands into the soil. She fanned herself with a fashion magazine and reached for her lemonade on the side table. Her bare legs were propped up on a stool, feet crossed. Even dressed in only a pair of tiny shorts and a tank top, the late-afternoon heat bled sweat from her skin.

"Why is it so damn hot?" she complained.

Mags snorted, reaching for a flower bulb. She had on a whale-sized sun hat, her silver mass of curls held back by a simple hair tie. She wore black cargo shorts and a black sleeveless shirt. In any other setting, she'd look like an old assassin, ready to melt into the shadows.

She looked up, patting the bulb into the earth. "I dare you to say that again."

Adeline increased the speed of her fan. "What? Ask why it's so friggin' hot in this godsforsaken—"

A small flower bulb bounced off her cheek suddenly, landing in her lap. She stared at it, dumbfounded. She snapped her head up, feet slamming on the porch.

"Listen here, ya old biddy." She picked up the bulb and threw it back. "Don't start a war you can't finish. Don't forget, it's my turn to cook dinner tonight."

The bulb landed inside the rim of Mags' hat. She reached for it, smirking. "I warned you."

"What did I miss?"

Kennedi stood outside the gate, her creamy skin flushed from sunshine. Twin braids fell down both sides of her freckled face, and she wore dark overalls with a red bandeau top underneath. Adeline popped up and hopped down from the porch. Mags groaned as she stood up, slapping her hands clean.

"You're here!" Adeline said.

Kennedi laughed and opened the gate. Adeline flung her arms around Kennedi's shoulders and squeezed. Kennedi returned the hug with equal excitement. They pulled away from each other but kept their hands on each other's arms.

Adeline's chest warmed. Having people who finally cared about her was incredible. Adeline brushed Kennedi's cheek with a kiss. "I'm okay. Still a little sore but otherwise good. You?"

Kennedi bit her lip ring. "Pretty good. It's hot as hell though."

Mags raised an eyebrow and placed her hands on her hefty hips. "Are you two going to continue making kissy faces or will you help me plant this shit?"

By the time the soil was stuffed with bulbs and pouring a healthy serving of water on top, Mags looked like she was about to collapse from the heat. Kennedi didn't look any better as she wiped a dirt-caked hand across her sweaty brow. She stood, kneading her fists into her lower back with a groan. Adeline smiled, dropping the gardening tools into a bucket.

"Doesn't it feel good to have put in a hard day's work?" Adeline teased, offering a playful grin. Kennedi wrinkled her nose.

"You know, I came here to ask you to grab a drink with me." She sighed, smearing more dirt down her cheek. "I guess that plan is shot to hell."

Adeline was about to tell Kennedi they could still go for a drink when a truck pulled up to the property. Adeline's eyes widened as Ryker stepped out, sliding off a pair of silver aviator sunglasses. He wore a warm purple V-neck, khaki beach shorts, and dark leather sandals. His short beard was a little longer than the other day, but still well groomed.

Kennedi tossed Adeline a glance. "Um, who the *hell is that?*"

"Yoo-hoo! Mr. Hero Boy!" Mags flapped her hand in his direction, her other arm supporting a wicker basket filled with fresh vegetables. Adeline rolled her eyes. Mags had looked about to die only three minutes prior, and now suddenly she was a spry chicken.

"You rang," he said dryly, stopping in front of Mags.

"Well, hey there, stranger," she said with a smile. He returned the grin and looked down, appraising the harvest. Adeline could've sworn Mags leaned in to smell him.

He swept the sunglasses into his hair. "You're all hot and dirty, Mags. Just like I like 'em."

A devious smile pulled at the edges of Mags' lips. She seemed to Adeline like a wolf walking up to a fresh kill—eager and hungry. Kennedi and Adeline exchanged a look.

Kennedi leaned toward Adeline and whispered, "Who's that?"

Adeline loudly whispered back, "That's Mr. Hero Boy. He's the one who helped scare off Alexander the other day."

Kennedi's tongue spun her lip ring. "You didn't say he was smokin'."

Ryker cleared his throat as Mags' smile turned feral. Finally, the wolf snapped at its prey.

"My dear child," she said, stepping closer, "you couldn't handle my hot and dirty." She snapped her teeth as if biting the air. Ryker flinched. "I know things we could do with these veggies," she said while caressing a large cucumber with one finger. "Especially this one. Excellent bumpage."

Kennedi choked on a laugh. Adeline gaped. "Mags!" She let go of Kennedi's hand and stomped over to the old woman, who was cackling like a *very* pleased witch.

Adeline snatched the basket off her arm. "Your phallic vegetable privileges are revoked."

Meanwhile, Ryker looked like he'd just been told pigs could fly. All three women paused and waited for him to do something— anything. It started in his rib cage, shaking his chest and traveling up his throat before exploding into the loudest guffaw Adeline had ever heard. His entire face scrunched up as he heaved for air.

Mags grimaced. She stage-whispered, "Do you think he's broken?"

Ryker clasped his knees as he sucked in deep gulps of air. He held up a hand. "Sorry—" More laughter. "—Sorry, I just. *What?*" He straightened and wiped away tears. "Mags, what the hell have you done with— No, don't tell me. I'm not drunk enough for that information."

Kennedi seized the moment and lunged forward, holding out a hand. "Hey, I'm Kennedi. Her best friend." She flashed a grin at Adeline. He shook her hand, politely ignoring her beet-red cheeks, which had nothing to do with the heat.

He gently pulled his hand back, giving a wry grin. "I need that back."

Kennedi faced Adeline again. "Excuse me, but you knew about him"—she threw a thumb over her shoulder—"for *two* days and you didn't tell me about this?" She motioned up and down his frame.

"Um," Ryker looked between the three of them. "Can we go inside or something? It's scorching."

Mags looped her arm through his, brushing past Kennedi and Adeline.

Kennedi fanned her face. "What the hell just happened? And is it just me or is that dude *hot?*"

Adeline grabbed an eggplant that had fallen onto the pathway. Mags and Ryker were already on their way inside. "Yes," she agreed.

"He's super-hot. But I'm not sure if I can be objective. He did save my life, after all."

Kennedi tapped a finger to her chin. "Would it bother you if I flirted with him a little?"

Adeline chortled as they meandered to the front door. "I'm not sure. You're welcome to ask him yourself."

They walked in on a bizarre scene: Mags lifting her cats, holding them up like prizes as she informed Ryker about each one. In her hands was a blue short-haired cat, its legs swinging. A deep feline scowl, paired with a deep, rumbling snarl, made Mags *tsk*.

"Bitzy, knock it off. You're being rude." Mags put the cat back down, and it bounded away. "She once broke a priceless vase. We've had a tense relationship since then."

Ryker's pleading eyes darted to Adeline, then Kennedi. "Help me," he mouthed. Smiling, Adeline shoved the wicker basket into Mags' arms before she could find another helpless cat. "It's *your* turn for dinner."

Mags wrinkled her nose. "Now *you're* being rude." She sighed loudly and marched down the hallway, muttering about purposefully overcooked eggplant.

Ryker sighed with relief. "Thanks for the save."

And then there was silence. The three of them stared at each other, hoping someone would break the awkward moment. It was Adeline who spoke first. "Sooooo, why are you here?"

They hadn't seen each other since the other night, but his reaction to her story still warmed her insides. There hadn't been an ounce of judgment, only empathy. They didn't exchange numbers before he left, which was probably why he'd randomly shown up.

He shoved a hand in a pocket. "I just thought I might show you something before the sun sets." He glanced at Kennedi. "You can come, too, if you'd like, assuming Addie even wants to go."

They both looked at Adeline. "What?" she said. "You haven't even said what this thing is you want to show us."

"A really special place."

Adeline looked at Kennedi, who shrugged.

"I love a good surprise."

Adeline stepped aside then, sweeping her arm toward the door. "Well then, lead the way, Mr. Hero Boy."

As they followed, Kennedi whispered, "Whatever happens, I'm here to support you. The moment you're uncomfortable, just say the word and I'll get us out of there. Okay?"

Adeline smiled. "He seems like a good guy—Mags is practically feral for him and she hates everybody. But I promise to say something."

The three of them got into his truck and crammed onto his bench seat with Kennedi, the smallest of them, nestled in the middle.

Kennedi's head swiveled. "It's pretty clean in here. Cleaner than any guy's car I've ever seen."

Ryker started the truck and buckled his seat belt. "I'm dirty for most of my life, so I like things to be clean where possible."

Kennedi shimmied closer to him. "Oh, do tell. What keeps you dirty?"

They pulled away from the curb, heading toward town.

He cleared his throat. "Uh, I'm a lumberjack."

Kennedi straightened. "I'm sorry, you're a *what*?"

"A man that chop-chops with pointy things all day?"

Kennedi turned to Adeline. "Is it too early to ask this man to cleave me in half?"

Ryker choked, hands gripping the steering wheel tightly.

Adeline rolled her eyes. "That's a weird visualization. You know he can hear you, right?"

Kennedi smiled wickedly. "I hope so."

They settled into a comfortable silence as Ryker weaved through the streets. Relaxing back into the seat, Adeline watched the world go by as the truck passed down the different streets. The sun was setting, golden clouds igniting a new fire in her heart.

CHAPTER SEVENTEEN

Kennedi pretended to overheat, fanning her face as she and Adeline took in their surroundings. All around were homes, each custom made to its owner's tastes. Some were impressive two-story structures, while others were short, ranch-style homes.

Confused, they followed his lead and got out of the truck. The neighborhood was peaceful, with the sound of a lawnmower not too far in the distance. Adeline smelled honeysuckle from a massive bush in someone's yard. Ryker motioned for them to follow him across the street.

"Are we allowed to be here?" Kennedi whispered, nervously looking into windows as they passed. With the sun's reflection obstructing their view, anyone could watch them and they would be none the wiser.

"I know the guy. He lets me come by whenever I want. He's out of town right now." Ryker reached for a rusted handle barely attached to a worn wooden gate. It was connected to a yellow house on the left. It creaked open.

"Ryker," Adeline hissed. "What are we doing?"

"You'll see."

Adeline didn't move, looking around for danger. Kennedi paused, giving an uncertain look. She reached for Adeline's hand. "It's okay. We're two bad bitches who know how to rip out his gonads if he acts stupid."

Adeline searched her instincts and felt nothing alarming. She knew shitty men, and Ryker didn't give her the 'I'm going to torture you' vibes. She squeezed Kennedi's hand. "Okay, let's do it."

They followed him into a massive backyard, un-mowed grass glowing in the light of the setting sun. Something in the grass scurried away. To their right, a few hundred feet away, was an enormous weeping willow rustling in the gentle breeze.

Streams of sunshine played through the branches, causing beams of light to dance in the air. The true magic, however, was in front of them.

The far end of the yard dropped gently to the edge of a lake that stretched for at least a mile before abruptly turning into wide swaths of lush pine trees. The orange tint of sunshine sparkled against lolling waves, melding into the sea of grass in front of them. It was an impressive optical illusion that made Adeline's heart stop.

Ryker watched their faces, not missing a single detail. His black hair was more of a deep bronze in the golden light. The warm sunshine made his eyes glow like honey. Seeing them speechless, he winked at them.

"This is stunning." Adeline devoured the beautiful scene; she'd never seen anything like it. It was like heaven had carved a slice out of her world.

Kennedi leaned over and brushed her palms over the grass. She looked up at Adeline, face full of child-like wonder. Adeline turned her attention to the lake. Ryker fingers wiggled in invitation.

Together they waded through the tall grass, following the crushed trail as he led them to the edge of the lake. Kennedi gave Adeline's hand a double squeeze. Adeline looked up to see Kennedi jerking her head toward Ryker, giving an incredulous look.

Before Adeline could say anything, they were at the water's edge, their toes hitting fat, gray stones. Itty bitty waves lapped at the shore. Adeline sucked in a breath as Ryker leaned down to untie his boots. Kennedi immediately copied his behavior.

Adeline sputtered. "Wha-what are you doing?"

Ryker used one foot and pressed against the heel of the other. "Taking my boots off."

Adeline looked around wildly as Kennedi kicked off one shoe. "Why?"

He chucked the first boot over his shoulder and turned his focus to the other. "To put our feet in the water? It's going to feel great in this heat."

Adeline kicked off her slip-on shoes. Ryker dropped his butt onto the stones at the water's edge, close enough to wiggle his toes into the water. He drew up his legs, casually leaning on his knees.

Kennedi sat down next to him and stretched out her short legs, leaving a choice for Adeline: sit on the opposite side of either Kennedi or Ryker. She weighed the options. Remembering how Kennedi had drooled over him, she plopped down on the other side of Ryker and wiggled her eyebrows at Kennedi. They shared a grin before turning their attention to the water.

Adeline stretched out her legs. She sucked in air at the unexpected warmth of the water. "That's the perfect temperature."

"It is," Ryker agreed.

The three of them stared out into the distance. Adeline enjoyed the comfortable silence. She startled as a fish jumped and landed with a loud splash. Drawing in a deep breath, she memorized the smell of the musty water and wet earth. Ryker shifted closer.

Her skin prickled and she snuck a glance, surprised to see him watching her again. Adeline gave a sheepish grin and looked down at her toes. Her sternum strained against the well of emotion exploding in her chest. After four years of cruelty delivered at the hands of men, Ryker was both a breath of fresh air and terrifying. Was she even ready to spend time with a man alone?

"Let's play the question game," he quietly declared. Kennedi, who'd been staring off into the distance, perked up. "Actually, let's make this fair: I ask one of you a question, and that person asks the other person a question."

"Sure," Kennedi chirped.

Ryker looked at her first. After a moment, he asked, "If you could change one thing in your life, what would it be?"

Adeline sucked in a breath. She leaned forward and was shocked to see Kennedi staring at her.

"Easy," Kennedi said, never looking away. "I'd talk my dad out of moving away."

Ryker looked at Adeline. "Away from you?"

Adeline nodded, a ball of emotion lodged in her throat. As if she could sense where Adeline's brain had gone just then, Kennedi said, "There was nothing we could do. It was a horrible time to leave you, and I knew it. Your mom had just died. I knew your dad was becoming more controlling. But I should have fought for you." Her voice was fierce, eyes shimmering.

Ryker turned to look at her, frowning. She had shared some details, but not all of them. "How old were you?"

"Eighteen," Adeline answered, trying not to cry. "You couldn't have known," she whispered to Kennedi. "He asked you to join him to open the bookstore. It was a dream you both shared."

Kennedi wiped away a tear, sniffling. Ryker kept his eyes trained on Kennedi. "She's right," he said softly. "You couldn't have known. All that matters is that you keep her safe now."

Kennedi blew out a breath and gave a watery laugh. "I know. Sorry. That probably went deeper than you thought it would."

Ryker stretched out his legs. "It was kind of a deep question. But maybe the next question should be more fun."

Adeline nodded. "So, does Kennedi ask the next question?"

"Yep." He tossed a stone into the water.

Kennedi rubbed her jaw. There were still dirt smears on her freckled cheeks. "Okay, I have a question," she declared, tossing a braid over her shoulder. She narrowed her eyes at Ryker. "Are you into her?" She jerked a thumb at Adeline.

Adeline and Ryker froze. "What?" they said at the same time.

Kennedi clapped her hands and laughed. "I mean, he saved your life. Once would be understandable, but why else would you come back around, Mr. Hero Boy?"

"I…" He hesitated and looked at Adeline. "I guess after the other night, I thought we were friends?"

Adeline twisted to face them. "I didn't say we weren't. That one—" she stabbed a finger at Kennedi "—decided to ask such a weird question. I think we're friends, although we don't know each other that well."

"Well, you don't know me well," Kennedi offered.

"What do you mean?" Adeline said, surprised.

Ryker's head wagged between them—they spoke over him as if he didn't exist.

Kennedi shifted to sitting on her heels. "I mean, we're into each other. We love each other, but we're still catching up. There's still so much to learn about each other, and to continue learning about each other. How is that any different? People can become friends in a second. Friendship isn't measured by sharing every single truth. It's made of moments strung together."

Ryker and Adeline stared.

"Where the hell did all of that wisdom come from? Are you secretly eighty years old?" Adeline joked.

Ryker said. "I thought being raised by a therapist made me all wise and shit, but I think you just outpaced me."

Kennedi leaned over and picked up a stone. She chucked it into the water. "Maybe a meme? A strike of temporary genius?"

"She has a point," Adeline said, drawing Ryker's gaze. Her skin prickled as she felt those deep citrine eyes burning down her spine. Only this moment existed; everything else faded away. She was used to men leering, but this was different—Ryker was observant.

She hated it—and absolutely loved it.

Adeline gulped. Feeling flayed open, she reached for another stone. As she pulled back her arm, ready to fling it away, she saw Kennedi hold up a finger to Ryker.

"You didn't answer the question, sir."

Ryker played coy. "What question?"

"Are you into Addie?"

Adeline threw the stone, pretending to not be curious about the answer. The sun was sinking down; twilight was settling in. Deep purples flayed the sky, casting the clouds into shadow.

Ryker dragged his tongue across his teeth, then admitted, "Truthfully? Yes. Even in the short time I've known you—" he looked at Adeline "—you've shown a strength I've never seen before. You're beautiful, too. I'd be crazy not to be into you. But I also don't want to overstep; I know you've been through a lot. I'd be cool with being friends, but if you ever want more, I'm game."

"Okaaaay," Kennedi said. "Didn't expect *that*."

"Does it make you jealous?" Adeline's heart skipped, not sure what answer she hoped for.

Kennedi cocked her head like a curious puppy. "Is that your question?"

"Yes." Adeline responded immediately, holding her breath.

Kennedi's mouth twisted to the side. She brought a hand to her chest in mock surprise. "*Moi?* No, ma'am. I'm not afraid of a little competition. In fact—" she waggled her eyebrows "—I wouldn't mind joining in."

Adeline exhaled. The conversation had taken an unexpected turn. She looked at Ryker, an amused look in his eyes.

He tilted his head and raised his eyebrows. "You aren't going to hear any complaints from me."

"We aren't hearing any encouragement either," Kennedi pointed out.

"I'm not the one setting the pace," he reminded her.

Adeline looked to the ground and wrapped her arms around her knees. It was hard to say how she felt about actually dating a man. She'd spent the majority of the summer working through her pain. Her journey was far from over, but she couldn't remain frozen in time.

She had to admit she'd noticed how attractive Ryker was, but didn't even get the vibe he felt the same way. The fact that he was attractive to her, but held back to not scare her, was thrilling in an unexpected way.

But was it too soon? She had always found men attractive; that had never been the issue. The issue is that her feelings had never mattered. Now they did. Maybe, just maybe, Adeline could find progress here.

She looked up. "Can we take it slow? I know I might struggle, but I'm tired of living in a cage of fear."

Ryker gave a slow nod. "You get to set the pace, always. If you want me to go away, just say the word. I won't even touch you without your enthusiastic consent."

Consent. Adeline almost laughed. That word hadn't existed in her vocabulary in years. That single word thawed her unlying fear. In its place bloomed an unfamiliar sensation that felt like trust. "Thank you. That means a lot to me."

They sat quietly, letting the conversation drift off. Finally, he stood up. "I'm sweaty. The lake looks like a great way to cool off. If either of you wants to join me…"

Adeline and Kennedi stared as he took off his shirt. Even in the dim light, Adeline could see the muscular indentations of his abs; cutting wood did a body good, apparently.

"Holy Ax Man, what in the foresting-destroying world is happening and how do I make it continue?" Kennedi breathed. Adeline could barely speak to agree. That stomach was a far cry from the middle-aged paunches of her father's associates.

Ryker peered down at them as he unbuckled his belt. Kennedi was up in a flash, shirt flying into the grass. Adeline remained locked in place. Kennedi laughed and motioned to Adeline. "When was the last time you skinny-dipped?"

"N-n-never," she stuttered. "I would have never been allowed."

"Well, I'm not getting naked. Just getting down to my boxers." Ryker continued to remove his belt. It was a methodical removal, avoiding any leather-snapping sounds. Adeline knew he was doing so to avoid any trigger sounds. His awareness was dizzying.

"Well, no pressure," he added. "Looks like Firebomb and I are going in, but you can just hang here." He gave her a solemn look. "Seriously. No pressure."

Adeline's armpits itched, a spike of adrenaline. What was this moment if not what she'd always hoped for? A way to live—to truly *live*.

With a voice the size of speck of dust, she whispered, "What if I trigger?"

Kennedi leaned down and put a hand on Adeline's shoulder. "Then we'll help you throw a famous Mags Throat Punch at it."

It was as good an answer as any. "Fuck it," Adeline muttered, popping up. She shoved back nerves and had her shirt off in a blink. They stood facing each other, no shirts to be seen. Adeline resisted the urge to cover her breasts, even though they were tucked into a sports bra. A slight breeze licked at her stomach. The sun had escaped past the horizon.

"Would it be okay if I kept my bra and panties on?" she asked. Kennedi and Ryker nodded. She heaved out a breath and unbuttoned her pants. "Okay. Let's do this."

"Can I be naked?" Kennedi asked.

Adeline slid her pants past her knees and kicked them off. "Sure. I don't care."

The smooth edges of the stones dug into the pads of her feet, an unwanted deep massage. She averted her eyes as Ryker stepped out of his shorts and waded straight into the water.

Out of the corner of her eye, she saw a flash of black briefs. Adeline stepped toward the water, catching a glimpse of two dimples above Ryker's ass before it dipped under the surface. *Jesus.*

Undressing faster than a speeding bullet, Kennedi held out a hand. The full moon stretched above the trees on the opposite side of the lake, its light accentuating Kennedi's soft curves. Adeline felt a deep urge to claim every inch of them. She grabbed Kennedi's hand and let her take the lead.

The warm water greeted Adeline's skin like a lover's caress. It slipped along her bare calves and thighs. The stones gave way to soft sand. She dug her toes into it, feeling a weed rub between them. Kennedi let go of her hand and waded over to Ryker, who was watching them. Adeline followed, bouncing over to them on the balls of her feet, the water kissing the bottom of her sports bra.

Once again, the three of them faced each other. And once again, Kennedi broke the silence. "So, what now?"

Ryker smiled. "I don't know. I hadn't planned past this point. I really was just super sweaty."

Kennedi smirked. "I mean, I've always wanted to go skinning-dipping *and* make out with someone…"

"I volunteer as tribute!" Adeline offered, bobbing over to her. A grin split Kennedi's face, and she nodded enthusiastically.

"I'm definitely into that idea." She was instantly in front of Adeline, like a fish in water. Adeline held Ryker's gaze as Kennedi wrapped her naked body around Adeline's waist. The moon caught the light of water streaming down his muscular torso as he dipped down and stood back up. His loose curls flattened against his skull. Before Adeline could think of anything else, Kennedi's mouth was on hers.

It was like falling off the edge of a cliff. The air whooshed out of Adeline's lungs as Kennedi's breasts pressed against hers. Instinctively, her hands reached around to cup Kennedi's ass, bringing them closer together. A zing of desire crackled up and down her spine, igniting every nerve ending.

Kennedi's nails trailed up her neck as their tongues explored each other. It was the sweetest pain, wanting to take Kennedi right then and there. Water rippled—Ryker drifted closer but kept a respectful distance.

Adeline's eyes popped open as she ran a thumb along Kennedi's jaw. Kennedi pulled back, still latched onto Adeline like a monkey. Kennedi's eyes landed on Ryker. The murky water hovered right above his belly button, blocking any view. Still clutching Adeline's neck with one hand, Kennedi reached for Ryker, waving her fingers in invitation. He hesitated, glancing at Adeline, asking for permission.

Adeline's heart thrummed at an unfamiliar cadence. Even the silent request for consent was jarring, at odds with every experience she'd ever had with men. A sliver of her mind shivered with apprehension, but feeling Kennedi in her arms kept the demons away.

Adeline nodded. Ryker's shoulders relaxed, and he moved closer.

"Come here," Kennedi said, voice husky. Ryker paused, knowing he'd be invading Adeline's space. Adeline nodded again, heart crashing against her rib cage. She dug her fingers into Kennedi's ass cheeks, causing Kennedi to wriggle against her.

Adeline jolted—she realized Kennedi was rubbing her pussy against Adeline's belly button. *Jesus fucking Christ.* It must be a fever dream, because there was no way this was Adeline's life. Three months ago, no one would have been able to convince her that something like this could happen.

As Ryker leaned down to kiss Kennedi, Adeline couldn't help but grin widely. Even if it was a dream, she'd revel in every second of it and carry it with her for the rest of her life.

Ryker put a hand to Kennedi's face, tilting her head back as his mouth claimed hers. Kennedi's back arched, her breasts rising out of the water, an offering to Adeline. They were heavy; her dusky nipples perked, ready to be devoured.

Tiny pearls of water reflected the moonlight on her sternum. Adeline took her tongue and dragged it from the bottom of her sternum to the top, lapping up the water. Her mouth trailed to one of Kennedi's breasts.

Kennedi groaned, and her hips undulated, sliding against Adeline's stomach. Swept up in the sexual energy, Adeline switched to the other breast and started greedily licking and sucking the soft flesh.

Kennedi broke Ryker's kiss, tossing her head back as Adeline slid a hand up her spine, the other clutching her ass for dear life. Adeline came up for air and looked at Ryker. His eyes were heavy with desire.

Contracting her soft, ample belly, Kennedi was once more flush against Adeline. She dived in for another kiss. Her scent mixed with Ryker's, a heady scent that made Adeline moan deep in her throat. The fire sparking life inside of her threatened to turn into an inferno if they continued.

Kennedi broke away from the kiss. She stared at Adeline. "Do you want to kiss him?"

The hope in her tone was impossible to ignore, but Adeline knew she wasn't being pressured. Kennedi wanted her to feel included, if she was comfortable. It was because of this that she felt brave enough to say, "Yes."

Kennedi's legs still wrapped around her, Adeline tilted her head up, eyes wide as Ryker moved closer. His warm skin brushed against hers. She sucked in a breath as he leaned down, lungs freezing as his mouth hovered right above hers. Even in the dark, his eyes were as bright as embers.

"You know you don't have to do this, right?"

"Yes," Adeline breathed. She brought her lips to his. They were soft and warm. Kennedi shifted to one side, giving him more room to invade their cocoon. With both hands he cradled Adeline's face, tongue against Adeline's lips, encouraging her to yield.

They fell apart, and she gave his tongue room to dance with hers. At the same time, Kennedi peppered kisses along her neck, sucking gently here and there. Ryker made a tiny sound of pleasure and then deepened the kiss. His beard rubbed against her mouth. Kennedi's mouth lingered on her throat and nibbled.

An alarm bell skittered across her brain, jabbing in there like a knife. The sensations were overwhelming suddenly; they pressed against Adeline, tightening like a vise. Her brain screamed *danger!* and she succumbed to the instant terror.

It was too much. Memories slammed into her like bricks, one after another.

Greedy mouths. Grabbing hands. Teeth drawing blood. Pain. So much *pain.*

Letting out a cry of fear, Adeline jerked her head back and shoved Kennedi off her before falling backward into the water. Water engulfed her as she slipped and fell backward. Adeline coughed and sputtered, swallowing water; the panic increased. Kennedi fell back into the water, but Ryker caught her.

Coughing violently, Adeline burst into tears, humiliated by her lack of control. She was so broken. It wasn't even possible to do something *fucking normal.* No, she had to be a *freak.* She'd always be a freak. Unwanted. Unloveable.

Gripping her shoulders, Adeline shivered violently as she attempted to rein in her unrelenting insecurities. Ryker and Kennedi watched, brows furrowed. It only made her feel worse. "I'm so sorry. I don't know what happened."

"Hey," Kennedi's tone was soothing. She approached slowly, holding out her hands. "It's okay. We're okay. You're safe right now."

Adeline slapped her hands to her face, trying to hide her shame. "I'm so embarrassed." She looked at Ryker from between her fingers. "It doesn't have anything to do with you. It's all me. It's all my fucked-up insides. I'm so fucked up."

He nodded slowly, taking a step back to give her more space. "I understand. It's really okay, I promise."

"Can I come closer?" Kennedi asked. Adeline couldn't stop crying, overwhelmed by their kindness and patience. She dropped her hands to her sides in defeat. Would she be this broken forever? Had her father ruined her for life?

"Yes, please." She sniffled and fell into Kennedi's embrace. Her reaction didn't have anything to do with Kennedi—only Ryker. She didn't want to admit this to him, in case it hurt him further. He had been so open and understanding; he didn't deserve to be treated like this.

She pulled away from Kennedi and looked at him. "I'm sorry for disappointing you."

His head jerked as if she'd slapped him. "What? Disappointed me? How?"

"By not continuing. I know you thought we would—"

He cut her off. "I expected nothing. I'm not disappointed in the slightest, Addie. After everything I've learned about you, I am *proud* of you."

He was proud of her? Dumbfounded, she tried to say something, but her mouth moved without a sound. Why would he be proud? She stopped him. Men didn't like it when you stopped them. In fact, they hated it.

Kennedi brushed her fingers against Adeline's face. "I'm proud of you, too. If you'd like, we can get dressed and head out. I need to head home, anyway."

As they dressed, Adeline's thoughts swirled with shame and confusion. Would she be like this forever? The idea of having these issues for the rest of her life made death sound more appealing. Surely it would get better. Maybe if she continued to face it head on, it would get better. It was worth a shot.

Just not tonight.

By the time they'd dragged their dry clothes over their wet skin, Adeline's pounding heart slowed. The shivering subsided. She still struggled to look at either of them, the shame branding her insides, right next to all the other invisible scars.

They walked silently through the tall grass, Kennedi beside her the whole way, a steadying presence. Ryker led the way again, glancing over his shoulder every thirty seconds. She could still taste them both, which only increased her anguish. Her brain ruined what could have been an amazing moment. How typical.

None of them spoke as they piled into the truck, Kennedi in the middle again, now a welcome buffer. It wasn't that Adeline didn't want to be near Ryker—because she did—but she was positive *he* wanted nothing to do with her now. The most surprising part of it all was him not freaking out or coercing her into complying. In fact, his non-reaction was shocking.

He cleared his throat at one point during the drive and peered over at Adeline. "I'm not mad. I promise."

"How could you not be?" she said, leaning her head against the window. The shame marched along her nerves like fire ants, pecking at her shattering heart. He was just saying this because he felt like he had to. He didn't mean it.

Undeterred, Ryker reached across Kennedi, offering his hand. "Because your worth has nothing to do with what you might offer. My mom figuratively beat it into my head that the way people treat you rarely has anything to do with you. I don't know all of your stories, but I do know that I don't judge you for any of them. I also know that you made a solid step forward tonight, even if you didn't land where you wanted to."

His words seeped into her mind, interrupting the scalding shame. Maybe, just maybe, he isn't like the others. Adeline hesitated, then took his hand. His grasp was firm and comforting. "Thank you."

His gentle smile soothed the jagged edges of her fear. "Anytime."

Kennedi placed a hand on theirs. With a wiggle of her hips, she grinned as she said, "I just want to feel a little included here."

The joke evaporated the somber mood, the energy shifting into something far more comfortable.

They stayed like that until they arrived back in front of Mags' ostentatious Victorian home. It was pitch black inside, lending an eerie feeling as the moon rose above the roof. They piled out of the truck.

Kennedi kicked a stone. "I gotta head home." She looked at Adeline. "Call me tomorrow?"

Adeline nodded, and brought her in for a tight embrace. Kennedi stepped back and turned to Ryker. "Can I get one from you, too?"

He grinned and opened his arms wide. "Absolutely."

Kennedi fell into his embrace, squeezing tight. "Thanks for the make-out sesh," she said into his T-shirt. He patted her back good-naturedly.

"Anytime. Just name the place."

Kennedi laughed and headed down the sidewalk. "Bye, you two. Don't do anything I wouldn't do."

Adeline felt her anxiety unfurling as Kennedi walked away. She looked at the house, uneasy with the lack of lights. She turned to Ryker and cleared her throat.

"It looks super creepy. Would you mind walking me to the door?"

He swept a muscular arm down the walkway. "Of course. Lead the way."

Atop the porch steps, Adeline hesitated. The hairs on her arm rose, and Ryker motioned for her to stop.

"Something's wrong," she murmured, a sense of knowing punching her in the gut. Familiar, awful energy crackled in the air like the signature of a serial killer.

The house was silent. No meows, no Mags. Ryker reached for the doorknob and twisted it slowly. It clicked open and swung inward. Leaning forward, Ryker flipped a switch and light flooded the foyer.

They were met with a swinging mass of fur hanging from the chandelier.

Ryker lunged for her as her knees gave out. Adeline barely felt anything as the ground clawed upwards and dragged her down into darkness.

CHAPTER EIGHTEEN

Adeline awoke to find herself in Ryker's arms, his face clouded with concern as he spoke on the phone to the cops.

"Adeline! Are you okay?" He sounded frantic as he brushed hair from her face. Shadows danced in her vision and she groaned, bringing a hand to her head. "What happened?"

"Someone attacked one of the cats," he said grimly. 'Can you sit up?"

As he helped her lean against the bannister, Ryker pulled out his phone to dial 911. She drew herself up into the fetal position, rattled from the turn of events. Alexander's energy floated around the porch like a specter. She knew the feeling of it as she knew the feeling of her own. The game was no longer paused—her father's patience was at an end. This was a message.

Within minutes, sirens and flashing lights careened to a stop around Ryker's truck. The sheriff, who Adeline recognized from the other day, put on his hat and strode over to them, eyes on the front door.

Ryker helped Adeline into a wicker chair in a corner of the porch. He stood guard as the sheriff and a deputy swept the house, checking every room and closet. They reappeared after five minutes, looking troubled. The sheriff pulled a notebook from his back pocket and approached Adeline. Deputies passed in and out of the house, peering over at her. She felt like an exhibit. *And over here, boys and girls, is a woman who was her father's prisoner, and when she escaped, he went around killing cats to teach her a lesson.*

"Is this your father's doing?" Sheriff Teer peered down at her, his dark eyes soft with empathy. Adeline bit the inside of her cheek to focus. The copper taste of blood centered her.

Mags, who showed up almost immediately, was on the other side of the yard, raging near a planter box full of ripe tomatoes. If she hadn't wanted her father dead before, the murder of one of Mags' cats sealed the deal.

The sheriff waved a hand, catching her attention again. He repeated his question. She shook her head.

"It's definitely my father. He's behind everything, I'm sure of it." The sheriff's mustache twitched. He made a note.

Mags hollered something at the poor deputy tasked with taking her statement. She was waving her hands around and almost smacked him in the face. Adeline smiled. Mags was poised to cause the ultimate amount of chaos. She'd left for her knitting club and came back to a dead cat—her father was unaware of the war he'd just begun.

Adeline's knees ached. She stretched her legs. The sheriff snapped his notebook shut and shoved it into a back pocket.

"We're still gathering evidence inside, but we'll be done soon. Will you be staying the night?" he said to Ryker.

Ryker nodded, placing a hand on the back of Adeline's chair. "I can. I'll ask if they wouldn't mind if I crashed on the couch."

Adeline stood and shook the sheriff's hand. Her legs wobbled like jelly—Ryker reached out to support her by the elbow. "Thank you. I'm sorry you've had to deal with this."

Sheriff Teer gave her an odd look. "Miss Addie, none of this is your fault."

The words were a vise around her heart. It was all her fault. Every bit of it.

A small, soft body swerved into her ankle. Adeline looked down and gasped. Aslin peered up, large yellow eyes blinking. She mewled again.

"Aslin," Adeline murmured, bending down and scooping up the soft feline, shoving her face into the tufts of silky fur. Aslin purred loudly. Mags, done berating the deputy, stalked over to them, wrapping an arm around Adeline's shoulders.

Sheriff Teer tipped his hat. "Ladies, I'll leave you to it. I'll have a deputy stay in front of the house for the next couple days, see if anything pops up. Mags, let me know if you hear anything."

Mags waved him off. Adeline grinned as Ryker walked over. He offered a small smile.

"Who wants a drink?" Mags said gruffly. She stomped inside without waiting for an answer and loudly declared that everyone needed to "get the fuck out." Adeline didn't think cops could move that fast. If she ever wanted to rob a bank, she'd bring Mags along just to demand the tellers to hand over the money. Tucking Aslin closer, she followed Ryker inside the house.

They found Mags in the kitchen, muttering loudly about cat killers, whiskey, and chopped-off appendages. Three shot glasses slammed onto the kitchen table. Aslin pushed against Adeline's chest with and tumbled from her, landing on her feet. The calico scurried to an empty bowl of food and stared at Adeline. Another loud, demanding meow.

As Mags poured the amber liquid into the shot glasses, Adeline found the cat food and poured a small amount into the bowl. Aslin crammed it down her throat.

Ryker and Mags sat down at the table. Adeline joined them a moment later and reached for a shot glass. A bit of liquid spilled over the edge and onto her fingers. Mags held hers up.

"To the end of men."

Ryker went to raise his glass but faltered. "Of all men?"

Mags' upper lip curled. Her hair was as wild as Medusa's, curls springing into the air. She threw back the whiskey, slammed the empty glass on the table, and leaned toward Ryker. "We'll keep you as a handsome pet. How's that sound?"

Ryker glanced at Adeline. "If I'm *your* handsome pet, I'm down." He threw his back and smacked his lips in satisfaction. Adeline did the same.

Mags continued to pour shots, each time making more outrageous toasts. By the time Adeline was ready to pass out, she was positive Mags' destiny was to destroy every cis-gendered man on the planet. And she wasn't sure that was necessarily a bad thing anymore.

Ryker entertained her rants, sometimes pounding the table and hollering, "Hear, hear! Down with men!" to which Mags would cackle and screech, "To the rise of women everywhere!" Adeline bowled over laughing.

When everything had gotten a bit too fuzzy, Adeline stared at the two Rykers right in front of her and grinned. Her vision swam, and her head wobbled. "Do you think… Can you check my bedroom? I don't think I'll feel safe entering it alone."

Ryker stilled. "Are you sure you want me to go to your bedroom?"

Mags squinted, then widened her eyes, trying to focus on their faces. "Make it quick. I need my hag sleep. Ryker, you can sleep on the couch."

Adeline frowned. "Don't you mean beauty sleep?"

Mags stood, her chair almost toppling. "No. I mean hag sleep. Who wants to be beautiful when being a hag means you can do whatever the fuck you want?"

They filed down the hallway, Mags leading the way. She trailed a hand along the wall for balance. Ryker followed close behind with

Adeline in the middle. She could feel the heat of him on her back. It reminded her of earlier, at the lake—before she freaked out. Kissing him had been nice… until it wasn't.

Turning left into her bedroom at the top of the stairs, Mags turned and glared at them. "I mean it. Make it quick."

Adeline was too focused on the hulking hunk behind her to care about Mags' warning. Her gaze was locked on her bedroom door. She'd left the light on earlier, but it was dark now. Thank goodness she invited—

Suddenly, a memory exploded in her mind:

A man's hands on her shoulders, guided her into a room. Dread knotted in her belly, and her feet felt so heavy. This wasn't the first time he'd brought her to his house. She doubted it would be the last. He leaned down and smelled her ear.

She jerked her head—

Ryker slammed into her from behind—she'd halted in the doorway. He reached for her arm and caught her before she face-planted on the floor. *Don't let him touch you*, a voice in her head screamed.

Adeline lashed out, still blinded by the memory. Dug her nails into his forearms. He grunted. She wriggled out of his grasp and landed on the floor, and crawled away. A sob lodged in her throat. She could see only the floor. Reaching a corner, she faced him, crouched like a wild animal.

Hands. There'd been so many hands. Mouths. Teeth. Pain. Screaming. Crying. Numbness.

Adeline sobbed hysterically, wrapping her arms around her torso, rocking back and forth. She panted like a dog, desperate to escape this sense of drowning. Old cigarette scars felt new on her flesh. The scar on her neck throbbed. Hidden wounds scraped claws against her thoughts, shredding her sanity.

Ryker stood as still as stone, eyes wide, hands still in the air. He lowered his hands slowly, palms out, fingers spread.

"Hey." His voice was quiet and even. She flinched as he lowered himself, hands still up to show he meant no threat. Stars sparkled in her vision; hyperventilating wouldn't help the situation. Slowly, the room came back into focus.

"Hey." He put the tips of his fingers on the floor, balancing as he inched forward deliberately. She bared her teeth and hissed; he paused. "Addie. Come back to me." He raised a hand toward her. She drew back, eyes wild like a feral animal. He didn't drop his hand.

"Addie. It's Ryker. You're safe. No one is going to touch you."

A tiny kernel of awareness within her sparked. She grasped at its flickering light, digging claws into the deep darkness of her mind. Clawing and scraping for an inch of sanity in this chaotic world.

My name is Adeline.

I escaped him.

I'm safe.

I broke Alexander's nose.

I'm not helpless.

As Ryker patiently waited, prostrating on his knees as her reality stitched itself back together, Adeline lashed out at the demons in her mind. This was *her* life. *Her* body. It belonged to *her*. Lucas had no right to it. He never did.

Adeline's body sagged as the terror eked out of her, little by little. Clutching a hand to her chest, she focused on her breaths, reciting the alphabet backwards.

Z. Y. X. W. V.

Her heartbeat slowed. Fresh air coated her lungs in a gentle caress.

U. T. S. R. Q. P.

The tears slowed, drying into salty streaks on her cheeks.

O. N. M. L. K. J.

Her vision cleared, allowing her to finally see Ryker's concerned expression. Shimmering pools of unshed tears line his dark lashes. His hand still reached for her, steady and unwavering.

Unfurling herself, Adeline leaned forward and placed her hand into his. Slowly, his fingers curled around her palm. An anchor back to this home; this room. She was safe. Everything was fine.

"Can I touch you?" Ryker's voice was barely above a whisper. She nodded, then shivered, needing his warmth. She squeezed her eyes shut, bracing herself. It wasn't what she expected; she'd assumed he would wrap his arms around her, but he scooted to her side. Their legs and shoulders were flush together. She almost sighed at the sensation of his skin against hers. She leaned into him and took a deep breath.

"Can I put an arm around you?"

She rested her arms atop her knees and dropped her chin. She nodded, hoping against hope that it wouldn't make things worse. He gently draped an arm around her. He held her firmly but didn't press them together. She relaxed into his hold. Felt his breath roll across her wet cheeks. She sniffled and brought the back of her hand up to wipe away the remaining tears.

"I'm sorry," she whispered, staring straight ahead.

"Don't apologize. You have nothing to be sorry for. What just happened is perfectly normal. You know I hadn't expected sex, right? You're way too drunk for me to even think about kissing you. I'm a lot of things, but I'm not going to even kiss a woman without sober, enthusiastic consent. Do I want to? Hell to the *fucking yes*. But not if this is where you're going to get hurt. I had just planned on making sure it was safe and putting you to bed, Addie."

Each word melted a little more of her fear. He hadn't planned on doing anything; he'd intended on putting her to bed. She'd never met anyone like him before. She turned to look at him—to *really* look at him. His face was filled with concern.

He smiled faintly. "Hey."

"Hi." Her voice was raspy. Had she been screaming? He squeezed her closer.

"Do you want to get into bed?"

She nodded. "Yes, please."

He helped her to her feet, gently pulling her up. She craned her head up, taking one last look at his face. She breathed in the scent of wood chips and petrichor. "Thank you."

He brought a hand up, stopping an inch from her face. She closed her eyes and rested her cheek against his palm. It was dry and warm. She sighed. Her eyes fluttered open again as he leaned down and pulled back the comforter. She lowered herself onto the mattress. When the blanket was tucked tightly around her, he gave her one more look.

"I admire you."

"Why?" Her eyes were growing heavy.

"You have the kind of strength that no one should ever need, but you wear it beautifully regardless."

And then darkness swept over her.

CHAPTER NINETEEN

Adeline wiped her brow, beaded with sweat from the late-spring sun, and watched Mags square off a few feet away. The woman stood a little above five feet, but the crackle of energy around made her feel like a giant. She'd tossed her red glasses to the side, and the normally large bush of gray curls was tied back in a wild bun.

"Don't tell me you're giving up," Mags jeered, casually tossing her knife in the air. She spun it and caught the soft leather handle with ease.

Adeline sneered and brought up her blade, flipping it upside down. Her arms ached, feeling heavier than cans of paint, but she wasn't ready to admit defeat. "Bring it, you old bitch."

Mags grinned. "That's my girl." She took two tentative bounces forward, testing Adeline's reflexes. Raised one eyebrow sharply when Adeline didn't budge. "Feeling brave, eh?"

Adeline stepped forward, taking the bait. Mags responded: a flurry of swings and footwork. Adeline ducked and parried, gritting her teeth as their forearms slammed together. She did a *Matrix*-esque backbend as Mags swept her blade across where her throat would have been.

As Mags flipped her knife and swept back, Adeline ducked into a squat and positioned her knife pointing up. Her thighs screamed as she flexed them, driving upward, aiming for Mags' throat. A hand was planted suddenly against her skull, preventing her from moving. In an instant, Adeline flipped her blade upside down again and landed a blow against Mags' rib cage. If it hadn't been a dull training blade, the old woman would have had a new hole to breathe through.

They froze, panting. From the corner of her eye, Adeline saw Mags' blade resting a hair away from her throat—they would have killed each other. They broke apart, and Adeline stood up straight.

"I almost had you," Adeline pointed out.

Mags waved her away, fanning her soaked T-shirt against her chest. "You're better, but you still would have died." She squinted at the sun. "It's lunchtime. Let's eat."

Adeline tucked her blade into the holster strapped to her jeans. "I'm dying of thirst. Do you have any lemonade left?"

"I think Ryker finished most of it. I'll split it with you."

Adeline groaned. "He's so dead when he gets back."

Mags smirked as she tucked her blade away. They practiced in the backyard under some old oak trees. It was normally a beautiful setting, but the day was too hot to appreciate the bright flowers and ripening vegetables.

The porch door screeched as Mags opened it. A burst of cold air hit Adeline's face, and she sighed. The kitchen felt too clean, Adeline thought as she plopped her sweaty ass into one of the seats.

Mags limped over and opened the fridge, hissing at a cat that almost tripped her. It scattered out of the way. She reached in and grabbed the pitcher of bright yellow lemonade, her wiry arms shaking as she carried it to the table. It was almost empty, with barely a cupful left. Adeline pushed over her glass from earlier. Mags did the same, and they split the remaining amount, giving Adeline just a tad more.

"Thank you," Adeline muttered. She tossed the sweet, tart liquid to the back of her throat, swallowed, and melted into the chair. Everything hurt, and at the moment, she wasn't even sure she could stand. Mags finished her ration and then collapsed into the chair across from Adeline.

"Not bad for a couple months of training." Mags appraised her. "How are you feeling?"

"Like pulverized beef." Adeline smiled. "Ready to take on the world, maybe."

"At least ready to take on Lucas?"

At the mention of his name, Adeline's skin prickled. "Hopefully. Battling the world might be easier than going hand to hand with him. Especially if Alexander is there."

Mags stood on wobbly knees. How she was able to keep up with Adeline's younger body was astounding. Adeline watched as Mags headed to the hallway. Another cat rushed past her legs. She turned and put her hands on her ample hips.

"Again tomorrow?"

Adeline was about to beg for a day off when Lucas' face—his leering grin flashed through her mind. "Yes. Again. Tomorrow."

After a quick shower, Adeline checked her phone. She smiled, seeing a text from Kennedi.

Want to go get ice cream?

Adeline glanced at the time. ***It's still morning***

That's why you get a waffle cone

Adeline chuckled. ***Touché. Meet you at the shop?***

See you in fifteen

Adeline threw on a shirt, some shorts, and a pair of sandals—as quickly as her tight limbs would allow—and hustled downstairs. She bounded for the front door, but the smell of coffee beckoned a detour. She hurried into the kitchen. Mags hummed as she whisked something yellow in a bowl. A bit of the liquid splattered on her ruddy cheek. Mags looked over to Adeline.

"You look like shit."

Adeline glared as she snatched a travel mug from the cabinet and poured coffee into it. She stuck out her tongue. "It's all your fault."

Mags shrugged and looked back down at the batter. "I have no regrets. Where are you headed?"

"Ice cream with Kennedi."

To Adeline's shock, the cantankerous woman didn't launch into a rant about her needing an escort. Instead, Mags said, "I left a knife by the front door. Put it somewhere safe."

Adeline rolled her eyes and walked away, relishing the first sip of scalding bean juice.

Mags yelled, "Remember: dicks are the best soft spot!"

Adeline barked out a laugh as she reached for the four-inch switchblade on the end table. The dark brown handle had swirls of pearl inlay from top to bottom. At the end of the handle was a pearled letter "A." She pressed a tiny silver button and gleaming metal popped out like a Jack-in-the-box. Its edge honed to peak sharpness.

"I had it made for you."

Adeline turned and saw Mags leaning against the kitchen doorjamb, a tea towel slung over one shoulder.

Adeline looked up, eyes glistening. "When?"

"When you showed up looking like the Devil had kickboxed your face."

"Thank you," Adeline whispered. Mags nodded once and then disappeared back into the kitchen.

It was the nicest gift Adeline had ever received. Better than all the diamond-studded necklaces and jet-setting experiences combined. Wiping away a tear, Adeline tucked the blade back into place and pocketed the weapon. Snatching her pale pink purse, she opened the door and breathed in the fresh air.

To her surprise, it was raining. It hadn't rained in Menforth since her arrival—it seemed weird. The normally vibrant garden was now different shades of gray, with dirt sliding off the white picket fence. Soaking wet cats darted past her ankles, desperate for dry shelter.

Adeline sneered at the weather. She turned and—

"JESUS!" Adeline shrieked as she almost bumped into Mags, who stood inches away, holding up a black umbrella.

"Don't get too wet." Mags flashed her teeth and handed over the umbrella.

"What the fuck is wrong with you?" Adeline grumbled, snatching the umbrella and storming out the front door.

"Play nice with the other kids!" Mags hollered, smirking when Adeline looked back.

Adeline stuck out her tongue once she'd passed the gate. "Don't go outside. Wouldn't want you to *melt*." She gave her the finger. Mags' cackle faded as she closed the door.

The air was warm, and her shoes were quickly soaked through. That Kennedi invited her to go anywhere in this weather was confounding. Adeline sunk into her thoughts as she walked, mulling over the past seventy-two hours: an almost-threesome in a lake. A dead cat. Freaking out in the bedroom and humiliating herself.

"And the hits just keep on coming," she muttered, ducking her head.

It would be nice if life would just lend her a break. Cut some slack in the noose around her neck. Send a miracle or two her way.

It was all about perspective though, she supposed. Walking in the rain and soaking her shoes would've been unthinkable under Lucas' watchful prison. It was a miracle her father even wanted to play this game of cat and mouse; that she even had the opportunity to walk in the rain and have ice cream with someone she loved.

Years of torture had taught her that even the smallest things, like the smell of rain or soaking wet shoes, were wonderful. Normally, her father was so wrapped up in making everything perfect, which meant avoiding bad weather. He was obsessed with things being just-so. He had to be pretty bored with her to even give her this kind of attention and freedom.

Adeline was so caught up in her thoughts that she almost careened into a light pole. She looked up as her feet made contact, barely avoiding a broken nose. She laughed at herself.

The ice cream shop was only feet away. Outside she saw Kennedi at a table, her legs crossed, thighs pressed together, popping out of her shorts. Kennedi shook her head slowly at something on her phone. She typed something furiously with both thumbs. Adeline thought she looked like the cutest thing in the whole world.

"Hey."

Kennedi looked up. She laughed when she saw Adeline's soaked features. She stood, beckoning Adeline into the ice cream shop.

"Hurry, I'm starving for waffles."

The door jingled, and the rich scents of cream and sugar made her smile. Her stomach grumbled. "You mean ice cream."

Kennedi shook her head. She hopped over to the counter, rocking on the balls of her feet as she read the flavors. Behind the counter was an older woman, about Mags' age, wearing a dark purple-and-white-striped dress. She seemed bored, her eyes glued to a TV in the corner.

Kennedi pointed at a bucket of ice cream. "Can I have a scoop of raspberry and a scoop of chocolate on one of those sprinkle-covered waffle cones? And more sprinkles. With some marshmallows. And a little caramel." The woman looked appalled. Kennedi added, "Please."

The woman—her name tag read *Terry*—shook her head but went ahead concocting Kennedi's request. Kennedi slid over to Adeline, who was stuck trying to decide.

"I haven't had ice cream in years," she whispered. "I don't even know what I like."

Kennedi was quiet for a moment. "Okay," she murmured. "Do you remember what you used to have?"

A memory rattled loose. "Bubblegum, I think."

Kennedi pointed at small containers filled with various toppings. "Anything there look good? You can get as many as you'd like."

Adeline leaned forward to get a closer look. "Gummy bears? And some strawberries?"

Terry reached over the counter and handed Kennedi her cone. Kennedi's eyes focused sharply on her meal. Terry looked to Adeline. "What'll it be?"

Adeline gave her order and looked away when Terry showed obvious judgment at her choices. Kennedi stood beside her, tongue pink, a rim of red already lining her lips.

Adeline grinned. "You look ridiculous."

Kennedi shrugged. "So? Why does eating ice cream have to be serious? It's literally flavored frozen milk. With sprinkles. I'm gonna get us a table."

She walked off, leaving Adeline to wait. When finally she had her cone, she turned and found Kennedi sitting at a table by one of the windows. Kennedi had already finished the scoop of raspberry. Adeline sat down across from her.

"Kennedi… you're supposed to eat it, not inhale it."

Kennedi glared, curling her tongue into the chocolate. "Shut up and eat your ice cream."

"Bossy." Adeline did as she was told, taking a lick. She jolted at the immediate sensation, sugar slicing her taste buds. Memory upon memory slammed into her, bludgeoning her senses.

Puffy clouds skimmed the blue sky, the sun turning them the color of fresh snow. Addie giggled to herself.

"What are you laughing at?" Mommy bumped her with a shoulder, grinning and taking a lick from her strawberry ice cream cone. Addie returned the grin, feeling the cold, sticky bubblegum-flavored cream on her chin.

"Just imagining the clouds made of snow."

Mommy nodded, looking ahead of them. The sun beamed through the green trees above, warming their shoulders. They sat on a green park bench and started people watching.

It was a secret ritual, sneaking out for ice cream together. Her daddy would hate knowing they were gone, though she didn't know why. He would enjoy some ice cream, too. She didn't know his favorite flavor, but she bet it was chocolate.

A family walked by, the mom pushing a stroller. Inside was a fat wide-eyed baby, its cheeks rosy pink. The mommy and daddy looked at each other and smiled.

"Mommy, why doesn't Daddy come for ice cream?"

A shadow passed over Mommy's features. "Daddy is very busy."

Addie knew she wasn't allowed to ask a lot of questions, but she pushed anyway. "Why can't we tell him? Did you ask him to come?"

Mommy's eyes widened and gave a stern look. "Addie, you must never tell Daddy we do this, okay?"

"But—"

"I mean it." Addie startled at the harsh tone; Mommy never spoke to her like this. Ice cream dripped down her cone, pooling around her thumb. "Promise me," Mommy insisted. Addie didn't like the way her voice sounded.

"Okay," she whispered. Mommy stared at her long enough that Addie shifted uncomfortably on the bench. The backs of her knees ached. She wanted to go feed the ducks.

Mommy's shoulders relaxed, and the scary look in her eyes was replaced with a beautiful smile. Mommy had the best smile. It was wide and safe. Mommy popped the rest of the cone into her mouth, the end of it sticking out. Addie giggled and did the same.

"Doyouf wan tof go for awalk?" Mommy sounded so silly.

"Yef pleaf." Ice cream sprayed out Addie's mouth, sprinkling her bare legs. They chewed furiously, as if in competition. Addie won and crowed with victory, throwing her fist in the air.

Mommy smiled so wide her eyes almost disappeared. "Good job, little fox."

Little fox. Addie loved that nickname. Mommy said it was because she was clever. That made Addie proud. She stood and wiped the droplets of ice cream off her thighs.

Mommy stood too, towering over her. She held out a soft hand. Addie reached for it, smiling as their fingers stuck together. They walked down the path, swinging their arms. Mommy looked to the sky and pointed at a cloud.

"What do you think that one looks like?"

Addie scrunched her nose. "A cloud."

"Yes, but if it could be anything else, what do you think it could be?"

Addie stopped and stared hard. Finally, she said, "A dragon."

Mommy's eyes popped in delight. "I see that, too!"

They spent the rest of the afternoon pointing out different clouds and feeding ducks. When the sun set below the horizon, Mommy took her home, sneaking through one of the servant's doors. They tiptoed upstairs, and when they reached Addie's pretty pink room, Mommy tucked her into bed. The last thing she remembered was feeling a kiss on her forehead and the words, "Sleep well, my little fox."

It was then Adeline noticed the drizzle of ice cream sliding down her fingers. Kennedi waved a hand in front of her face.

"Earth to Addie. Come in, Addie."

Adeline startled, and the ice cream almost fell off her cone.

Kennedi looked surprised. "I'm sorry. I didn't mean to startle you."

"No, it's just…" Adeline stared at her ice cream, shaken by the memory she had buried deep and forgotten. "I just remembered something."

Kennedi reached for some napkins and tried to wipe away the stickiness. "That you prefer a different flavor?"

Adeline took another tentative taste, and this time she smiled. The flavor continued to remind her of fluffy clouds, and of her mom. She took a bigger bite, rolling the freezing dessert around her mouth. "No. Just something with my mom I hadn't thought about in a long time."

Kennedi stood up. "Give me a second. I need some water. My fingers are sticking together like glue."

Adeline happily chewed on the gummy bears, her shoulders shimmying with contentness. Kennedi plopped back down in front of her with a glass of water. She dipped a napkin into it and ran it over her fingers. "So, what's this about your mom?"

Adeline took another lick. "Just a good memory. At least, I think it was good."

Kennedi tossed the used napkin onto the table. "Do you want to talk about it?"

Adeline crunched down on the cone. "Maybe." She ate the rest of her ice cream before responding.

While wiping her sticky fingers, she said, "I miss her." She swallowed hard. "I never even got to say goodbye. That's the hardest part."

Kennedi leaned against the table. Glancing outside, then back at Adeline, she said, "I get that. When my mom walked out on us, I thought the whole world was ending." Her eyes widened. "I'm not trying to compare traumas. Sorry. I'm just saying, I get the whole not-getting-a-goodbye thing."

"I get it." Adeline crumpled up the napkin and huffed loudly. "Does life ever just fucking stop?"

Kennedi shrugged. "Hell if I know. What I *do* know, though, is that Ryker is a total hottie. What happened when he took you home the other night? Was he a gentleman?"

Adeline tensed. "Uh." *Shit.* She'd forgotten to tell Kennedi. "Yes? Sort of? I mean, there wasn't any time for really anything to happen, because we found a dead cat hanging in the house."

"*What?*"

Terry glanced over, irritated at the outburst.

Adeline grimaced. "Sorry. I mean, it was crazy, and then I freaked out and went to sleep. And Mags has been training me to use a knife these last couple of days, and…it completely slipped my mind."

"Start from the beginning," Kennedi demanded. Adeline filled her in on the previous night's events, shuddering at the memory of the poor cat hanging from a piece of rope. She grew quiet as she went over the freak-out in her bedroom.

"You should've seen it, Kennedi. I was a right fucking mess, and he just stood there, like I was… I don't know. Like I wasn't some hysterical freak."

Kennedi rested her head in her hands. "So, he's hot, a good kisser, understands consent, and doesn't mind emotions? Who is he and what terrorist organization is he from?"

Adeline huffed out a laugh. "For real. It was pretty amazing." They sat there quietly, watching the rain.

Kennedi bit her lip. "Can I ask you something?"

"Sure."

She paused, unsure if what she was about to ask was okay. Taking a deep breath, Kennedi asked, "What was it like? Going through all of that? Without anyone?"

"I don't know how to answer that," Adeline admitted. "No one has ever really asked me… Putting feelings to something like that, thinking about those moments…" She trailed off. "It was incredibly lonely. Staring at four walls all day every day until I was allowed to come out. And even then, despite wanting to leave my prison, I knew it would never be good. It would always lead to something terrible, no matter where we were in the world. All I wanted was to die. I tried once, too. Swallowed a ton of pills."

She motioned to herself bitterly. "Clearly, I failed. I'm not sure how much longer I could have taken it. If he hadn't let me go for his own sick games, I would have never seen you again."

Her eyes burned, the truth crashing into her like an angry wave. She had been an absolute fool to think she had escaped. Kennedi reached out and grasped Adeline's arms. Adeline continued, her bottom lip wavering. "I've put you in danger. And I'm so sorry for that. I'll do anything to stop him. I'd leave, but I'm too weak to leave you unless you ask. It's selfish, and I know it, but I can't just leave you now that I've found you."

Adeline hiccuped a sob and bowed her head. *Don't cry, don't cry, don't cry.*

Kennedi squeezed her arms tighter and leaned closer. "Hey."

Adeline looked up through moist lashes, a tear slipping down her cheek.

Kennedi smiled softly. "Having the person I love come back to me, even in a very-not-ideal situation, is one of the best things to happen to me. I have zero regrets. Whatever happens, it's me and you." She paused. "And maybe Ryker. Even if he's just cutting down some wood." She winked.

Adeline laughed loudly. "You're incorrigible," she hissed, earning a quiet giggle from Kennedi—and a glare from Terry. Adeline took a deep breath, her emotions receding for the moment.

Kennedi glanced out the window. "Well, now that we've had lunch, what's next?"

"I don't know," Adeline admitted. "I'm so sore from sparring with Mags. She's a ruthless teacher. I might just want to go home, stretch, and maybe curl up with a book."

Kennedi stood, holding out a hand. "Let's get you home then, shall we?"

They exited the shop. It was still pouring, so they walked under awnings, scuttling quickly between each and laughing as the rain pelted their heads. They stopped in front of each shop and looked through the windows.

The town square was mostly empty, thanks to the weather—it felt as if they lived in their own world. Until they spotted Ryker unloading wet wood from the back of his truck. They halted beside a clothing store, entranced by the sight of his arms hoisting a pile of thick planks as if they weighed nothing.

"Good gods," Kennedi whispered. "Do you think he could lift me like that?"

"When was the last time you had sex?" Adeline whispered back, leaning up to Kennedi's ear. "You're like a total horn dog."

Kennedi gave a sidelong look, one eye still focused on the lumberjack. "A hot second. But I mean, *look* at him."

Ryker's forehead glistened. He grunted as he lifted another pile of wood and walked it into the hardware store. He wore tight-fitting jeans and a plaid red and black short-sleeve shirt that barely contained his bulk. Years of chopping wood honed him like a Grecian god.

Adeline had to admit: he looked good. Those muscles were hard won, unlike the pampered men she was used to who had expensive personal trainers.

Kennedi gave a low whistle. Ryker turned, arms full. He smiled.

"Beautiful day, huh?" he teased. Kennedi and Adeline scurried to the next awning, stopping by the back of his truck. He eyed their soaking-wet clothes.

"Aren't you a bit old to be playing in the rain?"

Kennedi retorted, "Aren't you a bit too sexy to be carrying wood?"

Ryker readjusted the hefty load. "I carry wood everywhere I go."

Adeline groaned and slapped a hand to her forehead. "You're both absolutely ridiculous."

Kennedi glared at her. "Did you somehow forget the lake? I'm barely satiated."

Fair. Adeline shook her head. Directing her attention to Ryker, she asked, "Do you need any help?"

He flashed a smooth smile. "No, I'm good. Almost done here. Where are you headed?"

"Not sure," Kennedi said. "I think this one—" she hooked a thumb at Adeline "—needs a nap."

"I don't need a nap," Adeline protested. As if on cue, she yawned, then narrowed her eyes as Kennedi and Ryker laughed.

"Be right back," he said, and took the wood into the store.

Kennedi turned to Adeline. "Want me to walk you home, Ms. Exhausted?"

Adeline sighed, twirling the closed umbrella in her palm. "Yeah, it's probably for the best."

Ryker came back out, slapping his hands together. "I'd love to hang, but I have a few more deliveries to make, and some other shit to do."

Kennedi gave him a tight hug. "'S okay. I'll walk her home. I need to relieve my father at the store, anyway. Stupid inventory bullshit."

"Then let's hang soon," Ryker said. "I'll text when I'm free again."

"Sounds like a plan." Kennedi declared.

Adeline popped open the umbrella. She took one last look at Ryker. "Thank you again for the other night."

His features softened. "Of course. I'm glad you're okay. Can I hug you?"

She nodded and stepped into his embrace, breathing in the scent of wood chips and rain. His arms enveloped her body, holding her firmly. He kissed the top of her forehead and let go.

"Don't fantasize about me too much."

Kennedi stepped closer to Adeline, trying to fit under the umbrella. "No promises," Adeline said. "See ya." She wiggled her fingers goodbye and they stepped out into the pouring rain.

CHAPTER TWENTY

The rain was a drizzle by the time they reached Mags' porch. Adeline shook the umbrella dry and rested it by a rocking chair. Kennedi leaned over and shook out her wet hair like a dog.

Adeline laughed, holding her hands over her face. "Down girl!"

Kennedi straightened up, laughing. "Why didn't we use the umbrella right away?"

With the gloomy weather, the porch was more shadowed than usual, lending it a sense of intimacy. They locked eyes, the tension between them growing taut. Adeline thought of the book store and the lake. Both encounters had been too brief and hadn't satiated her hunger. As kids, they had never really experimented together. Just a cautious, awkward teenage version of love. Now, Adeline ached for something more.

Adeline came closer, their toes tapping. Kennedi looked up at Adeline with flushed cheeks. She blinked off a droplet of water and smiled. "I just realized I have to walk home like this."

Adeline took another step closer, her breasts brushing against Kennedi's chest. The energy between them crackled. Adeline swallowed. She ached to dive into Kennedi's entire being.

Kennedi whispered, "Did you like your ice cream?"

Adeline's lips hovered above Kennedi's mouth. "It was delicious." She felt Kennedi lean closer, their bodies pressing together, closing the distance between their lips a little more.

Adeline savored the scent of sugar on Kennedi's breath. A fire ignited in her chest, her heart a frenzied gallop. The hairs on Adeline's arms raised as she cupped Kennedi's face with both hands. Kennedi's breath quickened. She placed her hands on Adeline's hips, jerked her closer. Molten desire pooled in Adeline's core, and she bit back a groan.

"Can I kiss you?" Adeline's words were raw with desire. Kennedi gave a slow nod.

Half of Adeline's brain recognized how utterly cheesy the moment felt, but the other half—the half completely consumed with said moment—didn't give a *fuck*. She brushed her lips against Kennedi's, the soft pink flesh parting, making space for Adeline. It was gentle. Their tongues danced in sync. And then a ball of heat roared from Adeline's core, rising up through her throat, singeing her insides.

The kiss was no longer gentle.

She devoured Kennedi, who responded in kind. Hands swept each other's curves, lingering in the best places. Adeline nipped Kennedi's throat, eliciting a hum, then a low groan as Adeline pressed her fingers between Kennedi's thighs, trailing them against the seam of Kennedi's jeans.

"Jesus fuck," Adeline groaned into Kennedi's ear, hips jerking forward. Kennedi hummed in agreement as she trailed her tongue along Adeline's neck. Adeline ducked her head to catch Kennedi's mouth with her teeth, jerking back when Kennedi bit her lower lip.

The pain surprised her, but oddly enough it didn't frighten her. Instead, her blood roared with excitement. For the first time in her life, Adeline emitted a guttural growl, pinning Kennedi up against the front door.

Kennedi ground her hips against Adeline, who curled forward and inhaled Kennedi's scent. She pushed a leg between Kennedi's thighs. The top of her thigh fit perfectly into Kennedi's groin, eliciting another moan. The sound urged Adeline to continue. Starting slowly, she moved her hips back and forth, sliding her thigh against Kennedi's clit. She groaned and pushed with force as Kennedi yanked her closer, their hips now moving in time. She slipped her own hip forward at the perfect height to crash against Adeline's growing need.

The entire world disappeared around them. Their bodies rolled together, hips grinding almost painfully. Adeline dragged her thigh against Kennedi clit, again and again, picking up speed. She felt Kennedi's hands tighten against her back, nails dragging down.

"Addie," Kennedi panted. "Addie, I'm going to fucking cum."

"I know." Adeline honed in on Kennedi's body, on the tiny signals she sent. She hissed as those thick thighs clenched together, anchoring her into smaller movements and causing Kennedi's hip bone to settle perfectly against her own bundle of nerves. Kennedi's moans quickened, becoming loud and breathy. She dug her nails through Adeline's shirt.

Then Kennedi went over the edge, giving a hoarse cry as she orgasmed. With one more thrust against Kennedi's hip, Adeline crested through the growing heat that consumed her center. It burst through her, washing over her in waves of indescribable pleasure. She had never felt anything like it.

They breathed, foreheads pressed together. Then, slowly, their muscles began to loosen, and the world around them returned.

Adeline straightened and took a small step back. She smirked and bit her bottom lip. "Did we just cum together?"

Kennedi blew out a breath. "Sounds like it." Her eyes widened. "Wait, we just did that… here… on the front porch."

Adeline looked around. "You don't think Mags has us on camera, do you?"

"YES I DO," Mags said from the other side of the door.

***

The rain lasted for three days. Afterward, languishing in the sticky humidity, Adeline sat in an old wooden swing hanging from an impressive oak tree in the corner of Mags' front yard. In her lap was a small metal bowl full of ripe green grapes. She popped a plump one in her mouth, enjoying the explosion of flavor. A sliver of sweat dripped down the inside of her thigh.

"Why is it so fucking hot?" Ryker complained. He was lying on the bright green, covering his eyes. Wearing a black tank top, Adeline enjoyed every bulging muscle.

Adeline munched on another grape. "You're wearing jeans. What did you expect?"

Ryker scoffed. "That's too logical."

Adeline swung back and forth slowly, rocking on the tips of her bare toes. "Suit yourself." She looked over at him, eyes lingering on the tantalizing slope from the barrel of ribs to his stomach, where his other hand rested. Maybe she should start chopping wood. "Are we doing anything today or do I need to resign myself to getting fat on fruit?"

He didn't move. "Want to play a game?"

"What kind of game?"

One of his fingers twitched. "Twenty questions, but only deep questions."

"And you can ask anything?"

"Anything," he confirmed. "You can go first if you want."

Adeline's brows pinched. "What animal did you want to be when you grew up?"

"Ferret."

Adeline almost spit out a grape. "A *what*?"

"A ferret."

"*Why*?"

He lifted his arm to peek at her. She loved the way his muscles rippled with the movement. "Because they're genius noodles. Super smart and resourceful. Plus, they're kinda soft." He lowered his arm again. "Why? What's yours, oh mighty one?"

She leaned her head against the rope. She pushed backwards. "A bird. So I could fly far, far, far away."

He lifted his arm again. "Did you just quote *Forrest Gump* to me?"

"Technically no, it was Jenny that said that. But she had it right; birds are the quickest at escaping something. Your turn."

His biceps stretched as he brought his hands behind his head. Eyes still closed, a smile bloomed across his stubbled chin. It lit up his whole face, making his golden skin shine. She raked her bottom lip against her teeth—he was looking surprisingly tasty today.

Staring up through the tree branches, he said, "If you could accomplish anything in this life, what would it be?"

Her response was automatic: "Have a family."

"Why?"

She frowned. "Why do I want a family?"

He hesitated. "No, I guess that makes sense. But does it make you afraid?"

She stuck out her tongue. "That's two questions. What about you?"

He sighed and rolled his eyes. "I want to run my family's company. My mom is always focused on her practice, and my father is getting too old. My brother certainly isn't interested, and besides, he's off… somewhere." He made a vague hand gesture before putting it back behind his head. "I just love being outside and helping people build things."

"Don't you run it now?"

He took a hand to his chest, scratching it absentmindedly. Adeline watched his fingers, the way they traced across his pecs. "Yeah, for the most part. But I want it to be official, you know? My father can't understand the concept of sustainable forestry, but I'd love to create a bamboo forest and get into the more ecologically friendly sector. The opportunities are endless, but he won't let me do that until he retires. Knowing him, he'll be as stubborn as the Queen of England."

Adeline toed the dirt. The bowl of grapes was almost empty. "That would be super cool to see happen."

"It's what I hope for, anyway. Okay, my turn: Does having a family make you afraid?"

She scrunched her face up in dislike. "That question is too deep."

"Why are you avoiding it?"

"Fine. Yes, I'm afraid," she snapped. "I'm afraid of turning into my father. Sometimes, I get *so* angry I feel like burning down everything around me with a cheap match and a lot of gasoline. I want to *hurt* people, just to share the pain inside me. I would never forgive myself if I brought that onto my family. Maybe it's a pipe dream, especially since he's still alive, but I hope one day to be watching the sunset with people I love, just enjoying the day without any deep, buried terror that my father might show up. That's how I'll know I've made it."

Ryker was quiet as he studied her expression. He sat up. "I don't think it's even remotely possible for you to turn into him. Something inside him is very, *very* broken, but despite everything he did, you never broke."

She let out a bitter laugh and looked away. "Whatever. You've seen my freak-outs. How is that not broken?"

"Existence is hard and freak-outs are mandatory," he said simply. "All things considered, you've done a great job at healing yourself. You're taking responsibility for your own actions and trying to work through things. Leaning into the pain is the fastest way through it."

"But I want him dead," she whispered. "Doesn't that make me super fucked up?"

His features darkened. "I want him dead, too. If that makes you fucked up, then we're in good company."

She smiled, finally looking at him again. "Thank you."

He raised an eyebrow. "For what?"

She offered him the last grape, but he shook his head. Popping it in her mouth, she said, "Actually, remind me to thank your mother for teaching you to be like this."

He let loose a belly laugh. "Don't tell her that. She's too smug already." He checked the time on his phone and smiled. Standing, he held out a hand.

"How do you feel about getting a dog?"

"*A dog?*" Her mouth slackened.

"Yes, a dog. I know Mags would prefer a gun, but I think this might be the better option. At least, it's the fuzzier option."

He had a point. "Where are we going? Shouldn't we ask Mags? With all of those cats it could be a problem."

He glanced at her with amusement. "I already took care of it. The dog we're getting has been raised around them his whole life."

Excitement fluttered in her stomach. "What kind of dog?"

"You'll see."

She scrunched her nose. "I don't like surprises."

"Well, maybe we can change that." Adeline gave up after asking three more times after they climbed into his truck. She sighed and looked out the window, focusing on the thick, lush forest sweeping by. To pass the time, she pulled out her phone. She pulled up Kennedi's number and sent a text.

RYKER IS TAKING ME TO GET A DOG

Text bubbles immediately popped up. ***WHAT.*** Then: ***You need to send me photos ASAP. I can't believe he's didn't ask for me to go. I'm going to send him a picture of my boobs and threaten to take them away if he ever does this again.***

Adeline giggled. Ryker glanced over.

She turned and glared. "What?"

"What made you laugh?"

"I thought you liked secrets?"

He huffed. "I like surprises."

"Same thing," she said sourly.

"Touché."

Her phone went off again. ***Send me photos of the puppy!***

Adeline typed, ***Love you.***

Love you too.

Adeline's heart pitter-pattered with delight. Those words would never get old. With a sigh, she tucked her phone away and watched the miles pass.

It hit her like a brick, the realization that in that particular moment, she felt happy. Even with impending doom catapulting toward them, happiness had clung to her heart. She began to grin like a maniac. She must've made some kind of sound because Ryker gave a loud, theatrical sigh. This time, she beamed when she looked at him.

He raised an eyebrow. "Are you going to tell me this time?"

She released a breath. "I just . . . I just realized that I feel actual happiness right now."

He put his hand in her lap. She grabbed it. It was warm and rough. Steady.

"I'm happy to hear that," he said.

She looked out the window again. "Me too. Meeeee too."

CHAPTER TWENTY-ONE

The truck pulled into a worn-down police station. Outside the front door stood a burly older guy next to a full-grown German Shepherd. The duo watched the truck pull in then glanced at his handler. The man grinned broadly as Ryker stepped out of the vehicle.

"Look at what the cat dragged in!" They shook hands and pulled in for a hugging with rough pats on the back.

"Charlie, ya old git. Looks like time hasn't been on your side." Ryker grinned. The old man hooted with laughter.

"Boy, I have tighty whities older than you. Keep it up, and you don't get ol' Lance here." The dog looked up at Charlie expectantly, ears perked. Adeline walked over timidly. She was intimidated by the large dog—the only dogs she'd ever met had been mean and definitely not for keeping in one's home.

Charlie regarded her. "You must be Addie. Nice to meetcha." He reached toward her with a large hand, and she shook it.

"Is this guy Lance?" She looked at the dog, whose head came up to her hip. Despite the graying on his muzzle, his eyes were alert, and she could see his muscles under his shiny coat. Charlie reached down and ruffled Lance's head. The thick furry tail wagged away some leaves scattered on the pavement.

"Sure is. Retired K9 officer. He's eleven and was forced to retire thanks to some hip issues. Guy's still got it though, don'tcha buddy?" He affectionately grabbed the dog's mouth, and Lance playfully nipped his fingers. "He's the best guard dog you can ask for. Plus, he's older. Needs less exercise. *Plus*, he was raised alongside cats his whole life." Charlie spoke like a proud father. It was cute.

Lance wagged his tail, tongue lopping out of his mouth. Charlie handed Adeline the worn leather leash. It felt like butter. Lance stood and took a step toward her. She reached for the top of his head and tentatively rub his sleek fur. Lance leaned into her touch and looked up at her with big brown eyes. Love at first sight.

Adeline looked between Charlie and Ryker. "Thank you," she said tearfully.

Ryker's grin was so wide his cheeks made him squint. He looked like a sun-kissed god, and for the first time, she wanted to kiss him.

"Here's a list of commands." Charlie handed Ryker a sheet of paper. "It's all in German. Less confusing than English when a perp is screaming." He chuckled at his own joke. Ryker and Charlie shook hands once more, and before Adeline knew it, the three of them were loaded into the truck cab. Lance settled into the backseat, head thrust between theirs, staring out at the road ahead.

"*Sichern*," Ryker ordered. Lance immediately obeyed. Ryker smiled at Adeline. "Already off to a good start."

After a quick drive, they pulled up in front of Mags' home. The lights cast shadows across the dark garden. Lance perked up, sticking his head between them again. Adeline smiled and scratched below his jaw, and Lance licked her cheek. They unloaded, and Lance jumped to the curb.

"*Sitz.*" Adeline felt a rush of excitement as Lance obeyed, sitting as quickly as two magnets connecting. She hadn't given an order in over four years. It felt good to have something in this world to listen to her.

"Talk to me like that and you might find yourself another guy willing to be obedient," Ryker teased as they walked up the pathway.

"Down, boy." Giggling, Adeline gave him an admonishing glare. It was met with a boyish, dimpled grin. A heart stopping one, too. It fanned the growing flames of safety she felt around him. Ryker was patient and kind. Empathy practically oozed from him. Her distrust was almost faded, being replaced with something new; young. Now he colluded with Mags to get her a protection dog? It melted her heart like soft wax against a flame.

Feeling lighter than a glistening soap bubble, Adeline opened the door to find a beaming Mags already squatting down to greet Lance.

"Oh, who's a good boy. You're a good boy. Sweet boy. Big boy," Mags cooed.

The baby voice seemed out of place, but it made Adeline grin. Lance aggressively flopped onto the floor and revealed his soft tummy to Mags. A couple of cats came up to investigate and were immediately insulted as he tried to lick them. Yeah, Adeline thought, he'd be just fine.

"Leftovers in the fridge," Mags called after Ryker and Adeline as they headed to the kitchen. Sure enough, two plates were set aside, featuring leftover pot roast. Adeline's mouth watered. They pulled out the food, and Adeline spotted Lance waiting patiently for his own serving. She looked at Ryker.

"Do you have food for him?"

"Check the second shelf," Mags hollared from the living room. Adeline found a bowl of boiled chicken and rice ready to go, too. She pulled it out and showed it to Lance.

"Want some of this?" The handsome dog sniffed it and wagged his tail furiously—a stamp of approval if she ever saw one. Popping the bowl into the microwave, Ryker set their places on the table and filled two glasses of water. Adeline set down a bowl of water for Lance and put the food next to it. The three of them sat in the kitchen, eating in comfortable silence. This moment in time would be titled, *Peace*.

She could get used to this.

When they were done, Ryker collected the plates and began washing them in the sink. It was such a strange sight, seeing a man doing something domestic. As he focused on drying off their plates, she watched his fingers as they rolled the towel around the plates' edges. He had nice fingers. Nimble like a pianist but thick enough to give her dirty thoughts.

He caught her staring. "Like what you see?" he teased.

She bit her lip and nodded slowly. In the recent weeks, she'd found herself more at ease around him. The triggers seemed to have faded to the point that only occasionally did she need to take a minute. In that time, he'd been so patient.

But she also desperately didn't want to trigger in front of him again. Objectively, she understood that people can't move on without stepping forward first. At least she was positive he'd be fine if she did happen to freak out again.

Regardless, it took serious willpower to ask, "Do you want to go upstairs with me?" The question made her palms sweaty.

He slid the last plate back into the cupboard and tossed the dishtowel onto the counter. He faced her, leaning back. His expression was a mix of curious and guarded. "Are you sure? Last time was difficult, and I don't want to upset you.."

She winced. "I can't keep living in fear, Ry. I don't know if it's going to be any better, but if you're up to it, I'd like to go upstairs with you."

His expression softened. "Of course. Do you want to do anything differently?"

She stood. "I mean, maybe don't walk behind me this time?"

"Is there a better way?"

She shook her head. "Not really. My experiences have… But maybe… " Maybe what? She'd been introduced to her father's business partners in so many ways, from being led, to leading them, to—

"You don't have to," Ryker said softly. He stepped closer, looking ready to leave if she even hinted at wanting him gone. He truly wanted her to be happy, in any form. Her comfort was a priority, something no man had ever done. Even her father, offering all the comforts in the world, a little bit of her always knew there would be a cost. It took her years to understand this. As a kid, it was impossible for her to articulate the fear, but she watched her mother with him — she remembered their fights. Her mother's fear. He'd always give her expensive gifts or experiences. when she hit puberty, and she expressed gratitude, he began to say, "Thank me later."

It didn't properly sink in until the end of the first year of incarceration, what he meant. When she realized it had never been a joke, she could barely eat for two weeks.

Ryker was here, ready for whatever she was okay with. She could ask him to sleep in the kitchen pantry with her, and she bet he'd say yes.

"Would you sleep in the kitchen pantry with me?" she blurted out. Immediately, her cheeks reddened. "Sorry, that was a stupid—"

"If it makes you feel more comfortable, sure."

Stunned, Adeline stared at him, mouth parted. And just like that, her doubts flew away. Smiling, she held out a hand. "Just lay in bed with me?" She gave a cheeky grin. "Maybe without your shirt on?"

His eyes twinkled with amusement as he took her hand and followed as she led them upstairs. Lance followed closely behind. Reaching her room, Ryker commanded him to stand guard in the hallway. The dog circled for a moment before settling into a tiny ball against the wall.

When they were finally in her room, Adeline breathed a sigh of relief—they'd made it this far without a freak-out. Maybe Lance helped break up the trigger. Lucas had never incorporated animals into her services, although it was probably inevitable. Especially as she got older—humiliations evolve.

Adeline walked over to the bed while Ryker closed the door. The sound made her freeze. A million memories bombarded her senses at once. Her body went rigid and her heart jumped into a gallop. The sound of blood pumping in her ears made it hard to hear him say, "Are you okay?"

She turned around stiffly, fighting the urge to lunge at him; claw his eyes out.

I am safe. He isn't going to hurt me. I am safe. He isn't going to hurt me.

She repeated this while attempting to get a grip on her emotions. Ryker waited by the door. No fear or judgment in his eyes. The air in her lungs quickened, and she dug her nails into her palms.

Ryker relaxed, turning his shoulders away from her. It shrunk his bulk, making him appear less threatening. He crossed the room slowly, headed for the opposite side of the bed. She swallowed a scream of pure rage. Since her father began selling her, she'd kept these emotions safely locked away. Showing it—ever—led to painful and terrifying experiences.

She'd felt like a caged beast, full of fury and grief. Without her father keeping her in check, the emotions were overwhelming, like hot coals threatening to burn her insides to a crisp. Stars danced in her vision as she watched Ryker bend down and pick up a pillow. He held it out to her.

"Want to scream into it?"

The question was so surprising, her anger ebbed for a moment. "What?"

He motioned toward her with the pillow. "Scream into the pillow. It helps me sometimes, when life just sucks. Plus, you can't hurt its feelings."

Impulsively, she snatched it out of his hand and slammed her face into it. Utter darkness consumed her as she roared again and again into the downy pillow. The release of so much emotion caused her knees to buckle, and she fell to the floor, the wood cracking against her knees. The pain was a speck against what she felt.

She continued to scream until the rage was spent—for now. It seemed like an endless pool of fury, the only thing holding it back being the shell of her own mortal body. She came up for air. The pillowcase was soaked from her tears. She wiped her cheeks and looked at Ryker. Twice now, he'd stood in this room and given her the space needed to feel every raw emotion possible. Even in the moment, his eyes followed her every movement. His hands flexed repeatedly, and she noticed the tension hardening the line of his lips. He looked like he wanted to join her in the war against her demons.

If only it were that simple.

"Thank you." The words cracked on her tongue, her throat sore from screaming.

He exhaled deeply. "Of course. How do you feel?"

She assessed herself. "Like shit."

He nodded in understanding. "Do you want me to leave?"

A part of her was desperate to say yes, but she shook her head instead. "No. If you're okay with it, I'd like you to stay."

"Do you still want my shirt off?" Nothing in his face even hinted that he was teasing.

"No, not right now. But... " She looked over at the bed. "Will you lay with me?"

He nodded. "Absolutely."

Sweaty strands of hair stuck to her forehead. There was no way she could stay fully dressed. She took off her pants, avoiding his gaze. As she did this, she saw him reach behind and remove the pistol tucked into the waistband of his jeans. He placed it on the nightstand. She'd so many weapons, it didn't even phase her. It might've even give a bit of comfort.

Adeline pulled back the top sheet and slid underneath. Ryker waited until she patted the space beside her before settling on top of the sheet. They turned to face each other, their bodies so close his heat radiated onto her skin. She breathed in his scent, enjoying the smell of fresh rain on earth and wood. She settled a hand under her cheek as she searched his face. He rested his head against the inside of his elbow.

"Is this okay?" he whispered.

She nodded. "Yes." After a pause, she said, "Thank you."

"For what?"

She wiggled slightly closer but still avoided his touch. "For letting me lose my shit. For being patient. For listening."

His expression turned serious. "Addie, you are worth it. The more I know you, the more I want you safe. You're incredible."

He swept a strand of hair from her cheek. She ducked her head.

"I'm not incredible. I'm just trying to survive."

He brought his forefinger and thumb under her chin and gently tipped her head up to look at him.

"To survive is to be incredible." He swallowed hard. "And you don't just survive; you're fighting back. I admire that."

She instinctively leaned into him. "Can you just hold me?"

He wrapped one large arm around her torso, and she snuggled closer, her face nestled between his pecs. He stroked her back slowly, causing her to release every last bit of tension. Before she knew it, she'd fallen into a dreamless sleep.

CHAPTER TWENTY-TWO

So how are you feeling?" Kennedi nervously shredded a paper napkin into tiny pieces. It was her turn to stay with Adeline while Mags and Ryker ran errands and went to work, respectively.

She had on black corduroy shorts and a Nirvana T-shirt. In her hands was a big mug filled with almost more milk than coffee. Adeline looked over from the eggs sizzling on the stove and cursed when a glob of fat singed her arm. Lance's ears perked up—he stood guard five feet away, making sure all dropped food received immediate attention. So far, he'd been disappointed.

Adeline sighed. "I don't know anymore. I almost never know how I feel, honestly. After years of trying not to feel or react, sometimes it's impossible to do either."

Kennedi took a sip of her coffee. "Makes sense. Has it been getting better?"

Adeline removed the pan from the stove and forked the eggs onto two plates next to slices of bacon. She grabbed two pieces of toast from the toaster and plated them next to the eggs. "I've been painting more, trying to access those feelings. Mags swears the more I paint, the better I'll feel." She shrugged. "I'm just trying to trust the process."

It was undeniable: her work had improved. It wasn't about perfection, but the colors, the texture, the overall feel had grown brighter with every passing week. Healing from trauma wasn't linear, as evidenced by the shredded canvas left in a corner of the art room, sliced repeatedly with a butcher knife. Mags stood in the doorway as she'd done it, cackling like a witch, going so far as to give Adeline the weapon. That moment was called *Enabler*.

Kennedi moved her coffee aside to make room on the table for her food. She grabbed a fork and began digging in as Adeline sat down next to her.

"What are we going to do about Lucas?" Kennedi asked with a mouthful of food.

Adeline tore off a piece of bacon and tossed it to Lance. Popping the other half into her mouth, she said, "I might have to try and strike a deal or something. Because you're right; he isn't going to stop. Why would he? To him, I'm a toy gone rogue." She hesitated. "I'm considering calling him."

Kennedi's eyes flashed with alarm. "Are you sure that's wise?"

Adeline stabbed at her eggs. "No, of course not. But the only other option is to wait around to see what happens next. I'm tired of waiting in fear. I've been afraid for so long. It's time to be done with it."

"When do you think you'll do it?"

Adeline stared at her plate. She chewed the inside of her cheek. Was it too early to start drinking? "After breakfast, I guess. Get it over with."

Kennedi stayed silent as they finished their breakfast. When they were done, Kennedi cleared the plates while Adeline filled the cats' bowls. The horde rushed in; the sounds of meows and hisses sent Lance fleeing down the hall. Adeline laughed.

Finished with the dishes, they went upstairs upstairs, and closed the door to her room behind her. Adeline flopped onto her bed with a groan. Lance curled up on a carpet by the bed. Kennedi crawled onto the bed, facing Adeline, and nestled her head into a pillow.

"Should we tell Mags?" Kennedi asked, stitching her brows together in thought.

Adeline quirks a smile. "Probably. But I need to do this for myself. I can't let her be my defender, forever, you know?"

Kennedi didn't look convinced, but Adeline pushed aside the doubt. She could do this. She broke Alexander's nose.

Adeline scooted closer, dropping her head to the pillow, their knees brushing. "Thank you for being here," she whispered, sweeping back one of Kennedi's curls.

Kennedi blushed. "When my dad made me move, I knew you'd come back to me. A part of me always waited. Of course, I never would have dreamed—or wanted—it to be under these circumstances, but I'm happy to be around you no matter what."

"You're all I've wanted, too," Adeline breathed. She reached for the quilt and dragged it over them. Kennedi giggled and burrowed closer. She pulled the blanket over their heads, cloaking them in darkness.

The tension was immediate. The darkness and the scent of Kennedi returned Adeline to a place of innocence: hours spent telling ghost stories in blanket forts, trying to scare each other; shadow puppets and secrets.

It had all been so innocent, even when they first realized they wanted to try kissing. Awkward teens, too nervous to admit their feelings, until one night, Adeline looked at Kennedi and it all changed. The yearning for that one moment made her heart sing. She had carried it with her; it had kept her sane.

"Do you remember our blanket forts?" Kennedi whispered.

Adeline closed her eyes. "Yeah."

Kennedi snuggled up to her. "Do you remember the first time we kissed?"

Adeline laughed softly and inched her face closer. "You were so surprised. I almost thought you wouldn't like it and we would stop being friends."

"I've always wondered…" Adeline heard the silver lip ring hit teeth as Kennedi sucked in her lower lip. "I've always wondered why you did it. Why did you kiss me?"

Adeline searched her mind. They were freshmen at the time, still trying to figure out puberty. Kennedi worried she wouldn't know how to kiss Blake Vernon, the cutest boy in school. Seeing Kennedi there, under the tower of one of their blanket forts, fretting about accidentally licking Blake's nose—Adeline had just kissed her. Her mouth crashed onto Kennedi's so hard, they'd both yelped.

Where Adeline had expected rejection, Kennedi had rebounded with a second, eager kiss, one that didn't hurt. After, when their lips were sore from kissing so much, they gorged themselves on chocolate and cereal. They never spoke of it again. Adeline assumed it to have been a fluke, a late-night exploration by teenagers.

But she'd never forgotten about it, and when Kennedi wrote that letter, when she said she had feelings to share . . . Adeline had spent years wondering if that kiss had had anything to do with it.

Adeline found her way to the present, to the absolutely perfect person in front of her. "I kissed you because another second without your lips on mine sounded impossible." Adeline brought a hand to Kennedi's cheek. "And if you're okay with it, I'd like to continue avoiding the impossible forever."

"I only want possibilities." Kennedi's words were wisps of tenderness. Adeline grabbed a handful of Kennedi's hair and tugged, baring Kennedi's throat. Kennedi arched back, a hand to Adeline's shoulder.

The first taste of Kennedi ripped through Adeline, eliciting a deep, carnal moan. It was instantaneous and unforgiving. Waiting and taking their time was off the table—Adeline needed her *now*.

She trailed her fingers up one of Kennedi's thighs, stopping at the top, playing with the edge of Kennedi's shorts. Kennedi's hips gyrated. Adeline nestled her free hand between her delectable thick thighs, enjoying the way Kennedi's hips moved in time with the slow circles she made with her fingers, pressing gently on her clit.

Suddenly, touching Kennedi through her pants wasn't enough.

"Take those off." She tugged at Kennedi's shorts.

"Only if you do."

They both giggled as they sat up and wriggled out of their clothes—first shorts and shirts and then bras and panties. Kennedi's body took Adeline's breath away. Her skin was pale, a complete contrast to Ryker's deep golden brown. Her breasts were luscious, her light pink nipples begging for attention. And those *curves*. Adeline's mouth actually watered. She reached for Kennedi but the red-head dodged her hands.

"Please let me touch you," Adeline pleaded. Kennedi tilted her head like a predator considering its next meal.

"No. Me first."

Adeline's breath caught. "Are you sure?"

Kennedi's eyes glittered as they roved over Adeline's body. "I'm positive."

Kennedi pushed Adeline onto her back and straddled her hips. Adeline gasped sharply as Kennedi's slick heat brushed against hers.

Kennedi settled her weight onto Adeline, who couldn't stop herself from sinking her nails into every inch of ample flesh. Adeline's shoulders flexed as she yanked Kennedi's hips forward and pushed them back again. Felt her thick ass cheeks rubbing against her clit, pleasure igniting her every nerve.

Kennedi rocked her hips with impressive force and dropped her head back, eyes closed. Adeline watched, mesmerized. She licked her thumb and brought it to Kennedi's clit, enjoying Kennedi's sharp hiss as she made slow circles. Groaning, Kennedi slid her hands from Adeline's hips to her breasts and tugged her nipples roughly.

"Gods, you're beautiful," Adeline whispered, running her free palm up Kennedi's sternum to her neck. Kennedi moaned so loudly that Lance popped up to make sure she was okay. Adeline laughed and shooed him away. Kennedi stared at Adeline with hooded eyes.

"You haven't seen anything yet," she panted. Then, before Adeline could register what was happening, Kennedi swung off and tapped Adeline's knees. Adeline obeyed, pulling her knees up, letting them fall to the sides, baring every inch of her pussy. Kennedi settled on her stomach. Her curls brushed against Adeline's inner thighs. Adeline dug her fingers into the quilt as Kennedi's warm breath swept across her wetness. From between Adeline's thighs, Kennedi peered up. Adeline moaned, trying to resist squeezing her thighs shut.

"May I?"

All Adeline could do was nod. No one had ever done this before. She wasn't even sure she would like it.

"Hold on," Kennedi warned. *Hold on for what?* Adeline wondered. But her confusion was short-lived. Stars exploded in her vision, pleasure thrumming through her in tidal waves as Kennedi's tongue leisurely swiped through her folds.

"Holy fucking shit," Adeline yelped, her backing arching so hard, she thought her spine might snap. Just as Adeline felt her body begin to relax, Kennedi's mouth vibrated with a chuckle, and Adeline went taut again. There was no way she could endure much more of this, and she said as much.

Kennedi looked up, mouth glistening. "You're gonna learn today what a good mouth-fucking feels like."

Adeline allowed herself to sink into the sensations, eagerly meeting every new feeling with a sense of gratitude. Each nip, suck, and lick dragged her to the heavens. Kennedi swung an arm around Adeline's hip, pinning her pelvis into place.

Just as Adeline felt like she was getting the hang of things, she felt a finger at her entrance. She whimpered. Clutched the brass headboard for dear life. It was one of the most exquisite experiences as Kennedi's finger slid in at a torturous pace. She was ready to beg for more and almost screamed as Kennedi dragged her finger in and out, taking her time, clearly enjoying Adeline's reactions.

"Jesus fucking Christ, I don't know how much more I can take!"

Kennedi ignored Adeline's desperation and began to pick up the pace. Her tongue swirled more furiously, turning Adeline's pleasure into a whirlpool that drilled into her core. When Kennedi added a second finger, this time plunging it inside without hesitation, Adeline finally screamed unintelligible words. Her hips bucked with such velocity, Kennedi had no choice but to rise and fall with her. She never once lost touch with Adeline's pussy.

Those magical fingers pistoned with skill, knowing exactly what she needed. Suddenly, reality exploded into sharp shards of ecstasy, and Adeline's core thrummed with a level of euphoria that seemed impossible to bear. The bed frame creaked under the strength of her pull, but she didn't even notice. Kennedi slowed her pace as Adeline came back down to earth. She slid her fingers out gently.

The room was silent but for their panting. Kennedi sat up, moving like a satiated cat. She popped two fingers into her mouth.

"Mmm," she murmured, taking time to lick them clean.

Adeline was a puddle of nothing and everything. She grinned. "My turn."

Kennedi stilled as Adeline gently cupped her swollen breasts, thumbs rubbing the pebbled nipples. Adeline licked her lips and sucked on one of them, grazing her teeth against the sensitive flesh. Kennedi gasped and rocked forward. The sound blazed through Adeline's core, and she groaned, desperate for more of everything.

Adeline brought her mouth to Kennedi's, swallowing each tiny moan as she dragged a finger lightly against Kennedi's slick folds. She yanked Kennedi's head back, demanding more. Kennedi eagerly offered everything she had, their tongues dancing and clashing with unsatiated needs.

Adeline hesitated as they both came up for air. Kennedi's eyes popped open, scanning Adeline's face. "What's wrong?"

Adeline's cheeks burned. "I'm desperate to taste you, but I'm afraid of being really bad at it."

She let go of Kennedi's hair, cringing at her own admission. Even though she knew Kennedi wouldn't reject her, there was still a little niggle in the back of her brain.

A slow grin spread across Kennedi's face. "I can take charge, if you want?"

Adeline sighed with relief. "That would be awesome."

"Can I be bossy?" Kennedi's eyes twinkled with mischief. "You can tell me to bring it down a notch at any time. Until you set a boundary, I'm going full throttle, cool?"

Adeline raised an eyebrow. "Sure?"

Slowly, Kennedi shifted off the bed and stood. Adeline's eyes were lustful as she basked in the glory of Kennedi's curves. She settled on the patch of hair between Kennedi's thighs. Every inch of Adeline ached for this stunning woman whom she had spent years craving, missing, and wishing for. Standing tall, Kennedi beckoned with one finger.

"Grab a pillow."

Adeline obeyed, grabbing one of the pink-and-brown floral pillows. Kennedi motioned to the ground in front of her.

"Kneel."

Adeline was eager to do what Kennedi asked. If it had been a man, it was unlikely she would be eager to obey, but it was Kennedi— the safest place she knew of. She tossed the pillow to the floor and got down on her knees so that Kennedi's pussy was eye level. The heady scent of her arousal only intensified Adeline's cravings. A bead of dew was caught in the patch of hair. Adeline licked her lips. Kennedi raised Adeline's chin with a finger, loving the massive silver-dollar eyes that met hers. The pad of her thumb played with Adeline's bottom lip before inserting itself.

"Suck."

Adeline's velvet lips wrapped around her thumb, sucking greedily.

"Are you hungry, Adeline?"

Adeline's eyes watered as she nodded with the finger in her mouth. Kennedi slipped her finger out of Adeline's mouth and swung a leg up, perching her foot on the edge of the bed. Her pussy was open, slick folds spreading like an invitation.

"Do you want to continue?" Kennedi said softly. Adeline, incapable of looking anywhere else, gave a stiff nod. "Say it," Kennedi ordered.

"I want it." Her voice was ragged; her lungs were barely able to function.

"Then I want you to feast on my pussy. You have five minutes to make me cum."

That caught Adeline's attention. "I've never done this before. How could I possibly—"

"Someone is wasting time," Kennedi chided. "Just use your tongue, spell the alphabet with it, pretend the only way you can breathe is if you suck on my clit hard enough."

Kennedi shifted her hips, inching forward. Needing no other prompting, Adeline leaned in and started eagerly dragging her tongue from the bottom of Kennedi's soaking wet slit up to the nub, like Kennedi had done to her. Kennedi rocked her head back, eyes closed.

Encouraged, Adeline melted into the experience, exploring Kennedi's body with her tongue. She raised a finger and swiped it through Kennedi's wetness before sliding it inside past her entrance.

It sank into the wet warmth like a hot knife through butter. Kennedi's knees threatened to buckle, but Adeline's other hand came up and grabbed her ass, offering support as she added a second finger, sliding them in and out vigorously.

"Faster," Kennedi urged, hips undulating furiously. Adeline obeyed, humming with satisfaction, sending Kennedi over the edge. Feeling Kennedi's pussy pulsate around her fingers was the greatest thing she'd ever felt. She fell into delirium, reveling in this pulsating pleasure. Kennedi's hips jerked forward, desperate for every last drop of paradise.

When Kennedi's orgasm finally abated, Adeline carefully slid her fingers out and peered up, still on her knees. It was like nothing else, locking her gaze on those glittering green eyes.

"You are a fucking goddess," Kennedi murmured, bringing her leg down from the bed. She reached down and helped Adeline to her feet. Upright again, Adeline leaned down and kissed Kennedi on the mouth. The mix of their flavors sparked that same ember of lust all over again.

If sex were like this every time, they'd never get anything done.

CHAPTER TWENTY-THREE

Adeline stared at her phone. She and Kennedi sat on the bed, fully clothed, their post-coital bliss fading with every second. Twisting her hair into a bun, she weighed the pros and cons of calling Lucas.

Pro number one: She'd be standing up for herself.

Con number one: It could make her father go berserk. He might show up and gun them all down. Or have Alexander do it, while Lucas watched on the lawn, smoking a cigar.

Pro number two: She'd finally start standing up for herself.

Con number two: He might recapture her, sterilize her, and possibly actually sell her to someone so he wouldn't have to deal with her ever again.

Pro number three: There didn't seem to be any other pros.

Con number three: There were so many, she didn't want to take the time to consider them all.

Her heart drummed at an impossible pace. Taking a deep breath, she focused on her lungs expanding.

"Are you sure you want to do this right now?" Kennedi asked, sitting on the edge of the mattress. She put her hand on Adeline's still-sweaty thigh.

"I don't have a choice." *Liar.* Adeline had plenty of choices, but she was choosing the road less traveled.

Kennedi brought her hand to Adeline's back, rubbing up and down. "I'm here for you." Adeline offered a faint smile in return, swallowing the impulse to vomit.

Kennedi paused her hand and gave a serious look. "If you're going to chuck, please give me time to at least grab the trash can."

Swallowing bile, Adeline picked up the phone. She inhaled sharply and dialed the number she had memorized. He answered on the first ring.

"Hello, pet."

At that single word, all of Adeline's confidence unraveled, dark memories opening inside her like a yawning void inside her very being. She exhaled lungs deflating like a balloon. Kennedi patted her back, motioning with her other hand, trying to get Adeline to say something.

"Hi."

Did she really just say "hi"? *Brilliant start, you idiot.* Her palms moistened. She cleared her throat. "I mean, we need to talk."

"Hmm," he purred. "That's never a good thing to hear. Are you about to try and break up with me?"

She winced. Fresh beads of sweat rimmed her hairline, adrenaline like a pickaxe to her nerves.

He sighed. "Pet, why did you even call me? To heavy-breathe and hope that something good might come of it? Why don't you just come back to me today, and I promise nothing else bad will happen to your friends."

Old familiar rage roared from her gut, incinerating every hesitation. She sat up straight and clutched that rage that festered inside her.

"I'm going to come find you, and I will fucking kill you."

Her father laughed deeply and then sighed with amusement. "Oh, I hope so. I mean, Alexander will gut you before you even come close, but I like that you still have fire. I thought I'd suffocated it all. What a joy to know my daughter has the same tenacious spirit as me."

Adeline ground her teeth and snarled. "I'm going to make you regret what you did to me."

"I welcome the excitement. Come find me, pet. Oh, and tell Kennedi I'm glad she's feeling better."

The line went dead. He'd hung up.

Adeline's rage was a living thing—a furious beast with a fiery gullet, ready to devour and torched everything in its wake. It burned from the center of her being, the years of thick chains holding it back finally cracking and shaking loose.

She needed to *do* something. Destroy something and channel her fury. Adeline threw her phone so hard against a wall that it shattered into a million pieces. Kennedi cried out, surprised. She reached for Adeline, only to be shrugged off as Adeline bolted out of the room and rushed downstairs.

Lance yipped, trailing after her. Kennedi called out to her, telling her to stop, but Adeline's need was compulsive—she had to put this furious energy into something. She swept past a startled Mags and made a beeline for the backdoor. Outside, she dashed into the garden and snatched up a shovel.

All the while, she screamed and raged and sobbed. Her thoughts were only wailing sounds, more feelings than thoughts.

It was all so fucking unfair. She hadn't asked for any of it. What she'd thought had been a perfectly idyllic childhood was merely grooming by a man with a twisted sense of ownership. Every single nice thing that twisted man had ever done for her had been tallied—what he felt she owed him. And for years, even through her aching need to escape, she felt that pull of duty; of owing.

Adeline drove the shovel into the pliant earth and began chucking mounds of dirt behind her, crumbs of it raining down on her face. Each swing of dirt, worms, and weeds stoked the inferno, cremating every single feeble part left inside. For four years, she'd been isolated, raped, beaten, and degraded.

She'd lost out on so much—Lucas had *stolen* so much from her, and would continue to do so if she didn't do something about it. Waiting around for him to act only gave him the control he craved.

A small hand tentatively touched her shoulder. Adeline halted in her frenzy, turning her head to find Kennedi staring down at her. A sob breached Adeline's fury. She felt a chunk of dirt fall off her cheek and onto the grass. Kennedi reached down and cupped one of Adeline's dirty cheeks.

"He took so much from me," Adeline croaked, every muscle shaking.

Kennedi's face twisted with pain. "I know."

"He isn't going to stop." Her lungs burned with each word, exhaustion already seeping into her joints. She dropped the shovel, unable to hold it any longer.

Kennedi trailed her hand up to the back of Adeline's head and brought their foreheads together. Adeline's shoulders sagged with defeat. Kennedi's free hand grabbed Adeline's dirty one and squeezed.

"Whatever you need, I'll make it happen. It's you and me, Addie."

"And me." Mags sat on the porch steps, watching the exchange, a fierce glint in her iceberg eyes. "Family is there for each other, no matter what."

Family. Adeline almost choked on the surge of emotions. She had a real family, people who would stand by her side until the end. Pulling away from Kennedi, Adeline wiped away the grime on her forehead with a filthy hand, smearing it. "I'm going to kill Lucas."

Mags grunted and crossed her arms, the creepiest expression unfurling as she raised her red glasses and rested them on the top of her head, then rolled up the sleeves of her light pink painter's shirt. "Well, it's about time, girly. Got a plan? 'Cause I have plenty."

***

Adeline didn't expect the amount of enthusiasm that Mags and Kennedi brought to plotting a murder. Scratch that—Mags' blood-thirst was a honed skill. There was a spark in her eye that almost made her feel bad for Lucas. *Almost.* The unexpected part was Kennedi's bringing equal amounts of determination to the planning process.

While Adeline brewed tea, Kennedi and Mags sat at the kitchen table with notepads, stickies, and pens strewn across the kitchen tabletop. Post-freak-out, exhaustion had gripped Adeline's bones. Functioning felt like wading through mud. As the kettle reached a boil, she heard Kennedi whisper something to Mags.

Mags responded, "Do you think Ryker would be into that?"

"I don't know if we should bring Ryker into this," Adeline said flatly.

"Shouldn't you let him decide that?" Mags challenged. "He's been game for everything to this point. You're doing the boy a disservice by not at least asking him."

Adeline stared at her dirty hands as she filled a mug with water and then added a green tea bag and watched it sink to the bottom.

"You're right, but I need to think. We aren't just dealing with my dad; Alexander will be there, whenever 'there' ends up being. You've never met the man—he's a walking, evil lump of fuckery."

"All the more reason to have a man involved."

"I need time to think." Mags opened her mouth to ask a question, but Adeline stopped her with a raised hand. "I need to take a shower and think some more before we come up with some diabolical plot."

By the time she was upstairs—Lance dodging past as she closed the bathroom door—she heard them arguing about whether or not they should skin Lucas alive. *Alexander will gut you before you even come close.* Whatever they ended up planning, they had no choice but to account for Alexander, too. She shivered at the thought of the two men on Mags' front lawn.

Right before she stepped into the shower, she sent Ryker a text.

Big developments. Mags is excited.

He responded within seconds: ***If Mags is excited, I'm in. Do you need me right now? I have some vendors showing up for orders.***

Lucas wasn't going to suddenly show up—probably—so murder plotting could wait. **Yeah, it can wait.**

See you tomorrow.

She stepped into the shower and sighed as water trailed down her body. She grabbed a bottle of shampoo and lathered up, enjoying the smell of lemons, and watched the dirt swirl down the drain—a makeshift baptism.

It had been almost three months since she'd escaped. In that time, everything had changed. Not just her surroundings and friends, but something integral inside her had shifted.

She was ready to go to war.

CHAPTER TWENTY-FOUR

Steam roiled over the edge of Adeline's mug with the smell of Baileys mixed with coffee. She took a sip and savored the way it burned. It was probably too much booze, but it was the only way to smooth the rough edges of her anxiety. A bird dropped onto a hanging feeder nearby, catching her attention.

The morning light was hazy with cloud cover, revealing bright light that was quickly covered by thick clouds. In the back of Mags' yard stood tall pine trees, the branches spaced out enough to let brilliant golden light dance along the beds of marigolds and sunflowers.

The beauty couldn't hold a flame to the constant unease. It had been a week since the phone call with her father, and they were all on high alert. Mags had taken to sleeping on the couch with her shotgun by her side. Ryker slept in the rocking chair in Adeline's bedroom while Kennedi slept in the bed with her. During the waking hours, they plotted, knowing their plan had to be absolutely perfect.

Unsurprisingly, Ryker had been on board with everything.

Mags and Ryker sat in their rocking chairs a few feet away, huddled together, narrowing down the different plans they had mapped out, while Adeline just stared at the garden. Bone-weary and worn down, the anxiety made it difficult for her to think.

She was grateful for how enthusiastic they were about wanting to kill off her father—an odd thing to appreciate—but all she wanted to do at the moment was curl up and sleep. The reality of the situation had fully caught up with her; it gnawed at what little peace she had attained.

A selfish part of her was glad she didn't need to face her father alone anymore. A shared burden always felt lighter. In the corner of her eye, she saw Ryker shooting furtive glances her way, between taking notes and brainstorming with Mags. The two of them could plan whatever they wanted—Adeline was in no frame of mind to plan an unsolvable murder. At that moment, she was too fried to think.

She rocked gently in the dark brown rocking chair, the sound of old wood creaking soothing the raging inferno scorching her insides. The wall she had built around her deepest, darkest feelings had come down. It was time to embrace her pain. The way to get over pain was to move through it.

"—what do you think, Addie?"

Ryker's voice hauled her back to the present. Adeline startled, realizing they were looking at her.

"Sorry, what?"

Mags smiled patiently. "We're just discussing your father's murder. We were wondering what you think about any of these plans."

Ryker offered Adeline a piece of paper. The words were clumps of letters her brain couldn't process. She handed it back. "Whatever you think is good."

Ryker frowned, placing the notes on his lap. "There's a lot that involves you, Addie. Literally all of it. And we haven't narrowed anything down."

Their stares drilled into her. She sighed and put her coffee down. Drawing in a deep breath, she looked each of them in the eye. "Whatever it takes to get me in the same place as him. I don't care about anything else. I want to watch the life drain out of him. I want to move the fuck on. I *want* to want things and *get* them."

"What did I miss?"

They looked to the backdoor, where Kennedi's face peered through the screen. Her normally unruly hair was damp and braided. She came outside, a glass of water in hand.

"Oh, not much. We have a list of ideas, all of which involve the death of you-know-who," Mags responded dryly.

Kennedi disappeared then reappeared with a chair, which she brought out to the porch and set between Ryker and Adeline. She plopped down, snatched the paper in Ryker's lap, and started skimming their plans.

"I like the first one, convincing him to meet us in the middle of nowhere. Taking out Alexander first is a solid idea. I also like the idea of holding them at gunpoint and making them dig their own graves." She glanced at Adeline. "How would we get them there?"

Ryker gave Adeline an uneasy look. "What if I called him and said I'd bring you in for a reward?"

Adeline looked away, preferring to watch the marigolds sway in the soft breeze. A strand of loose hair tickled her cheek. She tucked it behind an ear and looked back at Ryker. "He'd like that, thinking someone I care about is betraying me."

"It's a good plan," Mags murmured.

Kennedi gave Mags a sharp look. "What if he reneges and kills all of us on the spot?"

Frustration lashed inside Adeline's chest. Even explaining how exhausted she was sounded exhausting. "He's going to try to do that regardless. It'll be about breaking me down into nothing, so I never fight back ever again. The only way that will happen is if all of you are dead."

Kennedi folded the paper and handed it to Mags. "That settles it then. Tomorrow, we decide on the time and place. Then Ryker can give him a call."

"I'd like to do some training tomorrow morning," Mags announced, standing with a groan. "You all need as much preparation as possible." She stretched. "I'm going to bed early. It's been quite the day."

"Understatement of the year," Ryker said under his breath.

Kennedi and Ryker looked at Adeline, waiting to see what she wanted to do. Adeline studied them, her heart cracking. She hadn't noticed how tired Ryker looked—there were dark bags beneath his eyes and his hair was unbrushed and stuck out at the sides. Kennedi didn't look much better. Her brow furrowed with concern.

Adeline asked, "Can we just go upstairs and cuddle?"

Kennedi nodded and reached out a hand. "Come on."

Adeline took her hand and let both of them lead the way. Mags was already in her bedroom, four cats meowing outside the door. It cracked open, and they scurried in, then the door clicked shut again.

Ryker looked at Adeline and nodded toward the mattress. "Do you want to go to bed?"

"Not really." Adeline walked over to her closet, shoving the doors apart. Inside were her meager amount of clothes, all hand-me-downs from Mags. The kindness was appreciated, but the lack of independence made her heart ache. Nothing was hers—nothing ever really had been, not even her own body. Every inch of her had been owned by her father. It was time for that to change.

Without thinking, she pulled her shirt over her head and tossed it in the laundry hamper. Her pants were quick to follow. She turned and put her hands on her hips, dressed only in a mismatched bra and panties. Kennedi's eyes trailed up her body, with more concern than lust. Ryker's darted between them.

"I'm tired of being this person," Adeline announced as she marched over to her bed. She sat on the edge, facing them, and patted either side. Neither budged. Kennedi cleared her throat.

"Uh, Addie? What are you doing?"

Adeline huffed. "I told you. I'm tired of being this person. Of being afraid. I can't do it anymore. This whole plan could fail, and I don't want to die without knowing what it's like to enjoy sex with both of you. Together."

Ryker's eyes widened. The tension in the room thickened. Kennedi peered over at Ryker with raised eyebrows. He felt her gaze and met it. Finally, Kennedi grinned and reached back for the bottom of her braid.

Adeline watched as those nimble fingers began untwisting the hair tie that held back the red mess of curls. Knowing exactly how it felt to have her fingers in those curls made a deep need zing inside her core.

"So, what do you need?" Ryker finally asked. Adeline licked her lips and stared pointedly at his groin.

He shifted on his feet. "Adeline, we tried… Remember?"

"Yes, but Kennedi wasn't here," she pointed out, slowly widening her thighs. He refused to look down.

"Yes… but…" He looked between the two of them, dragging his attention to Kennedi, who was taking off her shirt. She tossed it into the laundry hamper. A green bra barely held back her ample chest.

"Touchdown!" Kennedi undid her jeans, revealing matching green panties underneath. Freckles smattered across the milky white skin, with dots of moles creating unnamed constellations.

Ryker took a deep breath and slowly blew it out. "So, what—you want me to have sex with you right now? With her here?"

Adeline gave a curt nod, her eyes locked on Kennedi's curves. Mesmerized by the way Kennedi held herself with such confidence. "I'd love it if you wanted to be a part of this," she said. "But I'm not going to force you. If you'd like to hang out downstairs while I fuck this stunning creature, you're welcome to."

Kennedi's face lit up. She playfully flipped hair over her shoulder. "I'm the stunning creature, right?"

Adeline held out a hand, and Kennedi took it, letting Adeline guide her to the spot next to her. Adeline put her mouth to Kennedi's cheek, brushed her lips against the curve of her jaw.

"You're the most stunning creature I've ever seen," she whispered. Kennedi sighed and leaned into the words, eyes closed.

Ryker still didn't move. "Addie, let me know what you'd like to do. You're in control of everything."

Adeline turned her head and looked at him. She stood. He narrowed his eyes, wary as she approached him. She put both hands on his chest. It was all hard, hot muscle.

"Ryker, you have been nothing but good to me. I know you're worried, but I need to do this for myself. I'd love it if you were here, but I totally understand if you need to go. But if you stay, just know that you won't hurt me. That's why I want Kennedi here, too; she can ground me and help us through this process."

Just as she thought he was about to say no, a smile curled his lips. "Okay. As long as you promise this won't hurt you."

"It won't." Hands shaking, Adeline reached for the hem of his T-shirt. They slipped past the material, sliding against his torso. He wasn't ripped like some primped-up model, but he had enough muscle to stir up her core. His skin pimpled as her hands trailed farther up.

Adeline looked into his eyes, holding his gaze as her hands snaked around to his shoulder blades. He sucked air through his teeth as she dug her nails into his skin and gently raked them down. She brought her hands back to the hem of his shirt. He took the hint and lifted it over his head, baring his broad chest. A smattering of dark hair curled between his pecs. He had a light farmer's tan line on his tawny arms. A part of her had expected to see tattoos, but his skin was as virgin as the day he'd been born.

She reached for him again. He grabbed her wrists gently.

"You tell me if you need me to stop, okay?"

"I promise," Adeline breathed. She was itching to taste him.

Kennedi clucked her tongue. "Please tell me I get to play, too."

"I'd be disappointed if you didn't." Adeline glanced over her shoulder as Ryker undid his belt. They both stared at him. His body tensed, fingers poised at the top button of his jeans.

"Blink twice if it's okay if I sit on your face," Kennedi offered. He blinked twice.

Kennedi air pumped her arm. "Sweet." She patted the comforter. "Hurry up, hot stuff."

Adeline stepped back as Ryker slid his jeans off, revealing everything. He was completely naked; a speckled trail of short, black hair led from his navel to his cock. The thick shaft bobbed at attention, nestled within a small patch of black hair. The tip peeked out from his foreskin, already glistening with pre-cum.

Kennedi raised an eyebrow. "No boxers?"

He winked. "Always be prepared, right?"

Adeline smiled. It was already a heady experience, having a naked man in front of her, ready and waiting for direction. An unfamiliar sense of power boiled inside her. She shivered as Kennedi leaned over, curls brushing her bare shoulder and stage whispered, "Want me to help you order him around?"

"Yes, please." Nothing sounded better.

Kennedi gave a low chuckle and shifted closer. "Can I touch you while I do it?"

Adeline groaned, her legs parting instinctually. "Yes."

She jerked as Kennedi slid a hand from the top of her thigh to the tender inside, slowly sweeping toward the apex of her thighs. "Tell him to start touching himself."

Ryker watched her, craved her. Adeline swallowed.

"Touch yourself," she said, the words barely a whisper. Kennedi zoned in on the bundle of nerves, and Adeline's head fell back.

"Louder," Kennedi encouraged, drawing lazy circles with her finger. The motion was heaven, even through her panties. She opened her eyes and looked at Ryker again.

"Touch yourself." The words were stronger, more assertive. Without hesitating, he brought a hand up, fisting his length. She watched as it slid up and down around the head of his cock. His thick thumb swept across the tip.

She had seen so many men do this, look at her with this level of desire, but feeling Kennedi's fingers work their magic on her clit at the same time made it an entirely different experience. Having complete control of the situation felt like walking through a desert and stumbling upon a fresh spring.

Turning her attention to Kennedi, their mouths came together like magnets. Kennedi's lips were soft and puffy as her tongue did a lazy dance with Adeline's. Her breasts brushed against Adeline's arm.

Breaking the kiss, Adeline unsnapped Kennedi's bra with expertise only a woman could have. Keeping steady attention on Adeline's clit, Kennedi shimmied out of her bra. Ryker made a tiny groaning sound. Adeline reluctantly pulled her attention from Kennedi to check on Ryker.

He was breathtaking, standing there, his shaggy black hair partially covering one eye. His strokes were lazy. Too lazy.

"Go faster," she commanded. He obeyed, picking up the pace. She had never been so turned on by a man touching himself. Kennedi moaned as one of her fingers pushed aside Adeline's panties, finding only wetness.

"Dirty, wet little creature," she said in a choked whisper. She dipped a finger into Adeline's pussy. Adeline's hips jerked in response.

Kennedi chose a tortuous pace, enjoying the way Adeline slowly turned into putty. Ryker licked his lips. Feeling emboldened, Adeline beckoned him to her with one finger. He stepped forward, hand around his cock, its wet tip mere inches from her face.

"Can I suck you?" She swallowed hard, drinking in his palpable desire. He gave a silent nod and released his grasp, offering her his entire length. Adeline glanced at Kennedi, who peppered her shoulder with kisses. Sensing Adeline's hesitation, Kennedi's eyes flicked to her. Smirking, she nipped Adeline's collarbone.

"Do you want me to join you?"

Adeline smiled. "Kinda."

"*Kinda?*" Kennedi sat back, removing her hand from between Adeline's legs. The loss of it made Adeline's thighs tighten. She groaned. Kennedi chuckled and faced Ryker.

"Can you handle two mouths, handsome?"

Ryker could do nothing but gape at the two women sitting in front of him.

"Blink twice if we can both suck your cock," Kennedi teased. He did. Kennedi motioned to Adeline. "After you."

Adeline stared at his cock, finding herself frozen in place suddenly.

Her father's business partner stood in a corner of the room, while the man in the corner groaned as her father reached for…

Memories of the men who had raped her over and over again flooded her mind. Both Kennedi and Ryker stilled, ready to stop at a moment's notice. Adeline closed her eyes, settling into the pain that battered at the edges of her desire.

Her father had spent an enormous amount of time schooling her on the art of giving head. The revulsion made her gag. She white-knuckle gripped the edge of the mattress. *Z, Y, X, W* . . . This wasn't her father. *V, U, T, S* . . . Ryker wasn't those other men. *R, Q, P, O* . . .

"Addie?" The kindness in his voice made her heart crack.

No. She would not let her father steal anything from her ever again. Her body was hers. She exhaled slowly. The panic receded, calmness settling over her heart.

"I'm fine," she assured them. Kennedi looked unconvinced. Ryker opened his mouth to protest, but Adeline steeled her jaw. "Really. It's okay. Can I please continue?"

A pause, then, "Yes," His dark eyes glittered, his voice full of raw emotion.

Taking a breath, Adeline released her grip on the mattress and leaned forward, wrapping her fingers around his considerable girth. She moved with mindfulness, living in the moment, refusing to think about anything else. The old version of Adeline was going to die—it was time for a rebirth.

She flicked the dewy tip of his penis with her tongue and then dragged her finger along its underside, enjoying the way it jerked. He groaned, hips instinctively thrusting forward. She wrapped her lips around it and swallowed; she could barely fit half of him in her mouth.

"Fuuuuuck." Ryker's knees wobbled. Adeline hummed in amusement, earning another curse.

"May I?" Kennedi licked her lips. Adeline reached for Ryker's firm butt cheek and pulled him closer. Adeline raked her tongue against one side of his cock from top to bottom. Kennedi did the same to the other side. Ryker moaned louder. Sweat beaded across his flat stomach.

Adeline popped the tip of his cock into her mouth again, swirling her tongue against the underside, flicking the tiny bit of flesh that always made men go crazy. As she did that, Kennedi took her mouth and sucked the edges of his cock with loud smacking sounds.

"Goddamnit," he groaned. He tugged Adeline's hair with one hand, his other weaving through Kennedi's curls. Kennedi took him in her mouth, her head bobbing furiously, while Adeline continued to lick his thighs and stomach, while reaching for one of Kennedi's breasts and squeezing gently. They were soft as silk.

Kennedi moaned, causing Ryker to jerk again, while Adeline pinched Kennedi's pebbled, dark nipple. There was a fire between her legs—her panties were completely soaked.

They took turns worshiping Ryker's cock until he let go of their heads and gasped, "I fucking need to be inside you. One of you. *Please.*"

Adeline pulled back, but Kennedi continued quickly and very enthusiastically sucking and pumping until he began to swell. She popped her mouth free and grinned. He narrowed his eyes at her.

"You're going to regret that," he said.

She wiggled her eyebrows. "Looking forward to it."

He turned his attention to Adeline. "How do you want me?"

Adeline chewed the inside of her cheek. There was no way he could be on top. Or from behind. That only left one option. "On your back?"

He gave her a half-smile. "Excellent." Knees shaking, she stood and let him scoot past her. He flipped onto his back and reached behind to grab the metal bedpost. He stretched like a lazy cat, his abs flexing deliciously.

"I have a condom in my wallet." He jerked his head to his shorts. Kennedi leaned over, pulled out the wallet, and plucked out a foil wrapper. She ripped it open with her teeth, pulled out the condom, and slid it on slowly. Ryker closed his eyes. A deep rumble vibrated in his chest at each decadently slow inch of his length being covered.

Adeline admired how his cock stood at attention. Even as she looked at him, enjoying every inch of his muscular body, she could feel terror creeping at the edges of her mind, ready to claw at her at a moment's notice. She mentally tried to push it aside.

"That's a beautiful thing," Kennedi said. She nudged Adeline with her shoulder. "You go first. I'll be right here the whole time."

Adeline's stomach clenched, nerves overriding her desire. "I'm afraid." Her cheeks burned.

Kennedi slipped a hand into hers. "Look at me."

Adeline's eyes watered at the tenderness. It took enormous effort to make eye contact. Her heart was beating so hard, it felt like her ribs might crack. She struggled to make eye contact, focusing instead on the smattering of freckles across the bridge of Kennedi's nose. Kennedi rubbed Adeline's cheek with her thumb.

"I'm here. He's here. No one else—it's just us. You don't have to do anything you don't want to do. No one will be upset. You just tell us what you need."

Memories of late nights in dark clubs, too-large hotel rooms, and her prison cell bedroom washed over her. What she needed was to replace those. She needed them to not define her.

Adeline could do this. She had survived too much to not grab her own life by the balls.

"I need you both."

Kennedi leaned forward and brushed Adeline's lips with her own. She walked to the other side of the bed and scooted onto the mattress, next to his hips. They both smiled as Adeline did the same. Ryker reached a calloused hand to one of her thighs, his fingers dancing against her skin.

Adeline swung one leg to the other side of him and poised her entrance above him. The tip of his length teased her exquisitely. Ryker clutched both hips.

"Give me you," he purred. His bronze eyes were like molten metal, shining with his need for her.

Those words undid her. She dipped down, and he slid into her. She gasped. He filled and stretched her in the most delicious of ways. When he was fully seated, she paused and closed her eyes. His heat flowed through her core, causing her to clench inside. She rocked her hips and moaned, his cock rubbing her sweet spot. Her back arched, driving him deeper. Leaning forward, she gripped his chest and dug her nails in. He groaned as she slid her ass upwards slowly, bringing herself down on him just as slowly. The teasing pace made his hips twitch.

It was a decadent experience. She turned to Kennedi, tilted her head. Scooting forward, Kennedi leaned in and kissed her ferociously. She gasped as Kennedi brought one hand between Adeline's thighs and started rubbing her clit in slow, methodical circles. A sharp spark of pleasure shot up through her spine.

"I need you to cum for me," Kennedi groaned. Adeline felt her jolt and looked down to see Ryker's skilled fingers playing Kennedi's pussy like a flute. Adeline felt herself teetering on the precipice of ecstasy, and she quickened her pace.

Ryker reached up with his free hand and palmed Adeline's breast with delicious roughness. She leaned into the pain. Embraced it. She dug her fingers into his chest, carving into his slick skin. He panted through gritted teeth. Adeline slammed down on his cock as Ryker swirled his tongue around her nipple.

And then she shattered. Adeline screamed and threw her head back. Every muscle, every nerve, every inch of her flesh pulsed with pleasure. The world disappeared.

Next to her, Kennedi's moans increased. As Adeline came down from her own bliss, she eagerly turned her focus onto Kennedi's body. Ryker continued to draw his fingers in and out of her. Adeline was shocked to see that he was using three. Kennedi's hips bucked uncontrollably, instinct forcing the thrusts. Adeline leaned in and nibbled on her neck and then her ear.

Then she whispered, "Do you want his cock, too?"

Kennedi's eyes flew open, her face split into a beaming smile. "Fuck yes, I do."

Sliding off his hard cock, Adeline moved to the side and settled into the same position Kennedi had just been in. Ryker's eyes shined, watching every movement. He brought a hand up and curled a finger, motioning her forward.

"Kiss me. I need to taste you."

As she leaned forward, Kennedi tapped her shoulder, and Adeline glanced, confused. A mischievous glint in those green eyes made her smile. As she eased herself onto Ryker—whose moan was sure to wake Mags—Kennedi brought a finger to Adeline's swollen folds and drew two fingers along the slickness. The sensation took her breath away.

The fingers came away soaked with Adeline's pleasure. Holding eye contact, Kennedi took her middle finger and slowly drew it into her mouth. She hummed at the flavor. Then she took her pointer finger, still glistening, and rubbed it against Adeline's lower lip.

"Let him really taste you, baby."

Something carnal unfurled itself deep inside her belly. Adeline obeyed, leaning down to Ryker, who took a hand and roughly grabbed the back of her head as he sucked on her lower lip.

"Fuck." His tongue swept against his lips. "*Please* let me taste more of you."

Adeline hesitated, not sure what he meant. Kennedi kissed her shoulder.

"Sit on that gorgeous mouth." The advice eased Adeline's confusion. She turned to face Kennedi as she lowered herself onto his face. It felt like she was about to suffocate him, and she said as much.

With a mouth full of her, he mumbled, "if I die, I die."

His tongue began to explore every inch of her pussy, flicking against that bundle of nerves over and over. Kennedi leaned closer, their noses almost touching.

"Fuck me," she growled to Ryker. His hands came up, digging into her thighs as he began to feverishly piston into her. The slapping sound mixed with their moans. Leaning one hand on his chest, Adeline brought the other one to Kennedi's clit, mimicking the motions she had experienced earlier.

"Fuck my cunt," Kennedi rasped, her lungs heaving for air. "Make it fucking yours, Ryker."

He slammed even harder into her. Kennedi's screams took Adeline's breath away, but she was quick to follow as Ryker flicked his tongue in the exact right spot. She came again, and this time, her orgasm was deep, almost aching.

She gave a low moan, and it felt almost impossible to focus on her pleasure while continuing to give Kennedi what she needed. Ryker's muscled torso flexed and released as he pounded into Kennedi, who at last came apart, screaming out his name as her orgasm rocked her. His muscles spasmed and his neck corded as he came hard, bellowing out words that sounded like their names.

They stayed in that position for a moment, catching their breath. Adeline moved first, swinging off Ryker's face. Cool air breezed between her legs and she felt the loss of his heat. Retying her hair into a ponytail, she watched as Kennedi and Ryker untangled. It looked and felt so natural to be with the two of them.

Ryker had a thick layer of sweat coating his body, and his hair brushed against his forehead in shaggy strands. He tossed his head, sweeping pieces out of his eyes. His eyes were the color of brilliant amber, but concern pinched his mouth.

He assessed Adeline. "Are you okay?"

She nodded. "Thank you." The words were barely a whisper but he heard them. She slid her hand into his when he lifted it toward her, enjoying the dry feel of his callouses. He had given her a gift few men could offer. It would be impossible to show the kind of gratitude that aligned with the magnitude of the moment.

"I'll always be here for you, lionheart." The nickname warmed her from the inside. Kennedi sat quietly, observing them. Adeline turned to look at the woman she was deeply in love with and a smile curled at the edges of her mouth. The red head looked properly ravished, her skin flush and hair wild. Her mouth was puffy and pink. Kennedi bit her lip ring and leaned in for a brief kiss. For the first time in her adult life, Adeline felt not only love, but hope.

CHAPTER TWENTY-FIVE

The morning arrived too fast. Adeline's body ached in the best way. She reached for the spot beside her on the bed, but Kennedi was already gone. A little warmth remained on the pillow. Ryker's makeshift bed was made as well.

Stretching languidly, she stared at the ceiling, reliving the night before. It had been glorious. Her lust and curiosity were thoroughly satiated. She was like a canary set free from its cage, ready to soar to whole new heights.

Adeline found Mags in the kitchen, whipping up some eggs and pouring them into a sizzling pan. Adeline opened the back door and let out Lance. The old woman gave her a knowing look and motioned to the table.

"Go on, you little minx. Sounds like y'all worked up quite the appetite."

Adeline's cheeks reddened. "I'm sorry if you—"

Mags shushed her. "You gotta live a little. Enjoy the delights of life." She winked.

"You're right," Adeline agreed, pulling out four mugs by the coffeemaker.

"Of course, I am. I'm as old as time. Lessons have been learned."

Ryker entered the kitchen, yawning and stretching his arms. His hair was still a mess. Adeline blushed again, remembering the way it felt to have him between her thighs. He greeted her with a deep, lingering hug and a kiss on the forehead.

"What's that about lessons learned?"

"That handsome men like yourself are dangerous," Mags chirped. He sniggered. Kennedi padded in behind him, looking equally tussled. She must have crawled onto the couch to lie with Ryker for a bit. Adeline searched for a pang of jealousy but found none. Society always thought jealousy was healthy, but the absence of it felt more right than anything else. The realization was a bright kernel, heating her up with happiness. She'd finally found her people.

Kennedi sat at the table, smudging her palm against a cheek and yawning. There was a scratching at the back door. Kennedi leaned back to open the back door. Lance trotted in and sat next to his empty bowl.

Ryker nudged Adeline toward the table and filled the four mugs with coffee. Chuckling, he said, "You have no idea. I make a mean cheese-and-broccoli casserole. It's been compared to a nuclear fallout."

"That doesn't make any sense," Adeline pointed out.

He shrugged. "I agree. It's unfair for everyone on this earth to have never tasted the cheesy ambrosia."

"Yeah, that's totally it." Adeline threw a tea towel at him, which he easily dodged. He brought a mug to Kennedi and kissed the top of her head with a loud smack. Mags turned off the stove and started doling out the eggs and bacon.

"Grab a plate, ya heathens." Mags threw the pan and spatula into the sink. "You're all too sassy for this early in the morning." Adeline opened her mouth to say something about pots and kettles, but Mags glared. "*No*, you don't get to use me as an example. Eat."

Only the sound of forks scraping porcelain could be heard until all food was gone. Sighing, Adeline pushed her empty plate forward and patted her stomach.

"Okay. Hours of sex, bacon, coffee… What else can we do today?"

Kennedi downed the last of her coffee then stood and walked to the dog food container, to fill Lance's bowl. "I'm off work for a couple of days. We could have a picnic? Maybe repeat all of the above?"

Ryker stood and began collecting plates. "Why don't we go to my site? There's a spot that my family has always loved. It has a really beautiful view."

Kennedi clapped her hands while Lance devoured his food. "Really? I'd love that!" She looked at Adeline. "What do you think?"

Adeline cracked a smile. "That sounds amazing, actually."

Mags sighed. "Oh, to be young again." Todd, the fattest of her cats, jumped in her lap, purring when Mags scratched behind his ear.

Ryker rolled his eyes as he brought the coffeepot over and refilled Mags' cup. "We won't be gone long. Just lunch. We have a bullshit murder to execute, right?"

Adeline's stomach knotted. In her bliss, that simple fact had disappeared for a time. Now, suddenly, she didn't want to go on a picnic. It felt crass, as if they were thumbing their noses at danger.

She looked at Ryker. "I don't think—"

There was a quiet knock at the door. Lance bristled, emanating a low growl. The four of them looked toward the noise.

Mags looked at the clock on the wall and frowned. "It's too early for Mormon bullshit. Or someone trying to sell me a vacuum."

Tension seized Adeline.

"I'll go see who it is." Ryker sounded anything but excited. Mags stood and moved toward the hallway.

Looking at Adeline, Mags asked, "Do you have your knife?"

"N-n-no," Adeline stuttered. "It's upstairs, in my purse."

Mags glanced down the hall, then back at her. "It'll be fine." She turned to Ryker and squared her shoulders. "Let's go."

Adeline waited in the kitchen with Kennedi. Mags paused at the hallway closet and quietly retrieved the shotgun. Lance stood behind Ryker, ready for his next command. Mags pumped the weapon and motioned for Ryker to open the door. He spared a look toward the kitchen before turning the knob and—

It was Bruce, the old man Adeline had met at the bookstore.

Mags harrumphed. "Jesus, Bruce, what the hell are you doing here?"

Mags lowered the shotgun as Ryker widened the opening.

Bruce snorted. "Hello to you, too, old friend."

Lance sniffed the air, snorting with approval. Mags snickered. "It isn't the right season. You get my winters—it's still summer. A bit early to warm my bed."

"Mags!" Adeline chided, striding down the hallway. Kennedi was close on Adeline's heels. "You're so rude. And weird." She looked at Bruce. "But really, you scared the shit out of us."

Bruce's eyes glinted. "So, there's still magic under this old hood, eh? Been a long time since I've been able to scare someone." He reached into his back pocket and pulled out a piece of paper. He handed it to Mags as he stepped inside. Ryker closed the door behind him, watching him warily.

Bruce approached Lance and held out the back of his hand. "Hiya, boy. I'm Bruce, your auntie's lover and best friend. Hang around with me and I'll slip you some food." Lance walked right up to Bruce and licked his fingers.

Kennedi yawned loudly. "I need to go shower and get dressed." She looked to Adeline, then Ryker. "Join me?"

"Hell yeah."

"Fuck yes."

Kennedi smirked and headed upstairs. Adeline hesitated, watching as Mags finished reading the note. The old woman stared at Bruce again.

"Seriously? I need the whole list, not half."

Bruce held up his hands defensively. "Sorry, my guy doesn't dabble in the bigger stuff anymore. I'm trying to make a new connection, but it's gonna take time."

"When can the outside cameras be set up?"

Adeline's ears perked up. Ryker paused halfway up the stairs.

Bruce sighed. "If you want, I'll get it done today. I gotta go get my tools, but I can make it happen." He raised one eyebrow. "For a price."

Mags crumpled up the paper. "Oh, for fuck's sake, really? You want me to fuck you for a security camera set-up?"

Bruce threw his head back and laughed uproariously. "Maggie, you can get that for free, even during the summer. No, what I want is some fresh veggies. You have a nice haul from the garden. But now that you mention it… "

He put one hand on Mags' cheek. Adeline was shocked to see Mags actually shiver. Their mouths almost touched as Bruce leaned over and whispered to her words Adeline couldn't catch. Whatever it was, had Mags whirling around, face fire-engine red as she stomped upstairs, past both Adeline and Ryker. Mags halted at the top of the stairs. Turned and stared at Bruce, eyes ablaze.

"Are you coming, or what?" She folded her arms. Bruce gave a deep, low chuckle and winked at Adeline as he climbed past.

"That woman is absolutely feral," he said under his breath.

"*I heard that, you bastard.*" Mags stormed into the bedroom and slammed the door. Bruce chuckled again. He entered Mags' bedroom and closed the door behind him.

Ryker's eyes slid to Adeline. "Did that just—"

"Yup."

"And they're going to…?"

Adeline burst into laughter, Ryker quickly joining her.

CHAPTER TWENTY-SIX

Sweat lined Adeline's brow as they hiked up to Ryker's lumber site. Though practicing with Mags had toned her body, the backpack of food was still heavy. Kennedi, wearing overall shorts and a white T-shirt, held a large blanket, and Ryker, in a dark blue tank top, carried a backpack filled with other supplies.

They marched behind him silently, Adeline taking the time to enjoy the sounds of nature. The trees were dense but offered enough space for them to weave through. Lance trotted through the low brush, sniffing everything and keeping a watchful eye.

"Get'em Lancey," Kennedi encouraged when Lance spotted a squirrel darting away. "Teach them big bad squirrels a lesson."

"Well, he's definitely enjoying himself," Ryker said.

Adeline wiped sweat from her brow with the back of her hand. "Speaking of enjoying oneself, are we almost there yet? I'm kinda over this whole sweating-and-walking thing."

Ryker glanced over his shoulder. "Don't be such a baby. We're almost there."

"Can't you just pretend I'm a log of wood and carry me?" Kennedi complained.

Ryker snorted. "It'll be worth it, I promise. We're almost there, anyway."

True to his word, they arrived at the clearing a couple of minutes later. What Ryker had neglected to mention, probably on purpose, was that the clearing actually fell off into a ravine. Lush, green trees swept for miles in front of them, the bright blue sky blanketing the landscape of tall grass and wildflowers. A gentle breeze—Adeline sighed with contentment.

Ryker swept a hand out over the clearing. "Ladies first."

Kennedi marched through the grass, squealing as a grasshopper launched itself at her. She batted at the air frantically. "Jesus. I *hate* it when they do that." Lance jumped, trying to catch it in his mouth.

Ryker chuckled. Kennedi stopped closer to the edge of the cliff and turned back to them. "Is this good?"

The tall, lush grass swayed in the breeze; Adeline wanted to sink into it and take a nap. Ryker nodded and off-loaded his pack. Kennedi unfolded the blanket.

Adeline dropped her backpack and rolled her shoulders. "All of this food better be gone by the time we're ready to leave, because I'm not carrying it back down."

Kennedi patted her stomach. "I could eat a stampede of horses."

Ryker unzipped his bag and started pulling out plates and cups. "Don't you mean a herd?"

Kneeling beside him, Adeline placed the food containers in the middle of the patch-work blanket. Lance settled on one side of the blanket, watching them.

Kennedi plucked a water bottle from Ryker's bag, scoffing. "No, because I'd want them galloping right into my mouth."

Adeline burst out laughing, envisioning Kennedi's jaw unhinging. "Please don't ever say anything like that ever again."

Kennedi moved like lightning, snatching a piece of fried chicken and taking a huge bite. Mouth full, she said, "Try me, bitch."

Ryker poured them each a glass of white wine. "Now, children, calm down and eat your food." He pulled an apple from Adeline's pack and began to slice it into eighths. Kennedi inspected the surrounding area, taking a sip of her wine.

"So why haven't you or your dad cut this place down?"

Ryker glanced around. "Look at it—it's too beautiful to destroy. We aren't the type to choose money over nature. My family used to picnic here when I was a kid—my mom felt it was one of the most beautiful places she'd seen."

Adeline popped a grape into her mouth. "Does she not come here anymore?"

Ryker laid the apple slices out on their plates. "I'm sure she does, but I haven't been invited since I became an adult. I think she and my dad come out here to bone now that their three kids are out of the house."

The chilled, tart wine was refreshing on Adeline's tongue. "Wait. Your parents had sex here?"

Kennedi looked down. "Maybe right here, on this spot?"

Ryker stuck out his tongue in disgust. "I really fucking hope not."

A shrill cry came from above. Adeline looked up and saw something brown with rust red tail feathers.

Ryker brought up a knee and hooked his arm around it. "Red tail hawk."

"It's so pretty," Adeline breathed. The hawk cried out again.

Ryker crunched into a slice of apple. "I've always wanted one as a pet, but I can't bring myself to stifle something like that."

Kennedi stretched and lay down with her hands under her head and her knees up. "Let's come here all the time," she said, staring at the clouds.

Ryker took a deep gulp of wine and nodded. "I'm down."

"But only if we can christen it with some d and v," she added slyly.

Ryker almost choked on his next sip. "Excuse me? You want to fuck in the same spot my parents might have fucked?"

"Yes," Adeline and Kennedi said at the same time.

Ryker sent them each a withering look. "No."

They both sat up straight. Ryker's jaw dropped as Adeline reached for the bottom of her shirt, pulling it off and tossing it away.

"What are you doing?"

Kennedi unbuckled her overall straps. "What does it look like we're doing?"

His face darkened, but Adeline caught the hungry glint in his eye as she kneeled to unbuckle her shorts. He looked at Kennedi, who was doing the same. Adeline wore a bra and panties; Kennedi was topless.

"How are you feeling right now, bad boy?"

Ryker wrinkled his nose. "No. It's too weird. Put your clothes back on."

Adeline unhooked her bra and tossed it onto his face. "I'm not wasting an opportunity to have sex on a cliff in the sunshine."

He clenched his jaw, eyes darting around. "I mean, maybe they haven't done it…"

Adeline crawled over to Kennedi. Adeline nuzzled her nose against Kennedi's cheek. Kennedi cupped the back of Adeline's head and brushed her plump lips against Adeline's.

Heat shot to Adeline's core, and she whimpered in her throat as Kennedi kissed her with slow, lazy strokes of her tongue. Adeline leaned her hands against Kennedi's thighs, loving the soft give of her body. She gasped as Kennedi palmed her breast and started gently massaging it.

Breaking apart, Kennedi looked to Ryker. "What about now?"

Ryker gazed at their bare flesh. "Isn't it a bit taboo?"

"Only if you imagine me as your mom," Adeline joked. She got on all fours and started wiggling her ass playfully. She kissed Kennedi again. Ryker groaned loudly.

"Fuck it," he muttered. Adeline laughed as he tossed his shirt into her face. Under the bright sun, his dark bronze skin shimmered. She ached to reach out and run her fingers through his black chest hair. He shimmied out of his shorts, already ramrod hard.

Adeline licked her lips in anticipation. Ryker shuffled behind Adeline and gripped one of her ass checks, kneading it like soft dough. He ran a finger down the crack of her ass, following the fabric of her thong. The light touch arched her back, and Kennedi kissed her more fiercely, swallowing up Adeline's moan.

Balancing on three limbs, Adeline pushed against Kennedi's chest. Kennedi adjusted, getting on her back and raising her hips to the sky as her underwear slid off her thighs. Adeline loved the way she could see wetness pooling under the red curls.

"Spread your legs," Ryker commanded as he pulled off her thong. The breeze tickled Adeline's sex. She obeyed, positioning her thighs farther apart. He flipped onto his back. She jerked when she felt his head slide underneath her.

With his hands on her hips, he lowered her pussy to his mouth. Lightning struck every nerve as his tongue swiped along her slit—very, *very* slowly. Battling the urge to buck, Adeline lowered herself down on her elbows and placed her eager mouth to Kennedi's slick heat. The first lick of her tongue elicited a loud, long moan.

It took every ounce of Adeline's determination to not devolve into a pool of lust. Ryker fingered her, licked her, his tongue circling slowly around her clit. Her thighs quivered. She flicked Kennedi's clit, then inserted her own finger, sliding into Kennedi's tantalizing heat. Kennedi's hips undulated with each thrust.

The redhead panted and grabbed her nipples. From between Kennedi's thighs, Adeline watched her repeatedly tugging and releasing them. Behind her, Ryker picked up the pace with his tongue. Kennedi's insides tightened; Adeline felt her own orgasm building—her senses were overwhelmed.

Kennedi heaved for breath, moans coming quick and fast. Adeline increased the pace of her fingering, enthralled by the way Kennedi's chest flushed as she grew closer to cumming. Adeline whimpered as Ryker stopped and scooted out from under her.

"What are you doing? Come back," she pleaded over her shoulder.

Kennedi reached out and dug her nails into Adeline's arm. "Don't. Stop." Kennedi grit the words, fingers to her clit. Behind her, Adeline felt Ryker push her ass upward. The sound of a condom wrapper, a pause, and then he was pushing at her entrance. Placing one arm under her hips, he began thrusting at an excruciatingly slow pace, using his palm to focus on her clit.

It was utterly exquisite. As Adeline drove her fingers deeper into Kennedi, Ryker quickened his pace, grunting each time her ass bounced against his hips. Her orgasm rushed toward her like a tidal wave. Kennedi core tightened further.

"That's it, baby," Adeline panted, trying desperately to keep pace with Ryker. He growled and, putting both hands to her hips, began fucking her even harder.

Kennedi's fingers circled her own clit furiously, moving faster and faster until she screamed. Her thighs shook around Adeline's shoulders, clenching her into place. Adeline felt Kennedi's muscles, waves of pleasure squeezing tightly.

Ryker increased his speed. "Fuck, Addie. You feel so good."

While Kennedi continued to melt into bliss, Adeline gently slid her finger out of her and lowered her head to the ground, right by Kennedi's ass. Gripping the soft blanket, she screamed with pleasure as Ryker drilled her so hard, she thought he might drive her straight into the earth. He completely possessed her, and she wanted nothing more than to give him every inch of flesh and soul he demanded. This time, it was her choice. No one else. Finally, her power had arrived.

"Harder," she groaned, closing her eyes. Her core was molten, welcoming each thrust of his hard cock. He hit every single spot she didn't even know existed. So consumed, she didn't notice Kennedi sit up and scoot to Adeline's side.

A bolt of bliss strung through her insides when Kennedi's fingers found Adeline's clit, bringing some of the wetness created by Ryker to rub over the swollen bud. Adeline screamed out both of their names as the orgasm smashed into every corner of her being, ruthlessly invading reality and shattering it into pieces. Ryker roared with satisfaction, giving one final demanding thrust.

Adeline shuddered, a complete pile of jelly. For a moment, the only thing she could hear was heavy breathing. Then the hawk screamed again. Opening her eyes, seeing the lush blades of grass, Adeline smiled.

She felt as free as the hawk.

***

"Okay, so tomorrow, we call Lucas? Make him think Ryker is turning Addie in?" Kennedi asked between heavy breaths.

They were making their way back down through the forest as twilight fell. Adeline ached everywhere, but it didn't bother her. Thanks to her backpack being lighter, she practically floated as she followed her two partners.

"Yeah." Ryker glanced over his shoulder, looking to see Adeline's reaction. "I think we should do it at one of our oldest sites. The trees there were cut a year ago. It'll be years before they're looked at again for harvesting."

Adeline didn't really want to think about planning a murder though. "Can we talk about this when we get back? I'm still on cloud fifteen. I just want to bask in it."

Kennedi nodded. "Truth."

Lance walked beside them, the retired cop looking as tired as the rest of them. Adeline reached down and ruffled his ears. He looked up, tongue lolling out over his sharp teeth.

Adeline sighed, exhausted, when finally they reached Ryker's truck and hopped inside. They paused, staring out the windshield.

"We just had sex on a cliff." Kennedi sounded grave.

A bubble of joy popped inside Adeline's chest. She laughed, surprising Kennedi and Ryker. They looked at her curiously. She shrugged. "What? It was as epic as it sounds."

Ryker started up the truck. "Agreed."

"Your mom would be proud," Kennedi quipped.

He glowered, narrowing his eyes to slits. "Watch it."

She stuck out her tongue. "I did. Multiple times."

Ryker put the truck into drive and they started heading down the mountain. "Maybe I'll blindfold you next time."

"Yes, please," Adeline quipped.

He sighed. "You both are trouble."

The drive took twenty minutes. With each mile, Adeline felt the ecstasy from earlier fading, anxiety nestling back into its usual place. Tomorrow, they'd try and trap her father. Kill him and Alexander. Bury them somewhere.

She wasn't sure she could handle killing Lucas. If it came down to it, could she be the one to pull the trigger? Would she regret it if she wasn't?

Pulling up in front of Mags' place—she supposed it was hers now, too—they filed out from the truck, practically falling through the front door in a heap. Mags looked up from the couch, scrutinizing their appearance.

"Where the hell have you been? You left hours ago."

Ryker walked upstairs without responding. Adeline and Kennedi followed.

Adeline smiled at Mags. "It was a good picnic."

Mags snorted, returning to her book. "I bet it was."

Later, after showering, the trio cuddled naked in the bed, just to be near each other. Ryker was fast asleep; Kennedi traced her nails along Adeline's skin. Nestled in the middle, Adeline stared outside the window. The moon was already high in the sky. She put a hand to Kennedi's hip.

"You okay?" she whispered.

Kennedi shifted in place. "Yeah. You?"

Adeline thought about the question. Either she was going to die or she wasn't—that wasn't what worried her. She feared things would go horribly wrong and the people she cared for most in this world would die with her. Or even worse, if Lucas killed them and kept her alive, to exist without the rest of her heart.

"I'm scared he'll hurt you all. What if he brings more than Alexander with him? We're assuming he won't, but he might know it's a trap. Then what?"

Ryker moved suddenly, throwing his arm around Adeline and bringing her closer. Kennedi paused, waiting to see if they had woken him, but he continued softly snoring. Adeline smiled.

"Then we deal with it," Kennedi said. "I think we've agreed—he won't leave any of us alive, so we need to bring him here, to our home court, and be done with it. Just imagine: in under two days, you'll be free. No more perverted psychopath father chasing you down and selling you to other perverts."

Adeline ran her fingers along Kennedi's skin, their arms crossed as they touched each other. "You're right. I just hate it."

"Me too, baby." Kennedi kissed Adeline's forehead softly. "But we'll get through it together."

Their hands came together, fingers intertwining. The moon was high and illuminated the room. Adeline stared at the person she adored more than anything else in the world. "I love you, Kennedi. All day."

Kennedi inhaled sharply. "You remembered."

"It always meant 'love' to me. I didn't even know back then how much I loved you. And how much more I would love you. But I'll love you all day, every day."

Kennedi whispered, "It always meant that to me, too. It just wasn't clear to me until you were gone. You were my first kiss. Even if we didn't know it then, I think a part of us always did. I mourned on the date of your last letter. I'd go get a sundae, play your favorite songs, and hope every single second that you were okay. Finding out that you weren't… It broke my fucking heart, Addie. When I got that call from you, it took everything for me to not lose my fucking mind. I didn't rush to you because I didn't want to scare you. I was too terrified."

Adeline never imagined she would hear her own feelings vocalized. "Can you believe I did the same thing? I had a teddy bear named Jack."

"After my dog?" Kennedi's voice tightened.

Adeline felt a tear slide down her cheek. "Yeah. He kept me company almost every day."

"That's…" The word caught in Kennedi's throat. "I was always with you, just like you were with me."

"All of the seconds and minutes and hours."

Kennedi pressed herself closer, mouth searching. They kissed. It was full of anguish, hope, and love. Regret and anger tinged, too—all of them pouring into Adeline, filling her to the brim.

Kennedi caressed her face. "All day, my love."

"Every day, baby."

CHAPTER TWENTY-SEVEN

Adeline woke in the early morning hours, the pink of dawn just peeking over the horizon.

Today was the day—she and everyone important to her would take down Lucas Oremen. Her father. It felt surreal, knowing that the day's outcome was impossible to predict. They'd planned so many details, but Lucas most likely expected her to try something.

What would the freedom from him feel like? She expected to feel some sense of regret—patricide was no small thing—but all she felt was excitement. The last few days had cultivated a level of confidence she luxuriated in. The newly founded support system was everything she could hope for. Whatever the day brought, she was ready for it.

She reached in front of her. Kennedi was gone, but the sheets were still warm. A furnace—Ryker—still lay against her back. She nuzzled his morning wood with her ass and felt him stir.

"Don't you tease me." His voice was a low rumble, the sound of it curling her toes.

She smiled. "Who says I'm teasing?"

One of his hands draped along her thigh. Into her neck, he whispered, "How are you feeling? Are you still sure you want to do this?"

"I've never been more sure about anything in my life."

He traced a finger along the hem of her panties. "Is it twisted that I want to make sure my scent is on you while he dies?" He moved his arm then and pushed his hand between her thighs. They opened willingly.

"Not… twisted… at… all…" Adeline gasped out, then moaned into her pillow as two of his fingers found her already wet and waiting for him.

"Fuck, Addie. You're already so fucking ready for me."

"Yes," she said through another gasp as he stuck both inside, pumping them slowly. She squirmed at the slickness of her pleasure. A wave of shame wriggled against her senses, and she froze. He froze with her, fingers paused.

"Are you okay?" His voice was smokey, still full of sleep, but his tone was concerned.

"I think so. I just feel…" His fingers began to slide out, but she reached for his wrist, stopping him. "I just feel… scared." She loathed the words and how they made the shame more intense.

"We can stop."

Adeline shook her head. "No. Keep going, okay? I want this."

"Tell me if you change your mind."

"I will," she promised.

Satisfied, he moved his hands again. Her legs widened even more, and she took a deep breath, relaxing her core to let him in further.

"That's it, baby," he crooned, breath rolling off the shell of her ear. "I'm so proud of you, working through your demons." His fingers moved upwards and trapped her clit, using them to rub both sides. "You're so beautiful, fighting for yourself. I've wanted you since the first moment I met you."

She groaned, turning her head to bite the pillow. His words were going to combust her into orgasmic flames. Making lazy circles with his fingers, he continued. "Helping you move through this has been an honor. I cannot wait to be there the moment you fly. I'll stay on the ground forever just to watch you soar."

A loud sob ripped from her throat. "You don't have to say things like that." If he didn't mean them, she would be crushed. He'd help her grow in ways no one else could have; any kind of lie would be instant destruction.

He paused and rolled away from her. While she heard him rip open a condom, she took slow breaths. He wouldn't hurt her—she was positive he was safe. But accepting his words as truth was a level of trust that would be reality leveling if he wasn't who he claimed to be.

But she also knew that she couldn't just borrow problems from the future. Currently, life was spectacular. In that singular moment, as Ryker repositioned himself behind her and thrust inside her, she knew what true perfection felt like.

The smell of cedar enveloped her, helping sharpen her focus. His lips brushed against the back of her neck. "I want to be inside you when I tell you this."

He pushed deep inside her, and she arched, trying to take him deeper. He took one of her legs and hooked it over his hip, helping him find the deepest part of her. The next thrust hit a point that had her moaning and biting the pillow again.

"Adeline, you are the most beautiful person I've ever met."

Thrust.

"You've surprised me at every turn, your ferocity and strength giving me a newfound appreciation for life."

Thrust.

"I want to watch you grow for the rest of my life."

Thrust.

"I love you, Adeline."

Thrust.

She whimpered, bringing her free hand back to grab his hip. He couldn't be deep enough. He scraped his teeth against her neck, and she bowed her chin.

His deep voice throbbed inside her core when he said again, "I love you."

Thrust.

"You are enough, and you're loveable."

His fingers came back to her clit, circling in time with his thrusts. She let out another sob, years of terror, shame, and desolation crumbling inside her. He soothed her with quiet shushes, keeping the same decadent pace as she crumbled. It was the first time she'd ever made love with a man, and it was one of the most exquisite experiences. Each purposeful thrust told her she was safe and worthy of love. His warm body cradled her, rocking into her very being.

"I want you to come with me, baby." His fingers began to pick up the pace, but continued thrusting at the same pace. The difference stirred up her core, the feeling of desire scorching. While she wept and the sun rose, Ryker made love to her in a way she knew she would never forget. His flavor of love branded her for life.

She hoped it was a good thing.

***

After getting dressed, Ryker followed Adeline down to the kitchen where Kennedi and Mags were chatting.

"Well, hey, sleepyheads," Mags said.

Ryker looked at Adeline. "Coffee?"

"Yes, please." She sat next to Kennedi. "How did you sleep?"

Kennedi chuckled. "Like I slept on a bed that wasn't made for three people. Almost fell off three times."

Adeline grimaced. "Sorry if that was my fault."

Kennedi waved it away. "Nah. Just restless. Today is stressful, no matter how we dice it."

"Which is why—" Mags breezed past Ryker with a pan of sizzling bacon "—we need to eat up. Full stomachs and no excuses. No meal, no kill."

Adeline reached for a slab of bacon. "Where the fuck did you get that from?"

"Iraq."

Ryker's eyes bulged. "What the hell were you doing there?" he asked, putting Adeline's mug down in front of her.

Mags placed the hot pan back onto the stove. "I was a war photographer."

"Lucas makes it sound like you did more than that." Adeline hummed at the smell of coffee. She took a sip and closed her eyes.

Mags began cracking eggs into a bowl. "Sometimes. It started getting me into trouble when I photographed the wrong people. That's how I met Bruce. That idiot saved my life once or thrice. When we turned fifty, we left that life behind, before it killed us."

Kennedi grabbed a muffin. "And you both moved here to Menforth."

Mags poured the eggs into a pan. "As you might have noticed, we have an interesting dynamic. It works for us. We won't marry, but we don't need to."

Ryker sat down at the table and poured sugar into his coffee. "Will we be seeing more of your lover?"

Mags gave a withering look. "Maybe. But if you're an ass about it, I'll make sure you never find out. But he'll be here in ten minutes or so. He wants to walk through the plan with us one more time before—"

There was a confident knock at the front door. Mags rolled her eyes. "Fucker likes to pretend to be formal just to mess with me."

Ryker popped up. "I'll get it."

Kennedi opened her mouth to say something, but the sound of Lance growling stopped her. He stood at the end of the hallway, hackles stiff. The three of them froze as Ryker reached the door.

"Who is it?" Silence. Ryker looked through the peephole. "Hello? Bruce?" No response. He sighed and opened the door.

"Who—"

There was a squelching sound. Kennedi screamed and scrambled back from her chair. Mags and Adeline rushed into the hallway. Froze.

Ryker turned to them, hands clutching the blade protruding from his stomach.

"*Run.*"

He barely got the word out before falling to his knees. Alexander appeared and toppled him to one side with a kick. He grinned with feral hunger. He stepped into the foyer, looking around. Lance growled, fangs bared, ready for a command.

Alexander eyed him warily. He raised the gun, and Lance sprung into action, charging forward, teeth gnashing. The gun gave a deafening boom, and Lance squealed. Adeline cried out as blood poured down his shoulder, but he didn't stop. Alexander tried to shoot again, but the bullet soared wild, hitting a wall by Mags and Adeline. Kennedi cowered by the bay windows in the kitchen, screaming.

Lance lept at Alexander, latching onto the arm with the gun. Alexander roared and tried to shake him off. He let go of the gun, and it clattered to the floor, inches from Ryker's outstretched hand. Lance shook furiously, digging his teeth into Alexander's meaty flesh.

Blood gushed all over Alexander's arm and onto the floor. With his free arm, Alexander punched Lance in the face so hard the dog crumpled to the ground. Adeline cried out, fear vibrating against her bones. Mags held her back, her grip hard as steel. Adeline watched as Ryker crawled toward the gun. Alexander leaned over and grabbed it.

"Nice try." he sneered. Standing straight, ignoring his injured arm, he calmly adjusted the lapel of his black suit jacket, unruffled. Ryker groaned, clutching his stomach as blood oozed through his fingers.

Alexander bent down, grabbed Ryker by the neck. Mags lurched forward like she was about to stop him, but she backed up again when Alexander dragged Ryker down the hallway, leaving a bloody trail in their wake.

Adeline dry heaved then as her father stepped through the doorway looking like a well-cultured demon. He wore an impeccable blue suit, with a crisp white-collared shirt and a deep blue silk tie. His hair was gelled, and there wasn't a speck of stubble on his jaw. Mags grabbed Adeline's arm and dragged her backwards. Adeline started to sob. She reached for Kennedi, pulled her up and hugged her tightly. Mags placed herself between them and Alexander, hands on her hips.

"You're very fucking rude, Alejandro. No gifts?"

Alexander smirked. He dropped Ryker to the floor.

"Ryker!" Adeline lunged forward, but Kennedi held her tightly, refusing to let go.

Mags whispered over her shoulder, "Remember what I've taught you."

Alexander stepped forward, cracking his calloused knuckles. "Whatever weapon you grab, I'll use it to cut your hands off."

And then Lucas stepped into the kitchen, a pitch black blight in what had been serenity. His sinister eyes locked onto Adeline's face like a lion ready to pounce on its next meal. Alexander stepped aside, ever the obedient mutt. Lucas slipped a hand into a pocket and whistled as he peered around the kitchen.

"Damn, pet. You really do have a cushy set-up here. It's nice. Too small for my tastes, but still nice."

Adeline shoved Kennedi behind her and bared her teeth. "What the fuck do you want?"

He clucked his tongue. "Pet, I've told you time and time again what I want. This is the problem. You never listen. It's extremely tiring, the way you just do whatever you want." His eyes glinted ferociously. Turning to Alexander, he commanded, "Tie them up. And don't forget about Magda Deanlight. That bitch doesn't expose an entire mafia ring with just her good looks."

Before Adeline could react, Alexander stalked up to Mags. The old woman, to her credit, ducked at the first swing and expertly pounded her fist into his gut. Alexander let out a sharp breath but rebounded instantly and planted an uppercut before Mags could weave. He slammed into her jaw, and she twirled backward, landing on the floor, knocked out cold. Adeline let go of Kennedi and rushed over to Mags.

"Mags, wake up!" She shook her. Mags' head lolled to one side like a broken doll. Adeline glared up at Alexander. "I'm going to fucking kill you."

He rolled his eyes and leaned down to pick up Mags. Adeline lunged, sinking her teeth into the arm Lance had already shredded. Alexander backhanded Adeline so hard she crashed into a cabinet.

Adeline brought a hand up to her injured cheek. She ground her jaw as she stood, motioning for Kennedi to stay behind her. It was time to show her father how disobedient and defiant she could be.

Voice cold, she said, "Let them go. This is between you and me, you stupid fuck."

Lucas chuckled. "It's cute how you still think you can make a difference." He glanced at Alexander, who wrapped a length of rope around Mags' torso, lashing her to a chair by the kitchen table. Adeline looked at Ryker, horrified. His skin was pale, and a puddle of blood was growing out from under him. The desperation in his eyes cleaved her heart in two. At least he wasn't dead—yet. But he needed help soon, or he would bleed out.

Alexander tightened the final knot around Mags and stood next to Lucas, ready for his next command.

"Do you remember the consequences for misbehaving?" Lucas said to Adeline.

She growled. "Having to listen to you talk too fucking much?"

His eyes lit up, and he clapped his hands. "Oh, pet. This lesson will be so much fun! Come now, Ms. Murphy. We have a game to play in the other room." He held out a hand to Kennedi, as if she would willingly take it. Kennedi sobbed and shook her head violently. Adeline moved, blocking Lucas's view of her.

"You fucking touch her and—"

"And what?" He stepped closer. "Pet, you don't have a chance. Here's what's going to happen: I'm going to let your little friend over there bleed out. While that happens, Alexander is going to fuck you on every surface in this beautiful kitchen while Magda Deanlight watches. I'm going to take Ms. Murphy to the other room and make her wish she was dead by using every one of her orifices. Then, when she's begging for oblivion, I'm going to let Alexander fuck her into a coma. While he's doing that, I'm going to make you eat your own tongue. And while you bleed out, I'm going to fuck the inside of your skull through that hole in your face. Then I'll leave all four of you in this home to rot and let all of these fucking cats eat your corpses."

Kennedi's sobs intensified. Adeline was aghast. Instead of cowering, though, she raised her chin at him. "You've been practicing that lame speech the whole ride here? Did Alexander give you pointers?"

He swung at her, and she blocked the swing. His eyes widened with true surprise. Taking advantage of his momentary shock, she thrust her fist upwards into a wicked uppercut. His chin knocked back, teeth snapping together. Before he could collect his thoughts, she landed a right hook into his ribs.

As she went to knee him in the gut, his fist crunched into her face. The familiar silver rings left a deep imprint she could feel without having to see. She stumbled back, almost stepping on Kennedi. Adeline held up a hand, trying to hold back the blood gushing from her nose.

Kennedi screamed and attempted to step around Adeline to defend her. Adeline held out an arm and stood her ground. Sneering, she let her blood trickle into her mouth, staining her teeth. "You're a pathetic, short, little man with a misplaced god complex. You're a sadist who needs to give pain to others so you can hide that no one loves you and never will."

The words only skimmed what she ached to say for years, but the satisfaction was still sweet. Lucas's face turned the color of a ripe plum; she continued. "You spent four years trying to break me, and you failed. No matter how many drugs, how many beatings, how many men, you could never break me." She spit on him. Then one of her hands flew up, and she backhanded Lucas as hard as she could.

Alexander growled, inching closer. Lucas held up a hand. He pulled the pocket square from his breast pocket and wiped his face. He regarded Adeline coolly, eyes like endless pools of death and darkness. "So spicy." He jerked his chin to Kennedi and Alexander sprang into action.

Adeline darted in front of Kennedi, parrying some of his attempts to hit her, but Alexander shoved her aside effortlessly. He yanked Kennedi up by her throat. Kennedi tried every tactic she'd learned to break his hold, but his grasp only tightened.

Adeline lost it. A visceral, primal part of her snapped, and she rushed Alexander, aiming her thumbs at his eyes, but punched her in the chest. She felt something crack, air heaved from her lungs. Turning his focus back to Kennedi, he did the same, then threw her at Lucas's feet.

Alexander moved to Adeline, but she was ready. As he turned his head, Adeline grabbed the toaster from the counter behind her and slammed it into his temple. He grinned and shook his head as if he were a dog. The pain spurred him forward; he grabbed her by the hair. She clawed at his hand, kicked wildly and landed one on his knee. He seethed, pulling her closer and bit her shoulder hard. Pain consumed her as she watched Lucas drag Kennedi down the hallway, ignoring her pleas for mercy.

"Stop!" Ryker yelled, trying to crawl forward with one arm. "Please! I'll do anything. Kill me instead. Torture me. Just leave her alone."

Lucas threw a sneer over his meaty shoulder. "Don't worry, pretty boy. I'll make sure to twist the knife when I'm done. Now shut the fuck up."

From behind Alexander, Mags stirred, her head moving from side to side. Adeline, trying to distract Alexander, forgot about her need for oxygen long enough to slap him across the face. It did the trick. He hurled her down so hard, one of her ankles buckled. Adeline screamed, scrambled around on all fours trying to reach the knife block.

A massive hand dug into her hair again, grabbed a thick clump, and yanked her backwards. She slammed onto her back, losing her breath again. Alexander loomed over her, face contorted with fury. Kennedi screeched over and over again in the living room while Lucas laughed raucously.

Alexander glanced to the hallway and smirked. "I was told to make sure you listen while he rapes your little friend. In fact, he told me I could rape you at the same time."

Mags stirred, her hazy eyes watching the scene but not processing it. Adeline knew then: rescue wasn't coming.

Kennedi screamed and screamed. Lucas met each with a joyful cackle of his own. Nearby, the pool of blood under Ryker slowly grew, signaling the distance between life and death swiftly closing.

Adeline couldn't stop trying. If she were about to die, then Alexander would have to work for it. She roared with fury and reached forward to punch him in the dick—and missed when he casually stepped back. His boot collided with her chest as he fell to his knees, grabbed her hips and flipped her over. The sound of metal and leather tunneled her vision. She clawed at the tile, ripping the skin off her fingers.

"I know all of your moves, you fucking piece of meat. Just accept what needs to happen, and it'll be over faster."

"Liar," she spat, trying to flip herself over again. He yanked her hips into the air with one arm. The sound of his jeans unzipping chilled her blood.

Suddenly, there was a crash from down the hall. Lucas bellowed. Kennedi screamed again.

There was a loud slap and then silence.

CHAPTER TWENTY-EIGHT

"KENNEDI!" Adeline howled and bucked her hips violently. The silence consumed every atom of her being.

Alexander leaned forward and whispered, "Sounds like he's going to be fucking a corpse."

Adeline's shorts tore in half with one rough pull. She felt his cock against her ass cheek, the feel of it sickly familiar. Adeline heaved, vomit spilling up her throat.

"No, no, no, no, no," she moaned, digging into the tile even harder, splitting a nail off one finger. With his free hand he widened her thighs, fingers curling around the weak material of her underwear.

"Are you ready?" he purred. Then his hand stilled. The other arm, the one holding her hips up, fell away suddenly. Adeline fell over and scrambled onto her back, crab walked away. She saw the towering giant, still on his knees, clutching his throat. His fingers wrapped around a short, arrowhead-shaped knife jutting from his artery. Blood pumped with each heartbeat. Behind him stood Mags, venom in her gaze. She locked eyes with Adeline.

"You want to finish it?"

Ignoring every aching inch, Adeline clambered upright and hopped over to Alexander. His skin was already ashen. She wrapped her fingers around the small dagger and yanked it out. Blood flooded out in torrents, rivers of it gliding down his torso. He had only seconds left; she didn't hesitate and bent down and sawed his cock off. His mouth widened, eyes filled with a form of agony that resonated deeply within her. She brought her face close to his, reveling in the terror permanently etched into his features.

"Open fucking wide, you whore." And she shoved the bloody chunk of cock into his mouth.

He collapsed to the floor like a wet bag of cement. Adeline hobbled quickly down the hall, past Ryker, who leaned against the wall for support.

"Kennedi!"

Right then, a loud, disoriented moan came from the living room. She stopped at the closet, wrenched it open and snagged the shotgun inside. It was heavy in her hands, the unfamiliar metal cool against her skin.

"It's loaded!" Mags yelled from where she was crouched next to Ryker. Adeline pumped a cartridge into the chamber. Another moan, the sound of a belt…

Adeline continued down the hallway. Rounding the corner into the living room, Adeline planted her feet and pointed the gun at Lucas.

Kennedi was under him, clothes torn to shreds. There was a shattered lamp on the floor next to him, and blood trickled down the side of his temple. Kennedi stirred, her head moving side to side.

"*Hey*," Adeline growled. Lucas's head snapped up, his expression twisted with excitement, with lust, until he noticed Adeline with the shotgun.

He raised his lip in disgust. "Where's Alexander?"

"Waiting for you in hell."

Kennedi moaned again. Lucas looked down at her. He looked up again, and Adeline's stomach sank—there was something more he could take, and he knew it.

"Don't," she warned, raising the barrel higher.

He laughed. "You've never shot a gun in your life. And if you shoot me, you shoot your precious whore, too. Then what would be the point?"

Adeline's protective instincts kicked into high gear. She stepped forward. "Get away from her." He watched, eyes wary. The barrel was only three feet from his face, but she knew hurting Kennedi was still a possibility.

"Stand up." To her shame, the words were pleading.

He smirked. "Or what?"

"Or I'll—"

He lurched forward and knocked the shotgun to the side as she squeezed the trigger, exploding chunks of wall and picture frames. He seized her wrist, jerking her downwards. The shotgun clattered to the floor. His face was close enough now that she could see the size of his pores. The dark depths of his eyes bore into her.

Then Mags screamed, "Duck!"

She obeyed as Mags appeared behind her holding a baseball bat. She flipped it expertly in her hand and then swung from the left. Lucas barely had time to register what was happening before the wood cracked his skull.

Dazed, he fell to the side. Mags tossed the bat to Adeline, who caught it and raised it above her head.

She slammed it down onto his head. He put a hand up in defense. She raised the bat again and brought it down even harder. "This is for my life."

Cracking, part of his skull caved in farther. The bat was soaked with blood as she brought it down one final time. "And this is for my family."

An unfamiliar sound, like a melon being crunched, and bits of brain matter flew across the room. It splattered the walls, Mags' face, and Adeline's hair.

Lucas's body was still.

Adeline looked over at Kennedi, who groaned and reached for her head. Adeline sobbed.

Mags hefted the bat over one shoulder, examining the blood stain. "Is that what they call a home run?"

***

Reality suspended for a moment. Kennedi's eyes fluttered open. Adeline knelt over her, cupping her face. Seeing Kennedi's bright green eyes land on her, Adeline finally wept. Full body sobs that racked her whole being, shaking off the intense experience. It had been less than ten minutes of chaotic hell, but it had felt like a lifetime.

"Are you okay?" Adeline's fingers hovered over the split in Kennedi's cheek—familiar marks from silver rings she knew all too well. The wound was already bruising. Kennedi grimaced and sat up, placing a hand on her cheek.

"Yeah, I think so." She looked down and realized she was half naked. Mags walked to the couch and laid a blanket over Kennedi's body.

"I'm going to check on Ryker and make a call," the old woman declared, turning on her heels as if she'd just announced she was making dinner. Adeline's gaze shifted to her father's body. She expected to feel *something*, but the only thing she felt was emptiness. Maybe that in itself was a feeling. She was a murderer now. She'd delivered the final blow to both of her abusers.

And she felt nothing.

There was a meow. Adeline looked over and saw Aslin gently prodding Lance's nose with a paw. Adeline's breath caught at the sight of the dog's bloody shoulder.

"Lance?" she called. An ear flicked.

Kennedi touched her shoulder. "Go check on him. I'm okay right here."

"You sure?" Adeline searched her face for a lie, but Kennedi gave a reassuring nod. Heaving herself upright, careful to avoid putting weight on her ankle, Adeline limped over to Lance. Aslin peered up and meowed.

"I swear if you're asking for food…" Adeline muttered. She dropped to her knees and put a hand on Lance's ribs. He was breathing. Lance's eyes popped open, and his head jerked toward her with a loud whine.

"Shhh," Adeline soothed. She started feeling him over for wounds. The bullet had grazed his shoulder, and there was a lump on his temple, but otherwise he seemed fine. Aslin brushed against Adeline's leg, purring loudly.

"Brave boy will get steaks every night for the rest of his life," Kennedi said, trying to stand. She hugged the blanket to her bare body. Adeline glanced down the hallway. Ryker was leaning against the wall, legs splayed, still clutching the knife in his belly. It looked like a small pocket knife—it hopefully didn't pierce too deep.

Mags stepped over Ryker's legs as she stomped from the kitchen to the foyer. "Bruce'll be here in a couple of minutes. I've also called the cops. Lucky for us, they started it and tried to kill us all. No need to cover up a murder now." She stopped at the entrance to the living room and stared at Lucas's corpse.

"That fucker is going to stain my carpet." She shook her head and stomped away again, muttering about bleach.

Adeline gave Lance one last pat and then went over to Ryker and sat next to him. "Are you okay?" She winced. "Sorry, dumb question. Can I do anything for you?"

Ryker shook his head. She hated how pale he looked. "As long as I stay still, it's okay." He looked at Mags, who was busy slamming cupboards, grabbing cleaning supplies. "How long until the ambulance?"

"Three minutes. You'll be fine." She didn't wait for an answer as she stepped over him again. Lance slowly stood and shook his head before limping into the living room, presumably to cuddle with Kennedi. Adeline looked back to Ryker. Her eyes watered.

"I'm sorry this happened. It's all my fault. None of you deserved this."

He took his free hand, covered in sticky blood, and grabbed hers. "Stop. You didn't invite him to come over and try to murder us. You had—*have*—every right to try and live your life. And we're all alive." He looked down at his wound. "And this is going to be a sweet scar to impress all the ladies with."

Adeline gave a watery laugh. She kissed his cheek and brushed back a strand of his sweat-soaked hair.

"I'm so glad I met you," she whispered.

"Me too." A corner of his mouth hitched. She wiped her cheeks with the back of her hand, smearing blood everywhere. Making a face, she tried to wipe them on her shirt, but it was already a red Pollock painting.

"Don't bother," Ryker teased, sucking in a breath as he bit down a chuckle. "Jesus, this fucking hurts."

They both startled at the sound of a knock. Adeline watched as Mags opened the door and stepped aside, revealing Bruce. The big smile on his face dropped immediately as he took in the scene. Lance limped over to him, sniffing. Bruce looked down and swept a hand over one of Lance's ears.

"Look at you, big puppy." He leaned to the side and saw Lance's bullet wound. Then he looked to his left, to where Kennedi sat, to Lucas's body, and then to where Adeline and Ryker sat huddled in the hallway. His eyes narrowed at the knife. He looked at Mags and sighed, slinging off a backpack Adeline hadn't noticed before.

"What the hell have you gotten yourself into, woman? I thought there was a plan."

Mags jammed her hands onto her hips. "Excuse me? Why do you assume this is on me?"

Bruce pulled out gauze and some bottles of vodka. "Because it's always you."

"Just *one* time in Morocco—"

"Do you even want me to mention Budapest? Istanbul?" Mags crossed her arms. His voice remained friendly as he looked at the others. "Who needs help the most?"

Adeline pointed at Ryker. "He's been stabbed."

Mags huffed as Bruce walked away, giving his back the evil eye. "We aren't done."

"We never are," he murmured as he knelt down on Ryker's other side, letting Adeline stay where she was. He reached into the backpack and pulled out a pair of medical shears. He paused, the shears hovering over Ryker's bloody T-shirt. "This is going to hurt. Do you need a drink?"

"I'll get it." Mags hurried to the kitchen, careful to step around all of them. The sound of alarms came from the distance. Adeline watched as she ignored Alexander and the enormous blossom of drying blood beneath him. His flaccid penis still protruded from his mouth. Dead, he'd lost all of his menacing energy. Adeline swallowed, trying to sense even a sliver of guilt. There was none.

It had been one of the most satisfying experiences of her life, a close second to spattering her father's brains all over Mags' living room. As long as she lived, she'd never forget the look of fear in Alexander's eyes as she shoved his dick into his mouth. The sound of his choking on it.

The only regret was that the moment hadn't lasted longer.

EPILOGUE

Sixteen Months Later

The bookstore had never been so packed. Every aisle was full, and the front of the store had a line threatening to snake out the door. The sounds of steaming milk and coffee grinding blended with customer conversations. Addie stood by the front door, admiring the sheer success of the store's grand re-opening.

Behind the counter, Kennedi and her father rang up one purchase after another. Kennedi glanced up and grinned at Addie, who waved enthusiastically. Peter, Kennedi's dad, looked up, grinning when his eyes landed on Addie, then looked back at the customer piling books in front of him.

Ryker was down an aisle, talking with an old man. He wore a blue-and-orange plaid shirt, sleeves rolled up. His beard was a little shorter than when they'd first met, but his roguish lumberjack charm remained intact.

He caught her eye and winked while nodding at something the man said. Addie approached the cafe, settling into the line. All around her, people chattered. She caught bits and pieces, every word making her heart sing.

"...so fantastic. We've been needing one…"

"I had no idea this was here, and I'm coming all—"

"They talked about a book tour for that woman who wrote all them vampire—"

Addie looked at Kennedi again, pride swelling. Kennedi had spent the last few nights fretting over how this day would go.

Surprisingly, adding a cafe hadn't been too difficult. Thanks to a hidden trust fund that Addie's mother had set up, which was released the moment she turned twenty-three, Addie was more than happy to invest in what she knew was a great idea. When the money arrived, Addie made sure to set some aside for future expenses while donating a percentage to a local domestic violence shelter. On Tuesdays, she and Mags taught women how to fight. It was rewarding and a great way to keep busy.

"Hey, Addie, what would you like?" Addie broke from her thoughts, smiling at Marybell, the head barista. She was blonde and wore a deep purple apron, matching the bookstore's aesthetic.

"Hey, Marybell, I'd like a white mocha with no caffeine."

Marybell rang the order up. "Isn't that just a white mocha hot chocolate then?"

"I guess that's true." Addie handed over some cash, but Marybell waved it away.

"No, ma'am, you own this place. Bosses drink on the house."

Addie offered a generous but firm smile. Pushing the money forward, she said, "No, I don't. Kennedi does, and I want to support my wife."

Marybell chuckled. "Fine, fine. Your drink will be ready in a jiffy."

Addie added a dollar to the tip jar and stepped aside. She checked her phone. The day would be busy with appointments, including a check-up later that afternoon. Ryker had promised to take her. Checking her email, she was thrilled to see a message from the university she'd applied to. She sucked in a breath, afraid to move, and opened the message.

Dear Mrs. Avila,

We are pleased to inform you of your acceptance into Hilltmon University's Bachelors of Criminal Justice program. Enclosed are the documents required. Please—

Addie squealed and thrust her phone into the air. Ryker and Kennedi looked to her, as did the rest of the store.

"I GOT IN!"

Kennedi jumped up and down with a shriek, clapping excitedly. "MY WIFE'S A COLLEGE STUDENT!" she hollered.

"WAY TO GO, BABY!" Ryker yelled. Addie felt all eyes in the room bounce between the three of them. They didn't hide their relationship, but it was still unusual enough that it caught most people off guard.

Addie wilted slightly under the attention, but Kennedi—always one to try and bring a little levity to a situation—clapped. She looked encouragingly at various customers, who joined in.

In seconds, the whole store was clapping. Addie tried to scowl but couldn't hide the enormous grin spreading across her face. She was accepted into her top choice—an absolute dream come true. The end goal, she'd decided, was to become a pro bono lawyer, helping humans in trafficking and domestic violence situations. She wanted to help elevate their voices and bring down people like her father. She put her phone away and grabbed her drink.

"Hello, love," she said, approaching Ryker, sliding her hand through his arm. A burst of love warmed her insides as he looked at her softly. He grabbed her hand and kissed the back of it.

"Hello, wonderful wife. How are you feeling today?"

The timbre of his voice always made her toes curl.

"Pretty good." She held up her white mocha. "Got my drink."

He chuckled. "You've had about six of those this week alone."

She pouted. "Excuse me, but I'm allowed to eat whatever I want." She patted her round tummy with affection. "I'm a slave to this one's hungry whims."

He faced her, placing his steady hands on each side of her bump. He looked down at her flower print dress and rubbed the soft curves beneath.

"Probably an eater like their daddy."

"Yeah, well," Addie huffed, already feeling tightness in her back. "I need to go sit down. Mags and Bruce should be here soon."

Ryker leaned down and blessed the top of her head with a kiss. "Dinner's on me tonight. Homemade pizza?"

It'd been two hours since her last meal; her stomach grumbled at the mention of food.

"See? An eater. I'll see you at home." With one more kiss on her cheek, Ryker walked back down the aisles to help others. Addie watched him for a second before turning to find a spot near the couches. She'd just hefted herself down onto a soft chair when the door opened loudly, followed by the sounds of a bickering couple as Mags and Bruce walked in.

"Maggie, I told you the heater needed to be replaced."

"And I," Mags seethed, poking his shoulder, "said I was going to get around to it. Who would have thought it would die so soon?"

"*I* did, woman."

Addie caught Mags' eye and waved her down before they scared off business. She pointed at two empty chairs beside her.

"Sit down. You two are going to embarrass Kennedi."

They did as ordered, spearing each other with dirty looks. Mags wore a light purple painter's shirt with jeans. Bruce wore a tan shirt, khakis, and a brown utility vest. Since the day of the attack, Bruce had been coming around a lot more. The Victorian house was full to the brim every day—Kennedi and Addie had moved in permanently, and

Ryker came over most nights, when he didn't have to stay on-site for his company.

Addie took a sip of her mocha. "I got into university. My top choice."

Mags' eyes shined. "That's amazing, Addie. I'm so happy to hear that." She winked at her. "I'm surprised they didn't deny you for being pregnant."

Addie rolled her eyes. "That's illegal."

Bruce gave Mags' shoulder a gentle shove. "Maggie, don't be rude. She's pregnant, not an invalid."

"She decided she needed to carry around a parasite. In any other circumstance, she'd be given meds to remove it. Like that tapeworm you got in Tanzania."

Addie winced—a kick, right into her kidney. "Keep it up, old woman. You'll get zero bouncy baby giggles."

Mags stood with a huff. "I told you, being a parent is a trap, but being a grandparent is a gift. You get to return the parasite after. I'm going to get a coffee."

Bruce watched her walk away. Turning to look at Addie, he said, "That woman drives me mad, but she's also the most wonderful person I've ever met."

Addie adjusted herself; her tailbone was almost never comfortable anymore. "Then why did you never marry her?"

He shrugged. "Ask her. I've asked over a dozen times. She's always saying something about being free." He glanced around, making sure the coast was clear, then leaned forward. "So have the cops given anymore trouble about him?"

The "him" being her father. She shook her head

"No. Once they saw the scene and looked into everything I told them, there was no reason for them to suspect foul play."

Bruce gave a thoughtful nod. "At least the fucker wasn't able to dissolve the trust your mom had set up."

Addie finished up her mocha and pushed herself up, with Bruce holding his arms out in case she teetered over. She laughed a little, feeling like a wobbly cow.

"Thanks."

He looked for Mags, spotting her still in line. "I'm going to go drive her more insane. We'll see you at home later."

He walked off then. Addie looked to the counter to see Kennedi ringing up purchases, chattering with patrons. She tossed her empty cup in the trash and waddled over.

"Hello, my sweet wife."

Kennedi turned and her eyes lit up. With a ring sparkling on her left hand, she motioned to Addie and spoke to the customer in front of her, "This is my wife, Addie."

The customer nodded politely, taking their bag of books and leaving. Addie kissed Kennedi lightly and nodded to the register.

"How are things? Seems crazy busy right now."

Kennedi smiled at another customer and started scanning their books. "Fantastic. If it keeps up like this, we'll be in the black by the end of the year." She looked to the side. "Looks like the cafe is a serious hit."

Addie grabbed a plastic bag from under the counter and handed it to Kennedi. "I told you it would be. My white mocha was amazing."

Kennedi filled the bag with books and rang up the purchase. "Awesome. I'll be done soon. Dad is gonna take over once things die down." She flashed a grin. "Then I can take my wife home and rub her feet."

Addie almost groaned at the thought. "Fuck yes. I swear my ankles are the size of houses."

With a final kiss, Addie left Kennedi at the counter. She searched for Ryker again, caught his eye and motioned to the front door to let him know she was leaving. As she walked to the door, she saw Mags and Bruce standing side by side in line at the cafe. She saw Bruce wrap an arm around Mags and nuzzle into her gray, springy curls. Mags leaned into it, eyes closed. Bruce pinched her butt then, and Mags' eyes sprung open with indignation. She returned the pinch, smiling good-naturedly and making Bruce laugh.

Addie relished in the perfection of this moment. Everyone important to her was happy and healthy. The door jingled behind her as she stepped out into the street. Menforth was receding into fall. She could almost taste the cider, smell the smoky fires.

She could barely contain her excitement—her baby would be there by the holidays, born into a world of love and adoration. It would never want for anything. Never in a million years did she think she would have a life like this, and she didn't want to waste a single second of it.

After all, it was the kind of life people would kill for.

THE LETTERS

Dear Addie,

It's been only two weeks since I last saw you, and I'm over it. We've been friends since forever, and it's so weird not seeing you all the time. Your father is a weirdo, putting you on some crazed social media lockdown. He's cray-cray. My hand already hurts from using this dumb pen. Who writes letters anymore?

Complaints aside, Dad and I have settled into Menforth just fine. It's soooo freakin' small, but he really thinks opening a bookstore here is a good idea. I won't hold my breath. But I guess the people around here will want to read books too, right?

I thought about what you said before, about wishing we had more time. I didn't say it then, but we're on the same page. It never feels like enough time with you. All through high school, we made sure our classes were the same until they wouldn't let us anymore. Homework and cheerleading, and even going to prom together so we didn't have to take any lame-ass boys. Now? Now I can't even see your face. What is this bullshit anyway? In your next letter, you must tell me when you can visit. I might shrivel up into a ball of trash if you don't come and see me ASAP.

Do you remember that sundae we had right after graduation? There's a diner here that can make sundaes just as good. They also have this burger special that is to die for. I'm not a fan of being in the middle of nowhere, I heard there is this crazy cat lady not too far from me. My dad told me to stay away from her, but why would I want to stay away from someone with cats? Does he even know me?

Well, I need to go unpack. Write me soon! I'll do jumping jacks until you do.

All day,

Kennedi

Dear Kennedi,

This snail mail bullshit is annoying. I think I've developed carpal tunnel just by writing these words. I'm glad to hear Menforth is okay. A crazy cat lady sounds exciting. I've never even been near a cat, so if you get a chance, pet one for me!

I miss you so much. Things aren't the same without you around. I wish you were here to watch some stupid romcom with me and make fun of the main character.

My dad has gotten stricter lately, even though I'm about to turn eighteen. I'm not even allowed dessert lately. You know how he's always been, so this is weird. Sure, I didn't pass with a 4.0 GPA like he demanded, but is that really grounds for whatever the fuck he's doing right now? I asked him about going to college last week, and he got weird about that, too. Remember how insistent he was about me taking my SATs and going to a good college? Now he's refusing to discuss it. I can't figure out why.

Yesterday, I was looking at that photo of us with my mom when we went to that park. Not gonna lie, I cried. I miss her as much as I miss you. I know I've already said that, but I feel so alone without you.

I'll be wasting away until you write back.

All day,

Addie

Dear Addie,

We opened the bookstore! It's super cute. I told him we should open a cafe, but he said not now, maybe in the future. When you visit, you'll get to see how adorable it is, and maybe you can help me convince him that adding a cafe isn't the same as inserting a Starbucks.

I also started some online college courses. I don't know what I want to major in, so I'm just doing the basics. Did your dad ever let you find a college to go to? I remember how insistent he was, so that does sound weird. Hopefully you're starting classes too! Do you still want to be an English major? I know it's only been a couple of months since we've seen each other but snail mail makes it feel like foreverrrrr. How did people do this for a billion years?

I miss you. I have that photo of us and your mom, too. She was so nice, way nicer than mine. Speaking of, good riddance to that bitch. Dad says she promised to email me but that was months ago. I'm not holding my breath. What kind of mother has a kid and then decides after fifteen years she just wants to go live a different life? I've promised to not even talk about her. I'm over her selfish bullshit.

So, tell me everything! I want to know about your life. Mine is a bit boring right now. Hopefully, my next letter will be more interesting!

All day,

Kennedi

Dear Kennedi,

I'm so excited about the bookstore! That happened so fast. Give me all of the glorious details—what color are the walls? I miss going anywhere. Maybe send some photos in your next letter? My dad isn't letting me go anywhere. He told me there are security issues. Having a rich dad isn't what reality TV pretends it is.

He still won't discuss college; however, he is letting me hold a party just for fun. I mean, we're only inviting people he knows. I asked if I could invite you—it's not like we can't afford to fly you out—but he told me no. Said it was mostly for his business friends, but he promised to get me a nice outfit. It's in a couple of days. I'll see if I can have a maid take a photo of my outfit and print it out.

Did you ever pet any cats?

Mom's deathaversary is in a couple of months. Three years since that wreck—can you believe it? Do you want to go to her grave with me? Maybe if we keep asking our dads, we can convince them it's important. What do you think?

Okay, the tailor is here for my new dress. I need to go look fabulous. Send me photos! I miss you so much.

All day,

Addie

Dear Addie,

I got to pet a cat! Actually, a lot of them. The crazy cat lady is named Mags, and, um, she's definitely crazy. She looks like a nice enough lady, but then she opens her mouth and you immediately wish someone would feed her a pleasantry pill or something. She yells at her garden when I walk around for exercise. I literally heard her threaten the tomatoes with a wire hanger if they didn't grow faster. Total Mommy Dearest vibes.

The bookstore is so amazing! I'm including some photos. What do you think I should put in that empty corner? I convinced dad to let me put an itsy-bitsy coffee corner by the cash register. People seem to like it. One step closer for all bookishkind!

I'm loving my college classes. Believe it or not, I love science. I know, I know, I hated it in high school. But maybe I just hated Mrs. Kelper more. She was a bitch. She hated our sitting together, remember that?

Sorry, this is so short. I have to go through inventory bullshit and then study. I can't wait to see the photos of your dress! Tell me all about the party. I bet you were beautiful.

All day,

Kennedi

Dear Addie,

It's been a month since I've heard from you. I hope everything is okay. I'm sure you're busy. I've been super busy, too. Why is being an adult like this? I feel like all I do is work and study. We were so eager to grow up, but give me Saturdays with cartoons any day now.

In my free time, I actually hang out with that lady, Mags. She's not so bad, if your skin is thick enough. I'd love for you to meet her one day. She really has the weirdest-looking house. It's all brightly colored, and she has an art studio inside.

I aced my science class, by the way. I think I want to major in criminology. Is that crazy? It's crazy, right? I've been getting into true crime. Some of these stories keep me up at night. I've been obsessing over some podcasts and books. Can I send you some books? I'm sure your dad hasn't become *that* strict … Right?

I gotta go, but write me back ASAP. I miss you so much. All of this distance is showing me how much I care about you. What you mean to me. I hope that doesn't sound weird. Just get back to me. Maybe we can do a phone call?

All day,

Kennedi

Addie,

You're scaring me. It's been six months. Are you getting these letters? I've sent dozens without getting an answer. Google says you still live in the same house. I'm starting to freak. Dad says you're probably just living your life and that the post office is lame, but something doesn't feel right.

Sometimes, I can't sleep because I keep thinking you might be dead. Then I cry, because I realized all of the things I should have said and done but didn't. Feelings I didn't understand. But I care about you, Addie, and I need to hear from you. Please write back. Please tell me everything's okay.

If you need me, call me at 555-1234. I'll never change the number.

I miss you.

All day. Every day.

Kennedi

ACKNOWLEDGMENTS

First and foremost, I want to thank my twin flame, Josh. I never expected to have such an excellent sounding board. One of my favorite things to do is come to you with a plot hole and flesh it out in less than thirty minutes. Thank you for keeping me fed, focused, and supporting me through it all. My stories are better because of you. I can't wait to bring to life your idea of a Western with dinosaurs. Here's to thirty more. Lovers you.

To my friend Kristina, thank you for re-reading this book like five times. Each version was different, but your feedback was always glorious. I appreciate you on so many levels. When I wanted to kill off Ryker, you told me healthy triad representation is important—his resurrection is due to him and I'm sure he's grateful. I know I am.

I had quite a few beta readers, and this story wouldn't make as much sense as it does without you. Shout out to Katia for reading the first few chapters and bluntly telling me I was holding back. I took it to heart and fileted myself for the literary gods.

To my bestie Cassie, thanks for taking a read and making sure it was a clean finish. You are one of the best people I know, and I'd be insane (and a hermit) without you.

And thanks to that one beta reader that disliked my book so much, your feedback was angry enough that I almost gave up for two whole days. Then incorporated your feedback, because it was all valid.

Finally, to the bookish community. About 99.9% of you will never know I exist, but the enthusiasm for tropes, twisty stories, and solid book recommendations shaped how I approached this book.

If you, dear reader, made it this far… Thank you.

www.ingramcontent.com/pod-product-compliance
Lightning Source LLC
Chambersburg PA
CBHW021233310726
48971CB00006B/1807